A COUPLE CALLED MOEBIUS

Eleven Sensual Stories

A COUPLE CALLED MOEBIUS

Eleven Sensual Stories

Carol Bergé

THE BOBBS-MERRILL COMPANY, INC.

Indianapolis / New York

ACKNOWLEDGMENTS

"The Water Ceremony"—*For Now*, Donald Phelps, Editor

"The Farm Woman"—*The Unfolding*, Frank Murphy, Editor

"The Kitchen"—*The Unfolding*, Frank Murphy, Editor

"KOU, or, Coming to Meet"—*Measure*, Don Ross and Howard McCord, Editors

"HUAN, or, Dispersion"—also appears in *A House of Good Proportion: Images of Women in Literature*, Simon & Schuster, Inc., Michele Murray, Editor

The Bobbs-Merrill Company, Inc.
Indianapolis • New York
Copyright © 1972 by Carol Bergé
All rights reserved
Library of Congress catalog card number: 72-80797
Printed in the United States of America
Book designed by A. Christopher Simon

This book is for
those who have kept with me:

ANNE PEPPIS
WARREN BOWER
JUDITH SHERWIN
IAGO GALDSTON
JANE NORTHUP
DWIGHT and RUDY HOPKINS
RAÚL MEDINA MORA

CONTENTS

from "Four Short Essays on Vuillard," by Max Kozloff

Somewhere in his journal, Jules Renard writes that night is the day gone blind. Vuillard was alive to those artifices that kept the blindness at bay . . . he tends to adopt one of two mutually contradictory views of matter as illuminated by light. The first is to conceive of an already given, populated world cast in darkness, lit dramatically and interruptively, that is to say, *articulated* so that various crucial surfaces emerge in high relief from concealment. The second is to assume that the painter's marks themselves create the world . . . constantly materialize appearances . . . All location, fluid or crystalline, exists in a separate continuum of luminous energy . . . Thus Vuillard bestows—one would almost rather say emblemizes—landscape as part of the decor of apartments necessarily closed off from nature. In these cavernous zones, night and day, that which is near at hand compared with that present only in memory, coexist on their different levels of reality.

"The Light Within" (II)

—Artforum, December, 1971

A COUPLE
CALLED MOEBIUS

Eleven Sensual Stories

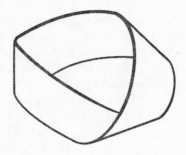

THE WATER CEREMONY

I.

They were both made of metal, almost the color of the water. Now that night fell in chunks, the water formed blocks that worked against their oars. They fell into a lack of rhythm, their flesh working against themselves, against the self, and so against the rhythm of the waves surrounding them. Off to their left, left of the bow, the island lay, metallic and dulled against the water. It was an unknown metal, perhaps lead; the idea was somehow to transmute the two of them into lead too, and let the water serve as magnetic ore, to perhaps pull them toward the island. The tide was turning. Neither of them knew these waters enough to guess the character of that hour as a surface; the light was going as if it could be poured and set solid, the water seemed to grow solid. The woman saw his face briefly in profile, sharp and carven, stress lines, away from his own nature, and she fell away from her oar. His oar slipped from its lock and pierced upward and back into the boat. She spat slivers of fear. The island was unknown. She was an inland woman. He knew a bit more, but her shape confused him.

They had left the motor of the dinghy at the bottom of the shallows, tangled mercilessly in a seine just offshore another island. It had made a breaking sound when he loosed it and dropped it, not the bubbles of a live thing, but the unprotesting of hard into soft metal. From that time they both moved unnaturally, pushed into a reliance they would not otherwise have chosen. He was from an island; he was an Englishman and could sense the way of the water when it was his own choice; but she was from inland, a city like Mexico City where colors and fabrics were not derived from the sea. There had only been visits like this one, to lakes nearby or to an alien ocean. No bays or coves, no shale cliffs; the weathered people who moved on water were different from her own people. His people were more akin to these, his hands on the oars became part of their wood, at least at the beginning. Until the motor's descent, he had felt secure about oars and hands, his own hands. And until he had brought the unwilling oar into air against its own rhythm and his, she had been secure about the strokes they were making toward the island. In what was left of light, she stared at his profile, forcing him to turn his head and shrug off what was left of his unity with the boat. Nothing remained of their previous days, the warmth of bodies, the long comfortable conversations, walking, a certain softness of looks between them which had shaped them, the building of their more generous possibilities, recognition of their different lands as able to shape a similar music. They were sharp against the water, the first move away from the nature of the place and from the tenuous and firm way they knew they could move together. There had not been much time for them to gauge whether they were rowing in true unison, really; it might have worked out, if the tide had not begun to turn, or the wind had not risen just then, but his stroke was shorter and wider than hers, the boat would veer and one would have to backwater while the dinghy righted itself.

There was no choice now. The metal water grated on the sides of the boat, her mouth opened and bits of her own metal spat out toward his profile, they sat staring across at the dark statue which was the nearest island. No lights on it. But he knew there were houses on it, not near their shore but on the opposite side perhaps. The words hurtled between them, no singing now, and the decision to move with the tide until they would reach that island, whatever it held would be better than this cold oven, with its possible treacheries. As they started to row with the shore current toward the island, the moon disappeared. It took less than five minutes for the bottom of the boat to strike rock. The tiny pieces of phosphorescent sea animals were sparks of the metallic landing. Neither of them were levelled with themselves or the rocks in that minute. When he jumped out onto rock and into water, he took her hand to help her out of the boat, but his hand screamed the gesture and he pulled her sharply onto the wet kelp with a terrible urgency. There was nothing left of the feeling of clean bodies or towels or white sheets and a set table. They did not see the available lights, the rocks were in complete darkness and their shapes were the texture of nightmares.

But there was some vestige of their having been together: she reached toward him at the same instant he put out his arms and they stood that way, their feet in a tidal pool in the rocks, they might have stood thus if they had been strangers or enemies in that pool, that moment before the work of getting to safe land began. The fierce gratitude for any kind of rock, after water's hour. Any man and woman might have moved thus, and then moved apart in sudden awareness of the tide moving in fast. He left her while he

3

moved with the boat along the island edge. He would have
wanted her to walk with him, near him, until he found a
higher rock on which to anchor the boat, but she was immobile in her fear and could not even respond to his questions. He was angry then, no memory of their conversations
or of her nature, just a fury at her immobility, he moved
along the rocks in his blindness, the wet rope wound on his
hand. It was one of their possibilities now, this boat-shaped
piece of wood he was towing, and it had in it bags of groceries
they had gone to buy for the kitchen of the house he had
rented for them. When he climbed back to her, he had hands-
ful of cigaret packs, matches, a packet of chocolate bars from
the grocery bags. She was blind, immobile, shifting too fast
from sharp thinking to the need for release from the need for
such thinking, and as they stood on the rocks without a vision
of the island they were near, she uttered words that had no
meaning, to prepare him for the electricity lighting up her
brain, and he put out his arms in time to catch her as she
fainted. It was brief, again, this stance of theirs, together in
the tidal pool where they had first stopped briefly. Her Mexican sandals grated on the mussel shells she knew were underfoot, his leather oxfords were by now filled with seawater, he
had stepped waist-deep into the sea while trying to secure the
boat's line, and the wind was still rising, the tide was turning,
water moving fast till it was the large water itself that filled
the tidal pool, cold water replacing the sun-warmed water,
they stood rooted in horror knowing they had to move to
find a shelter on the dark possibility of land in front of them.

He pulled them across the rocks, blind leading
blind, they fell and slid over the kelp-rocks toward the dark
grey shadow of the land, they clanked when they fell as if
they were a sort of metallic robot whose sight mechanism had
short-circuited but whose basic instructions were still functioning. There were perhaps fifty feet of rocks to cross. There was
no way to gauge distances there. They tried to move on a high
ridge of worn shale that seemed to have less kelp adhering

than the lower, fewer tidal pools to slip into. The wind was high and cold. In the darkness it seemed that there was a low cliff before them, with trees at its top edge. They knew they would have to reach for the trees but they knew nothing else. Water had soaked his thin denim slacks to the waist, had long since filled his shoes and spattered his shirt like the ore from smelting-pots, spots with irregular edges. He was not connected with the earth under his oxfords in any direct way. And she had no connection with water or earth, they both had no memory of having moved as part of it most of their days together. They looked back only once, from the rocks across the clashing water chunks of the bay, and he saw the lights of perhaps Brighton while she visualized perhaps Acapulco. His shoes were the wet hide of animals, leather-bottomed, and her sandals had rubber soles, more slippery than gripping on these rocks.

By the time they had moved far enough to feel rocks underfoot that gave some traction to their steps, he moved with more sureness. She put out her hand in the dark and studied the surface of the shale outcropping. Their next ten steps put them into a crevice of the cliff. They were both crying and touching the first grass under the shelter of the land rocks, it was done, they had reached dry land, it was possible to stop at this place and become another kind of creature, she remembered a friend telling her, there are four lethal instruments in the wilderness; knife, ax, fire, and ignorance could destroy. Now they could add the fifth: panic. The panic ebbed and their minds moved again, creaking, logical, wise. They decided that the underbrush in the crevice was truly above high water, she looked at him in the dark and still could not recognize him as anyone she knew well, nor could he remember now what woman this was beside him. But as a man and a woman they fell depleted into the narrow end of the crevice, and with their wet-cloth thighs against each other's, they rested. He breathed more evenly and realized that she had fallen asleep, her head warming his arm. But he was soaked through, and there were too many angles or curves of his body which the land-bound wind was reaching, too few places where he was warmed by her weight on his limbs or her flesh through her clothing. He began to shiver uncontrollably. He had to waken her and make another move for them both. From this angle, looking out over the iron-colored water and upward, he thought idly that the stars looked cold, that there was surely no life on them, not of any kind which humans could visualize. He felt his own flesh moving in shivers, moving of its own accord and with no instructions, and he felt his mind moving in to take charge, it was perhaps the woman's body that shifted his balance, those lines of his flesh along which she rested seemed to bring him out of it and into a way of being with which he was more familiar. He had a minute of sensing even this land as metal, or himself as formed from a substance hostile to earth though part of it. And then she woke, his shifting had disturbed her from the intense sleep she swam in.

She woke with the new way open to her as well. His terrible coldness, his tremors which were not visible to her but were moving her as well, woke her, moved her in a way similar to when they made love in their house on the shore. It was his moving that shifted her from her isolation and metallic way of being alien even to herself, that brought her in some fast way back to him and his flesh, his presence as a man beside her. She did not yet realize who he was or remember what they had been to each other. It was only necessary to make him feel comfortable somehow, he was so hideously cold and shaking, with only a denim shirt and even that was spattered with wet. She had borrowed one of his sweaters for the boat trip but she knew it would remain on her back, that he would not accept it for covering now. There would have to be another way. At the same time that it occurred to her that their laundry was lying in the boat, their laundry clean and copious, he told her he was going down to the boat for some candles and fruit juice he had remembered were among the groceries.

There was a wide dark cotton rebozo in among that batch of clean clothes, and an old woolen sweater she had dared to wash, one that had come from Toluca and had always been too large for her. The sweater had not dried in the town's dryer, but the rebozo was dry, enough for him to put around his shoulders over the wet denim shirt. He wound it thus. She was thinking of a way to dry the sweater for him, they both knew that a fire was the next thing to do, not a specific thought of building a fire but the vague gratitude that there had been a dozen or more packs of matches in the groceries and that there were candles. He lit a candle, its light making them stare at each other like stone *idolos*. They looked and broke, spun into laughter, they laughed in a shaken relaxed way for the first time in many hours, his shivering stopped then, she was able to move again. He wanted to move away to explore, perhaps find a shelter, a shack or cave or place farther from the water, perhaps a place with a roof, or one where they could have shelter from that wind. So he began cautiously along the cliff, his hands moving branches away, the thorns of the growth getting caught on his socks and sleeves, the small branches of higher bushes catching on his hair and beard. His eyes could not get accustomed to the absence of light, but anyway he was beginning to move with a rhythm across the rocky edge of land, his own natural rhythms working, moving his long legs, letting him put down his heavy shoes with a kind of sureness which he had not felt for some hours. There was a cave: it would do for them. But he was not sure. His hands found it too smooth inside, none of the tough sharp uncomfortable bushes which grew above high water, none of the comforting tufts and patches of tough grass which they had found on the floor of their original crevice. He made his way back there.

She had come awake fully and wanted a fire. She

7

would not hear him when he wanted her to come with him to
seek out another shelter, perhaps something better than the
crevice where they crouched now. He thought that she was
afraid again, could not move again as it had been when he
moored the dinghy on the rocks and she had had to wait. He
spoke softly, firmly, explaining from his sureness, but she
would not or could not listen, all she seemed to want was a
fire, he must go and find firewood, not driftwood, which she
said would bring him too close to her enemy the water, as it
made its slow way toward their unseeing place. He wanted
driftwood, it would be dry and he felt sure he could go and
return without her knowing, he could safely fool her if he
went. She let him go, seeing his dark outline against the
stars as he climbed up the ridge above them and headed into
the forest.

   He returned with a long heavy board which she
knew must have been waterworn, but his other arm held
branches of dead land trees, and it would have done no good
to protest, his gesture was made. He had birchbark in one fist,
dry and curly; by the candlelight it looked the opposite of
the clams they had eaten that day, the clams with their
hardness over softness, their muscular or pulpy form, their
alternation of idea, and this birchbark had a spiral quality of
a conch, but it was all different, the clam was an alive thing
or dead but this birchbark had the quality of a possible
Moebius belt, it could be alive and dead and alive again, by
being a fire-thing, the fabric of the beginning of their fire.
That water near them had clams and mussels, invisible for
now but alive there, identifying with the undulations of the
incoming tides. But this birchbark and the dry wood, they were
in keeping with the land, or with fire as a land-thing, and the
hands of the man and the woman moved on the wood and
bark with the same quality as a finger would trace the curve
of a Moebius belt, the same delight or wonder. As if it were
flesh, as if it were the earth in which corn is planted, as if it

were what it indeed was: a container for fire, for the warmth they wanted and needed.

II.

In the time it took for the man to build the fire, the woman had found the dry leaves he needed. He had begun to break some of the larger branches and set them while she arranged small slabs of weathered slate to form a windbreak for the fire's survival. They worked silently and in unison. They had recovered much of it, that way of working together or being two parts of the same animal which they had achieved before tonight. It was no effort to make the necessary gesture, they worked quite rapidly, the crackling of the branches being broken to size, the small clatter of rocks they displaced in moving on the slanted floor of the crevice. He looked across the beginning flame of the fire at her face, wondering as he had done before at their difference, his face and hers, how her dark, straight hair hung in bangs near the oriental gloss of her eyes, the contrast of his own sleek oval close-cropped head with her small skull's typically Japanese configuration, his hair browner even in this light than hers, his broad, compact frame that of the mountains he came from. The rough bristle of his chin, unshaven since that morning in the safety and comfort of the hotel room, how many miles he had thought since then, since they had gone into the city to buy clothes. She was crouched flat-foot at the edge of the fire, arranging the heavy cotton robe so that it might dry, so that he would be able to wear it and be warmer. He wondered briefly if his sweatshirt was keeping her warm enough and saw that her hands were moving surely with the small twigs, she was not shivering any more, the sweatshirt seemed enough.

They built the fire against the smoothed side of the crevice, with the heavy board of driftwood as a vertical base for it: branches arranged tepee-fashion against it, so that the large board might catch fire in the steady wind. She moved quietly, watching to complement his moves or gestures, to supply him with the right wood for the building of the fire, or to move the robe so that its heavy folds would spread in turn toward the heat of the fire. There were no stars, the water was level and calm in the same dread windlessness which had prevented them from sailing directly toward this side of the mainland. She wanted to say something to him, to comfort him, but in her way she reached out to touch his face, keeping her silence, in keeping with the quiet of the water and the man himself. They were both reserved people, people who did not make acute gestures. She thought about what it might be like if they made love, if it would be as she imagined, a long time from now, when they had learned to move together in some sort of way that matched how they were making this fire. His calmness and her silence, the occasional sound of his voice the texture of wood, and her own answer which was of the consistency of a reed. It would be like the pruned trees of her own country, a delicacy and choice of structure, each gesture valid and each sense refined. But he was an inland man, his was a terseness of another kind, he moved more heavily than she, his frame was broad and thick-boned. The flesh from the ankle to the Achilles tendon was thin and stretched thinner at her foot, and his was firm and thickly filled in, and they walked much differently. He could not crouch as she was doing now, at the fire. He felt himself to be wholly of wood, even his flesh, not yet warmed by the fire, was porous and had soaked up too much of the stranger seawater. His own shirt was still quite damp, its textured silk clinging stickily to his skin under the thick folds of her obi. He felt almost wooden, as he had identified with the wood of their sailboat when they had tried to tack into the wind which was not there, in the early night. He felt somehow it would be dangerous for him to get his hand too close to that young fire.

The thick board caught fire soon. The man took

off his sneakers and socks and hung the socks on a branch near the fire, turned the tongues of the sneakers out so they would catch heat and dry. The woman took off her zoris, placed them some distance from the fire so that their wooden bases might dry out slowly without scorching in the direct heat; she knew they would not crack this way. Her cotton tabis were hung next to the man's socks on the same branch. Their double layer would take longer to dry, but that was all right, she was warmer to begin with than he was, she could wait. The two toe-sections of each tabi were filled at the ends with the fine white sand of the beach where they had landed the sailboat, and her dress and the dark tabis had flecks of the white paint of the hull and fragments of the rope of the hawser. Her left hand stung from the rope-burn, getting the boat up onto dry sand, pulling while he hauled the tiny craft. He knew he would have great trouble getting that ripped spinnaker fixed properly; after the great gusts of late afternoon had thrown them off course, it was impossible to do anything other than try to get it down in a hurry, and it was inevitable that it should catch in a gust and rip badly on the nearest cleat.

The man pulled out his pipe and the leather-and-plastic bag of tobacco and lit it from the new coals of the fire. He was considering the damage to the sail and whether the tide would reach the boat where they had left it. But the woman was sleepy, tired, dreadfully tired, she felt faint again and told him so, asked if they could possibly eat something, could they manage with some of the kelp from the shore or perhaps some of the three apples he had stuck into his pockets from the boat's supply. He silently gave her an apple and took one for himself. When she had finished the apple, she began to gather boughs for a makeshift bed on the floor of their cave. He tended the fire while she went. It was not his spirit to go out and she was apparently able to move away from the fire more naturally than he, and so he kept feeding the wood they had both found, the bits and chunks of driftwood from that long beach, two dried-out pieces of buoys, branches white with age and water, barnacle-encrusted small logs, branches with dried kelp wrapped in strands around them.

The man leaned back against the packed earth or almost rocky end of the cave, his feet toward the windbreak of branches he had set up toward its mouth. She moved into his arms, wound her legs around his near leg and, with her head on his chest at the curve of the armpit, fell instantly asleep. He remained awake. Above the branches, he could see the constellations of this part of the world and could identify some of them, but they looked oddly cold, as if they were surely uninhabited, at least as far as he could consider life forms. Yet his own body at this time did not seem a kind of life he could feel sympathetic toward: all of it save those segments which touched the woman were wooden; where her flesh touched, her head rested or her thigh adjoined his, he was flesh, but the rest of him was immutably wood, his spine the mast of the craft they had sailed to this place, his pelvis the boom, pivoting him into danger when it could move in other ways toward safety. Treachery. He could not trust his own body, moving as it did in ways involuntary and unbidden.

But as he shivered and his moves splintered against the woman's body, she awoke and turned to him, her thigh against his longer thigh, where the flesh was thick and had warmth. She was terribly cold now, shivering, at this distance from fire. They turned to each other, their bodies moved until he covered her and moved her skirt aside, and for the first time they knew each other, his warmth went through him to her as he entered her, and his body renewed itself into flesh again. Although it was the first time they were together, they moved with a grace that was seemly with the natural elements. She was an island woman, she moved with a blood knowledge of the way water moved as it sounded near them; and though he was an inland man, he knew trees, how they went into the wind and remained firmly strong, that instinct which lets things happen and does not make things happen. The lifegiving quality opposite to panic moved between them; no thoughts, a wilderness which was mindless, logical, wise. Their sounds were animal and in neither of their acquired tongues.

It did not matter that there had been many women for him before this night, and no man for her until now; they were moved outward toward each other from their woodenness until they turned to flesh again together. When they rested on sea-grass, the wind was lower and the fire had dropped to embers along the piece of driftwood. She slept again, her smooth head nested in his armpit as before, while the man again remained awake. The tide had changed along the beach, it was moving out with the first greenish grey of morning light, so that sea and sky were for a few moments the same color, no horizon line, no stars. He thought about the morning, about shelter for them, how far they might be from other people, the sensation of being separate from all people but this woman in an unreal way, as he had felt seeing the distant lights of boats too far across unfamiliar water in the deep night of their landing. The distance between himself and his own country, between himself and the earth he lay upon, was in reality only the distance between his flesh and that of the woman next to him, who was not alien to him in any way he could sense.

III.

He had gone to search for other people. At first the woman protested, not wanting to be left alone, a remnant of feeling from the night's hysteria. But the sun penetrated her still-damp clothing; she could visualize resting or perhaps sleeping on the rocks while he reconnoitred the island. Her mouth's inner surfaces tasted metallic and strong: she had chain-smoked most of the early part of the long night. Even their singing had sounded to her like the utterance of forced machines, so unlike the way they usually sang about their work in their cabin. The sound of the tide as it had risen toward their rock-cleft perch had awakened her too many times, it was a repetition of some old nightmare, even her man's warmth beside her did not comfort her immediately. She had remembered her father telling her that fire and water were good servants and poor masters. So that when they were almost ready to sleep and the man was already settled into the crevice of rock, his back braced against slate and his arms ready to receive her, she took time to bank the fire carefully, so that no spark could toss upward in wind onto the nearby twiggy bushes. Now, in the clear morning light, she began to renew the fire, stirring it so that the almost-buried live embers could rekindle, using the birchbark swirls the man had tucked into the rocks where she crouched.

They caught like cellophane. In a few moments she had the fire going, built against the unburnt section of the huge piece of driftwood he had brought. The wind was from the land now, it blew smoke to where she perched on the rocks above their crevice, but in her exhaustion she put her head onto her folded arms and slept. Heat from the sun and heat from the fire surrounded her, she fell into that small and intense dreaming sleep that knows itself to last briefly, she folded in upon herself until his return with some sort of news. The need for other people on this island did not come strongly to her. She knew that the area was well-covered days by lobster-fishermen and sardine-fishermen, the knowledge made the more sharp by their having tangled in the seine and thus lost the motor of the dinghy. But for now, with the panic of the night's isolation behind her, it was enough to know that the man would be returning, carrying his own thoughts and his own idea of himself and bringing back as well his idea of her as he saw through his clear blue eyes.

While she slept thus, he moved to the left of where they had beached the now-marooned little boat, gauging the possibility of dragging it down to the low-tide water. With the water as calm as it now was, and the tide not due to change sharply for at least an hour, he thought it one way to leave the island: to try to row in the gentler water, across the miles of bay to the mainland. But he and the woman were changed after the night. He felt crackled, as if he had been subjected to a heat or stress unusual to the natural fabric of his being, so that the surfaces of his face and the deeper matter were stricken into odd lines, in an unfamiliar pattern. He thought of the dry ground of playas, in the desert, those places where flash floods run, where the clay-and-sand earth dries too fast into hexagons, as expected in shape as snowflakes and as logical for their time and place: heat things, dry-after-flood things. The sun angled onto his back as he moved through the woods, branches catching on his hair and beard, thorns of the undergrowth getting caught on his socks and the drying cloth of his sleeves. He noticed that he was on a sudden path, grass beaten down in a regular curve along the high shoreline, and then there was a house: shuttered, closed-in.

He followed the path further. It turned into the inward part of the island, away from water, and in a grove of pine and spruce, he found the second house. The sharp, angular smell of evergreen lifted him toward it, there was no presence of the sea here, he could be in the heart of an inland forest and nowhere near the sea, save that there were clam-shells here and there along the path, curled to the air like the clear morning air itself solidified, made visible and tangible. The pine-needles underfoot gave off an almost solid aroma, musty, thick, the years or decades of needles under his feet gave him a perspective of his own time and how he had spent it until now. The woman had remembered, during the terrifying time before they had built the fire, she had had a surge of memory that day, many scenes from her years suddenly rising to the surface of her sunlit day, night memories, faces of people about whom she had not thought in years, and now the same feeling suffused him, the pine needles under his feet gave him doors into other times he had walked with this scent in his nostrils, and unexpected places slid through his eyes during his walking. That nearness to death had moved them both sideways through their lives, scenes and memories had oddly occurred from past days, friends, the look of sunlight during a certain autumn when he had gone to a football game with one girl, the angle of evening lightbulbs at a party she had gone to with one man, those long-gone times which came alive again as backdrop or precursor for this intense night of water and rock and cold wind, threatening to both of them in the quiet context of their lives as they had been until then.

The evergreens thinned at the edge of a clearing and he saw the second house. An old woman responded to his knock at the door by jutting her head from an upstairs window: she was old, unable to be of any help to them, but some distance away he would find a couple who lived in a large red house and who had a functioning boat. Her head inclined toward another shore, the curve of which, if continued further, would have brought him full circle to where the woman was waiting and asleep on the rock shore. He moved along the grassy path as the old woman suggested and after the next turn saw the huge old red house with its grounds bent toward the waters of the bay. As he moved toward the door he heard the putt-putting of the first lobster-boats moving out across the bay to pick up and set out their traps for the new day. His knock was answered by a tall man whose resemblance to himself was marked: yet his own English accent was shaded off into the local speech of the Maine area where they were, and the man was clean-shaven, slightly shorter, broader in stature, less tree-like. He opened the door wide and took the man in at once.

His woman come out to them. She was a small, blonde woman of delicate structuring, with a strong Spanish accent and the fine aristocratic features of the landed classes of some countries: the high-bridged nose, skin so fine that the fine wrinkles near the eyes were mostly suggested, not quite visible. Her handclasp was stronger than the man expected. The rooms of the house spread back of her, he saw worn furniture, a massive stone fireplace, a hooked rug covering an oval diameter of the wide golden floorboards: to him, the place was civilized, more than that, it was tasteful and genteel in a familiar and comforting way. He saw himself reflected in their eyes, his beard matted and twiggy, clothing hanging damply, in fact he still had her rebozo wound over his denim shirt. But as he grinned his explanations, the man led him to a chair and the wife went to the kitchen for coffee and toast. Never in his life had he felt so grateful for walls, for the house-smell which held him like old memory of youth. He felt the chill beginning to sift outward from his marrow, he smoked the cigaret proffered by his host, and they talked a bit, discussing the details of his experience on the far side of the bay and the other side of the island. The wife came in with a tray of coffee and toast, the toast burnt mostly but lathered with butter and accompanied by the first truly English marmalade the man had tasted since leaving his own country years before. It was delicious.

The couple had two boats moored down the hill in an inlet of the bay, and since one of them had a working motor, the host volunteered to come around the curve of shore to where the woman and the boat waited. The man thought of his woman back there and went to get her. It was fitting for her to share the delight of such coffee after their night. He went back along his former path, past the houses, to where the woman slept across rocks, head on arms. Again she woke from heavy dreams: she was a child, in a dark Mexican village where streets were ruts, cloudbursts turned them into rivers, teaching her the nature of water's threat. She looked quickly toward the banked fire, instinctively checking its intense heat with her hands, and the feeling from her youth returned, yes, this heat was just right for the maiz, it would burn the edges of the tortillas but would cook them right, the thin layer would puff and rise into bubbles of heated air and they would be good to eat or take to the kitchen in clean napkins. How long it had been since she had come to this country or had eaten a fresh tortilla, how caught she had become in the netting ways of this country and of this man who himself was both alien and familiar to her. Her throat was thick with longing for her own country, to be speaking her own tongue, her throat burned with too many cigarets from the night's ordeal and with the thousand unused phrases stopped there while she spoke a language only vaguely resembling her own.

But her man was telling her of coffee, and toast, and the couple who awaited them. She had to turn to flesh again from the smoke world she had slid into. Together they doused the fire with seawater and gathered the assortment of clothing, candles half-burnt, and cigaret-packs. She let him lead her over the higher rocks and into the woods, along the path and through the inland forest. It was refreshing, hot sun into deep shade and always the firm, crisp smell of the pines, almost like the thinner stands along the Toluca highway, whose scent rarely came out, except during the dense afternoon rains of summer and spring. They walked single-file, passing the first and second houses, she realized her exhaustion and stumbled as they reached the grassy path of the large red final house.

The tall Maine man again met them, took her hand briefly and introduced his wife. The women moved quickly to another part of the house, first the kitchen, for fresh coffee and more toast, then to sit drinking and eating near the two men on the capacious porch which overlooked the Maine bay. From there they could all see the island which had been the dinghy's destination: three miles out, it was shrouded in ideas and not quite itself. The women spoke in Spanish, but with sure barriers between them, the blonde head inclined at a certain angle toward the dark head, a reserve between them, a certain compassion from the fair woman as she ministered to the two visitors. The Englishman watched his dark woman as she spoke Spanish, he had never heard her thus, he glanced at her between the practical sentences of the men's conversation. She seemed to be moving out sharply from her terror, she had a look of a bird now, her head inclining in a way so familiar to him from their own calmer conversations. He could tell that she did not like the fair woman but had decided to trust her completely.

They were offered a warm bath before the trip to the island would be assayed. When he was in the tub, he held his hand lightly on the surface of the water and considered the skin of water, its almost metallic quality, how much more liquid it seemed when warm, a mercury, not the molten quality of last night's icy sea but the wanton nature of a metal which was at the same time liquid. His own body floated like wood toward the surface of the warm water. And when the woman had finished eating, and took her tub, it seemed to her that this house was a ship, a boat of some kind, that the air was itself water and she was at that moment immersed in a natural element called air, this was air that was cleansing and easing her muscles after that terrible night, when she stepped out of the tub it would be to move back into water somehow. She shut her eyes and let her body float to the surface, a linear current, perhaps at the level where stratus clouds form. She thought about cirrus clouds, how they curved, and about the curl of the birchbark, how alike the two shapes were. The element moved in such a swirl when she turned her arm and hand, the way the oar had responded last night. She knew clearly that the terror of last night would grow thin and thinner as her days passed, until she would no longer look out into the saltwater and feel her throat constrict, her toes turn as if to dig more surely into earth.

They dried their hair before the huge stone fireplace. The plan was to go around the shoreline to the far cove where the dinghy was stranded high on rocks. The Maine man would fasten a leader to it and would tow it, empty except for the groceries, out to the island, while the Englishman and his woman would ride with him in his motor launch. While the fair woman cleared away the food and gave fresh coffee, the host put on the phonograph, first the Bloch Concerto Grosso for Strings, then a Schubert Quintet. He mentioned his wife's training in the London Conservatory as a pianist, and her performances in Barcelona and Nice, they had met while he was in the army in London, where her father was serving with one of the diplomatic offices. The Englishman had a vague memory of the name of her father, that name which she had used professionally herself as a pianist briefly in London. But the Mexican girl chose the music now playing, rather than to acknowledge the other woman's past as present in that room. Her own Barcelona was Guanajuato, her own memories linked with colonial silver to the baroque university buildings there, her own studies which had not included music except as an adept listener. It was her Englishman who was the musician. She could watch them and at the same moment be completely involved in the Schubert, its thick swells of cello moving like tides into the fine edges of the violins. She did not need to talk. But her man's face was bright as he talked with them, his beard soft and reddish in the firelight.

It was almost midmorning when they rose to go down the hill to the inlet where the fit and unfit boats were moored. The blonde Spanish wife stayed at the house, she watched them leave and made her gracious goodbyes, inviting them to return at an early and less harried time, her manner was immaculate and somehow gentle, her eyes deeper-set than they had noticed. And there was something else. A reaching out to them, a touching which had no explanation. The smooth manner of her goodbye was surface for some thought or sensing, for which she had no words. The Mexican woman acknowledged this by turning, halfway down the hill, looking past the two men, directly to the face of the other woman.

But by then they were near the boat. The water near the boat was rainbowed with oil, its seat was hot and dry. The two men got them off the mooring, one working the motor, the other shoving at the wooden dock to give them that slight turn or impetus of direction. His hand scraped the edge of the dock, so that a red mark appeared diagonally across the heel of his hand, with tiny droplets of blood near the imbedded bits of wood of the dock. The woman handed him a cigaret and the boat's owner gave him a clean handkerchief to bind the hand with. They moved around the long, Manhattan-shaped island toward the rocks where the dinghy lay. The men talked of tides and the Englishman pointed out the place, fully a mile away, where they had dropped the motor the previous night. The host offered to pass by that spot, with a view to try to salvage the motor, even though it might have been found already by the owner of the seine in which it had become entangled, since it was of a certain value, and this was their course. They moved over the water of the bay, moving rapidly so that the space seemed far less than it had by black night. The woman did not want to stop for the motor, she wanted to go straight to the island, to their little house, their own land things. But she did not say any of this, and they continued smoothly across the bay.

When they reached the place where the seine had been placed, there were no cork markers from the shoreline. The little motorboat moved closer in to shore, plying back and forth in an attempt to perhaps find some sign left by the owner of the seine, or the seine itself, or perhaps a marker indicating where the motor was. In this bright sunlight, the island should have been a known quantity, yet it had a quality of mystery about it, the absence of the seine or any sign of the seine or motor, and the waters nearby were oddly clear of the usual fishing-boats. It was past the time when the lobstermen trolled past, laying their boats into the wind to retrieve their full traps, it was not yet time for the sightseeing boats to move on their routes through the richer islands. It was quiet, quiet and hot, the water had the metallic sheen of between-tides, of noon, it had a tension at its surface which made it seem like a molten metal in this even heat.

The two men seemed more ruffled than necessary. Without looking at the woman, they leaned their heads together and talked, looking from land to water, from surface of water to depths of water, each man looking into the other man's face and then to the land or the water. It had become important to locate the motor, more important than the motor itself. The woman's hand rested on the wood of the gunwale, creating a small pool of shade in the intense heat. Their craft's motor was turned off, there was no wind, and suddenly the sun fell behind clouds. At that moment the Englishman turned and looked at his woman, where she sat across from him. Her face was taut and uneven, the look she returned was odd, his insistence on this part of the trip was against her instincts. A shred of last night's panic crossed between them, against logic. Each saw the other with water as background and there was a terror in the repetition.

A wind began. The boat's owner reached to start its motor and stopped. The same oil which had rainbowed near the dock was spread in a swirl or curve around the bow of this craft now. The tide had begun to shift. The three knew it would be no use to try to start the motor, and so, with the wind rising and the sun so long behind clouds that the air was chill, the Englishman put his handkerchief-wrapped hand down, past the bailing-can, to the bottom of the boat, where he knew he would find the oars. Oil was all around them. The woman's hair, clean and fresh, fanned out into the wind, but did not change its smell to salt, it flowed to one side of her head and then across her face, blurring her eyes and sifting across her mouth. He handed her an oar.

1964

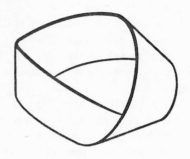

THE FARM WOMAN,

or,

The Powers of Magic and Earth

It was possible that the Farm Woman had burned the house down. In her thirtieth year, having decided to be done with at least some of it, she lit a cigaret (she was not accustomed to smoking) and set fire to the farmhouse by allowing the cigaret to fall. And simply not picking it up. She watched it begin with a hole in the wide old floorboard of the big main room of the farmhouse. The building to which she had come as his bride, eleven years ago. It did not occur to her to destroy the house in any other way, in a less passive fashion.

She undeniably had a certain aura. Before the burning of the house, the Farm Woman had already been twenty-nine, had already been in the Baha'i movement for a year . . . had had four children, all very difficult births (she a big woman, and so it was against nature to have a hard child-bearing, against the earth itself; she being so big-boned, everything looked as if it would be so easy). But there had been no orgasm and the last child was a breech-birth, he weighed over ten pounds and was, at least at his birth, all bones, no fat. Unlike the pigs in their shed, who gave only ten dollars' profit to the family at sale. They had to be fat and weigh high.

Not her concern, really, whether to burn the house or leave it to strangers. The pigs went about, smelling from the yardshed, the flies went from manure to her kitchen with grace and no distinction. The same little white pills cured an upset stomach or the croup or the flu. The same women came to see her, well or ill, the same numbers on the cover of the telephone book in her kitchen.

The building had a room in the cellar which was perhaps a hundred and fifty years old. The walls were two feet thick, ideal for insulation but not so valuable for burning. She forgot about those walls while she performed the slow ritual of watching the burn on the front-room floor as it widened . . . as the burn grew wider, it became the mouth of her mother, telling her to shut up, shut up, get to work, every day: a strong woman, that one, a teacher, to other children anyway . . . her own thought her soft, if they considered her at all, lately. Or maybe some of them simply noticed a burn charring oval into a wood floor she had cleaned too often.

The Farm Woman did not know Shakespeare, but he had once known her, quite carnally, in the way a playwright of great toughness knows his people. In his hands. Through the ends of his fingers, through his sexual parts, which functioned the same way. When she slept, her hands made the motions of kneading her bread. Awake as well. She had no knowledge of why she'd married Robert, and no particular pride, except in the widow's peak of the oldest child, who sometimes resembled her.

She weighed a great deal, even for a big-boned woman: two hundred pounds. In her world, the weight of things was important. More than the proportion. Quarts of milk from their cows were weighed by the pound, the cans of foodstuffs from the A&P were packaged by Heinz for hotel use, sometimes there were sixteen at dinner and always extra folks coming by. Two of her four children were huge, massive, and one of these was truly ungainly. He had a habit of pissing his bed at night; he was the size of a small bull or horse, or an unknown, unnamed large animal. He weighed a hundred and fifty-two pounds and was just eight years old, stood a bit over five feet tall. When standing next to his bed nights, turned, pissing quietly in his sleep. As her sleeping hands kneaded dough, he was in the next room, pissing the covers through. His future was not sure, and she sensed this, but this was not in her reason for burning away at the house . . . not ultimately. For he did know his figures well, he did, and called her 'Mommy' well.

If giraffes or lions or other complete strangers had appeared at her kitchen door, wearing nothing or loin-cloths but identifying themselves as being from her Baha'i group, she would have asked them in at once, offered them a place at table, dinner, the big meal, but all the time wondering, inside herself, if she would give them her fat boy, should they ask. What if they should invoke the name of the Baha'i founder, or quote from some important book they had just read and she had never read. Manners did count.

Well, it would be a pity, but she might do it; ruefully, though, because it might have been nice if the children had all had a chance to ride on a train, maybe just once. Never quite enough money for a train, or to go to the movies all of them together once a week; they took turns; every other week half went. She did not know the accounts of the farm but she did know it would be a shame to let the kids go before even a train-ride. So this feeling, then, would begin to be a reason for getting rid of the house. Some way to get out from under a weight. Starting with the big room. The biggest.

The cellar room was unused, mostly, though she

took visitors there to see it. The big fireplace was in scale with her, one could roast half a steer on it and have room. That spit! with its hook for the kettles! of such marvelous strong metal. But this room was unused. Her own kitchen was just above it and to its left, and had an electric teakettle, an electric stove, an electric mixer, an electric blender. It was so very odd to her, these slick appliances, so modern alongside the thick primitive farm faces and areas. Near the pigpen, near the barn, near her, near the milk cows, this same milk that went to make evaporated milk for the cities. Near all of them, her odd bovine face, milky white beneath freckles, jut-jawed, puzzled. She had a certain aura, though, she did; it came out mostly when the children were abed, and just before the fat one pissed, before she slept. It had vaguely to do with the cows, maybe, perhaps other animals, what, yes, animal-aura, nothing to do with humans.

The burn had the shape of a flower as it grew. A dark blossom, the round oval of clover but without softness; it had a fine perfume of its own, the scent of clean old fine wood burning, charring . . . the ideas burning through, finally. Why had she married Robert, why had she come to the old house, and then borne these thick children out of her pained body, how had she acquired this aura that she knew existed when she walked or shopped in the circular town. The town was like her: the plans for its layout had gotten confused with another nearby town, which had had a small lake or pond as its central focus. The plan for that town had been to build all the stores in a circle around the pond, and, for her own town, to build the stores in a gentle semicircle, with a view of mountains as a focus. But, the mistake having been made, the city fathers having gotten the plans mixed, the architects being on their vacations when the buildings were begun, the confusion: her town had a neat circle of shops which centered rather oddly around an office building and its dull, small, irregular lawn, thereby neatly blocking out the fine view of the hills, and the nearby town had gained a semicircular shopping district, though without a view, so that half the small pond was naked and awkward.

In one of the shops, a coffee-shop called The Busy Bee, she would pause occasionally. Was once seen there with her daughter, a loose-lipped, wide-mouthed child who resembled her maternal grandmother . . . though at times she resembled one parent or the other. But always the same quiet, sullen round face. The Farm Woman took her daughter with her into this Busy Bee once, to share the ritual of taking food and drink not prepared at home on her stove, in her own kitchen. This child, this daughter, for whom no bright future could be discerned . . . another reason for allowing the farmhouse to catch fire. The daughter was like the woman her mother, and unlike her. When the child dressed up in clothing given to her by the grandmother or an aunt, she seemed as skinny as a pine tree, and made no sense at all, even as a masquerader. The mother stared, and doubted she could explain Baha'i to such a child, ever.

In the cellar room behind the huge pile of kindling and near the larger pile of logs for winter burning were odd pieces of furniture and some loop-rugs made by her near aunt. O this aunt, so very handy with delicate work, things like sewing and weaving; o she was thin, even inside! whereas the Farm Woman was gross, and inside her lived the kind of small woman, birdlike, handy, like the aunt, like the creature who lived inside Dorothy Parker's gross mammy-character Pearl: petite, exquisite, a blossom finer than any clover. If the Farm Woman could have chosen another nationality, her inside-woman would have been of royal Italian birth (a quick, easy, tiny, slippery birth), those tiny sleek women who appeared to her lovely in a Sunday Supplement once each year in their light fabrics and Maseratis, stories of their hands easy and light with silks, jewels, powders, books; how she would love to touch that way, touch such jewels, colors, books! In the front room, on the long table near the widening charcoal stain, near to her, there were the agricultural magazines, with their tractors and their milking-machines, fertilizers, and pick-up trucks; and the Baha'i magazines and books, and the Reader's Digest &c., but no Paris Match, or Il Giorno, no examples of Garibaldi's force or Vivaldi's forms, no Dante. Most of the forms moving near her were as she, were large, firm, Michelangelo or Lachaise figures set into space.

But she would never learn to weave; it was enough to knead, and to cook; at least, these had been enough, before she'd joined Baha'i. Then it became important to have many more people in: once, at an open-house she'd had, there were thirty-eight Baha'i, culled for love like the wheat heaped to the wind on the open truck. Ah, one might wish, but couldn't ever have all the Baha'i people to the farm, there wasn't enough room at table, and so many strangers would intimidate her kids like so many unfamiliar beasts appearing suddenly: not things to be petted or played with, not relatives, not familiar. But some few did come. She was pleased with the new friends. Each one of them, it seemed to her, had so much good available, to be found and relished.

In trying to see much good in each person she met through Baha'i, she ran into the problem of being unable to see much beyond her own creases of flesh, the folds that grew near her eyes, then the ones that ran around her belly and hips, which prevented her from seeing the kids clearly. It was one thing to be philosophical about it, this trying to see everyone's good, and it was quite another if one's eye-folds or belly-flesh made it difficult to see the other person clearly at all. But it could not change. In this house. In this house, there were often no vegetables for the meal. Fine vegetables were grown in their gardens. But they were raised for sale at the market. A few would appear with each seasonal crop at some meal. But she baked a great deal, of course, using hundreds of pounds of white flour, not made of their own-grown wheat, and she baked her own bread, cakes, rolls, muffins, pies, biscuits, and cookies, carrying the kneading motion on into her sleep. Much of the time she was preparing bread or rolls in her sleep, as when awake.

It did not occur to her that she was destroying the house. She had already done so much this week, what with seeing to the feeding and hearty nourishment of over two-hundred-and-ten people (if you consider that she had around ten or twelve in to regular meals in summer, and each one counted as one mouth for one meal), not to talk about cleaning, and some chores, and many trips down-cellar. In the cellar, near the woodpile, was the freezer which stored some of the foods prepared in the kitchen, with the aid of all her electric machines. Many days she would go to the cavernous freezer, to see if she could find an idea, an inspiration for the next meal or two, and she called this 'getting a package of Frozen Ideas,' which usually worked out fine.

She had learned much of what she knew from watching her own mother around a kitchen. Always the mother's mouth, instructing, instructing, and the mouths of her brothers and sisters and the guests, mouths to be fed, around that other honey-colored kitchen table, day after day: those mouths resembled the dark oval blossom on the wood at her feet. Not like the dark night, which did not threaten, with its green grass dark and mildly illuminated to silver by the moon; this blackening wood made her shudder. The dark night had its own idea of forms and shapes: thin spirits. She had never been thin, even as a baby. As her own children had come, each had seemed to be an open mouth all the waking time: she nursed them: so that a shoe lying on the floor, a cookie darkly round on her table, or an empty cup, would appear to be a waiting open mouth, waiting for her copious milk. Waiting to take her energy. All the objects in any room which could look like an open baby-mouth . . . .

Robert's mouth was thin-lipped and calm: he had one tooth missing, toward the front, which made him look older than his thirty-seven years. He was quiet, quiet, he had this quiet even way about him, never did talk much about how he felt; in fact, until last year the wife had never really wondered how he felt, and he never said. Four children between them as flesh bridges, and she never knew how he felt about anything, except when he was physically hurt, like the time he caught his hand in the thresher. . . . Neither of them fell ill much; it was always the children, the small or large illnesses of childhood. When either of the adults was hurt, it was as a result of accident, and rare, took them under completely for a while, and then was done. Then, back to it, as usual, back to all of it, day after night. The comfort of his back and legs at night, his warm body, the sweetness of his bony face turned to her in sleep. But rarely when they were awake. And never saying . . .

It was the upstairs porch might have really begun it, this black burn on the front-room floor. After dinner, she had been sitting there, as often she sat nights after the children were finally asleep. This night realizing that she and Robert had never talked, she did not know how he felt, what he thought, wanted. How he imagined, what he dreamed, long nights next to her. Only last year she had finally learned that he did not like the animals part of farming, only the grains part. So then what did he want, him thirty-seven already and all these years next to her, slender near her wondrous bulk, skin tanned hard with hours under the sun on the combine, pale belly-skin, hair the color of and the way of oats and barley-beard . . . . on the porch, in the nights, she thought about his eyes.

About the word 'love' as it had never passed between them. Wondered if he reckoned her by gross poundage as with the animals and the milk. What if he were heard, some day, figuring it out, 'Now let's see, at better than two hundred pounds or so, with more in wintertimes, puts away, say, most half as much again as I do, or twice easily as even the fat kid, well, that would come to around . . .' and get to his annual figure. In that quiet way of his. What if. That

magazine at her elbow, The Farm Woman's Journal, nothing
in it about her Baha'i friends, but it had a story in it about
a New York City working girl and her lover. Many nights,
after the kids slept, she took a look at the story. The New
York man called his girl 'my darling' and 'my love.'

This idea of a lover. Reaching through to the
slender woman who lived inside, who wore silks and moved
gracefully, to whom Robert had never spoken, not with bodies
or with words . . . he and she were more speechless than
the animals around them . . . she saw herself in the dark
glass of the glassed-in upstairs porch: and her mouth gaped
open. Dark circle on pale freckled heavy face. Well then.
Enough. That damn open mouth on that damn face. It was
hands she wanted to see now, not kneading, but delicate in
some Italian way . . . she took her mouth and hands down to
the front room. Robert was out to the once-a-month lodge.
The children slept. She did not think about it. Found some
of his cigarets, awkwardly lit one with her mouth firmed oval
over it, then with those thick hands placed it on the wide
wood of the floor. Or let it fall.

Her eyes widened and took in the world as it
burned into a dark circle. Surely it would go downward, the
flower, through the ceiling to the cellar room with its great
spit and freezer; slowly, slowly. Then there was a small noise
at the door. The kitchen door. Not the front door where
company always came. The Farm Woman rose and moved
there, saw the two lions, they were at ease, so she greeted them
as they stood in their white loin-cloths, since they knew. She
knew. Without opening her mouth, she went to get the big
boy, the ungainly son, for whom they had not needed to ask.
Their expressions were perfectly clear, understandable. It was
so easy. . .

Leaving the other children sleeping for the while,
she went with the lions to the cellar room, past the secret
bedroom where she and Robert really lived, in soft dishevel-
ment, away from the tidyness of the rest of the house. Went

down the stairs; and then it turned out that when she'd let them in she'd missed noticing one Baha'i book: which was the one used by the near lion to start the fire in the wide, seldom-used fireplace. The kindling and logs were attended to by the other lion. The boy did not wake during any of this. Nor when they arranged him gently on the spit. She watched, knowing it would work out, and remembered how he called her 'Mommy,' how he knew his figures, how he pissed the bed, standing up, each and every night. . . . Somewhere around this time, her hands went involuntarily into the old kneading motion. One of the lions gestured toward the freezer. The Farm Woman went over, reached in, with hands that were becoming different. She got out a can of Frozen Ideas, and it was working out. Without a can-opener. It just came open in her changing hands. In their new way of moving. A new speediness, but with grace. As if they knew that right now Robert would be driving along toward the house, would be here soon, and it would have to be well along, all of this, by then.

The eyes were wider and now, finally, the hands were different. One of the lions tended the spit; the other went upstairs to check the blossom of char on the floor (it was beginning to smolder through to the ceiling beam above her head; it was going along just fine), and to move the three other children, still asleep, out of the house. To the cool silvery grass, other side of the farmhouse, away from the too-close pigpen and its inhabitants, who knew too much and not enough but were making their knowledgeable sounds. All right. About the trainride, well, she felt quite at ease about that, and about possible trips to any restaurants as well. There is something about a lion's motions which breeds confidence, or at any rate, a certainty of aura. . .

There was a gesture from them that indicated that she was to have her turn, and, while waiting, to gather the Baha'i books she kept in the front room, placing them near the dark smolder. Still no flame. She watched the wood and was careful to avoid meeting her reflection in the glass of the dark window back of the sofa. Then the second lion came in, to indicate it was her turn. She went with him down the stairs to the big cellar room, where she found the spit warm, empty and somehow quite cozy, not a brilliant fire but rather a warm and comfortable one, unlike the heat of the electrical gadgets in the kitchen. The boy was nowhere to be seen. She did notice, before she stopped noticing things for a while, that the charred beam above was about to burst into flame, probably a warm flame, not hot, soft-colored.

When Robert turned off the main road toward the farm, he saw the glow in the sky. Accelerated his motor. He did not recognize most of the people watching the farmhouse and barn aflame: but there was a boy who was familiar around the eyes, and there was a tall, pretty woman, a lady with oval-shaped, very dark eyes who motioned to him that he might join them as they sat. Although he had never seen her before, he was drawn to her. He commented to her that the flames looked like lion-manes or some sort of fur, and she smiled. He was not seemingly conscious that this was his farm. They sat together, watching the buildings turn to glass and then to smoke and to mist, and then, in an unconcerned way, watched the night go.

The woman reached into her purse, got out a golden cigaret-case, took out a cigaret, offered him one; he lit it for her, enjoying her perfume and the way she held his hand, just so, a touch, a steadying in the wind, when he extended the match. He felt he'd seen that woman before. But he could not ask her. He was very quiet. But she was quite chatty; told him she was a widow, from another county, with one child, the boy at her side. The neighbors decided afterward, in their fashion, that the Farm Woman, probably by some cruel accident, had perished in the house after a cooking-fire or some other kitchen fire, which had easily spread to the barn . . . it was discussed. A sweet woman, and such a healthy one, and them kids, all gone. . . . But

33

some other family took over after that; they seemed to know a great deal about the property; they were all bone and gave up on the livestock, sticking to the grains . . . and wasn't it lucky for poor Robert, to meet that widow just when he was so alone, and he thrived, got so as he could really tell a funny story, and him such a quiet one for so long. Seemed very much in love with the dark eyes of his new wife. In less than a year, she left him, and the area, and took her son, and went abroad to live.

1964

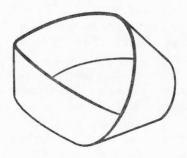

KOU,
or,
Coming to Meet

I.

She was pockmarked. She would be riding the bus and carrying a transistor radio, of black plastic, tuned to 'Downtown' or 'I Want to Hold Your Hand.' But the music would always be soft, not harsh or offensive like the cigar of the man toward the rear of the bus. Her eyes were astounding: insect-like in enormity, magnified by lenses for nearsightedness with perhaps a touch of astigmatism. And the poor brown shoes, worn, cheap, neat. Her cheeks, taut over the bones, were covered with the pustules of a late acne: my cousin had such skin cleansed with acid treatments when we were children in a Bronx slum. This girl: I stared at her: she reminded me of people I had known, no one definite, many people in my past, that girl in our 8th-grade class who had such bad skin and was shunted aside . . . but those eyes, and the alert set of her head—these reminded me of the rich, plain girl who was the daughter of a house-builder in a town I lived in later in my life. In every class of my school-days there was one such girl. She who had a beautiful older sister and who herself was absolutely plain; who was lovable and welcome because she was no competition. And these days, I see this composite girl on the bus, often, crossing the island we both live on now, holding my memory in her hands with the plastic transistor radio. She always sits up front, near the door, near the driver. She speaks with him.

II.

They live in such a way that even one who has travelled much in other countries is moved to exclaim. They are both massive, fine-looking, finely fleshed. The man reminds me of a shark, the woman of an unnameable soft-furred jungle animal; they are wildly civilised people; rain-forest people; Wall Street People; Ile St. Louis people; hidden-valley people; cocktail-party people. They are practitioners and purveyors of the purest evil I have ever encountered in human form. When one is invited to their home, to one of their parties, one is assigned an invisible small etched tag, worn above and between the eyes, to indicate the specific way in which one is notably distinguished from the human herd: achievement, into notoriety, is valuable to them. They themselves are not notables, their names hold no significance to those in the arts except in the light of their limited patronage. He does not know that she has a secret post-office box, she does not know that he has been faithful to her for all the years of their married life. I see her bangle earrings, from Sikkim or Siena or Samarkand, where they at one time lived; her soft body constantly pregnant, one dark baby after another curled into her wide arms or at her breast, her fair curly head bent over the baby head. I see her moving with the same grace at a dinner for twelve famous adults as at a birthday party for twelve tiny classmates of one of her children. I see her alone in a tiny, antiquated kitchen, her gourmet cookbook open for the children's party rather than for the adults' dinner; I see her tall, wide body enlarged by pregnancy and by the thick fur coat of an unknown animal (unlabeled; brought back from the latest country) and the latest two-year-old at her knee in a similar fur coat handed down from the child directly above, whichever sex. And I see him with my sense of smell: if my nose had hackles, it would tingle and they would rise when he moved into a room: the immense bulk of him, perhaps glandular in origin—but I have seen him poised eagerly before a steak that might feed four average appetites. He is a man of appetites. He is an angry man and a malcontent; he wants all that this society can offer him, and he has used his excellent and imaginative education toward this end: he has become a procurer, of sorts. Money can buy taste, and he has good taste to begin with; from there, money can equal fame. He is a collector, of furniture, of people, of weapons. And their taste is exquisite; such sherry, from an unheard-of city in southern Spain! such toys in the violet rooms of the children! such foods, flowing into the tiny, unmodern kitchen from all parts of this and other great cities! and flowing outward from her hands to that great trencher table at which the big man waits with his collection of guests and children! But a mutual friend also sees them clearly, and from a different angle. It does not surprise him that she tips the greengrocer ten cents for an order of seven dollars' worth of exotic fruits; and he summed up my sensings when he told me, 'With such grossness, they must live in this manner, to equate their forms; their tiny true natures live within and become evident.' And another friend, having been well-used and ill-used by the couple, added, 'They have no genus, no breed. A bit more coarse-textured, and they would be merely starfuckers, but what invisible label can we apply to this form of hunger?' Meanwhile, they are dabbling in the dangerous arts, and moving with Pergolesi behind them. And the laughter of many children.

III.

They are affectionate with their children. 'Not how often, but how much. . . .' My child plays often with them and I visit with the parents while the children play. Delores and I sit and talk about the offensive moral attitudes of the falsely emancipated American woman of today: she who has been convinced that independence is a fair price to pay for loss of femininity. With the children scattered near us, with the great hairy dogs racing through and seven alabaster kittens underfoot, we talk quietly, holding Courvoisier or pipes of Asian hashish. This Friday, my son fell in love with their second-eldest child, a finely-wrought girl who is not beautiful by American tastes but is a Vermeer sketch, a Botticelli portrait: the tiny chin, oval face, the long nose and straight fine hair. We often meet them at concerts; this mother is always late, as I am always punctual; it is a balancing; she is a bit less late now, learning from me, and I arrive a bit after curtain some of the time. I have wondered how her children feel, always arriving when the performance is well under way, or how my own child feels, always rushing with me to arrive early or à point. From time to time she tells me she wishes she, too, were writing. This is another factor that links us, and is why she looks forward to my visits, and is why he hates me. He sees to it that they rarely visit our tiny apartment, though it too has its evidences of travel and of ideas.

IV.

I have participated in a mixed-media and am returning home by bus. My child is beside me. After I see him safely to bed,

I am to cross town again, to join friends for the evening. The pockmarked young woman is seated at the front, near the door, near the driver. Her transistor radio is in her lap; she is eating from a bag of candy and is tuning the radio, munching the candy with a quick, animal motion of her head: updown, updown, updown, rhythmically. Her coat is thin, in relation to the brilliantly cold air of this New York City winter, and her hands are rough-textured and reddish and youthful as she waves them quickly up and down with the candy. Her enormous eyes are those of a lemur, resting on me for a brief second without evidence of recognition. You could almost say that she didn't see me. When I leave the bus, she remains, maintaining the silence and absorption of her usual life. I go home, see that the boy is safely abed and that my sitter is comfortable, and leave the house. On the two-way street where the bus travels, I see the bus I will catch: and she is on it, she is on it, although barely an hour has passed. I see her straight, pulled-back hair and the thin face, pointed toward me, where I stand in darkness, waiting; she is clear, she is illuminated, and she is the only passenger. The bus starts East, passes, going toward its last stop, whence it will turn and come to where I wait. And it does. And as I board, I see her: she is still there, still the only passenger; but she has changed her clothing, she is wearing a heavy coat now, a woolen plaid, and a worn pair of black shoes. She is hatless, gloveless, *sans* candy but with the transistor radio. And at this point I begin to see her: there is a tautness, an electricity here, some aura between her and the driver of this bus. They do not speak, they have never spoken in all of the times I have seen her here. But it is always she and this one driver, always this same driver, all the times. On this short route, almost a local affair, the drivers are acquainted with many of the regulars, exchanging banter and pleasantries. But not this silent girl, not this driver. He is dark, sallow, stocky, a silent man with a warm expression. And I see her skull, with its skin taut behind the acne, until the idea comes: perhaps she is his woman, perhaps this is her idea of how love is, to ride the bus and ride, until she is noticed, acknowledged, until she becomes familiar to him, perhaps she wishes to be his woman; wherever her desperate clothing is hung, at the end of this busline, is not where she lives, but here, on this bus, on these endless, oval rides across an island . . . she rides, her thin legs crossed over her oval womanhood, her oval mouth firmed shut or opened for candies, her great round eyes immured in the hunger of seeking. . . .

V.

I am invited to one of their parties. He is the perfect host, smiling from beneath his delicate moustache with his toothy, predatory smile, waiting for the next personage to arrive, guiding the most recent arrival to the liquor or food or toward someone who is in the field most *apropos* for conversation. While she moves about warmly, wifely, in this exaggerated house; she moves thickly through rooms double the size of reality, where all the faces soon assume the quality of the blurred edges seen in the portraits of the family which line the walls. The herd of children runs distantly; now it seems there are at least twenty-five of them; I would not, at this point, be surprised to hear them announced as the next delicacy. After all, this society! with its ridiculous dicta . . . anyone in this room would consider this country provincial and a bit absurd. . . . Someone tells me that the poet Robert Lowell is here, and I see him, at the end of the long, narrow room, stretched in an unusual pose of ease on a chaise longue, under one of the huge portraits of Cecil and Delores (she with one of the children at each knee; he with his opium pipe; the many other children peering through nearby, like a Tchelitchew painting, one of his watercolor sketches that are studies for large oils). . . It is Robert Lowell there, and I want to speak with him. But Cecil tells me that it will be necessary to exact a certain fee, since I am a lesser personage; he explains carefully that these transactions are the method by which he pays his long-distance telephone bills. I am extremely annoyed. As soon as he leaves to attend a new arrival, I walk across the velvet carpet and introduce myself to Robert Lowell. Nothing further occurs: he is extremely drunk and cannot speak; you could almost say that he did not see me. . . . But Cecil has seen all of this; he is quite put out; he is such an angry man and needs his arrangements, and to have his arrangements honored. To have them go smoothly. He asks me to leave his home at once. He has forgotten that our children are in love. I leave by the back entrance, which opens onto a great formal garden, much like those at Fontainebleau, but now it is covered with snow, which, with its intense, unreal whiteness, shapes the careful cultivations into grotesqueries. The garden ends with another building, part of their property but at such a distance that I have never been to it. It is along the lines of Victoria Station, but slightly smaller, with the glasspaned roof snow-covered, extending as far as the eye can estimate. On entering this building, I discover it to be the children's playhouse, and filled with unusual toys: elegant dollhouses furnished with antique wood or porcelain objects; shelves of Fabergé eggs, other shelves of Ukrainian enameled real eggs; a thousand feet of the first model railroad, in what looks to be perfect operating condition; a miniature Bugatti; a tiny, perfectly formed Iron Maiden, with freshly greased hinges; a working model of an early steam engine; in a corner, a live Tibetan pony, and other, smaller pets. In the area, a few other guests are strolling about, admiring the collection. But none of the children are here. There are many half-uniformed men standing about: ordinary white shirts, grey trousers, with dark stripe down the side. I know they are guards. One of them, near me, leaning idly against a toy stock-market ticker-tape machine, remarks about the weather to me, in a mild, British voice. But he suddenly raises his hand, alarmed, gesturing toward the roof:

from the metallic rib above us, a curved plate, the shape and color of a giant armadillo shell, dark and shining, is descending rapidly toward where we are standing. We are mute. It is an emergency of some sort, and, as on a ship, the sections of the huge building are to be automatically divided. The guard, a man of about twenty-seven, swarthy, but with the intense blue eyes of many islanders, turns to me: he notes that the plate is moving too rapidly: we must move, and fast. But we cannot move, and I can only say to him, with a slowness that astonishes me, 'M oo ve m ee eee, I c a nnnnottt m ooo oooo ve. . . .' And so he does, quickly, firmly, tenderly, he drags and then lifts me, to a door I had not seen. I feel the rush of air as the metallic plate falls shut behind us. We move normally now, with a sweetly embarrassed silence between us. Outside, the lawn is a brilliant green. In the distance, near the house, I can see the great bulk of Cecil in his summer whites, talking to Robert Lowell and Edith Piaf; that lady, in her usual black, and Lowell's rumpled grey suit, complete a peaceful tableau. Near us, there is a wide table spread with delicacies, tiny shrimp, *pâté de foie,* limes, caviar; the guard and I are served by a slight young woman with a most unfortunate complexion, but with remarkable eyes, large and lustrous as a lemur's behind their corrective lenses.

1966

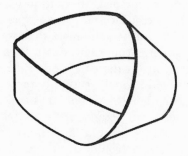

AN AMERICAN ROMANCE

In late spring, Ellen would get a divorce from Ari, to whom she had never been married. The idea was that she would then be free to marry Robert, officially, since everyone around the couple had assumed they were married. It was, Ari thought, a foolish idea, but then, as he fondly pointed out, he was never quite sure of Ellen's stability, much less her sanity. Ellen said it would add an element of surprise to their lives, and some reality, for a change; "Ridiculous!" said Ari, taking a slow sip of his Courvoisier.

Ellen sometimes agreed with Ari, having noticed that they should have been living their lives in any other time, in almost any other country—she was, as she told him, quite Seine, and would have done well (or at least *better*) in France, where people of taste would consider her a delicacy—or in Florence (she did say Firenze), where folks were numb, mummified, the antiquity you can recognize; or in Venice—decadence—anywhere—Spain, for instance, was never the place for her, any more than was this country; as she herself put it, "You know, Spain is so *sane,* even Gaudi wasn't enough to tip the balance or slide the scales . . ." to which Ari would lovingly, cuttingly reply, "You mean it's better in Grease? where they hate kings and the populace really wants the junta, not because of the uniforms, as designed by Gaudi I suppose (you would think that, dear), but as an old culture, those Greeks could overthrow anyone they pleased . . ." which got them both started for a two-hour dry-martini argument. "I'd do better in any country with a dictatorship," Ellen said, charming and being charmed. There was a Frenchwoman nearby who had taught her so much, a beautiful, withering lady called Anik, who was so fair, so fragile, that Ellen called her "the Licorice Lady." Anik had been Ellen's lover at one time . . . Ari's, at another. Through the Madison Avenue shops. The galleries.

Ridiculous to observe definition or amenity in these times, but it might happen. Ari might officially sue for any children resulting from some union at any future time if they did not get a divorce, said Ellen, not to mention her own possibilities. He was such a practical man. In the past, a lot of people thought they had him all figured out. He was short, thin, well-made, a very handsome man, vain, with bones as delicate as the dry bird-bones found in crevices in rock cliffs. He liked to keep things orderly and organized; it was a love of subtle power. For the many years before Ellen, he had cultivated the friendships of practical, mediocre-looking women who had talent in fields such as nursing, fashion, or journalism. Women taller than he by half-a-foot. He had an inheritance, well-invested, and could live very decently on his income; it was his pleasure to walk down the street of any city with his current average lady on his arm, delighting in the stares of passersby. His face was so beautiful. He was just a bit over five feet tall. Later on, he would grow fat with the pleasure of fine food, but just now he was still elegant, well-dressed, and took his pleasures with an eye toward keeping his looks intact.

Not too many perversions. He had never been poor; he was not fascinated with money; his sign was probably Libra. Remember that children's game that went, "He likes ——, but he doesn't like ——"? which went on until one deduced that the base of the game is that the person "likes" only things that begin, for example, with the letter W? It went this way with Wari. I mean, Ari. He liked cats, but he didn't like iguanas; he liked chocolate (especially Dutch) but not tea; he liked Loewenbrau dark beer, or, even better, Guinness dark, on tap, at room temperature. He liked elegance and never shabbiness; he liked to dance but he didn't like doing the Monkey; he liked curtains, drapes *and* blinds (if they weren't Venetian, if they were bamboo—ah, Venice again!) and he liked Alaska (baked), Bermuda (so British, tiny and tidy), Caracas, England, Greece . . . but when it got to Italy, he was disturbed, he began to reject. See?

Ellen came along to disturb some of his systematized theories: she was tall, yes, very tall, almost six feet tall; sturdy bones like a live seagull; beautiful, and clever enough. Talked a lot. Had an independent income of her own. Had never needed to work. They seemed cut of the same cloth. None of this "your house or mine, baby?" crap; the shorthand was both more subtle and more direct. They wanted the same things from life; they were delighted to meet. And stayed together. Marvelous, not to have to go through any preliminaries. Now, when they walked down any street, people stared, and then did a double-take. And in the bed—their pubes made a fine conjunction; the bones of the different birds very much in synch., meshing perfectly. Would they die of it? each asked, within, at different and the same times. It was lovely.

She wanted him to want to move about rapidly, to go places: perhaps live in a different country every year. She used the device of moving about to keep up her energy, what she called "her energy-wheel," because as it spun it renewed its own energy, and when it was stopped for too long, grass would grow between the spokes. He was languid, conserving his energy, of which he had an infinite supply. More than she, by far. But at times he was heavy-lidded; his disguise, because he could move faster than sunlight.

He knew she looked very good without makeup; he knew this before they got together. They had been neighbors in the same high apartment house, each with a different mate-of-the-moment: Ari was living with Jean, who could have been of either sex, a long-haired, civil, mild person with a considerable limp and a reputation in the literary world; Ellen (until recently called Alexandra) was living with a stockbroker who was forever urging her to go into modelling or night-club-singing (wanting to share her beauty with the world, he said). One day, armed with the knowledge that both Jean and the stockbroker were otherwise occupied, Ari knocked at Ellen's door, so to say, and, over a cup of neighborly espresso, suggested most enthusiastically that they would do better by far with each other.

When he left the apartment, Ellen smoothed her rumpled house, and immediately felt the inclination to call her stockbroker, or to masturbate; instead, she reached for the phone and called Ari; they left for the Laurentians at once, leaving notes behind in each apartment. (He had opted for a lodge he knew in the Alleghenies, but then gave in when he realized that the Laurentians were, after all, in Canada.) Ari's educated guess was right: they were good together.

The best glory was that neither was inhibited. Ari's rules stopped short of divination. He did not care for right angles, as you may imagine; he preferred acute angles. This might not be his own personal world entire, but as for

specific places, specific ways of moving about, he knew . . .
he knew. . . . He had an Aston-Martin. Pale cream color.
Sleek. On his side, the driver's side, it was altered to suit his
height: the seat moved forward and upward, the wheel
slipped up and out toward him. On her side, there was
enough leg-room for comfort. They were both interested in
William Buckley and couldn't stand Gore Vidal. Ari would
teach her a lot about cooking. He loved brains au buerre noir,
and oeufs en gelee, and any meat en brochette, so she would
learn to make them. And artichokes, and beets, and boeuf a
la boeuf, &c. She was a fast learner, had the natural bent
to be a good cook, a sensual lady, although her sensuality ran
to fine fabrics more than to fine foods (this pleased him: he
learned a bit, too, adding to his natural vanity when she
shopped with him in England for his scarves, in Finland for
his shirts) and they got along. They never fought, never
limited each other.

He began to feel fulfilled. He was suspicious of
the feeling. He would not consider marrying her. She had
never mentioned the possibility. He was not sure why. There
was that thin edge of fear sometimes. But they were both
geniuses at life, both specialists, with no degrees but with the
proof obvious in every gesture; the fear was slippery enough
to be put aside. It was so pleasant. Everything. When the
mundane obtruded, it could be made to slip into their ways;
one didn't need to stop at a Howard Johnson's, but occasionally they did, and enjoyed the reactions of the populace.
They figured out what they would order and eat well before
they arrived there, and enjoyed ordering and consuming three
chocolate butterscotch sundaes each, or two plates of plain
washed lettuce each, or half of seven hot plates between the
two of them; they thought of it as a flair for coping. It was a
sense of the life. Because life was ugly, it could be lived
beautifully, or at least dramatically . . . they did have a
choice. They took every choice.

And one must never lose one's sense of humor,

one's perspective. Acapulco; Cuernavaca; places where they did not need to notice the ugly or the poor. She bought him a Borzoi and bought him a stupid beautiful Afghan bitch; he added a pair of champion-stock miniature Bouviers (make of that what you will). People are what their chosen possessions are; people are how they dress, they show their true faces even when they think the mask is being worn; people are who their masks are. Is the woman who quotes Djuna Barnes equal to the woman who reads Jacqueline Susann, better than she who buys Doris Lessing and never reads her? Is the man who eats at Pen & Pencil the same as the man who shops for shirts by lifting the phone to London? Even Admiral Byrd had a feel for the luxurious; even Admiral Peary ate from real china with real silver on real linen in his summerhouse off Maine, between voyages. Every man is an explorer; some of it is how he sees himself, some how he spends his time; it is only the boundaries set that show the difference. "I will not stop now!" is one way to tell.

So then—with all so perfect, why should she consider their separating? The energy of the relationship began to wane. Ari was afraid, and it filled the air like an animal scent no deodorant could cover. Most of the energy seemed to be coming from Ellen, lately. Tudor City was boring to her; she knew Ari had begun dying his hair; when they smoked hash, it was Ellen who softly had realms to uncover and discover; Ari stayed in tight. Ellen became interested in rare meat, simply prepared. She was over ten years younger than Ari. He was spending too long in the bathroom. She had never thought to inquire about his past. He turned out to be Dutch. She thought he may have been an informer during the war. They both laughed at this, but the idea did not dispel.

Meantime, he began to look more closely at plain women he passed. Here he was, about forty years old, and very satisfied with himself, but always the old concept recurred, even when he was tanned and healthy: wasn't she getting more attention than he? It had gone on for several years. They were not given to bickering; they were too mature, too civilised to lose dignity that way. The sexuality would begin in a wave, would take them over, they relied on it with each other, they had no other lovers; this was their habit-pattern. "To hell with Margaret Mead" was their favorite motto; they had it embroidered on a sampler for their living-room, the one in Mar del Plata. They had few mutual friends but saw a lot of people. Or, accurately, they had a few friends and many acquaintances.

At one point, Ari saw an analyst (around the time when they were beginning to part). But he left after the second session, waiting politely until the end of that session to announce his decision to the doctor, because, as he put it, "I am sure you do not live like I, and you would have great difficulty in understanding how I live." In fact, the psychiatrist was a top man in his profession, and, even so, I can say the same to you: I am sure, if you are reading this, you do not live like Ari, and may have difficulty understanding his life, no matter how expert you are in your own profession. Or, as the ad on TV told him one night, you cannot buy another pair of eyes, you have but this one pair to do you for all of your life. . . .

Ari went to the house of one of his neighbors: a softly rounded, homely woman who lived with a professor of chemistry at Columbia. It was summer; she was wearing a thin skimmy shirt; her body was excellent beneath it; her professor was out teaching. "Why do you express interest in me, in my company?" she asked Ari. "It is rumoured you have an excellent relationship with Ellen, in any respect . . ." "Yes, but . . ." he replied. In his own eyes (the only pair he would ever have, for love or for money), he had no major character flaws. Right or wrong, he was always right. The new woman, the neighbor, rejected him, but not before he was permitted to see the honey-colored inside of her mind. He did not believe that the rejection was neither total nor permanent. He had so much to offer. Everything except time and a sense of perspective. But bitterness is not venom, forty is not old, and honey is not come.

The name Ellen began with a proper letter. The new lady's name was Eve; this was a satisfyingly logical progression. Ellen had high cheekbones, a marvelous high, smooth forehead, hair that was prematurely grey, silvery, with a fine natural wave. Eve was a brunette of the most ordinary kind: those middle-Mediterranean looks, dolichocephalic, dark: an invitation to the czardas. . . . She had a slight lisp which Ari found endearing. Eve was *grateful* for everything. It was her long suite. Whereas Ellen assumed she had every thing coming to her.

Ellen knew that Ari had begun to spend time with Eve, and she pretended it was all right with her if he did; she acted casual. But she had learned from Ari. She had developed a cool need to clean up loose ends. She had met many other men during these years. For one, there was Robert, who had very green eyes but was taller than she. Robert was more interested in making love slowly, and he'd been around enough so that his techniques, while seemingly sincere, were also interestingly kinky. He liked steak au poivre, very rare, that is, blue inside; he liked Lalique better than Daum and kept it about him in his violet-mauve-purple apartment. He, too, knew all the Inns, but he liked unbleached muslin sheets, he liked raw silk, he was very powerful and liked power. In fact, he was all about power, he had a massive handshake, he was probably Capricorn. And since Ellen was Scorpio, he was very attractive to her: she loved power, she was all about extremes and interested in kinky but direct lovemaking. So there was no question, on her part: it was pleasure, part of her "Pure Pleasure Principle" as she had explained it to Ari: ends justifying means, fidelity limited only by will and circumstance . . . her philosophy covered it all. Was adjustable.

Robert had a full beard, dark red and beautifully shaped (it looked untrimmed but it was carefully trimmed to seem natural or casual). Ellen found she couldn't foretell Robert's responses as she could Ari's. One afternoon, in bed with him (knowing that, elsewhere in Tudor City, Ari was doubtless in bed with Eve), she told Robert she was going to marry Ari. Robert neither laughed nor understood. She quickly explained that she intended to marry the other man in order to be able to divorce him, in order to be utterly free. Robert, being Capricorn, was not that interested in a concept of utter freedom; he was too staid, and rather too moral. He told her the whole thing made no sense to him. He was displeased, in some strong corner of his soul, with her becoming a divorcee; he had been pleased that she had never married —a kind of purity—why bother with it all? "Well," Ellen said slowly, grinning up at him, "it would be fun to go to Mexico again. . . . You've never been there. . . . Perhaps the four of us could go there together." She had it in mind to remarry immediately after her divorce from Ari became final and official. She was not yet sure whether she would remarry Ari or marry Robert. By that time, it would have worked itself out in one direction or another. . . . What a lark, said Robert dryly, not especially to her, just to himself and the pillow. He was not pleased. He was not whimsical. But it did sound pleasant, in a way unfamiliar to him. He had long ago divorced several wives, under increasingly unpleasant circumstances, and the idea of handling the whole business in this manner was new to him.

Ellen thought of Robert as a government undercover agent. He thought of himself as a connoisseur of women and of wines and intelligent collector of modern art. Not the tubes-of-fluorescent-light kind; the earth-works kind. His flat was filled with photographs of them; he had even commissioned several, through his friend, young Jack Gibson of the Gibson Gallery. Ellen thought of this as super-hip and therefore dull; interesting at the beginning, perhaps, but duller with each repetition. . . . What better guise than all this, for a J. Edgar Hoover man? In fact, Robert was a very direct man, not imaginative, not given to subtleties or subterfuge, and it was Ellen's overglamorization that gave him any aura of mystery. He was, himself, an earth-work: transitory, beautiful in an earthbound way, pragmatic. . . .

Yet everything in life is not as predictable as solid Robert would wish. . . . You wonder how they met . . . at a party, in Tudor City. Or near there. He was a neighbor. He had been living alone, was between affairs. He was more interested in himself, at the moment. He liked dark suits of the latest conservative cut; he wore boots, despite the fact that he was very well hung. This was refreshing for Ellen, who had grown accustomed to Ari's normal proportions. Robert chose to be careful with Ellen at the beginning, but she encouraged him to "be himself," in order for her to adapt faster. She really enjoyed his subdued violence. They saw each other regularly and considered each other exciting sexually.

They were a very goodlooking couple. But they were moving among goodlooking people, so they seemed average. Many of the people they saw were people who knew Ari as well. Knew Ellen-with-Ari. Ellen was considering it all, these days. She met and talked with Eve. Eve was busy being grateful for Ari, who was so different from her professor (tho, to Ellen, the two men seemed very much alike). Both with a boring need to overspecialize. One had the feeling, Ellen thought, that Ari and the professor could not maintain a civilised conversation; the professor would be concerned with the similarity of Ari to Eve's father, in skin tone, in length of skull, would notice that both men wore scaphoid pads for weak arches, that both had sunken sternums (sterna?) and were balding slowly. . . . The professor might ultimately suggest a marriage-counselor to Eve, in an attempt to keep her with him. . . . Ellen was thinking more of an encounter group, which might lead to a naked-in-swimming-pool session, for the four of them together . . .

But both Ari and the professor tended to avert, to avoid, when things got too comfortable; there was Chivas Regal for one and Courvoisier for the other. And Tanqueray in between, for the professor at any rate. "You can have her if you can get her, and if, after that, you can keep her for a month," the professor told Ari; at which point Ari decided he might not want Eve as badly as he'd thought . . .

Meantime, Robert was somewhat put off by Ellen's playful suggestion that they all go off together to Mexico, because he suspected Ellen might want to marry him there and he didn't wish to marry again, no matter how well he looked with Ellen on his arm. There was no room in his life for a strong, goodlooking lady with ideas of permanence. He was still young (he was thirty-one) and there was much time in front of him . . . and he lacked a sense of humor, you may recall. He told Ellen he would not consider the trip. She was not an adept at weeping but she knew how to sulk effectively, and did so, with a bit of pretty pouting thrown in; upon which Robert became aware that she might in time resemble her mother (there was a photograph of her mother in one of the first issues of Vogue which Ellen kept around her flat).

The upshot of it all was that Ellen and Ari stayed together; Ari decided it, to begin with (or thought he did), and Ellen seconded the idea, sounding calmer, less enthusiastic than she felt. She knew that she could live out her life more smoothly without worrying about details, and that not many men had Ari's lack of character; with the others it was subtle; in Ari's case all was known quantity, nothing hidden or assumed. They knew each other well. Flaws and virtues, virtues and flaws. They were both pleased. It would obviate the idea of the divorce. They went to Cuernavaca, and were married there, in the garden of a lovely old movie-star and her Italian industrialist husband, both old friends of Ari. A small wedding, with caviar and tropical fruits, coconut but no papaya, gazpacho with avocados and garlic but without onions . . . it was winter, and Merle and Bruno knew just the way to do everything.

1970

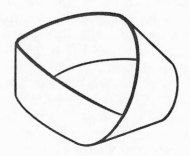

HUAN,
or,
Dispersion

The man was chopping wood. It was evening, after a day or two of rain, and the air was full of sweetness. He enjoyed the scent of the cut wood, of the wet grass, the night air. They needed the wood for the fire, but he was really chopping to impress the woman who watched: she would be delighted with the line of his arm and back as he raised and slung the axe. It was true: he was strong, and his half-naked body seemed suited to the sensual pleasure of the chore. She wanted to consider him as an intellectual being, as revolving around his intelligence; this he knew. And he was out to deprive her of this image. He wanted her to want him, to want his great physical being, to want him inside her strongly. His lust for her was continuous. And she would insist on refusing him, time after time. Until he was well beyond his own mind with it all, and became more a body creature still, and opposite to that which she thought she craved. He lived inside the body which people around him recognized as his own, more and more, rather than the spirit or intelligence she would have him be. They had been married for some while now. They lived in this very house, whose fireplace devoured the wood he hewed every day or so. Usually she watched him.

'Tea is ready, why don't you come in now,' she said, unable to permit him all of his physical existence. But if they were to have tea together, it would mean another conversation. And she lived from these: she seemed, these days, to care more for them than for the conversation of the bodies. He knew that this was not entirely true of her, that she was in some way lying to herself. But he could not reach her. He could not reach through her gloss, to where her own body lived. He gave one last whack to the wood and turned toward the house, toward the lit chamber where the woman waited. It was too damned bad about that woman. But he could not, would not leave off her. He had to reach for her flesh. As he came in, she was at the table, pouring. Her back was to him, the line of the nape of her neck set so that he had to touch. She recoiled from him, not a sharp gesture but more of a slight moving aside, as he had known she would. As she always did, of late. In that new way of hers.

He could not remember how it had started, this angular game they were in. They had moved to this house, maybe that was it. They had come to this house, away from most people, a month or two ago, when the season had turned. She was eager to leave the town where they had been living. It was really a small city, and the air was not clear most of the time, it was full of the smoke of the factories which supported the townspeople. But he did not make a living in the factories, although he found use for some of their products. He was a sculptor. He was a man of the mind, as far as that went: he would work on machines, yes, but of such exquisite conception that the ordinary people could not cope with even their sight; they elicited unfamiliar emotions and sensations: the effect of a hurricane, or the softness of wind just before dawn, or the sharpness of a city set into the softness of a valley. The man had a feeling for metal that was not akin to the way factory men worked with the same material. To him, the metal was alive, had its own life, was part of the earth and constantly alive, vivid. He was filled with pleasure at the possibilities of metal, and the languages open to him as he worked. He liked old metals, and often went to the town dump to find the rusted and altered pieces he liked. Their texture aroused in him a feeling he found hard to discuss. 'But why do you bring this back?' she would ask him, running her finger along an edge. 'I don't know, it makes sense to me, it works. It is something that has worked, has had one life, and is still working, is still alive. It is a continuation. . . .' And although she, too, worked creating things with her hands, he thought she did not understand. She did not question him further; she did not say anything to show that she was aware.

He wondered what she would think if he told her he thought of her skin's texture with the same feeling as when he worked with the pieces of metal. He had a passion for the metal, and for her skin. He was a man whose senses were overt, available to the world. Whereas she was obverted, presenting to the world directly but in such a design as she chose and planned. And if she could manage it, she would always send him to people rather than go out to them herself. He had no feeling of resentment about this; it was part of her way, and actually he considered it attractive. She made many such demands on him. He thought of it as her 'shell' and let it be. It was really all right with him, he liked to go out and talk to people, meet people; and if she didn't, then he would be glad to go. He did not consider himself to be imposed upon, since he knew all about her, her ways of being part of the world. But he did not really know her. It was that she did not like most people, and would rather not take the chance of meeting the kind she did not like and would not get along with. Not even the possibility of meeting those she might like was enough, by now. Most people offended her, with their coarse tastes, their manufactured ideas and opinions. She considered herself too fastidious for most of them and saw no need to reach out of herself. At one time she had been ready to like the people they were meeting, in a city or town where they lived, but it had changed for her. Her trust had been betrayed. And she had withdrawn from them.

Neither of them was beautiful, in the conventional sense. She had badly-made teeth, which protruded so that they distorted her mouth, the line of her lips. But the lips were pleasant and soft, and of course her marvelous skin was so pleasing. Her eyes were myopic and set a bit too far apart, giving altogether an almost rabbity appearance to her face. Her body was well-formed, round of bosom and round of hip. She took care of herself. Her clothing was well-chosen. She had dark, rich hair, which they both considered most fortunate, and she took inordinate pride in it, winding the great braid of it around her head every morning and night. One of his pleasures was to watch her in this ritual, even as she would watch him as he chopped wood or took his bath. There had been, not long ago, a great sensual pleasure between them. She had dropped back from him about the time they had moved to this house.

He thought about it as they sat drinking the tea. She wanted him to talk with her and asked him about his work, about the piece on which he was now working: 'Dan, how do you see that piece? Is it finished?' But he was unwilling. 'Yes. I think so.' But she insisted: 'I mean, it seems to me it has so much similarity to the one you did last month and that one went . . .' 'How can you know? That was that one, and this is this.' He had cut her off sharply. She stared at him. He was angry at her myopia, that permitted her, which forced him to accept the full power of her hurt look. But she was asking the wrong things of him. 'The work is my idea, and I know when a thing is done. Let me *be*.' It was one of the edges in a week of increasing tension. During the rainy days, they had been too much together, and he was full of the dreadful tension of having her body so much near to him and so unavailable to him. At night, he would reach for her, and she would withdraw, or recoil, in that quiet or subtle way she had. It was more than he could stand. He was becoming edgy and bitter. There was not so much he asked of her, he was willing to be what she wanted of him, most of the time, because it suited him; because his own nature was so close to what she herself needed of him. But their bond had been so much physical. He could not cope with her finality of refusal. If she were a cold woman; if she had never been close to him. But there was their mutual memory of passion. There had been much passion between them, until lately.

He walked away from the table, feeling her hurt. Well then, it was no use. It was impossible that she wouldn't know what he was feeling, what was happening with them. He could not imagine where she was. She was in another place, and he would give up rather than reach for her again. In the hallway, or the little space near the doorway, he stopped, catching a glimpse of himself in the mirror she had hung. His habit was not to stop there. This time, he saw her, as she was reflected, as he had left her. She sat at the table, obverted, her face turned bluntly toward him and not seeing him, her hands limp and at ease on the table. As he watched, she moved, not knowing she was being watched. She went to the window just next to the table, and leaned softly against the frame. Her mouth moved. She reached out and touched the frame of the window, so, and then the plant that cast its leaves' weight against the shutter. And then she stopped moving. It was as if she went rigid with a thing that came from outside her, and stopped her. He himself stopped, almost stopped breathing as he saw this. It was not like her, not like anyone he had ever seen, this kind of cessation of motion. She simply stopped moving. But she was an agile woman, an active woman who rarely was still, even in relaxation. Now he could suddenly recall other times when she might have stopped in such a way, just at the edge of his sight or consciousness. It was clearly a moving over into something else. If he had not known intelligently that this particular woman was a woman with whom he had moved for some years, was in fact his woman, he might not have recognized her. She was moved to one side of herself, in a way that seemed to remove her from his sight, and even from the room in which she seemed to be standing. It was not that she had any particular tension about her, about the way that she stood. She seemed, to his eye at least, at ease. It was another quality.

He watched. And then he realized that she had stood thus for quite a while, for perhaps six or eight minutes. Her slight gesture made him realize the amount of time that had passed. He turned from the mirror and went softly out the door. Once outside, he breathed deeply. There had been a strangeness about watching; he had felt like an eavesdropper . . . it was odd. It had been she who had wanted, or needed, to move out here. Was she in some way discontent with it all? It had been she who was pressured from within, who had needed to get out of that city; she who had found this house and urged him out to look at it. 'I have a feeling for this place. I feel that it will be a good place for us.' And he had agreed: it was a good house, solid, with more than enough room for the two of them and their equipment and interests. She could have a room for her looms, and he could use one inside room and that outbuilding for his work. There was a bit of fine land around it. The house itself was not in such good shape, but he could work at it slowly, without taking much time from his work.

They loved the house and decided to take it. It did not cost them much more than the house they left, and it was much more commodious. The only quarrel they had concerned the use to which certain rooms would be put. She had immediately claimed a southeast room for her own, wanting the light for her colors and her eyesight. But he found he had visualized using that room himself. Ordinarily, he would not argue about such a matter; he would usually give in, because it was a small thing, and it did not matter that much. He could even consider it whimsy, justifying not fighting her. But this time he had felt a pull toward that room, himself, had wanted it for himself. They became set against each other. 'But it cannot be so important to you,' she said shrilly. 'No, it must be mine. You cannot have it.' He became aroused and involved. 'What do you mean, I cannot have it? What right have you? What right to the room, and what right to speak in such a manner to me? I want it for the same reason you want it. I like the light in it, and the shape of the room. It suits me.' 'Well, but you shall not have it. I shall.' 'You won't get it with screaming,' he said. So she moved back, and to one side, and: 'Well, then, this is to be mine. There's no point in discussing it further,' in a soft, ominous voice. 'I'm not sure I like it, what you're doing, Della. I think we could arrive at our choices or agreements without . . .' 'You have all that space outdoors and I must work in here most of the time. I simply have to have this room.' 'Very well, then. But I resent the way you've gone about this.'

He had helped her move her looms and wools into the southeast room, but he could not get over being sullen and set against her, although he could not define his own need or wish for the room. She felt his mood, but she moved blindly, firmly, as if without her own will. In past places, she had had trouble always in deciding which was to be her workroom, and then in deciding what was to go where within the room. But in this room, she put things to rights at once, as if there had been a drawing on the floor, as they had on stages in plays, indicating where each object would go. He had noticed this, but had not commented upon it. It came to his mind now. From that time, she had left him, had started to leave him. 'You see?' she said, in a triumph, when the moving-in was done, 'this room is perfect for me. Perfect. I can work in this room.' He didn't like the set of her face then. It was a new look she wore, a kind of queer triumph, which set her against him and off to herself, left him without the grace of having bent to her whim, and shut out.

So it had gone: she would go to that room and do her work, and he would go out to his out-building, or his tiny workroom within the house, and do his work. He would take long walks in the woods near the house. Before now, all of it had been good: they would both be immersed in their work, much of the time, and come together joyously for meals, and to make love at odd hours, and to sleep together. They rejoiced in each other's work. He had great respect for her as an artisan, and his confidence in her pleased her. For her part, she usually knew what he was about in his work, and took pleasure in going with him on his trips for materials. He had more feeling for her work than she did for his, but that was all right too. He knew quite well what he was doing. He was secure in the work. She was a good wife, an excellent wife, withal. She was bright, alive, interesting, a fine lover. Until they moved out here, and she grew abstracted, moved into another way of being, away from him, away from their intimacy and smoothness together.

He did not think she was behaving to spite him. She seemed to be moving without herself, in some way quite unavailable to his understanding. She was not a malicious woman. But she would always talk to him, would want to sit with him and talk, she would question him, draw him out, as she had never done. She seemed pleased when they would talk about matters that had never before concerned her: matters of the world around them, things about business, about museums, about the stock market, about other countries, wars, civilisations. They had had a life pretty much removed from such realities; not by choice but by happenstance. If either had been concerned with the rest of the world, it had been Daniel, who would occasionally read a newspaper or talk with other men. She had not been interested. Her limit had been the magazines of the world of artists, mostly. When the men would talk, she would refrain, and move aside. It was not one of her needs, this discussion of the life outside of their lives. Until recently. Now, she would almost force him to bring her this kind of talking. She had a new voracity for knowledge which in itself was not that unusual; but as it was between them it made her seem a stranger to him. He was not used to this from her. She would perch at the edge of the chair, her eyes fixed on his face, while he would tell her whatever he knew and respond to her questions. He would give her as much as he knew. There was something unnatural about her at times, as if she had a high fever. He would watch her begin to shine, or respond, as she once had on the bed with him. But when they were in bed, there was no talking and there was no lovemaking. He was a whole man, he was at home in the world, he was at ease with it, he felt himself becoming involved in some delicate kind of perversion, the natural boundaries of his life with his woman were shifted radically. It was impossible to him. It made no sense.

And now he felt like an eavesdropper, a man watching a stranger perform an act or ritual which was somehow forbidden or sacrilegious and made him uncomfortable. He was drenched with sweat. He walked down to the stream that bordered his property. It had always had a quieting effect on him, this stream: he loved to stare into the moving brown water as it passed beneath the little stone bridge that had been there for a century. There was such a kinship between the water's motion and the metals as he worked them. His metals lived in that water, lived all around him. But now all he could see and feel was the image of his wife, as she had stood at the window. And the hurt look, when he had shut her up, before that. And he was buried beneath the month that had just passed, without the closeness of their flesh. He was full of the sense of his own body, as it curved around the need for warmth and contact. He had been given the right to expect this from her. What had happened to her, who had been that close to him! As the evening light slanted upon it, the stream seemed clouded with silt from the rains. He left it. He went to his workshed. He picked up the job he had left, a wide structure of curving shapes. Although he had thought it done, it drew him now; he went further on it, changing it, further into it until it expressed his chagrin, his anger, his dissatisfaction. In an hour, it was completely changed. It was an angry piece, it had much agony in it. He was satisfied with it. Now it was done. But damned if he would tell her that, if she should ask.

When he came back to the house, it was full night. The light was on in his wife's room. He saw her outline as she moved quickly past the window. He would not go to her. He would take some tea and sit in the kitchen. He would light a fire. But above all, he would not go to her. She had not done much work in the past couple of weeks. Had begun a few things and then dropped them, or so she had reported. And then just stopped. Even as she had at the window. There had been none of the usual restlessness about her; usually, when she was not working, she would be uneven and edgy, impatiently awaiting the time when she would feel like working again, until she would be at the next tapestry or hanging or rug. Nothing would absorb her at those times. But in the last few weeks, she would simply stop. Nothing would seem to be irritating her. She had a kind of calm, or lack of motion. Then she would start at another piece, and drop it without finishing it, and start at another, and drop it as well. And would go into that sort of calm, or absence of motion. She would go about her chores without irritability, without impatience. But she would not really be there. And she would still refuse him when he reached to touch her. Without a word, she would turn from him. What did she want of him, in this new turn of her being? He knew she wanted him. They had come together like animals, wholly, mindlessly, wonderfully.

He missed her, he did not want to feed her his mind any more. Yes, he had his work, and his land, and he was his own man, but he needed his woman. Her wanting him was important to him in his spirit. Although neither of them thought about it, he was slightly crippled: his right leg had been damaged in a childhood injury, so that the defect extended to his whole right side, giving him a severe limp. Between the man and his wife, this was a condition of their lives, and taken for granted. But the man had an unacknowledged need for her physical love, because of this. It was as if she accepted him as perfect. It might have been balanced out by her odd, unfortunate teeth. Yet they never discussed these things, they took each other very much for granted. They were in good health and oblivious to each other's faults. There were so many others around them who were misformed or damaged in ways far greater than they. And they were in a way of life which sought perfection in the art rather than in the person. It was a seemly arrangement.

He drank his tea and considered. He heard her moving in the room above. Their cat jumped into the curve of his arm as it rested on the table; he patted it absently. His wife had been pouring affection on the cat. When the cat was in a room where they were, it was the cat who got the attention, the affection. She would stroke it, coo to it, fondly. He wished they had a child. There would probably be no children. But she gave to the cat more than the gestures she might give to a child, because its demands upon her were far less. She would always shut it out when she did not want it around. Since they had moved here, she came from her strange withdrawals by accepting affection from the cat. And then not always; just when she pleased. There was an obstinacy about her. He was not sure what she was about. He could hear her moving above him: the steady, even rhythm of the loom, her steps as she went to get another skein or shifted the articulations. It went this way for perhaps half an hour: and then she came down. She heated water and poured herself a cup. She sat down near him. Her face was bright and fully toward him.

'How does it go?' he asked. But he was almost unwilling that she should answer. 'Oh, it's good, I want you to see it. If you want to. I like it.' He feared her. In her dreadful enthusiasms. She reached over and patted the cat as it lay encircled in his arm. He did want to see what she was working on. He did not expect to learn anything new, but this was this time and none other, and the first in a while that she had offered to show him her work. There was always the possibility. 'Yes, I would like to see.' 'Good. Come.' She got up, touching the cat as it rose when he did. He followed her up the stairs. The cat scampered past them both, and he tripped on it. 'Goddam that cat.' 'Leave it alone.' 'Oh I wouldn't harm it. You know better.' But he thought he might, by now. 'Come on, Daniel. Forget it.' She had left the lights on. On the loom was a large fabric, heavy-looking, about seven feet square. He recognized it as a blue piece which she had started and then deserted, about the time they had first moved in. It had been turned toward a corner of the room, half-covered, since then. It now was almost finished. It was a peculiar blue, very dull, but with a dark radiance, as with some metals; almost a gunmetal blue, he thought. In the center was a figure which was catlike. 'A cat?' 'Yes. This cat.' And she reached down and stroked their cat. 'What is this, then? A wall-hanging?' He had a certain irritability in his voice. But she did not notice. 'No, it will be a blanket.' 'A blanket. A blanket?' 'Yes. For our room. For our bed.' 'No. No, it won't. Impossible.' 'What do you mean? What do you mean, impossible?' For an answer, he reached out and slapped her face sharply. She recoiled, flinched: stared at him. 'You want to call it our bed, and you make a blanket for it, and you put a picture of the damned cat on it. Goddam you. Goddam you.' He was crying, in a fury, in a lack of understanding her, in his own anger. And slapped her again, wildly, a gesture that had some-

how a tenderness to it, a reaching-through. 'With the goddamned cat on it, eh? And where are we, you and I?' And she
laughed, having no other way available. 'Yes, it is the cat, and
it is for our bed.' It sounded to her quite sensible; but to him
it sounded like the same tone in which she had said, 'This is
my room,' in a kind of blind obstinacy. 'Well, my lady, if that
is what you still are, *I* think *not*.' And with that, he reached
across and swung his fist into the loom, and his other hand
raked across the weaving. The wood moved and hurtled. The
loom shifted and the shuttle spun loose, dragging a strand of
the blue into the room, across the room, into the air between
them. 'Cut it loose,' he said to her. 'I want it.' 'What for?'
'Just do what I say, my lady, if you know what's good for
you.' 'But it's not done. . . .' 'Cut it loose, I said. I know
what's good for you.' She saw his face clearly, and she moved
to cut the wool off the loom. 'I can always make another,' she
said, nastily. But he would not answer. His position was
changed. He simply waited until she had cut it loose.

When she had it free, he took it from her and spread
it on the floor, in a flinging gesture. 'All right,' he said, quietly,
firmly, 'now you sit on it.' 'Are you crazy? Have you gone
crazy? What are you doing?' 'I told you to sit on it. Sit on it.'
He reached past her and scooped up the cat from the floor,
put it out of the room, and shut the door. 'Now you may sit,
and be as quiet as you please. In fact, you must not move.
I wonder if you can do that.' 'I don't know.' 'Yes you do. Yes,
you can. You do know. You know how, quite well. Let's see
how it goes right now. If you can do it at will.' She stared at
him in that way of hers. 'You saw me. You've seen me.' 'I *see*
you,' he said. 'Now let's get on with it.' She sat on the blanket,
the unfinished blanket, toward one corner. 'No, my dear. Over
there. On your precious cat. In your precious room.' She did
not move. 'No, don't begin yet. Over there, my lass.' He
reached and lifted her and put her down squarely on top of
the woven image of the cat. 'And there you shall sit, my puss,

my own sweet puss, while I watch you in your ways of leaving me, and there you shall stay until we have done with all of this.'

'With all of what?' she said, smiling up into his face. She knew how to be charming. She had been too charming. She had no sense of timing, however. He reached out and slapped her again. 'Now shut up with that. No more of that. Talk when you are ready, but I don't want any of that intellectual smut you have been feeding yourself on. And you can bet I know the difference. Watch it.' She pulled into herself and sat. The time passed. He saw her become immobile in that strange way. He watched her working backward into herself, in that way which threatened and irritated him. 'All right then,' he said, breaking through it violently, 'what are you about?' And she broke: she looked up and saw him; she tried to talk, and stopped, started again: 'You have always taken things for granted. I never could. I don't have to, now.' 'Now what's that supposed to mean?' 'Daniel. Everything is new for me here, now.' 'It sounds pretty smug to me, and I still don't understand, and you'd damn well better make me understand, lady.' She did seem smug. Sitting there on that blanket, which she intended to be for both of them, as if she were planning their world completely, and were working from her own design. 'I wish I could tell you what I mean. It's that everything is different now. I see everything in another way. Things come to me, and if they don't, it's all right too . . . being out here. A lesson . . . I don't have to move, sometimes. It comes to me. Not as before. I want more, but I don't have to go after it. It comes to me.' 'What does?' 'Everything. The music. The colors. The pattern . . . the patterns. Do you see what I mean?' 'Not yet.' 'It's that everything is rather more simple than I had thought. So I don't have to reach. And I have room for more, and I want more.' But he was still a distance from her. 'Is that why you don't need me?' 'I still need you. But in a different way. Another way.' 'Where are you? All you've wanted is talk.' 'Not true. But what I want is different from what you've been giving . . .' He heard her, but he was still willfully not hearing her. 'It's this damned room. I'll move you out of this room.' 'Oh Daniel, don't be silly!' 'Don't ever say that to me again.' 'It doesn't matter . . .' and she smiled up at him, too quietly.

He stood over her, his foot at the edge of the blanket. 'Blanket, is it? For our bed, will you?' He reached down and turned her. In so doing, he stepped onto the blanket with both feet. She twisted away, as she had so often done, as if in habit, but he caught a weird little smile as she turned. He would not release her, he would not be bought again by her averting. Now it was becoming clear to him. 'Not now, missy. Not *this* time.' And he took her. On the blue blanket. '*This* is how it is. Yes. This. This is how it will go,' he said, into her open mouth, into her ear. Pulled his head back from hers and looked into her face, into her eyes, and said, from within her, 'This is where we are now.' She said nothing. But his taking of her brought out her violence, her wish for violence. She did not want him to take her, not in the old way they had had between them; but now she wanted him, she wanted this. She had a spirit to match his. She struggled and he consumed her, took her with him, he moved her in a way that was not familiar to either of them. So that she became mindless again, even while struggling and moving beneath him, went along with him into a wildness beyond herself, beyond her wish to goad him or remain reserved from him. They had been away from each other for a long time, so that they came together with a strangeness and a total familiarity. He was through to her, with his will as a man. She went with him and gave over to him.

It was good. She fell back against the rug, with her head on his arm. But she wept. 'Now you've spoiled it.' 'What the hell!' 'I won't be able to see as clearly. The work won't go as well. I wanted to do without, and keep the energy for the rest of the life. . . .' 'Oh, I *see*,' he laughed. 'Well, you don't have to worry. You won't lose it. You'll see.' 'I wanted to be *clear. . . .*' 'You aren't cut out for that. You wait and see. It's better this way, for both of us.' She was crying now. In relief from tension, in disappointment at her own flesh, she cried, sobbed. He held her, and he was still a bit angry at her, but he understood, and he was amused. He was angry for the time he had been shut out, and for her reasons. Very well then, they were her reasons, and they were her own way through to her life. If they had given her so much, he would leave them alone, although all of it seemed ridiculous to him. He knew now that she had wanted him to take her in just this way, and that she was into a real fight, with himself and herself as enemies, she would have to be convinced that she would not lose her spiritual clarity. Her reasons meant her life to her, but he could modify all of it. She did not need to leave off the body-life; it had worked for her till now, it was an answer, but it was not the answer. She had not been able to say any of it to him; not knowing how he would take it, what he would do. There was no way for her to discuss it before now. He had freed her, tonight.

He continued to hold her, awkwardly but firmly, with her legs still partly around him, her skirt bunched between them at their waists, her shoe indenting his calf. She was angry with her own flesh, for its betrayal of her, for wanting him as he took her. But it was no use. She was with him, in a new way, and she would have to be with him. It was over, that clarity she had found. Or maybe he was right, it would continue in another form. He had made certain that she would not want to stand in that kind of motionless removal any more. The blanket would be a blanket, as she had designed, but it would cover them in a way she had not foreseen. This pleased her. It pleased them both.

1966

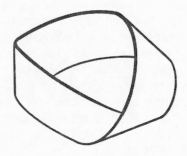

IN MOTION

I.

They would sit in their forty-five-foot living room, with its mild alabaster and marble statues and pale grey walls, and smoke Acapulco Gold until the statues looked like the Kama Sutra, until the walls writhed and undulated, until he reached for her, his own 19-year-old bride of two months, and they would make unconventional love on the huge round bed. Daytimes, she would go to B. Altman's and buy under-clothing, she would walk along upper Madison Avenue and buy exquisite Italian footwear, while he worked in his office on lower Madison Avenue. It was not, truth be told, an easy life they had. Actually, he was not quite old enough to be her father. It was just that she thought he was. And her psychiatrist had a time of it, second-guessing her moods and her dreams. Her psychiatrist was the son of the owner of a large shop like B. Altman's, and he had fantasies of his own. One of them was that he would one day marry a Bunny Playgirl. And this girl was an ex-Bunny. She was brilliantly fair, tall, long-legged, and Jewish. Her husband (they were legally married, had been married in a large room at the Sherry-Netherland) was short, muscular, handsome, and mildly Semitic-looking. You could never visualize this couple in Miami Beach: their taste was impeccable. This was what drew them together and kept them together, perhaps. When they woke in the morning, they had their morning cup of rich Mexican coffee and, later, laced it with either Guernsey milk or a fine brandy, depending on their previous evening's activity, and they smoked their first joint of the day. Then he was in shape to go up-town, and she was in shape to cope with the maid. She felt weird about giving orders to a woman who was obviously both older and wiser than she. Anyhow, how would a 19-year-old acquire a sound demeanor of authority? This girl had been raised wealthy; her looks had added to the tendency of people to find reasons to give her gifts; nothing had ever opposed her. It struck her as slightly ridiculous that neither of her parents had ever slapped her or kissed her. When she went to a finishing-school in Maine, she discovered sex and pot, simultaneously. So the most natural next step was to become a Bunny. Her parents thought she lived on Fifth Avenue, all that while, with cousins from another finishing-school.

She met her husband at a poetry reading. One of his concepts of himself that he first confided to her was his wish to be a writer. Of course, this was how he was now making his money; he had written a successful novel, and had been offered a job by a large public-relations house, on the basis of the novel's style and success: it having had to do with world problems in communication, and done in a reasonably journalese manner. But Len wanted to be a different kind of writer; he had been raised poor; he was full of a warped kind of social consciousness. Before he had written a line of the novel which succeeded, he wrote many poems, in which he had absolutely no confidence. He got the idea for the novel and wrote it in three weeks while on a yacht belonging to his brother, moored off the coast of Connecticut. From the day he took the job with the public-relations office, until the day he met Louise, he ran the small delicate circle of Dexedrine to stay awake and Seconal to sleep. Some nights, with his first wife, he was simply unable to attain an erection, no matter what. He maintained his weight and his clothing precariously.

Louise had a quality which he craved. He had a hunger for this long, blonde girl which he'd never felt with his other wife or his girls. Her good taste; her low-pitched, simple laugh; the way she put her hands on him before he himself knew he wanted her. He wanted her until he choked with it. And he was never sure of her. Perhaps that was it. He became hysterical at the thought that she might leave him and marry someone else, so he asked her to come and live with him. He had lots of dues behind him: the years of the war, the years in California, the damn novel, the damned poems, all those faces and bodies, alive and dead. It seemed to him he deserved a little beauty, a Louise. He could get lost in those light eyes of hers.

She did move in with him, after a fashion. She kept most of her things in the apartment she shared with her sister and brother-in-law, some ten blocks from Len's place. Her clothes blended in perfectly with Len's decor. The pale-grey walls expressed their life together perfectly at times: days and days of absolute Nothing, blank, going through the rituals they had temporarily set up to keep them from themselves and from each other (mostly) and from the outside world (most important of all, perhaps). They were both very bright people, very delicately structured people.

The pot and hash played an important role for them: it let them go, it freed them, it left them with no guilt about ruining their bodies (they were, of course, both inordinately proud of their bodies, of their physical selves, of their handsomeness and their sturdiness; Len, having passed through the ruining circle of the sleep-drugs and the fastmove-drugs, was caught up some with health foods these days). True, they drank quite a bit, but not enough to cause them to gain weight. Just enough to blur or to get a buzz on, and only when the mood hit them. Their first two months were a paradise. They began, after an evening of smoking and playing soft jazz, to move out from the sexual patterns of their previous lives. He would play with her in gently wild ways, she would come awake and alive and respond in kind; their love-making would carry through their days, underlying the tensions, loosening their hours among the people of the concurrent world. Len had begun smoking hasheesh in Algeria, during the war. He respected it enormously; it clarified him; sometimes it blurred him; always it smoothed out the red-hot points of pain back of his forehead. He could lose himself, or find himself, depending on his initial feelings, with the sweet smoke of the little pipe. He wished he could let his co-workers in on his secret; he was quite relaxed in comparison to them; so many of them were tightly wedged into their existences, and he had great compassion for them, he saw them as he saw himself, trapped in a system not of his or their devising.

Even so, he himself was trapped. He needed and wanted and loved money for what it could buy. He had no car; not that he couldn't afford one, but that he couldn't afford the idea of himself as the driver of a car and thus responsible for his own life and the lives of his passengers. When he thought about getting a car, it was with a lust like that which he felt for Louise. But he was able to realize his lust for her; it worked; it smoothed out, as if he could see or feel the dried and curled-up emotions unfolding and turning smoke-grey and easy and flowing. He began to wish he had another novel going, a real one this time, something that told about where he'd really been, not theory but what he had learned in his life, a sharing of whatever wisdoms he'd accrued. And, like the car idea, the idea of the second novel was turned into his relationship with Louise. They went into a phase of intensity, of running, of staying up most of the night with their Village friends, of making love before he went to work in the morning. In fact, he found himself ready for more love-making in the middle of the day, and had to make do with the lesser qualities of alone satisfaction, during this time.

Once, after they'd been seeing each other almost every day for a month, Louise had decided that she had to spend some time alone, doing some thinking or walking the city or just being (he was never to be sure of what prompted that space) and, without forewarning, never showed up at the apartment one evening. They had parted that morning in perfect accord. As the night progressed, and she neither phoned nor came, he swung mildly from concern through a calm realization that she, as a fellow human being, had needs which he could not supply or even guess at, to the edge of a jagged anxiety during which he recalled any of the small sharp differences between them which had caused arguments or disagreements in the past months and might be involved now. The day after that night was limbo for Len. Friends came over and stayed overnight with him, bridging the odd space left by the absence of her warm flesh in his big double bed. After all, wasn't he himself, they assured him, with his own life, his own ego, his own past and therefore his own present and future?

By the night of the third day without word from her, his equilibrium was lost. He came home from the office, and, despite the Dexedrine, lay down exhausted, with the hi-fi turned on loudly for company. He slept and woke after half an hour of dreaming about her, woke into the most terrifying feeling of emptiness, wild nameless shapeless terror, he'd ever known. Somehow, despite his defenses, his age, his experiences with women, this young woman had become so important to him, such a pivot-point for his life, that the possibility that she might never come back to him drove him past his own realities. He sat on the edge of the couch and sobbed until he retched. The doorbell rang six times. He stared past the grey walls, past the windows, seeing nothing. Seeing empty. Which was a red color. Or the same grey as the walls.

The friend at the door kept trying the buzzer, and finally Len let him in. Fortunately, it was a close friend, not a man Len saw often, but one to whom Len felt allied in deep ways, almost mystically. It was this man who helped Len through that night of desperate anguish. Len wanted any way out of this that he could find; he knew that it was his own skull which formed a cell with red-hot walls; but it was out of his control now. He loved her, whatever other names might be given it that was his name for it; it was possible she had left him, he noticed that her robe was not on the hook in the bathroom, that her blouse was not in the bureau, what was on her mind, jesus, did he really know anything about her, was he too old for her, what had they talked about the last time, panic, panic, anguish, the pain, Louise, your flesh, the flesh at the nape of your neck, my god, what will I do with my nights, if you gave a damn you'd call me, a word, anything, goddam you for not giving me a word to cling to, o god these rooms smell of her flesh, that table where we ate, what did I do wrong, christ, i can't stand this, even knowing it's done would be better than this, goddam you Louise I am so damn vulnerable to you, you know me, how could you do this, what are you doing, thinking, god, give me any word at all, no, this is incredible, not you, not her, you can't be gone. . . .

On the fourth night of her absence, he went out with friends to a bar in the East Village. It was a place many painters went to, and Louise's sister, a painter, was there. If Len hadn't been involved with Louise from the minute he met her, or if he'd met Ellen first, he'd probably have started something with the sister. Realistically, he knew Louise's temperament suited him better, but he enjoyed Ellen: she was lighter, less serious, she had less of the dark-lady moods of the fair Louise, about her; he felt easier with her really, than with Louise, although this might, of course, be because lovers are so seldom able to be friends. Ellen was closer to his age by a few years, Ellen was friendly, Ellen would dance with him to the discotheque music there; and Ellen could tell him something about what was on Louise's mind, some of the time anyway. But this time, she couldn't. She knew only that her sister was not communicative with her when she was in this shape. Louise had spent the last two nights practicing the piano. Not sleeping much, not going out or running around, just mostly staying in, playing the music she loved but could not accomplish well: most of the two nights.

On impulse, Len asked Ellen if she might want to drive up to Connecticut with him that weekend. She said, 'You're on!' immediately. He could spend the whole day planning for the trip instead of listening for the sound of Louise's key in the apartment door. This was good, this was better, he could run and get the hell away from this torment. Before they left the city that night, he connected for some hash, and the taste he took with his dealer lasted him until they were up in the country that night. They stayed in the cottage of friends of his, near the Sound. Ellen asked for some of the pipe; they shared it for half an hour, with Ernest Bloch and Miles Davis on the phonograph. They talked about music, and about the city, and then about Louise, which led them to men and women, and thus into Ellen's inability to 'be in love,' about what love could do to people like them (they both considered themselves to be 'destroyed' people, people too scared to be able to love fully or calmly); the difference, Len asserted, was that *he* was willing always to take the chance: he was not defeated; his years had not convinced him that he must not take the next chance into life, whatever the result; he would continue to take reasonable risks.

They were high before midnight and relaxed and

easy with themselves and each other. Like two kids, they got into pajamas and fell into the twin beds near the fireplace. Len got up and moved over to Ellen's bed. But when he began to make love to her, he found he still had the smell of Louise in his nostrils, her flesh echoed under his hands. He couldn't follow through with Ellen. Ellen knew where he was at; she held him quietly until they both slept. The next day, they swam in the Sound, walked the beach for an hour, ate with their friends, and went back to the city. On their arrival, he found that Louise had phoned him. The flat voice of his answering service noted that she had called at midnight the previous night. He knew that Ellen had gone out of the City with him in order to fill in the time of waiting, the anguish, and he was grateful to her; it welled thickly in him, this gratitude to her. But that was all he could feel for her, that and an affectionate companionship; simple as that. He was completely caught up with Louise.

When he and Louise saw each other that night, he was very careful. He waited to see what her reactions were, tried to sense her; more than he'd ever done; his nerves were cupped and curved around her like a radar antenna; he seemed calm and reserved. This control was the hardest to achieve of any act of his life. They walked to the nearby park. In the smooth night air, her face seemed concealed, and therefore more desirable. He asked her to marry him; she said, smiling, 'I will, but not just yet, not for a while . . .' and he was almost content with this answer. They walked back to his apartment. He was still trembling, it required a great effort not to tremble visibly. Louise asked him about the weekend with Ellen and he told her most of how it had gone, leaving out the days before his time with Ellen, those days during which he'd looked down the dark chasm of life without Louise, when he'd moved toward death and thought of it as cessation to pain (O Louise, he thought, why do you want to get mixed up with a sick, fucked-up, old cat like me? you who are strong and young and beautiful!) But Louise was still con-

cealed, still not saying much. He brought out what was left of
the hash and they smoked quietly for a while. His hands on
her seemed almost to pass through her, it was as if she were
sea-spray, and her mouth was salt to his taste. He carried her
to the bedroom, he took her, smoothly, beautifully, she gave
herself fully to him, her gown was transparent and like sea-
spray around them, he felt as if this were the first time he'd
had her, had any woman, her face shone near him, she felt as
if his face were the only face in the world now, her world
pivoted on him, they moved and swam free. He fell asleep
still inside her; she slept moments afterward. And she dreamed.

II.

When Lou finally rolled off her to his side of the bed, Elinor
almost laughed with relief. He was such a bull, he had never
been tender with her in all their years of being together in
this bed. She lay awake, listening to the night sounds. And
they gradually eased her. Yes, they were good, these sounds,
they always worked. The thick rustling of the cows' hooves in
the scattered hay on the barn floor. The coughing of the girls
in their beds in the next room. Even the ticking of the clock
in the kitchen below her. Night sounds. Yes. Reassurance. The
cicadas, the elm outside the window, the solitary whippoor-
will, the dog Taffy growling in a dream, the ponies snuffling
in the near field. Elinor was worrying, she was worried, too
many things she could not change, she worried them in her
head the way the coon hound worried a rabbit before he was
trained. O yes Lou disgusted her. It hadn't changed after six
kids. But there was always the thought that it would stop in a
few years, the kids would be all grown up, maybe Marie
would amount to something, maybe Billy would stop running
around with that trash in town, the twins would continue to
be sweet and good, it was good there were some of the kids
who behaved, it was good that Al was working with Lou and

helping him some on the farm, that youngest one was really a
trouble, him with his head out in the mountains all the time
and needed on the tractor and never to be found, if they
didn't get rain soon the corn would come short of what they
needed, the Chevy needed to be fixed, she would take it into
Kingston tomorrow, maybe Marie would ride along with her
and she could talk her into finishing high school, I'll tell her
we can buy some fabric for slipcovers and she can pick it out,
maybe she can come around and leave off seeing the Thomas
boy one night, I really think Al should marry that girl he's
been seeing, if he had any sense he'd get her settled before
someone else did, she'd make him a good wife, not many girls
would put up with his foolishness the way she did, O if that
first baby had lived he'd have been twenty-two, no, let's see,
twenty-three by now, baby, that baby, my god. I still miss that
little thing, funny how you never get over it, like I still
haven't got over losing mamma and pappa, I have to remember to buy a roast and order some more eggs tomorrow, we're
almost out, those twins are growing so fast they eat more than
a new heifer, god what if I got pregnant again now, I wish
sometimes they took the calves away from us and just took the
milk like we do, what if someone else thinks about that, get
us all freshening and then take the calves, like with my first
baby, well the one I would miss most now would be Billy,
I wonder if the others know he's always been my favorite, him
with his wild ways, Lou knows, and he holds it against me, he
likes the twins better, that man, bet that he thinks it was
some damn cleverness on his part made them twins, like more
cows in the barn or something, Lord, that man snores like a
goddam moose, you'd think a man his age couldn't get it up any
more, I wish sometimes mamma had taught me more about
women and less about cows, maybe I would've married a city
man, I bet they don't have so many kids, look at bunch of
city people down the road, wish I could understand how they
live, they don't say one blessed thing I can understand and
they wear jeans like they was a costume or something, and

with kids too, wonder what they think of us here, walk up to buy their milk and look at everything like it was something good to eat or they didn't know the name for it, I am so damn tired of all this, that man with the beard yesterday talking to Lou about Europe, what would it be like to just say to hell with it all and get on a boat and go there, and Lou looking like he looks wherever we go, wonder if they have corn-flakes to eat for breakfast in Europe, better to just stay put and grow the kids up, still, what would it be like, even go to New York for a week, say see the Fair, stay at a hotel, go to Radio City and see those dancers, must be three years since we went there, I bet Lou wouldn't want to part with the money, never saw a man so set in his ways, good man though, never looked at another woman once, and she reached out, put her hand on his stomach, the furry skin of his belly, feeling the hard muscles under the skin, and he woke out of his dream of mountains he owned, and turned toward her, and took her as a bull takes a cow, dreamlessly, his hard pizzle finding her soft and firm and open, and for the first time in her life she met him with a kind of passion, her own, her anxious wide thoughts converging on her cunt, and he sensed this and responded, changed a bit, kept with her, they moved royally in the big bed where they'd conceived six children, they got there together, she gasped and rolled, no words, and for the first time he fell asleep on top of her, still inside her, her face shining near his, O what is this new thing, to her this man had truly the only face in the world and her world pivoted on him, he slept still in her but not snoring, and, moments afterward, she slept. They both dreamed.

III.

They were married shortly afterward, in a place chosen by Louise's parents: the Sherry Netherland Hotel on Fifth Avenue. It was a gesture of deference, really, but one which annoyed Len more than he would show—god, such a gauche place!—and went to the west coast of Yugoslavia for a week's honeymoon. Louise was not adapting well to Len's kind of life, though: this being a Madison Avenue adman's wife. She didn't take to the structuring; it began to show on her face within a month after their return to New York . . . sure, she was superb at entertaining, but she didn't know much about cooking, really, and her small-talk was limited; besides, she was always unsure of herself with these polished and elegant people so much older than she. She tried not to let it all go more than skin-deep and she did not succeed. She didn't like the kinds of people they were under the façades; her senses were good and they made her edgy and irritable around Len's business acquaintances. She had a feeling that Len didn't like them any more than she did. But they both loved beautiful clothing, fine furniture, airplane tickets, good food. There was no compromise for them. This was the way it had to go. Len had less and less time to spend on his poems or the novel he'd begun. Louise was more tense each day. She had too much time to spend, too much money to spend, none of her activities seemed to fill the Big Empty, even the morning smoke didn't smooth the edge of the pain underneath. She thought of having a baby. Len liked the idea at the beginning, when she mentioned it. But was a bit scared by all the changes in their lives, all the shifting that would have to take place to make room for a kid. But then again, he was making enough now so that they could afford a nurse, or a full-time maid and governess; perhaps a kid wouldn't fulfill his ideas of himself as a man, but it would help Louise or she wouldn't have brought the whole thing up. Besides, he relished the idea of a son, and maybe it would be a blond kid, like Louise, that would be interesting, how would he feel about that! So many of his friends had married blonde girls when they were overseas and now had little blond kids running around and growing up. Two of his best friends, both New Yorkers and both Jews, both nervous and aggressive and hungry types, had brought back pretty French girls, girls who were also bright but with the gentleness of the provinces over there. And Len had looked enviously on those matches, which somehow had lasted longer than his own, than many other marriages he'd seen. Yes, maybe it was a good idea to start a kid, he was seeing the 'over 35' ads every time he looked in the mirror these days, maybe a kid wouldn't ruffle the surface as much as he feared . . .

IV.

They were married shortly afterward, at a little synagogue on the upper west side; B'nai Jeshrun or some such, he had little knowledge of the Hebrew language and had disavowed it for so long now; he remembered only the rose-window of the synagogue and how it contrasted with the rose-window at Chartres, as he'd experienced it many years ago. They booked for Grossinger's for their week's honeymoon. When they got near there, having followed the same directions as usual for getting to Liberty, they found that they could get no farther than a town near the giant hotel. In this town, the only hotel was a place which had been active in the Borscht Belt scene some forty years earlier. Since then, it had gone through its ups and downs, and had been purchased by a group of Spanish-Americans for a vacation-spot for those of that group who could afford to get out of New York for a week. At first, at the beginning, Len and Louise had a game of it: they lit up their pipe in the car and went wandering around the premises, Len remembering his youth, when he'd been to such a place. They tried out two of the rocking-chairs in the endless row on the frontporch of the place (all the seats were worn but empty; the whole place seemed uninhabited; yet the diningroom was set for dinner and the table was ready to serve fifty meals); the row of rocking-chairs faced an equally symmetrical row of pine-trees, no view of the road or the land beyond, just the chairs facing the trees, the dusty and even trees. It was deep summer. The heat was oppressive; Louise felt it on her spine; they were both soaked with sweat; the breeze which moved the print curtains at the upper windows of the huge plain building did not seem to extend downward to the grounds where they wandered. The lake of the place was swampy; tiger-lilies grew on its banks and water-lilies formed an island near the land where they stood. It was impossible to think of going into that water. In the lobby there were beautiful old prints in ornate frames, left from the time when the hotel had been a successful and busy place. But now the walls were dull pink; there were bilingual direction signs on many of the doors ('Favor de . . .') and the place smelled brilliantly of a strong disinfectant. Louise found huge pans full of oily food in the kitchen (which was also deserted). Bottles of Cerveza Dos Equis stood in cases in the corners of the kitchen and in one corner of the lobby. When they made a circuit of the lobby they came to the traditional counter where guests were tempted or cajoled into purchasing jewelry for themselves or each other, or gifts for those who, less fortunate, were not able to come to this hotel. Louise looked into it and wept. The case was filled with a dusty assortment of objects: plastic-flower earrings, celluloid toys, dried-grass necklaces; and, set in among these pathetic attempts at memorabilia, several of those sea creatures called 'diábolo del mar,' the ray-like animal whose skeleton so resembles that of a transmuted man, a human as interpreted by Bosch. Louise's hand had been on Len's arm as they approached the showcase; now, as she wept, her nails dug deep into his forearm. She had no memories to draw on; this place was all new to her; not an admixture of old jews and new puerto ricans, but a place of dissonance, of cacophony on her eyes and nerves. It did not make sense to her, in a most terrible way: she could not encompass it.

The car was out of commission. They would have to stay in this place. No one was in sight, no one, for directions, for registering, for food, for a room. They climbed the old, wide stairs, still with the original carpeting and polished dark wood newels. In the first corridor they came to, there was a room, door swung open, a tiny breeze moving the brash print curtains. The bed was made and seemed quite clean. Len shut the door and carried the weeping girl to the bed. They made love, like starved animals; and when it was done, they made love again, as a fending gesture. When Len fell asleep, Louise got up and moved to the writing-table in the corner near the window. There was a stack of small paper, blank, no letterheads. The pen was missing. She took her own from her purse and wrote:

V.

Please. I am on this island. In the other room, one of them is doing something which creates a noise which I cannot identify. Tonight, all of their daughters have gone to a ceremony, one which I think of as a sort of sorority dance; it is a puberty ritual, of sorts, surely, yet one which will culminate, this night, in the death of each of them. In the meantime I can see the lights in the compounds around me: the parents (if that is what they are) of these girls have gathered what seem to be friends and relatives from other villages or gathering-places, and are playing a game with paper; to me it looks like it is based on Tarot (but how can it be?) Their cries of delight or amazement or shock come to me in the humid air. On each of the doorposts of the huts is placed a card. This is designed to show the Spirits that only males of the household remain; although during my stay there has been no apparent sexual activity and no visible distinction between the people here, I suppose these are the adults of the family-group divisions.

In each grassy compound or enclosure is kept what appears to be a pet, a sort of baboon but with feathers as a ruff near the neck. This animal is not bound, yet remains in a circumscribed area and appears content. Its function has not become apparent to me as yet, although I have noticed the villagers offering teeth and locks of hair to the 'baboons,' from time to time. I wonder why the daughters are not permitted to survive beyond their teen years. On the table in one hut, I found a copy of Rilke's Duino Elegies; another has John Cage's book SILENCE, and another has Hesse. From these, I assumed at first a certain intellectual level, which was soon disproved when I saw that these were being used in a way not thought of in my own culture: they were shredded, page by page, 'unread,' and used as fodder for the animals kept near the huts. The animals enjoy this food, or let us say they seem to do so, mixing the shredded paper with some sort of liquid at midday. Perhaps there is a form of osmosis with which I am not familiar, in all of this. Certainly the pets seem to have a look about the eyes which I have not noticed in their captors or mentors.

The sons, which do show rudimentary male characteristics (disappearing, gradually, after puberty, I judge from the older ones), are kept dressed in white only. Their hair and toenails are either removed or bred out; are conspicuously absent, at any rate. When they go to the bathing area at the eastern end of the compound, it is seen that the 'males' and 'females' (the females' characteristics are more like ours, and thus more readily identified, or distinguished, although they might, in this place, actually be 'males,' I suppose, or neuters, depending on values in the subculture) bathe freely in each other's company.

There is a smell of honeysuckle tonight. I have been here several weeks, as I judge time. It is a matter of speculation as to what the locals think I am doing here. They have been trying to be kind to me; of this I am sure; but what will their attitude be when they discover that I am a female, and within the age-range which requires the death-dance as its conclusion? Yet the women seem gentle, and the men and small children keep a distance, surely with great effort, since they have some curiosity. They have shared a pipe with me once: a local tobacco, which had the same effect as . . .

Then Louise went to the bed where Len slept, and she too fell asleep, lying across his body, her legs slanted across his. The papers were folded casually into her purse. Afterward, those who knew her could not identify her handwriting.

VI.

When they awoke, the car was repaired; in fact, the motor was running. Since they had no luggage in that room, it was easy to leave the place. It seemed reasonable to continue on to Grossinger's; only a few hours seemed to have passed. But they had not eaten; they were starved. In the town of Ellenville they stopped to eat. Len, sitting opposite Louise in the booth, was once again totally absorbed with her small, intense face, the delicately structured features overwhelmed by the odd chiaroscuro of her spirit, behind the fine skin of her face. He was remembering a joke his sister Hannah had told him, at the time of her first marriage, many years ago: 'Sure, all of the mamma and pappa types want us to marry nice Jewish boys; guess they don't realize that the only way to get a nice Jewish boy these days is to be a tall thin blonde Gentile girl!' —this, as she was marrying a tall, slender, fair man from Mississippi, with her parents providing a background of dismay to the wedding. Maybe, Len speculated, this was part of his being so hung-up on Louise. All the symbolic things she was. She was a great combination; she was both in one. A perfect solution.

Once, during their brief courtship, he'd gone with her to her brother's house, to meet him and his wife and kids. On arrival, he'd found that her parents and her sister Ellen were there, and had been expected all along. He gave Louise a sharp, shocked look. Even in this short time, he'd thought they had worked out their definitions and terms: new people, family people and the like, required at least a warning or some preparation. But she had not considered this to be a really threatening situation to him, and she was partially correct. Soon after introductions were over and they were sitting around having pre-dinner cocktails, she thought, I don't have to protect him, he has enough veneer going to slide him through even a night like this, migod, he sits down to lunch with Gene Black of the World Bank and this General or that, in his day's work, what could he fear from these people? And she was, in a sense, right: somehow, he was already smoothly on his feet, and she wound up being the nervous one; he even seemed to enjoy the tension, the sizing-up, the delicate dance of it all, and met these relatives of hers with a poise and sang-froid that ended up offending her more than any clumsiness would. It somehow negated her role as a helpmeet, this way, not having to put him at his ease. He might at least have the grace to be ill-at-ease, or make a faux pas, or to be as reticent as he'd been among her loquacious and outgoing friends. . . . This way, she didn't know what her role was, she was almost unnecessary in the full, well-lit, comfortable room. Usually, Len made quite clear to her what behavior was expected under the given circumstances.

When the family embarked on reminiscences, Len sensed her annoyance and discomfort. He led her into the children's bedroom and asked for the hash-pipe. They smoked deeply of it, sitting at an open window and looking out on West End Avenue in mid-winter, the first heavy snowfall of the season making it almost romantic; the people below became quite simpático, they were all Salinger characters, or so it felt after a few minutes. Len talked softly to her about his youth, about the changing mores of their native land: had they been adults at the time of Prohibition, they'd probably have gone to speakeasies, and with probity; yet here, in her brother's house, they were criminals, subject to long terms of imprisonment in exchange for this soft pipeful of relief. The faces of Genet, Burroughs, Miller, Artaud floated into the room with the crisp winter air off the Hudson. A block away lived friends of Len, both writers; Len and Louise could easily walk out and see them this evening, but the courage was to remain where they were, with her relatives.

He realized that it had been an act of great courage, for her to have brought this group together; regardless of the means, it was a respectable result. Her relatives. The people who had conceived her, brought her up, shaped her. Well, it was unlikely that he'd try all this sort of scene, with his own relatives, for quite a while. They were critical; they were destroyers; when he thought of them, he choked on the edge of their critical eyes and voices. Enough, for now, to keep this his own secret: the full, dark secret of Lawrence, subsurface always, rich between them. What passed between their eyes, in such roomsful of people, was marvelous and was enough to sustain him for now. He didn't need to seek approval; and it would not be forthcoming, anyway, in all probability. Her eyes, though blue, were deep-set and almost violet in color, and they contained her passion, her pain, her love; her eyes were far too wise for a girl of nineteen who had lived in such protected circumstances. And Len had those dark, strong eyes of the Russian Jew, so that he'd been told more than once, 'You're too *intense*, Lenny,' to which he would respond sharply, 'No such thing as *too* intense; either you're intense or you're not, and I am.' He was always aware of himself, conscious of his voice-tone, of body posture, stance in a room, his own position in relation to the other people in a room. But he grew blind when faced with his closest forms of self-expression, and as blind as possible to his motives. Whereas he knew by now that Louise would try for such blindness but would often end up analyzing and magnifying. His escape was always in his sure feeling of his own indestructibility; not in his superiority (he was on to that dreadful product of the Hebrew mythologies, the Chosen People bit, where you have to live up to your own godhood or the eye of God would smite you, and it's always impossible to be just plain human and forgive yourself; all that guilt! which he used to spend his energy on!) but in the strength of his own spirit and body; his man-ness, his inner resource, that spurt into the concept of scope which pushed him out into what he thought of as The Big Picture, the country he lived in, the business he conducted as a logical and functioning animal in his society; his place in the world. Usually, the question boiled down to whether or not he was content with the way it was all going at the moment. Most often it was enough to have perspective, that sideways look in on himself and where he stood in relation to the world.

He was no longer young, but it didn't taste bitter; he had done a lot with his life till now, and having a girl like Louise was enough to balance out much of the ordinary agonies. In a sense, it was like being her parent (he couldn't think of it as her 'father,' exactly; preceptor, maybe), because she, at almost 20, at about half his age, had had the sort of upbringing which included the beginnings of excellent and discriminating taste, which he was most interested in developing and carrying further, and bringing out. She really had an innate sense of taste, he thought. Long ago, when he was around Louise's age and was going with a girl of 30, he'd looked around her East End Avenue apartment at the Daum-crystal-and-Lalique elegance and asked her, 'I *feel* it, but what does good taste *mean?* What does it *include?*' and her answer, her smile, her shrug: 'Good taste . . . well, good taste *knows.*' It had seemed, then, an enigma; now it made more sense. His own apartment, his clothes were in Good Taste; it was Good Taste that had made him see Louise and none of the other girls in the Playboy Club that first night; it was this that had soon made him see that she had enormous potential (sort of the reverse of seeing an old farmhouse and mentally remodelling it, he thought now). And then there was her physical self: her way of moving her body in a room; the tilt of her head across a street; the way she moved in bed; her nervous, high-pitched, crisp way of talking when she was interested in what was going on; the tense, instinctive way she waited until she thought he was damn near starving for it before she put her hands on him. A smart chick, this one; instinctively smart, she was, and he liked that. He thought of himself as Europe and of Louise as America, magnificent of itself but waiting to be colonized, civilised; full of natural beauty and natural resources, but unable to put them to use. How many of the others he'd known, gone with, made, even married once!— and he would marry Louise, or know the reason why.

Everything, even this night, was moving in the right direction. He wondered if she knew what a commitment it was, for her to bring him to this house to meet all her close relatives. That father of hers, with his genteel poverty, his academic accoutrements, the kind of man who would never make a buck, sure, but knew enough to give the kids a sense of taste and an aura of refinement; it was okay, it was just fine for him to work with, he could take it from there with Louise The father wouldn't have to worry. He looked over at the older man (not that much older, come to think of it; must be around fifty-five; it was those scruffy tweeds that did it) and caught the father in a deep glance; Len knew he'd intercepted the father's appraisal of him as his youngest daughter's possible mate. And he knew that the father would give her to him. It didn't matter that he was not a literary type like the old man, not able to talk about Proust or Dostoievski as they were now doing. He knew it would be enough that he was self-made (or at least had parlayed his family's small money into a sizeable amount, over the last fifteen years). To hell with culture, for the most part; anything older than 1900, unless it was furniture or paintings, didn't interest him except as an investment. The fact that Louise said she wanted to paint was not pertinent. He guessed she'd get over that, with all the travelling they would do, and with all that he could give her, and he trusted that the damn psychoanalyst she went to would back him up in this. Well, if she really had to, she would have the time, they could afford a maid and she would have plenty of time for a hobby. The only things he would expect of her would be to be well-dressed (not these nice but sad-looking casual corduroys she was now affecting; he could see her in a Cardin suit or a good fur; his mind's eye dressed her like a mannequin in the new hip fashions from the Frenchmen, and chopped off her mass of blonde hair to a sleek cap; then she would look big-time enough to move in his circles!)—and to keep the apartment in good shape. She had a good disposition and she was wonderful in bed; what more could a man want?

Not long after this particular evening, Louise met Len after his workday and they went to the Italian street-fair on one of the Village blocks near Len's apartment. The quality of looseness, of poverty, the remnants of raw peasant quality attracted them both: as long as they were sure they could leave it whenever they wished and return to Len's apartment, with its Rauschenberg paintings and Miles Davis records and of course the sculptures: DeNoto for smooth, Chamberlain for rough and cool, Bontecou for wise . . . Turning on was one way to get all of the delight offered by an evening out. And then going back to that apartment, so different from Louise's parents' place on Hudson Street. Louise had a warm affection for that drafty old place, cluttered with dried wood and peculiar fabric and furniture whose stuffing leaked out where the cats had clawed at it over the years, but to Len the place was in some ways too much like the apartments of his early years with his own parents; too scruffy, somehow, even though this one had books and a few things that were handsome to look at. He had smoked two joints of pot while still uptown and the edges of the day were smoothed down a bit for him by the time he met Louise on the corner. He had called her from the office today, his feet on the desk, his voice already softened and easy, 'O babe, I wish you were here, this is some of the finest Acapulco Gold I ever got near, I'll save you some, what do you say we go over to the street-fair when

I get done?' But on this night, as on most others, they wound up at a bar on the East Side where many writers and painters hung out. It was as much of a contrast for them as was the fair, moving in this community which also had its ease and its different way of being within the larger culture; all the couples of negro-and-white who were obviously just being together, as men and women, like themselves (one couple had even brought in their kids); all the loners (Len, to her, as two women came in: 'Now see, that's what I mean about the Loners, baby: those two are sure losers as I see it . . .' and his sudden grip on her arm as he realized that one of the women was his ex-wife . . .) all the lushes, and all the cause-joiners; the ones with dilated pupils and the ones with a soft haze between them and the world, the way Len and Louise were; the social drinkers and the frantic searchers and the calm ones. It was a good bar, and alive, for them; all the contrast with their world; as good as the Renaissance uptown, for them, sometimes, and often better by far. Something here was real and tangible and to-be-sought.

What would the Italian community we were just in, make of all this? Louise wondered. Probably put it down, the way they do the newer coffee-houses on MacDougal, too different from their Catholic way of seeing the world . . . what a funny marvelous city this is, last night we were at the Renaissance, all that red velvet and smoothness and gloss, boy what money can do, but I bet nobody there was real, too smooth, what do they do with their pain, look at all this real, what kind of real is this and what kind is that, I bet nobody there was real, how much real can you be or stand, are we real, am I, is Len? She stared at Len's profile. He was looking at a man at the bar, a man his age, bearded, tall, ugly, and not smiling. A man with paint on his jeans; housepaint. What was it made that man able to leave money alone, except what he needed of it to survive? I wonder if he's got a woman or if he's queer or what. Wonder where he lives. Probably near here. And Len was thinking, Bet that guy wouldn't trade his pad or these weird chicks in here for my pad and this chick, I'm not so sure about this little kid of a chick I've got here, yet; wonder if I could make a break, it's still early enough in the game, I'm not in too deep with her yet. . . .

Louise had been to the hairdresser's that day; she was studying the hairdos of the women in the bar. The black hair that had been conked into a style resembling her own new Sassoon smoothness; the little blonde who couldn't have been much more than Louise's own age but whose hair was like straw, bleached almost white, over her strained little face, I wonder what that faggot who does my hair does with his evenings, wonder if he comes here, it gets hard to make conversation with him when I'm in the chair, where will we go after this, god I want to leave this place soon, too hot, too much happening, music too much, 'Len, what say, you have to get up early,' and caught him in the middle of his early youth memory: the Bronx, Sedgwick Avenue, going rowing on a forgotten lake with forgotten companions, racing down the back alleys and falling in broken glass and getting the cuts that left the scars on his legs and chin and skull, sitting in the Park Plaza movie-house on Saturday nights, smell of that place like another world, cool, dark, groping on the lap of the girl he'd brought, and on the screen John Garfield off on some impossible mission and getting blinded in the War, the cool outdoor air outside afterward, his mother's smothering food, Hebrew-school, the jackets the guys wore with CHAMPS scripted across the backs in red, dirty drawings passed around the desks in class, riding the subway to Van Cortlandt Park, seeing the mansion and vowing he would have a place just as light, as cool, as clean, as lovely as that one, to live in, no subway, no El, no soot, no little dark rooms, and no dark labyrinthine hallways to get through before sanctuary . . . yes, today, yes, the clear expanse of well-lit halls, into the cool, calm apartment, the 45-foot livingroom, he did not have to sleep in any livingroom on any goddam lumpy couch, the pale-grey of the livingroom was like pale clean silk to him, a pale expanse of quiet evenness, all good taste and cool colors and immaculately kept up, it was his haven and defense, his way of getting even, his retort and response to the flats of his youth . . .

They left the East Side bar and rode the crosstown bus to their familiar street, the doorman, the crisp lobby, the rosewood-lined elevator, the wood-panelled door of the apartment. It was marvelously quiet in there. He breathed the filtered air with delight, touched the little Lalique bowl with gratitude, loved his furniture as if it were an animal waiting for his hand's caress. Good taste, yes, and more than that. In the bedroom, that place of worship of the flesh, he ripped the bedspread off the huge round bed and swung it across the room. He grabbed Louise's shoulder as if he were angry or possessed; then, gently, gently, he lifted her, and took her to the bed, and took her, but not gently this time. Urgently; filled with ideas of his ugly and dirty and poverty-ridden years, the crummy little girls of back-alley days, the scribbled words-and-drawings of the school yards; his mind that since then had learned to treasure the almost inanimate smoothness in things and people . . . the desire of possession of beauty . . . and then she slept, finally, her face still puzzled and troubled; her desire sated, but her mind like a gaping wound at the assault . . .

He thought about the novel he'd always wanted to try. Not the one that had gotten through, that had made his name for him: not the money one, that had gotten him all beauty for his own. He went to the typewriter and began, quickly, quickly, with the urgency of one who had never spoken; as if he had somehow, from birth, been deprived of speech, but had heard clearly, almost too clearly, the speeches and movements of those circling around his life, and had, in his mind's eye, thus perfected his diction and perspective. He wrote:

VII.

Story time. This is how it looks. Once upon a time, there were a boy and girl. They were 'all fucked up.' Not their fault. Fault? They came from a big city, let us say Manhattan, and they are still in Manhattan today. This is only part of the reason for their not being in such good shape. We want to talk about them because there are so many of them all around us. To begin with, they were children, both of them, though at the beginning they were children at different times. That is, one was considerably older than the other, chronologically. Each had a rich mother and a rich father. But the parents, all four of them, were not rich to begin with. They were originally poor. The original poor. Their name is Legion. We can call the boy's family name just that: Legion. Will it do? What was it changed from? Anyway, the parents, when they grew rich, became convinced that money was a cure-all, second only to 'a good night's sleep.' They kept small packages of money on their persons at all times and referred to it when their spirits sank. It was kept in leather sacks of one kind or another. They also kept vials of sleep on their persons. They used these as well. The containers were glass. There was a fealty arrangement made with the children, by which they could obtain some of the contents of the vials or the small sacks. Another substance was also involved in this arrangement. It was called 'love' by the parents, and one of its ingredients was termed 'affection.' This was a stuff the color of sunlight on a clear day, and it was kept just under the skin of the hands, in such a way that it could exude through the pores when required. There were a definite group of prescribed rules by which the children, and their siblings, could obtain this or the other substances. One of these rules was that they must at all times pretend they were not full-grown and had no intention of so becoming; in other words, that they would remain true to the parents' vision of them as children. The ideal age-concept for this seemed to be somewhere around eight years of age. They, the children who were not still children, soon became aware of what was expected of them in this arrangement, and learned to comply; for, after all, at least two of the substances kept by the parents, and seldom privy to the children, were essential to the well-being of humans. As a result, and since the substances were doled out according to definite rules, this particular boy and girl, having become adults, were not any older, just larger. 'What do you want to do when you are larger?' was substituted in their conversations with their friends, for '. . . when you are a grownup' and even so, they were careful when they spoke on this subject. Their ideas were chosen for them as carefully as their clothing. These were tailor-made to be of the same fabric as the outfits worn by the parents, and differed only in the cut of the garment. They were garments for a smaller person, but fitted loosely, so there would be room, in case the person became larger. There were several changes of clothing available: 'attitude toward the body,' which was quite dark and opaque, and of a glossy fabric, so that outside things would glance off it; 'attitude toward one's family,' which was made of metal in a square of boxy shape, and had, just inside the visor, a list of one's antecedents, which was removed when it could be proven that one had memorized the list; and a list of birthdays of members of all relatives by blood or marriage. There was an outfit called 'political attitude' which was made of a substance akin to the human skin: it had a ceremonial value, and was presented to the children when they attained 18 years of life. It was of the same color and shape as the parents' 'political attitude,' and therefore it had the peculiar quality of being able to change hue or shape a bit, depending on the current perspective of the biggest members of the family, which in turn depended on whom the current war was being waged with. There were many accessories available, and all were provided for the offspring: gloves called 'table manners,' shoes called 'how to conduct oneself in public,' eyeglasses called 'religion,'

&c., &c. The important thing to notice and remember is that everyone in one's neighborhood, and perhaps in one's city or village, wore the same or very similar 'attitudes.' At parties, the adults wore the 'political attitude' outfits if it was a cocktail party or an evening party without the children; in the streets, everyone wore the dark, opaque 'attitude toward body' outfit, spruced up by the appropriate gloves and shoes and eyeglasses. One could not tell who one's neighbor in a building was, but it was a reassuring thing, one was always sure where one stood, and the most valuable commodity was sameness, if not actual anonymity. All deviants were suspect; any deviation was frowned-upon and revealed in a discussion and lecture-session, and thus usually suppressed.

There were many many children who found this setup valuable; in fact, invaluable; they learned the rules early, and thus they thrived, receiving their rations of needed substances, their outfits for existing within the home and out among other people; often, they hewed so exactly to the system provided, that the process of individual thought was bred out and eliminated within a generation. But about this particular couple of children, the ones to whom I refer at the beginning of this Story Time: they are not of this breed. Something has gone awry, as in every system. Earlier, I used the term 'fucked up.' This needs explanation. It is a password, in effect, among those few in the small percentage of humans who are deviants. But it is not a term they use to refer to themselves. It is applied most often by those whose job it is to try to re-align the deviants to the norm. Let me tell you about the requisites of the members of this subgroup. First of all, it is necessary to have become aware, at some point in life, that there co-exists, alongside the group of parents and children and neighbors and relatives, all of whom look alike, a few humans who are 'different,' or who show some sign, however slight, of variation of dress as defined earlier. Once one has gotten the knack of spotting these slips in the system and the adherents, a whole new world opens up. One of the most carefully guarded secrets of the system becomes available. It is that secret which is most threatening of all the possibilities, to the parents. For whatever reason, the chance (ah—that is the key word, isn't it—CHANCE) that everything might not be predictable, and therefore Calm, and Manageable, and Structured—causes qualms of fear in the hearts of the members of the majority group. So then we find the parents' membership taking steps. Or should I say, Taking Steps. This is a ritual in which a ceremonial flight of stairs is made available to the non-conformist, in an attempt to re-align him or her to the Safe Way, if at all possible. One of the steps on the flight is called 'Getting You to See Things My Way.' This step (upward) is followed by one called 'Or Else,' and is a deep, broad step, involving much privation, whereon the deviant or suspected deviant is deprived of all the needed substances in the vials and pouches of the parents. A view of the World is projected against the stair-tread: it is positively sinister; or should I say, negatively sinister. It shows the deviant wandering alone and bereft in a dark landscape, forever. This, of course, is just a cheap trick; but more of that later. The third step is called 'To Disown or Disavow,' and has loud noises and sharp voices placed strategically. This third, or last, step is followed by a chasm, or what appears at first to be a chasm. In reality, it is a blind, or device with mirrors; there is actually no chasm at all. And here comes the Secret of Secrets: beyond the third step is really the other, or co-existent, world.

Now then, about our hero and heroine. You might imagine that they are among those who, at an early age, began to suspect, for whatever reason, that all was not as it seemed. They began to find clues. The most important early ones came to them in books. Not the ordained books they found in the houses of the parents. But in books they found in the schools, and at the homes of a few rare friends. The possibilities were concealed quite cleverly within the routine contexts of the material in these books. The second group of clues came through music. Not in the ritual pieces found in the homes of the parents, but in the recordings heard played while passing along streets at odd hours, off hours, when the rest of humanity seemed to sleep. And, once they had found these clues, many other things seemed to add to them. The boy would realize that, just back of the visor of his friend, his classmate, or his neighbor, there would be a glimpse of writing that was 'different.' Just a quick glimpse, but enough. Or the girl would notice that just before she and her friend would begin to talk about the prescribed subjects, there would be a few words, or a look, which would indicate that there was something else here; something unnameable which would appeal to something she was thinking or feeling, and for which there was no name in the language she had been taught. And over the years, these clues piled up

By the time we meet the hero and heroine, they have indeed grown larger. They have attained physical maturity. They have so continued to amass clues, and been so careful about their identities, that they have been able to identify and join the rest of the co-existers whose movements were not merely speculation any longer. In fact, by the time the hero and heroine were at this stage, their group had become almost as ritualistic and public an affair as that of the majority group. Still a minority, but gaining strength by virtue of membership in many countries of the world. There was a password, or phrase—'In motion'—which implied the desire for the new, the adventuresome, and evidenced itself in a mobility of the person, so that these people could be found in any city and all countries, recognizable and available. And there were artifacts or commodities which were commensurate with the leather containers, vials and bottles and jars, and skin-exuded emollients of the other group. Instead of money (of which they nevertheless had varying amounts, it being so necessary to certain elementary gettings-on), they kept small packets of a certain herb, which, when some of them smoked it, opened the door at which they were standing. Others of them kept the distillate of another plant,

similar in action or effect. Instead of the vials of sleep, they
kept on their persons small containers of essence of humor,
or laughter; and many of them carried, especially in cities, a
substance made of pine wood and leafmold which was called
'country air.' This last was of an addictive quality, whereas
the first mentioned were not. Many of the co-existers had to
leave the cities and form colonies in pine-forests because of
this substance. But for those who did not or could not, the
country-air-essence was always available and not high in price.
You see, these people operated mostly on a barter basis. They
would exchange books with one another (they had their own
printing-presses by now) and recordings of their music (ditto
for the music). And by far the most desirable commodity in
their aspect of the world was an exquisite liquid called
'imagination.' It was this substance that was most feared by
the other group, because it made all things possible; it made
any world available; it could automatically cancel out the
buildings, clothing, rules, and values of the majority group,
with just a few drops.

     Well, then. With all of this, all of these things and
people available to them, or on their persons at all times,
you might well ask, 'What is it that made the hero and heroine
unhappy?' Yes, it would seem that only wisdom and glory
would follow them till the ends of their days, and they would
dwell in peace in their own and their friends' houses forever!
—but such is, alas, not the case. As we look more deeply, we
find a fatal flaw, a schism, a dichotomy. We report that there
has been one vital ceremony, one ritualistic gesture we have
not recorded. There has been an incision made into the skull
of each of the offspring of the majority group (into which our
hero and heroine were born, as were most of the co-existers).
Into this incision has been placed a chemical called 'inculcation,' whose strength is renewed at certain ritual ages. The
first would occur at a very early age, and, depending on the
'religion-eyeglasses' style of the parents, is specifically cor-
related with a religious ceremony, such as 'baptism' or 'cir-

cumcision' in the very young, and 'confirmation' or 'bar mitzvah' in the larger child. Whenever you see a girl in a white dress resembling a bridal outfit in miniature, or a boy in a dark-opaque suit the exact replica of his father's, you may know that this has been part of it. The trouble is, the liquid of 'imagination' and the substance of 'inculcation' tend to work in chemical opposition to each other. Usually, one dominates and cancels out the other. The 'inculcation' substance is quite powerful, and its effect cannot be underestimated. However, the 'imagination' liquid is of such nature that it takes hold early and withstands the periodic renewal onslaughts of the other fluid. The origin of the 'imagination' substance, and a detailed history of its character in the human, are as yet a mystery, though its effects are readily traceable (in books and in music, in much the same manner as the co-existers identify each other).

In rare cases, as in that of our hero and heroine, the liquids continued at perpetual imbalance, with first one and then the other taking effect. You can visualize the resultant emotional state. Most of the time, the boy-man and girl-woman were able to see life as co-existers, whose company they preferred (without knowing exactly why). And yet, many of their acts and apparent desires were based on majority-group values or judgments. As we see them, the two are in a state of deep conflict. They have both, at different times, had to face the Flight of Steps, and have made it to the top and seen the world beyond—but both have backslid, in an attempt to reconcile their two ways of viewing the world. With the expected confusion. At the beginning of our story, they have met, and identified each other, with the passwords, with exchange of their barter-substances and (behind the careful disguise of the outfits of the majority-group, among whom they moved always) have begun to live together. But all is far from well with them. There are certain tensions which pull them . . .

VIII.

When he got to the last line, he pushed away from the typewriter and stared at the smooth, grey wall. The room looked
a hundred feet long. The hash was getting away, was beginning to wear off, everything was wearing off, he didn't like
what he'd just written. Like the first and only time he'd tried
an analyst, gone three times, and quit, because he hadn't
liked what the man had told him. Laid open for him. Top
off the barrel, and the contents smelled rancid; or so it
seemed from the pretty obvious distaste the man had had
written on his face, at Len's mention of pot and hash and his
reasons for using them. O god what it was like to be an
American male today. Maybe he was rancid. His mother was
rancid, she walked foolishly around that luxury apartment
which she thought of as 'a home,' looking slovenly and with
a Kotex pad sticking out of her housecoat pocket. How's that
for a symbol, huh kid. And his father still belched at the
table, the way he used to in the Bronx. What the hell. To
hell with it. With them. Those bastards wouldn't even let
him borrow their car for a weekend with Louise, just to get
the hell out of the city for a breath of *air,* jeezus christ, 39
years old, the goddam war in back of me, can you believe it,
they didn't even think I was competent to drive their goddam
fucking *car,* 'O I don't think your father would want to go
along with that,' when he mentioned it to his mother on the
phone one day, not dreaming she would refuse. Impossible.
It was impossible. Just touch them and you get your hand
scorched (the metal suits!) He'd see them dead and he'd still
flinch with their refusals, or would he go nuts, with joy, with
freedom, or would he finally grow up, and stop hurting from
these hurts, how did they know exactly how to get to him
where it hurt? And when they did these things, how did it always manage to succeed? Maybe it *was* something like what
he'd just written. . . . Too much, all of it . . . too long. . . .

He walked out to the bedroom. Maybe if he talked to Louise, he'd make some sense of it all. Although what a nineteen-year-old would be able to say to shed light . . . So if he thought that about her, what the hell was he doing with her in the first place? He felt a great gust of horror and amazement and pain. And then fury, and then numbness. This little kid, what was he doing with her? A Lolita bit, or what? Or maybe he was her age emotionally and that put them at a level? But his mind edged away from it, that gasping view into what might be the answers. He opened the bedroom door. The light at the bedside was on. Louise was not asleep; that is, she looked asleep, in a way, but her limbs were angled oddly on the bed, and her mouth was open in a way he knew she had never assumed when she slept or dreamed. The bottle containing his sleeping-pills was on the bed next to her hand. Empty. He would never forget the look of that bottle, or of her mouth as she lay there. Empty. The bottle was the emptiest thing he'd ever seen, it was somehow equated with the chasm down which he'd looked briefly ten minutes ago, this vial, this bottle . . . god, what was he doing, staring at the bottle! He lifted the girl and listened for her heartbeat, tore the silk gown open at the neck and put his mouth on hers, nothing, nothing, Louise, her mouth was dry and cool, his mouth met hers, tears and saliva and then her mouth was wet, he grabbed the phone, slammed it down, it was 4 a.m., maybe the doctor who lived on the next floor would be home. . . .

He was, and he examined Louise, and at first he thought she was dead. No, not believable, unbelievable, too short a time, and Len thought, She has left me again, why has she done this, why, what happened, what did she want, is this the same as the last time she left me, now what, what shall I do, is this the final leaving, and the room was full of her scent and another smell, the smell of fear or of shadows, smell of naked flesh but naked of all disguise, and sometimes

over it was Louise's perfume, strong or faint, and Len sat on
the bed next to her, and waited for the doctor to speak.

IX.

They were married by a Justice of the Peace in Amagansett,
Long Island. It was a strong gesture of security for each of
them, under their circumstances. They had decided, a while
after the end of the summer season, to go out there for a
last quiet weekend; the crowds of white-jeaned or blue-shirted
desperates would be gone; even their friends and the busiest
tradesfolk; but they wanted to see and smell the ocean again.
When they got to the little station at Easthampton, after the
long traintrip, there was no one there to meet them. But
then, they expected no one. There were no cabs, and the
nearest cars were too far away to hail. And the nearest motel
seemed deserted. From its lobby, they saw a room, neat and
proper, but when Len walked toward it, he found that the
door was actually shut, and that what he had thought he'd
seen as the interior of the room was a painting of an interior
of a room, painted on the door itself, a sort of trompe l'œil,
even to the windows with the sea shining beyond. He opened
this door. The room within was almost identical to that which
was painted on its door. They went into the room. While
Louise was in the bathroom, Len went to the windows; he
found them sealed shut; painted shut, in fact; stuck shut by
the paint used to portray the seascape view outside. He could
not move them. When Louise came out to him, he offered her
a lit pipe. They smoked silently; he could not tell at this
point what she was thinking. After the pipe they went out
to the lobby again, looking for food. There were two signs:
'Everything in these rooms is the property of the temporary
occupants, and is to be treated and handled accordingly,'
and 'Justice of the Peace.' They stared at each other and
laughed: a man and a woman alone in such a place, and

then, this sign! All the papers needed for their marriage were there. Louise and Len sat, like children, at either end of the desk and wrote out the information required of them. Then they went out of the anteroom, and shut that door (on which was painted an almost-real eye) and sat in the lobby, smoking their pipe, for the necessary time interval specified on the documents they'd just filled out. When Len went again into the anteroom, the papers were properly signified and notated and ready for them. Louise, laughing, put her lipstick-print at the end of the paper and waved it loosely in the empty sea-breeze. Then they went back to their room. The bed was turned down for them. They shut the door, or what seemed to be the door. Louise went inside to put on her gown; she was in a mood as light and playful as her gown. When she came out, across the long, bare floor, Len's breath caught, he had never seen anything as lovely. He reached for her; she moved away; he reached; she turned; he barely touched her; finally, he put his hands on her, and it was like holding sea-spray. To her, his body was like the ocean; she remembered a poem made by one of their friends, a young junkie: 'love is mandatory/the genitals/demand it/every gesture/fills a need . . . i love you/like surf, pounding the sandy shore . . .' It was good, their lovemaking, wild and strong, with deep currents, majestic. But Len did not sleep afterward. He looked down at Louise, her silk gown as soft around her as sea-marks on the shore. He moved to the writing-table in the corner near the sealed window. He put his head down on his arms. The form of a story came to him. Its nature was alien to him, to all of his experiences, but its form was sure, he felt it flow from him, the words swept out . . . he sat up and began to write.

X.

I am almost sixty. Eleanor has gone; she is dead; she has been gone for twenty years and it is as if she left yesterday. When

I pass the only mirror, my hair is almost white; the white of these walls which she so loved; these walls which are a foot thick; these wise and ancient walls, to which I brought her as my bride. Eleanor! her grace, her gentleness! how she still lives in these rooms! Ah, it will be another cold winter . . . already the birds are circling to leave. The dark and wonderful hawks, my brothers, their strong beaks and hard wings. If our child had lived, he would have been a man by now, he would walk the trails with me, this would be his sanctuary too, he would watch the whirling of the seasons with me, we would tag the birds together and find joy in their return at springtime, we would set the winter fires together, O the boy Lewis, if he had lived!—he would resemble his lovely mother more each year. If he had gone from me when my Eleanor left my side, I need not dream thus. But his skin and wide eyes stayed with me longer, his skin the shape of my dreams, his eyes the shape of my love's blood. And O these thick walls! that go grey with my words, each day I write to her, a few words, graven on the white walls she lived within for our small time and space together. Among her own people, she was never strong, but here she seemed to thrive, she was as one of the birds on my mountain, the delicate bones of her shaped like light through all my days. Eleanor, Eleanor! your dark hair as the birds on my mountain, your hair as wings outward from your silken forehead, how you seemed to grow strong as the hawks, when you were young in this house, how brightly we moved in storm and sunlight as if they were of the same fabric to us, O they were, Eleanor, it was all the same to us, remember! how we were fire and floss, we were the silver of the cloudy days, those days you loved most of all, the days which are thought to be sad or desolate, and were only lovely as the rest, for us. But my dear, there is a purity to this life now that you and the boy are gone; the seasons blend; there is a purity to the grace with which the human moves, or rests, solitary, against a luminous landscape. In this my life, there has been great love, and brief, and past; and smaller loves when I was younger. Through these, and since, I have remained my own friend. That I am alone now is only a part of beauty for me. For we are born alone into the world, and alone we stalk through it, and all closeness is a gentle delusion or a brightness which moves near and is but one ring in the space where we breathe our years. We are always, ultimately, alone; there is a dignity and a grandeur to the figure of the human walking or standing alone against a stark landscape; it has the balance of art and the beauty of original nature. O yes, there are the ways to turn against the self of the skull, and call it loving, there are names for going against the pure sense of being alone, and there are men who try for them, and some who never do. The prisoner in his sharp-marked cell is no less free than I, nor more, as I move through my landscape of rocks and trees. The friar in his solitude is my equal and a reasonable opponent for debates. Yes, even the Don Juan is my brother, for who could be as alone! And the dwarf, the cretin, the hunchback, in their limited worlds, hear the same thin music as I; the painter, the poet, the composer are my twins, and this, too, leaves us each alone; alone, separate, we move and live the days out. Having loved a woman and a child, I can say I have loved myself best, and thus could love you both so well, in our brief and spacious interval; yet now I remain, as before, in my own skull, whose corridors echo less and less as I age, and whose transparent walls share me with my fields and heritages of earth. Always, I am turned in a skull-shaped space of time to this: being alone: not again, but as always, a delicate and balanced form of being alive and human; a form with its own beauty, the beauty of its own nature. Eleanor! this is my earth I tread daily, with my circling thoughts like hawks, this mile of earth is my church. Sometimes, in deep winter, all is white and shades of white: my hair, and then the soft wall where the mirror sits; the snow outside, and the brilliant white air, and white is the thought of your fine delicate bones, fragile as birds' tracks, which have long since become part of the air I breathe. This

life, which will slip me out of these walls soon, first the walls
of my skull, then the thick walls of this our house, O this life
has been good, Eleanor! Each season is a rich and marvelous
event, and different from before, seen through the ever-wider
corridors of my skull. If you remember last Autumn! when
all my hills were hymnal, my stained-glass speeches filling the
eye! and my own legs marking out the rings of color descending each hill. O it is good, this being a man, this loving of
earth and the self; my lungs are filled with jewels, replenished
every Spring; my tendons are the same stuff as the hide of the
deer that come in Summer; Autumn, somehow the strangest
season, spins out my blood into song; and Winter, feared by
the foolish, has been my skin for all my seasons on earth. This
will be the coldest Winter . . . already the hawks are circling to leave. They are marking the sky as I mark out my
gentle messages on these walls. This winter I will let go of
life, with all its memories of urgency, and slip through the
transparent walls, each by each, and join the whiteness.

Then Len went to the bed where Louise slept, and he too fell
asleep, lying across her body, his legs slanted across hers. The
papers were folded casually into his jacket pocket. Afterward,
those who knew him identified it as his handwriting, and,
correctly deducing it as the tenth chapter in his second novel,
published it as part of his collected work.

XI.

When they awoke, the motel was filled with people. The windows were open, and the fresh sea-air streamed in. There was
a knock at the door; Len opened it, and found a man in
serving-jacket, with a tray of brioches and espresso for them.
Fine! God knows they were hungry, after that trip. They ate
cross-legged on the bed, with the tray between them, like

a picnic-blanket; and when the buns were gone, they called
for eggs, and ham, and more coffee. Oh yes, it was a fine idea,
this, to take a second honeymoon. Excellent. Especially after
that scare with Louise and the pills. Migod! She'd almost lost
the baby, with that bit. It was only luck, and her strong con-
stitution, that kept everything intact. Good thing that doctor
had been fast and right. Len reached out and touched
Louise's belly. He remembered the long days and nights of
her recuperation; all their talking, all their mutual reassur-
ances; the sudden shocking insight he'd had into his own
need for changing her from her own nature to suit his concepts or nature.

It was her psychiatrist, oddly enough, who'd given
them the first sharp push. Not the original, uptown man to
whom Louise had been going for a while before she'd met
Len; but someone new, recommended to them in the terrible
days just after the scene of horror with the pills: a youngish
woman who lived near them, in the west Village, a tall, plain,
sensible woman, who, in her humanity and her immediate
concern for Louise, had made time and room to see the girl
every day for two weeks, until the crisis had passed. She had
even managed to gain Len's grudging confidence, with her
warmth, intelligence, and obvious honesty in her dealings
with both of them. In the months that passed, they marvelled
together at the way this woman vindicated the whole tribe of
psychiatry: her unfancy way of talking, her incisive habit of
cutting through deception (even self-deception) until a clarity
was reached, her underlying compassion and unfeigned solic-
itude for her patient. Len came to admire her in a practical
way; he saw her as a sort of substitute wise parent for both of
them, or an accidentally found guardian. In his fantasies, she
was in some way like a government official, if there were a
sane and well-designed government; it would be composed of
men and women of great innate wisdom, rather than political ambitiousness and voracity for wealth and power. But
Louise saw her as a mystical figure: in the younger woman's

dreams, the analyst appeared in a blue dress and a strange sort of picture-hat, and was, at least at first, somehow able to move just a bit off the earth in her walking. This fit into what Louise knew of the theories of metempsychology. And, in line more or less with all of this, she believed that it was no accident that they'd met Miss Baer. She saw it as a preordained meeting, and she saw her doctor as a soul which was wise because it had lived many times before on the earth and had honorably won wisdom. For a short time, Len went to talk with her once a week, and he, too, became her patient, although that was never his own concept of the relationship. In his own way of needing to see it, he was merely cooperating with her treatment of Louise, and it was three months before he realized that, in beginning to trust Miss Baer, he had begun to discuss things about himself that in no way pertained to the current crisis with Louise and himself.

In one of these talks, Len told her, 'If you want to have anything in this life, you have to hunt damn hard before you find it, and when you find it, if it's less than perfect, you have to work damn hard to shape it up.' This was the beginning of the revelation that he had been unable to value Louise (or, for that matter, himself) as a human being, the self intact, with faults and virtues, and acceptable as such. He came to realize that it was Louise's resentment of his trying to mold her that had (among other, equally pressing problems, it is true) driven her to the point where she'd taken the pills. He remembered the one time he'd been angry with her, after that night. 'O you thought you were being so cute, didn't you, damn you, you knew I'd come in and find you and you just wanted me to baby you some more, you just wanted to test me and see if I really gave a damn, what a helluva trick to play, don't you know there's no such thing as a would-be suicide, or you'd have done it when I was out of the house, it's the same damn trick as not showing up that time before we were married, put me through hell then and that's all you were trying to do this time, I don't know why I put up with all this shit from you, I should have known better than to get mixed up with such a nutty chick in the first place . . .' He couldn't stop. She looked at him, stared at him, stunned and silent, her hand clenching into a fist as his voice grew more shrill. 'No,' she'd said, evenly, 'none of it's true, Len. I had to do it that way, and I had to do it then. Right then. Like I had to get away from you back in the summer.' She had talked about this with Miss Baer already, and she knew that it was her sense of self-protection, of protection of the innate nature of the self, that made her automatically withdraw from Len, when he became manipulative with her. Now he faced her, his fear of losing her making him furious, his vulnerability to her making him afraid and the fear driving him to anger. His face was clenched like a fist. She had never seen this side of him. But it was his own private pain, his own deep-set old agony, that was making him act this way, and if she responded in kind, it would only compound it. 'Len,' she said. 'Look. Once you said, I didn't know you yet, but when I did, I wouldn't like you. Well, let me tell you this: now, I begin to know you. And I like you. I like you more now than I ever have. This has nothing to do with loving you, I loved you and I still do. But you only just begin to be, outside, the guy I fell in love with, the inside just begins to come through now. I think that if you told me what's racking you up now, we could get through this.' And she watched him. Somehow, marvelously, she had gotten through to him. At least a bit. His face loosened and softened. But he was still caught in the anger. It was as if he valued his pain, his anger; he was so used to it that no one could approach it or remove it; it had become a part of him, of his way of being, like a chronic wound. She tried again. 'You know, we could make it easier if we didn't get so wound up; what do you say to smoking a pipeful?' He went into the other room and came back with the pipe. He lit it and passed it to her. They smoked and talked.

112

'Maybe if I told you everything I could about me, you really would get disgusted and . . . o, I see, maybe I disgust myself. . . .'

'Len, we have this good chance to be happy, or whatever passes for happy with people like us. . . .'

'I'm the one that's supposed to be giving you the encouraging speeches, *you're* the one tried the suicide bit . . .'

'It seemed to me then there was nothing else I could do. I was looking for some sense to life, or some way around or out or through and I couldn't see any. It was like living with a total stranger, with you, some of the time. It didn't feel right. Now it's better.'

'What makes people like us? I mean, I have this theory . . .' and he told her about the 'story' he'd written, the night she'd taken the pills. She was caught up with the ideas he'd tried out in it. 'O listen, Len, this really grabs me, and so much of it is true. That's one test of it: is it true? does it feel real?—and I know what you're saying in this. You know, one of the ideas I've thought about is, if I want to be adult as well as simply 'larger,' who can I imitate? For sure, I don't want to be the kind of woman my mother is; and I'm not like Ellen, she's a different kind of . . . well, I mean, her way is different. Miss Baer says there are choices. I don't know that many women who are even remotely like what I would like to be like.'

'Yeah, I know what you mean. No patterns around to study from. I feel like I've been walking around in a dark opaque suit all my life. And the damn eyeglasses and all the trimmings, they've fucked up everything for me . . . I don't know which I want, to swing with the co-existers (if I'm one of them to begin with, I don't even know that), or just take the easy way and stay with all the patterns.'

'You said the answer yourself. It isn't the *easy* way. You talked about those liquids, the imagination thing and the inculcation thing, and the conflict of them in us. What do you mean, the easy way? Seems to me there's more pain in trying to stay far in than in coming out and making a choice.'

'Damn right. I remember, ten years ago, when I was overseas, this buddy of mine in the same platoon, knew a lot, name was Parker. Only cat I could talk to in the whole damn bunch. Boy, did I envy him. My age, and he knew where it was at, had it all figured out, I mean he was *himself*, you could tell he knew what he wanted, knew who he was and which way he was going. O I don't mean he knew about the future, except the way you can guess at it from being awake to the past and present, and where you fit in, and extrapolating from there. He knew who he was, is what it is. I mean, in history, in a thing like a war, in his own country or in that one, you could tell he moved out from his own center. A feeling came off him. You know what I mean? I haven't met many people like Parker in my life. And he said to me once, 'You gotta stand up and be counted; that's what it's all about.' It made me pretty uncomfortable at the time, because I instinctively knew what he was getting at, but I didn't want to face it.'

'I guess that's where we're both at, now,' Louise said. She leaned over to him and put her head on his thigh. 'You know,' looking at him at right angles, 'we've got so much. Now all we've got to do is get it untangled . . .' She took his hand and moved it until it cupped her chin. 'Not so bad these days, Len. Much better. Maybe to just relax and let it smooth out.'

'My mind is crowded, god, I can't keep up with it all, it's not blurred, as if there were a million fine shards of ideas or thoughts, the memories and the possibilities of the new things I could be or do, and the things I've read or heard about or done, god, do you realize, I don't even sleep these nights, and I haven't been tired, just turned on and moving —I guess that's it, in motion, I feel like the world is spinning under me but I am finally going at the same pace as it's going

—ah, Louise, I'm sorry about before, screaming that way at you, I know better.'

'It's okay, babe. I know how you felt. Anyhow, better to spit it out than keep it in and get sick on it all. Besides, remember, I answered you, and part of what I have to learn is to talk back and keep myself talking back, not quiet and taking all the punishment, like when I was a little kid.'

'The thing is, we have to figure out what we want, and what we want to do with our lives. I bet you know what I want to do with our lives right now? Dig, Louise, I read this last week, I read this story about a guy who did nothing but read books and eat tuna-fish sandwiches until he was twenty; didn't talk to anybody; just picked his toenails and built up steam. Bright guy, too. Wound up going into the electric chair, because he spent all his energy at once, committed three murders. I wonder what that guy would've been like if someone had turned him on to hash or pot in his early teens. Or if anyone had taken the trouble to listen to him when he was a kid. I mean *really* listen to him. But what struck me as most incredible of all was, they said this guy hadn't ever had a woman. He wasn't gay, that wasn't it; he wasn't *anything;* he was sort of interested in women; but he just hadn't ever made it with a woman. God, think of it. To die without knowing about that! Incredible. It would be okay to go out at the end of a long life of making good love, even letting it disappear slowly, but what would it be like to never know?'

'How can you even guess! It would be like discussing the color red with a man blind from birth. Or the story of the seven blind men with their hands on a different section of an elephant. I can't get away from the image of 'blind.' Seems to me making love is like one of the primal senses.'

'I think that's the only time I've been able to be real. Most of the time, with you, and some of the time, with the others before.'

'I know. It's the only way it's good. Miss Baer and I talked about keeping a corner of oneself always to oneself—but that's the only exception. If you try that in bed, you're not there at all. I know what that's like. Awful.'

'Let's stop talking.' He covered her mouth with his. Afterward, he cupped her head in his palm, and told her, 'I've spent my whole life watching tenderness—other people—movies, plays, books, even friends—envying it—wondering—it was like a nearby country to which I had no passport and whose language I could barely understand, just intuit somehow. Thank you for living, lady—' And they slept.

XII.

They sat in their forty-five-foot livingroom, with its mild alabaster and marble statues, and they sold the statues. Between times, they smoked some Acapulco Gold and drank enormous quantities of Coke and ginger ale, and played Edith Piaf on the hi-fi. Then they sold the hi-fi. The apartment was crowded with strangers who had come to buy their things. Things they had decided they would not need. It was interesting to both of them to discover how many of their things were really unnecessary, now. The day before, they had gotten shaky at the hugeness of the move, to sell almost all of their things. But the ad was in the paper. Many of their friends showed up and ventured the opinion that they'd both lost their minds. It was a matter of opinion indeed. They certainly looked okay, and acted sane. In fact, several friends who dropped by to buy their Daum and Lalique were, in the months that followed, known to reconsider their own values.

The apartment was sold out within two and a half days. This was good, because it gave them a day to just relax and see New York, before their ship sailed. They spent that day at the Guggenheim Museum and walking in Central Park.

Joy in their voices. Over the past six months, in the same way that they had sifted out which of their things were simply relics of ideas of themselves which were really invalid, and then gotten rid of them, they had been slowly sifting through their own ideas of themselves and the world. But it was not such an easy job, surrounded with their friends, their relatives, their city, their history, their routines. So they had decided, with great joy, to leave, to get out of New York, for a year at least. In another place, the perspectives would shift, it would all come clearer. At the sailing, they looked down to the deck. A few friends, and Louise's sister Ellen, had come to see them off. Someone had given them a small silver alcohol-stove, made so that it condensed or folded itself compactly, and this would come in handy, since they would do the kind of simple living, at least at first, which meant living in a cheap hotel room somewhere. The only thing that Len had bought for himself, from the money after the sale of the furnishings of the apartment, was a portable typewriter. The rest of the money was held for the tickets, for the wherewithal to live without clock-punching for a year or more, and for buying a little car, after the first few months there, if their plans worked out. And for Louise he had bought a fine set of oil paints, and a portable easel. And, of course, for both of them always the same small pipe, with enough to smoke until they got there. It would be easier there, in places outside the States he knew that there were fewer restrictions, fewer legal hangups, fewer delusions about the nature of hasheesh as compared with alcohol. So they should have less trouble than here, and less worry about consequences.

As the last gangplank of the ship was being raised, and everyone on the ship was at the rail, calling or watching or just standing and feeling, Louise saw Ellen. She was standing just off to the side of the group of their friends. And when Ellen caught their eyes on her, she raised her fingers and made the gesture of the surgeon's snip of scissors. As at birth.

XIII.

They found a farm outside the town of Barbizon. It was late winter, and the light was cool and fine. When they'd arrived, in early fall, the town was just pulling itself together after the onslaught of summer tourists. A beautiful little town, with thatched roofs, mansards, cottages; almost too pretty. But they met and talked with the woman who was caretaker of the Millet studio, and she directed them to her friend, who owned an old farmhouse about four miles outside the town. It had only a well for water-supply, and the only heat was from a fireplace in the livingroom and a coal-stove in the kitchen, but it was set among the very fields that Millet had loved, and in the fall it was more beautiful than they could bear. By the time the cold weather had set in, they were ready to work with the minimal comforts of the house. They could afford it; Louise bought chickens and vegetables from the people who grew them; Len took long walks and, one day, began writing. Thereafter, he wrote almost every day, for a few hours, until he was so relaxed and involved that he quite naturally took care of the details of their survival and found time to continue with the novel. They bought bicycles, and went often into the town. They had first come to Barbizon with a Vietnamese student they'd met in Paris; he was the night-clerk at the hotel where they had a room, and told them he would love to have them join him on his occasional trips out into the countryside. Once, they picnicked in the woods between Versailles and Barbizon, on a shale outcropping which formed a clearing in the forest. To the Americans, their simple lunch of Brie, baguettes and saucisson andalouse, with vin ordinaire, was as luxurious as had been their dinners at L'Armorique in New York. And when they reached Barbizon, it was with the attitude of newcomers, if not actual tourists; neither of them was prepared to be taken over by the town and its spirit: to be made a part of its flesh.

While Len and Than went to see about gas for

Than's little car, Louise walked alone. In the October late afternoon, she turned in the road and found herself engulfed in the most brilliant color she had ever experienced: a great elm, red-gold of itself, which contained as well the red-gold light of the descending sun. This tree took her. It was a sensual meeting, a union, a consuming, with the great flaming tree and the girl finding delight; she was gradually lost into its branches, intuitively holding her own ground in the face of its deep heat and glorious illumination. Her face assumed a tinge of the red-gold, and her hair reflected it. But she did not know of this. It seemed to her that this was the only tree in the world, her world pivoted on it, she swam in its color and form, it sprang like a fountain from the darkened trunk and held her, thus, fixed in line with the trunk, consumed by the spray of the leaves. She gasped and moved slightly, feeling the brilliant tree, feeling the color as a tangible substance. But not as flame: as color, as she saw the sun. Not fire, but source. Thus she stood, and then she was aware that Len was beside her. Motionless, and just back of her left shoulder; she could not tell how long he'd been there. And, back of him and again left, near Len's shoulder, Than stood. 'This is a good place for you, Mrs. Louise,' Than said gently. 'What do you want, Louise?' Len asked. 'Yes. Yes. Here,' she said. Not talking to either of them, really.

So they found the farmhouse, through the fine lady who chatted with them in Millet's studio, and they settled in. That tree had opened up Louise's great appetite for color, in a way that nothing until then had done. For the first time since they left New York, she began to paint. Soft things, at first, and gradually the work moved toward the intensity of the tree. Her belly was now round with child. In the early afternoons, while Len was writing, she would take the easel and paints and go out into the fields. Often, while she sat in the cool air, she would simply sit in the midst of a field or a wood, with the easel unopened; she would notice the line of the earth under its thick foliage, or the way the granitic

rock held streaks of crystals in thick veins. Some of her paintings were quite detailed; they seemed based on the myriad
delicate forms she was discovering in nature: some were like
the structuring of the underside of ferns; one series of drawings was made after she had studied the ridge of rock that ran
through the hills above the farm. And she began a series of
studies for a portrait of Len. During this time, the motion of
the child within her was her constant companion, a motion
like the ocean, or like an irregular music. She was available
to the land under her and around her, and so it opened to
her. It was as if she had been blind, or unseeing, her attention
had been fixed on the artifices of Madison Avenue shoes and
vacuum cleaners and the masklike cocktails with faces painted
in back of them. Here, she was coming to life, the air was
bright with its own color and texture, she felt as if she were
living in the midst of a clear and brilliant tapestry, where
each thread was distinct and had its place in the scene. Not
the scene before her: but the scene in which she was an inte-
gral part. The baby would move within her, and she would
remember her own flesh, and its nature in relation to the
earth she stood on. She would light the little pipe, and its
sweet scent would become a part of the mulch of centuries of
leaves of the woods, the two plant odors mingling and naturally earthen. Some of the paintings seemed to bear little resemblance to the woods of France: they were echoes of her
city life, and she did not do many of this kind. They were all
angles and corners, and used the sharp, artificial colors which
are made of chemicals and seen in overcivilised places. She
was almost twenty-one; her age seemed unimportant to her
now, it was really the beginning of a new section of her life,
an opening-out, as if her mind were given a sharp-focus lens,
or, at times, a wide-angle lens. She knew that the habit of
analysing the minutiae of her problems was blending into
the simple living of the life itself. And she felt herself to be a
part of the countryside where she walked. Her limbs had
grown full, rounded, she had none of the taut, lanky slimness

which had been her pride in the cities. She had already, in her fifth month of pregnancy, gained twenty pounds, which was a delight to her doctor, the man who cared for the Barbizon townsfolk. Her body was sturdy and healthy to begin with, and showed every sign of a normal and comfortable delivery, and so of course she was relaxed and at ease with the changes in her body. She and Len ate well, with their limited funds: plenty of fresh vegetables and eggs; the local chickens and pigs, for meat; butter from the next farm. And they slept with their windows wide to the air, and spent most of their days outdoors. So their bodies thrived and grew clear-skinned, almost seemed to gain another dimension. Actually they ate a bit less in quantity than they had in the cities, so the flesh became firm and the muscles more elastic with use. They felt well: the water and the air were clear, they bought the thick-soled shoes the farmers wore, and found their feet widening, loosening; their tendons grew firm and resilient. Louise thought about names for the baby, while she walked or sat painting the fields. She thought of calling the child Ellen, if it was a girl, for her sister; it was also close to Len's name. That name seemed to have the color of earth, to her. At the end of October, she wrote to Ellen:

XIV.

. . . Now I love Len in a way that is deeper, different from anything we've had before. As soon as I began to really know him, I began to really love him. You know I love physical beauty, and we have this, but it was the deeper beauty we had going between us, which kept us together and brought us here, to this marvelous place, which keeps us together so richly now. A current of magnificent mystery—it binds us beneath the superficial structures of our day-to-day life here. Len is different from the Len you saw or knew in New York. He's still beautiful to see, with his dark intense eyes, diamond-shaped and as sharp as diamonds—but he's easier in his ways now. Fewer edges. His quick motions have purpose behind them now. I love passionately the way he walks, sometimes I watch him when he is coming back from the fields. Now, he almost strides. Imagine! And he is actually enjoying working on the novel. The skin of his forehead is easier, and wider somehow, the tension is dropping away. But to sit and talk with him, listen to him, is my special joy. To be with him and talk, for hours. His is a wisdom and a gentleness which delights me, always new, always a tender surprise. He is becoming a truly tender man, and he is finding the world a more comfortable place, and so am I. His face is strong and shows that he's had perhaps too many lessons before this place. What I mean to say is that I *see* Len now, and he sees me, and it is good. No more of moving in a trance, moving through life by rote; everything we do feels right, and you can't imagine how marvelous this is to me. My baby is moving now; it is strong and healthy; I like being pregnant. I wish all women had as easy a time of it as I am having, Ellen. I hope you do. It is such a joy. I never thought things would go this way. Now, I have a different way of looking at my life. Before, I thought there was a system, or plan, to account for every move or action of any of us. I still think this is somehow true, but now I see how the earth itself, the *nature* of the earth, and we as animals on the earth, are part of it. Or how we seem best to blend into natural surroundings. This place is so good to us. Here, we drop the masks or façades we must give to the world, and they ease and disappear; in their stead we have those nuances which make up that self which we save for the few in our lives whom we love. To love is so complicated, somehow, for people like us, Len and me, and you; once, Len said, at the beginning of all the breakthrough, 'You don't know me well yet, but when you do, you won't like me much . . .' and yet he came forward to me with love, and we both knew he was hoping that I would love him as he was, and he would love himself. I knew then that he had a deep

knowledge, perhaps instinctive, that we were beautiful together; that we are really the same age, because of our currents, the deeper things that bind us now and were underneath
for so long before then. We accent each other; we complement
each other; we can work well together and these days, we do.
This is a blend of the mundane and the exotic, this life: because we've come to it from the most sophisticated and yet
superficial ways of being a human—so everything is new, fresh,
strange, even the cooking of a chicken, or Len's cutting wood
for the fireplace. We make the discoveries: and we are always
coming to each other with new and wonderful things we've
found out about. Len says that you told him once that you
think you can't really love. Well, you and I come from the
same house, the same parents; so I have to believe that it is
possible for you to love, because I have learned to, myself;
at great cost, but it's real and worth it. Maybe you think this
is a naïve assumption, that my handicaps are less than yours,
or some such. But I think it's time and space and chance that
matter, and I think you'll make it up and out too. I wish
everyone could live these days! I couldn't begin to describe
this countryside, or the aura I move in. Perhaps the paintings
will say some of it.

      I'm sure that we'll be back in the States, at least
for a visit, when we've learned what we have to learn from
being here. My mind fills up with the city sometimes. Not
with longing, I assure you. But a kind of wonderment. I
wonder why people are *striving* so, there? And I was part of
that, such a short time ago; and you're still in it. Look at it.
Everyone trying to impress, to win, to gobble up; the nerves,
the pills, the indigestions, the angry patients and angry doc-
tors, the wild struggle to get out of the cities to get some fresh
air, that ghastly game of politics, god, it's incredible to me,
from here. What are the city people doing with their lives?
I mean, what are they buying that's half so precious as what
they're sacrificing, to coin a paraphrase! Even in small towns
in USA you find the same thing, only less bunched together

than in the cities. The boredom, the loss of sight which seems almost willful, the giving-up that you see on people's faces. This is what Len's novel is about. I mean, in the life we had, we and most of our friends never bothered about much other than clothes, a big salary to buy them with, a showy house to impress the cocktail drinkers. You couldn't tell our place or our faces from any of theirs or them, for sure. Especially Len, who played the game for so many years and now hurts the more for it. I wonder if it takes a major catastrophe to force us to take stock, or split open the shell, to get a man or woman to wondering if he is spending his life according to what he really loves, or according to a bunch of rules and ideas he never has evaluated but has merely succumbed to. I wonder if I myself knew there was a choice. I'm sorry, somehow, that more of our friends can't find this great way through to themselves. I know there has to be a balance of kinds of lives, or ways to live life, but I can't help theorizing that if there were some way for people to live 'out in the open' as we've been doing, simply, sifting out one's values and living by the ones that have proven of one's own choice or devising, there might be fewer wars. Maybe even fewer cities.

Of course, it's not all idyllic, as you might imagine. Len and I bring all our old angers and anguishes here, like a flock of albatrosses, and we had a simply smashing fight just yesterday, over nothing. But the point is, it *was* smashing; that is, it cleared the air, and got us through another of those official-type ideas which didn't belong to us at all. Len's a good teacher, and not just to me; he's made friends with several of the men in the village, and they look to him for the wisdoms he's accrued, and this is so good for him, and good to see. If you'd told him, a year ago, that he'd be sitting for hours, talking with a group of middle-aged villagers in a small town in a foreign country, and *enjoying* it, he'd have laughed you out of the room. But, of course, he learns immensely from them too; their wisdom comes directly from the earth, their values don't have to go through all the middle steps of over-civilisation, that is, the transmutation is easier, faster.

Last week, Len said, 'You remember the night we went to the street-fair, and the Annex? God, how little we knew each other then, compared to now—what luck—maybe your taking the pills was good—it brought us here.' And yesterday, in the middle of the screaming fight, he stopped, and leaned across the table, leaned right up to my face, and said, 'Look, it doesn't *matter*—all of this jazz—I almost lost you, or I almost never found you to begin with, and then the scene with the pills and I could have lost you without ever having found you. . . . This, this is more precious than all the things we fight about, all the things against us, against our survival.' What we had been talking about was my crazy idea, at the beginning of when I knew him, that he was strong and knew so much, had been around so much, and therefore I thought he could tell me who I am. Now of course I know nobody can, and this is a good thing. I walk around *being* me; I know now who the me is, and I like being me. I think he counted on my looking to him for finding out who I am; he was very manipulative. Well, out here there's very little of that sort of thing. We move on a level, each of us respects the search and the struggle of the other. I realize that he's learning from me too, but I couldn't put into words what the lessons might be. I just *feel* them. He needs to have me next to him, and his wanting me here is part of what makes me feel good and rich and full.

The quality of this, of the 'us' we have become, in this clear countryside, this finer air, stands in such contrast to the murky lives we tried to live in the city. For me, the Being of us, the intensity and calmness of every day here, underlines and absolves all our tragedies, past and present; I think what we have will carry us in whatever future we form for ourselves and share with our children. In all the franticness of those parties we used to run to, those bars, those restaurants,

I see everyone as just searching desperately for that way of being which Len and I have found; I think this is what everybody wants and what few people are lucky enough or driven enough, or maybe brave enough to get through to. Sometimes, I feel like it's all work, and it's all uphill. And I lose perspective. Found myself wishing I had a simple American washing-machine, the other day; or just one pair of really great Paris shoes (you remember my shoe-fetish-type collection!)—but then I saw where I was, and why, and the place I've been making here for us, and I had to laugh. It's not all luck (though finding this place was, and even so I have a feeling we would have found another as fine for us; that's my mystical streak still there)—but so far our luck is good. But you know as well as anybody, what hard work it's been for us to get in the clear. And as for its being worth it, it's worth everything, I tell you and I would tell everyone in every city if I could, in fact I would follow this wild notion I have (that Len says is so impractical, for economic reasons, but he likes it nevertheless!) of getting the US gov't to open out free land-grants to settle the great American plains and prairies, not just a sort of land-reform thing, but a population re-distribution. Suppose everybody who came here could get a farmstead, instead of hoping to try to make it in some 9-to-5 job in an office or factory! And from there it would be an easy thing to get back to the virtues of the land itself, as we're doing. To shuck off the shells of overcivilisation. What do you think? Maybe it would be good for at least some of the people, especially the ones we know. As for me, this is the greatest thing, this gift of an existence, this being a woman and moving next to my man; this is what I'm on earth for. I walk on the firm earth and I feel at home.

1965

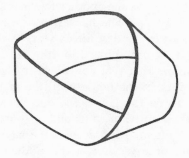

AND NOW, ALEXANDRA...

Now that she was pregnant, she felt she finally could give herself permission to eat as much as she wished, whenever she wished. She stood next to the kitchen table, reached for the jar of elderberry jam a friend had sent her (thoughts of the party they'd given that night, aura of the news, she had told the friends of her pregnancy when inviting them, this friend had known the fine luxury involved in sweets at this time, had brought an elegant collection of Swedish jams and tiny crystal jars . . .) She tipped the jar so that the jam trickled slowly toward the lip, toward her lips. A viscous, sweet river, she thought; this is a darker purple than my own favorite; this one fairly smells of the jam, I'd know it anywhere.

Difference between jam and jelly, she thought. Difference between me and Sally; she's jam, I'm jelly, she has

more silky substance than I—but I'll have more substance, I
will, just give me another few months. I'll be a very substantial lady. . . . She had always watched her weight carefully.
At least for the last fifteen years. A thin layer of jam, if at all,
on the morning toast. Martin had left for the office. She envied him that ride downtown in the morning air. She would
be stuck in the house until the maid came. This was Elsie's
day to do the house, the once-a-week that was saving Alexandra's sanity, or so it felt. Of course, they could afford Elsie
more often; daily, even; but that would be more of an in-
vasion of privacy than either of them would tolerate. Martin, a
Scorpio, could not bear to find his possessions anywhere other
than where he had left them. After Elsie left on Wednesdays,
Alix would go about re-creating Martin's ambience for him;
just the right amount of apparent disorder, just the right
casual robe thrown in a chair.

　　Making a baby, she thought, an orderly process,
lots of it out of my hands, and a good system at work. It
might be fun—if I could only do without the worrying. The
word pushed her to an edge of fear like an inkblot she'd
seen on a test once: worry, it is shaped like ink, or the mark
if this purply jam should spill and run on my damask. She
watched the thick jam release a bit of juice as it slid slowly
down the side of the jar. No spoon this time, she thought. To
hell with the rules. I'm going to have this baby. She put her
tongue into the jar to meet the sweetness. It was one of her
more familiar gestures, a sly reaching-out, she could have
spooned the jam out in thick mounds, or set it in a glisten-
ing sheet on the toast before her; or simply (an adventure!)
taken a tablespoonful and just eaten down through the little
crystal jar's contents, to the last globule. . . . Her pleasure
was always in the slow, the sensual. And in this kind of perverse disavowal: if she wanted something, she would not permit herself instant taking, instant delight. Nor any excesses.
Would rather have this suspense, this slow savouring. A sensual Gemini. She liked to make love slowly; would postpone

her climax so that it would be wider, stronger, deeper for the waiting.

Having this baby would be that kind of waiting. Nothing quick or sudden; a process to be enjoyed. A slow peace and a slow growing, and a pleasure in the knowledge. She was forty-two. It was her first child. And now she couldn't control any of this, the time it took, all of it was arranged, all she had to do was to avoid touching the edge of the worry-stain that was just at the edge of consciousness most of the time. Just sharpening into the soft edges of her dreams. Dark into light. . . . She loved the softer rhythms. She loved gentle surprises; hated shocks; it took her a while to accustom to change. . . .

Becoming this age had been a gradual shock; becoming pregnant was a surprise. At this age. And with only one ovary useful. Martin was a good deal older than she, and had never fathered a child. They kidded each other about it. He was surprised at her news; then pleased. Unaccustomed to the thought. She was hoping that the changes in her appearance would come so gradually as to seem barely noticeable. They had married well into maturity, were not interested in other people's children, their involvement with the jargon and rituals of parenthood had been minimal.

They were not concerned with being spiritually intimate with each other in their marriage and were not concerned with the obvious rituals of marriage and of housekeeping. For the first year of their marriage, they had sporadically considered living in an apartment-hotel. It was the third marriage for each of them. They liked each other, respected each other, moved in ease near each other, felt content with the smooth pattern that evolved beneath the smooth surfaces of their lives, their appearances. Martin was in the Market. A partner in a small firm. A compact, well-groomed man, also sensual, bright, he was a Scorpio who moved in gestures which had been disciplined for his own comfort, so that by now his experiments had been made and his paths chosen. He would be fifty-four in November. When they decided to take this East Sixty-third Street apartment, they both had great delight in furnishing it, in arranging the contrivances for comfort and for pleasure.

In her own mind, Alix was a compilation of the ads in her favorite fashion magazines. The long-limbed ladies who illustrated perfumes, bathing oils, lipsticks, fine resorts. Thus she saw herself, as she moved about the bright, spacious brownstone flat. She was rich now. She had not needed to marry Martin for his money, but it added to her own, it gave her the last dimension in elegance, and she felt totally guiltless in her enjoyment. Because she loved making love with him. Their temperaments were matched, in bed and out. But they did not congratulate themselves on the match. In that same gently perverse way of tantalizing, they would not acknowledge to each other that their marriage was smoothly delicious. It was in order, it was expected . . .

Sure. Ordinary and expected. To have finally met; satisfied; elegant in each other's eyes; to marry and find it excellent; and now, to conceive a child. They were astonished. But never gave it a name: in that ritual of foreboding: it was so finely made that it might be destroyed if they discussed any of it. Their conversation was light. They rarely discussed the past. Martin's first wife had been a delicate, primitive shrew from Arabia, with shaved pubes and an arrogant religion. His second had been a bright, sensitive Negro dancer, twenty years his junior. And now, Alexandra. He was pleased with her. He couldn't believe that he was comfortable with her. His ultimate jewel.

Alix had been, was a singer. The Plaza 7 type. Built by hand by a conscientious, conscienceless manager for the part. For the money. The teeth changed, the hair changed, the body shaped, the walk tutored, the eyes fitted for contacts, the speech pattern changed so that the regional accent slurred off, the biography doctored. . . . Edward, her manager, had rebuilt her. Had built her. She remembered the woman she had been before the process of change. Skinny, twenty pounds heavier, but still thin, and awkward in her world. She had wanted the change. But she liked the person she had been. But she desired to be more lovely. But it was hard to seem a new person.

She liked the new smoothness. She liked herself these days. Smooth as silk, smooth as jelly, as satins, as cocktail conversation, as moonlight through jalousies, as her own lipstick. Her first husband had been Edward. Her manager. Silly, she thought, a classic move, marry your manager and become Mrs. Whoever Built You Over. And get unmarried when the realities crowd in. When he discovers you are going to be the same girl you were before, when the bedroom door closes. When you discover he wants the money more than the marriage. . . . Her second husband had been one of the hotel men; a Jew, slick, easy-going, given to leather and horses and tweeds, ambitious for himself and for her; he had wanted her with him always, and he had wanted to keep her, had wanted not to be married to her, but she would not have stayed unless he made it official. It had sounded too risky. And it was: but not as she had predicted. This husband, this Harold, had invented a series of intricate games, sexual and social, to delude himself into getting and keeping an erection: she was his harlot, she was his bad little girl who needed a whipping, his Chinese houri who would suck him off whenever he so desired. That had lasted three months, which was too long.

She met Martin at one of Harold's famous house parties. While she was still married to Harold, seven years ago. Martin had been very gentle and very persistent. What the hell are you doing here in this mess, he asked, over and over. Over and under the week-long inundation of the partying. Get out, it'll ruin you. You look terrible. I see you, under the makeup, what the hell, you don't have to live like this, you don't have to live with him, you like it or what, you a masochist or what, do you love him?

No, she had answered, I didn't know what he'd be like; now I'm just waiting a certain amount of time. It's one of my own little games, I can't really explain, I know how good it's going to be when I'm through with him but I move slowly toward things I want a lot. I don't trust fast moves. Not that I like him.—I should hope not, said Martin. A woman like you. I can't promise his kind of pedestals or perversity, but I think we could get along. Listen, she said, I just met you. I don't know you. Hearing it as phony even as she was saying it, knowing that this was quite another sort of man. Don't be foolish, he said, you sound like you're sixteen and you must be at least thirty. Aren't you? Almost, she said, wanting to tell him the truth: a habit she'd almost gotten away from by now. Okay, he said, then stop playing games. If you can do that, you can have me to look forward to, and I can promise you an easier time. Something that feels more like you.

And it went like that, but with a bit more of a time-interval than he'd have liked: because she had to do things in a certain manner; slowly; sudden changes scared her. She didn't want to move to Martin immediately after leaving Harold. It did not seem fair to Martin. And the shock to her psyche. She had, after all, gotten used to a few things about Harold, she had to put some space between, she thought; and so planned an interval of a couple of months. During which she went to Europe and relaxed. Played one or two of the finer hotel supper-clubs. Appeared in Paris and London briefly. This was relaxing for her; she loved singing, loved the routine of it, the grind of it, the elegance of it, the gloss. She was only then beginning to reach maturity, and it came through in her voice, her bones. The voice was deepening, becoming richer; her body-structure, so finely-wrought, smoothed and filled in a bit. She was able to wear simpler designs. Her bones had become set, finished in their development; she was thinner than she had been in her twenties, had the elegance of a thoroughbred horse, the kind that improved with age. Seemed, finally, beautiful. To her own eyes.

Or *beautiful* was never the word, really: she had always seemed elegant, at least since Edward had remodelled her. Before that, she had been lanky and lovely in a hidden way. A model type. Potential for the easy stance. Edward had liked her voice, had remodelled, had managed, had been manager (as he was for few other women) and had married her (as with none other). How simple a pattern, she had thought then; all I have to do is whatever he asks me to do, and I shall have what I want out of life, and so will he. He was naïf and tender with her, and terribly strong, demandingly sure. Bent on a complete renovation. Only partly inside; mostly the façade. Just the outer girl. But she had needed to start analysis during that marriage. Had started diet pills, sleeping pills, tranquilizers.

She loved learning the way to sing for the particular kind of crowd at the clubs where she worked. Loved the singing. It was its own reward, her rapport with the crowd. She had a simple, anonymous relationship with the crowd. It relaxed her, it got her high, she enjoyed the tension, the feeling of being loved, Edward's appreciation of her as she came onstage each night. And the crowd of faces loved her, she was a symbol they had been taught to admire and to enjoy: desirable, unattainable, and untouchable. In the first months, she became addicted to the singing.

So that she would take on jobs even during the months between the marriage to Harold and the upcoming one to Martin. It relaxed her; she loved the exquisitely anonymous intercourse between her body and the crowd. Always different from her lovemaking with any man. The difference between jam and jelly . . . all of it sensual and therefore good. While she was in Europe that time, she changed perfumes. She had been wearing the scent Edward had chosen, but it was associated in her mind with herself as she had been before Edward, slightly bucktoothed and virginal, as she had been before the master dentist had worked on her. Before Edward. At her supper-club, she passed a French woman who was wearing something quite different; she stopped her, asked her its name, bought a large bottle of it that same day, and stayed with it. Until now.

Until forty-two. Until now. The familiar scent annoyed her. Nauseated her slightly. Was it the pregnancy. Prima-something, the doctor had said. Prima-part something, she thought, like apartheid, she thought, I am making something inside me that's a part of me and apart from me, apartheid, she giggled. Her doctor didn't bother to say the word to her, of course, it had been said to his nurse. In her presence. She wasn't sure she liked him. Martin said there was something strange about all g.y.n. types; she'd gone to a friend's doctor once, a woman, who'd turned out to be quite dykey, and Martin had given her a little lecture then, and had found Dr. Bob for her that week. But he was strange too, she thought. That way he had of tilting his head to the left and giving her warnings. What a weird bit. As if she could have any problems, beyond the constant gnawing edge of the worrying. Didn't he know she worried enough without his warnings. You're very narrow, he said. You might have some kind of trouble with this, but of course you might not; at any rate, you're very lucky to conceive at this age, and let's hope it all goes well; we'll do our best, eh?

As if he would really have anything to do with it beyond checking her pulse and her vitamins and the wrists and ankles to see if she was getting edema, or whatever that mess was that had made Sally's ankles swell out so hideously. I have absolutely no intention of getting that sort of thing, she thought. And: I wonder if the baby will come out looking like me. I mean the way I used to look. Before all the renovation. She thought of her own baby-pictures. A little fatty. But it would be a boy. What if it looks like Martin. Not bad. He's damn bowlegged, he is, very sexy, and probably cute on a kid.

But aren't all babies bowlegged; I ought to get a book . . .
but that would be just like every other new mother, she
thought. I hardly look pregnant and the book clerk would be
smirking. Funny lady, must be her daughter's expecting or
something. Yeah. No. No bookshops for Alix. Not now,
anyway.

She was very nauseous now. Maybe the jelly. Too
sweet and too early. But she held it down. If she threw up
now, it would ruin her eyes for the rest of the day, and she
had a luncheon date with friends at Caravelle. I'll wear the
dark-violet dress, she thought, that one with the wide collar.
And the transparent plastic earrings. Oh, very funny, she
thought. Like the jelly-glass and the jelly. God. Touching and
shying away from the big table at the farm, her mother's face
mornings, the jam-making, don't want to think about that
now. Maybe never. Hideous. But there was purple all around
her now. And her perfume smelled all wrong. She went into
the luxurious blue-green bathroom and threw up.

Mirrored image. With violet-tinged vomit spattered.
Antique silver faucets, spigot, towel-hooks gaped back at her.
She needed Martin now. If he were there she would not have
called him. Would not want him to see her like this. But he
would have wanted to help. But he was probably almost at
his office by now. He could ride right down the East Side
Drive; if he left after 9:15, as today, it was an easy ride. If he
left before 7 a.m., leaving her asleep, it was a magnificent ride,
little traffic and the fog still soft over the River . . . either
way, he loved the ride. Driving. In his copper-colored Aston-
Martin. Down the Drive, easy, sweet . . .

Or up the Hudson, for a sweet, soft walk around
the place they were buying near Poughkeepsie. Just a look.
They wouldn't finish closing on it until after the baby was
born. It was due in November. Another Scorpio for the world.
Dr. Bob would deliver, of course. Martin said he was the best
in the business. All the show biz girls went to him. But how
many of them had their first kid at forty-three, she wondered.

Their pictures all over his office walls, not haphazardly, but each one inscribed and framed: "To Bob, with gratitude, from Jayne," or "from Janis with many thanks for help with our wonderful baby Scott" and such.

What were their names before, she wondered. Remembering how she became Alexandra. She might have been Alicia; almost was; Edward considered it. But 'Alexandra' seemed right to Edward. He had gimmicks in mind. And, he said, Alicia was too cloying. This name had dignity . . . more dignity, at the time, than had the girl.

Huh. Edward. And then Harold. And now Martin. Edward Harold Martin. Not an imaginative name in the lot. But *she* had had to become Alexandra. From Alice to Alexandra in one fast leap. One slow, agonizing, strange remodeling, and then one day the new name. But it had worked. It was unforgettable, and it did fit her, the new her. She wore great strands of alexandrites, rings of huge stones, all shimmery and bright, matched her eyes exactly, or so said Edward, and, later, the reviews. The gimmicks worked. So said Edward Harold Martin, she thought, rinsing her face with cool water. Staring at her face in the oval baroque mirror. What a name, Edward H. Martin, Esq., maybe out of a bad John O'Hara novel, or one of those Sinclair Lewis jobs. A man from Boston, he would be, or maybe Dallas. No; not Dallas. Everyone out there had names that were *things*, she remembered, not places or ideas. . . .

She had been a fast success. The voice; the eyes; the alexandrites, the name. She had style and impact, and she loved the work. It took years. The husky voice, the long limbs, the attitude of her body to the work. After the initial success, it had taken her years, with Edward as coach. And then alone, and then to Harold. And now to Martin. Now to this baby. She would become bloated, or a kind of ugly (was it?) which would distort her achieved sleek form. Could it form into another kind of beauty . . . she studied her body. Her "figger," her British masseuse had called it. Her mother had called it "figger," too, but in quite a different way. The men, watching her, had no specific word for their appreciation. Many of them had round-bodied wives at home or sitting next to them in the clubs. Women these men would be in bed with that night. Not with her. She would be alone, in those days, or with Harold, or Edward; she was the familiar body to her own man, each knew her smell, her lines; but to the men in her audiences she was the fantasy, the art of womanhood, the art object. Unattainable. The ultimate refinement on burlesque. The socialite women, both wives and mistresses, would watch her, and might copy her style, and would learn from her. Martin never came to her performances. She was grateful.

Martin . . . affable, sensual Martin had few words but they were the ones she needed. "Lovely . . . my lovely lady; you're all the loveliness in my world." She felt this was almost true. He was surrounded by loveliness; he liked it. She liked his counting her loveliest among his possessions. She liked doing for him. She would consider really learning to cook. Maybe after the baby was born. In the meantime, he loved what she knew. Never had to ask her to suck him off; it was her pleasure as well. "Wife" was the word, and he sensed it. She never wore her wedding ring when she sang. "Let them think they can try for you. It's more anonymous," Edward said. "They like it that way. They reach. If anyone gets too close, I'll be around. Don't worry." But he had never been around, and he had never been close to her himself. And she worried. Her analyst told her it was normal to feel concerned.

Now she worried. The baby. Would it be normal. Dr. Bob told her it was normal to worry but that she should sleep more regularly and not let the worrying interfere with her nourishment and rest. This morning it pulled at her, this being within the belly. She was still slim as a branch . . . she felt that the men who watched her singing could see the new life she contained, and disdained her. In this culture, men did not covet pregnant women. She needed to be desired. In

Mexico, in Italy, pregnancy made a woman more desirable. An aroma of fecundity. The good woman is the fruitful woman. But not in these Anglo cultures. When her flat belly rounded, she would quit work, her body would seem somehow obscene, and the men would no longer desire her. Would no longer contrast their wives' roundnesses with her sleekness. The fabric of her as sleek as those she wore . . .

The vanity of her being was channeled into her daily rituals as soon as she quit work. She would rub creamy emollients into her stretching skin and would eat the loveliest foods she could purchase, and developed a habit of smoothing nourishing liquids from her foods into her skin when she finished the solid portions. If it was good for her body, and for the baby's forming body, it was good for her skin as well, she reasoned: and so she would rub whole cream into her skin, or yoghourt, or the cooking-liquids from fresh vegetables, or champagne, or sherry, or the water that came to her spoon when she ate a cup of custard . . . all of it could keep her lovely. She would not fear for her bones; her teeth were already capped; the thigh joints hurt her sometimes and she was concerned and took calcium tablets, but she did not discuss this with Martin. She was no primitive. She did not walk enough, she thought, and so began daily walks as part of her ritual. She did not gain weight. She refused to gain weight. Dr. Bob approved of this. He did not discuss this with Martin. He knew of the man's pride in his wife's appearance. He was determined to help Alix to maintain her figure and to regain it as soon as possible after the birth. Most of his patients had this attitude. He was used to it.

She was beginning to forget who she was. "Alice" was the name of a young girl; "Alix" sounded so much like it; she was a woman who was carrying a child of her own, finally; no one called "Alice" could be that responsible; she felt the baby move within her, she watched it grow. This was a job that no Alice could do. But she was still Alice. Daughter of a farmer. Martin arranged for the hospital: she would have a small private room at a small private hospital near their home; Dr. Bob had privileges there and was more than welcome. She wanted unconsciousness. She wanted to wake and find her beautiful daughter in her arms. Not exactly magic. But no pain. No more worrying. But an astonishment; an extension of that moment when her pregnancy had been confirmed.

She went to Saks and bought clothing for the infant. Then she took some of the blankets, and the tiny jackets, and boots, which were white, and had them dyed the color of the alexandrite. Martin thought this was a genius idea. Boy or girl, it would be a good color; she hated the ordinary pastels. Why didn't they make infants' things in moss green, she wondered, in burgundy, in velvet the color of champagne, how fine! and she had some made for her child. Instead of those insipid pale yellows and blues. A vivid blue for her child, the blue of the sapphire! and that rich red of the velvet cape she sometimes wore. And a deep primrose bunting. If children love bright colors in their toys, might they not also enjoy them this way, she thought. . . .

She and Martin looked for furniture for the child's room. They bought an antique brass crib, and an old oak rocking cradle; they planned that the child would rest in the cradle at first, and could move to the crib in a few months. . . . Alix bought a darkwood chaise to sit in with the baby. Visualized herself holding the child when friends came to visit. When it arrived at their apartment, she stretched out in it, her belly heavy and her leg-joints hurting, and she fell asleep, and had a dream: the baby was here, it was a boy, it looked like Harold, it knew her name was Alice, she did not know what the baby's name was. And Martin was there, he was angry, she had grown fat, he stood next to her and the baby and was angry because it did not look like him. When the baby turned it had a dark purple birthmark on the left cheek, from eye to chin. She was sorry for him but more for Martin. In her nervousness she dropped the baby. She would call him

Hartin. She would call him Marward. She would call him Edwold. She opened her mouth to call him and no sound came out. The baby stared up at her from the floor and sighed. "My name is Alice," he said.

Dr. Bob spoke seriously with her and with Martin toward the end of the seventh month. "You can probably look for the baby any time from now on," he warned. "We aren't sure when you conceived, and you're very narrow, you know. It's hard to tell what to expect from here on in." "But I feel fine. I mean, I feel really well." She did. Today, she felt energetic and confident; in fact, she felt better than she had for weeks. Months. The baby seemed very much at home inside her; she felt strong and sleek, as if she were about to go onstage. She felt she could move mountains. She stared at Martin. He was wearing the ascot she'd bought him yesterday; his face seemed smooth; his hair looked young and even; it was the same auburn as hers. They both attended the same salon. He told her once that he'd been a towhead when he was a baby. The day after they were at Bob the Doctor's office, she went into labor.

There was no doubt it had begun. As with many important events, Martin was at his office. It was a quarter to eleven. She spilled the orange juice she had been holding; she had just creamed it carefully into her skin as a facial. Forever after, she would associate the smell of oranges wtih this discovery. She called Martin. He was home in twenty-six minutes. As she picked up her valise for the hospital, she thought of her birth-control pills: the tiny aqua box was still in the bottom of her leather travelling-case. Man proposeth, she thought. Martin, the all-knowing, the great understander, proposeth, and then acteth, and God fucketh up, she thought, her teeth grinding with the contraction. Should she be angry with Martin or with God for this pain? God only knows, she giggled. Relief. And Martin smirked: "You seem to have a convenient sense of humor, lady." "Don't *smirk* at me," she snapped, another pain beginning. "I'm *not* smirking; *you* stop

snapping," he snapped. "If you start snapping at me now,"
she warned. "Yes?" he said, menacingly, with a grin. "Shut
uhh . . ." she started. It ran off into the next contraction.
"Get off me, I got no use for yer face here now," she said,
gasping, reverting.

The lobby of the little hospital was much like that
of the Tuscany Hotel or of any of the quality small hotels
nearby. There were good oil paintings on the walls and a
series of fine oriental rugs in an attractive pattern across the
floor. No telephone visible; a Breck-ad woman sat with crossed
ankles in a leather armchair near other couples, who were
talking softly; she asked their names, glanced at a small note-
book on her lap, and spoke, seemingly into the wing of the
chair, to announce their arrival. Dr. Bob would be there in
a moment.

Martin was calm. But he was not his own man
here. It was as if he had dreamed her dream too. Withdrawn.
He set the valise down in her room. It was a sitting-room facing the River, all in beiges and olive greens. This was not her
act. Nor his. She was uncomfortable. Wished Martin would
leave. He did. Dr. Bob came in, bringing the intern who
would prep her. Hateful business, she thought. "Will it grow
back as soft; or tough?" "Almost as it is now," the intern said,
obviously annoyed. "At first itchy and prickly." "And my
belly?" "Just the opposite. Now it's tough and hard; in a few
days it'll be flappy and soft; then you'll get it back to just
as firm as before you conceived, if you're lucky and you work
at it. If that's what you want." She had the feeling he'd tell
her about his wife's belly if she didn't shut him up. He looked
annoyed. She reached out for Dr. Bob.

He was busy. He was concerned. Put his gloved
finger into her rectum to find the baby's head-position. She
felt a sexual twinge at his gesture, professional though it was.
Ridiculous, she giggled. I'm having a baby and he's rimming
me and I'm remembering Harold the sadist rimming me dry
with that huge cock. I wonder if I'll come when the baby

141

does. . . . When the new pains hit, it became her act. She felt onstage. She was no longer thin. Nothing sleek about this work. Naked under the short, smooth hospital smock, her belly huge and convulsed, her breasts lumped and swollen toward the milk she would not give to the child (her figure might suffer)—her thighs taut, calves cramping with the effort . . . she was sweating. Not the delicate, fine perspiration of her days, not the scented heavy mist of making love or of singing: this was sweat, pungent, soaking her back, soaking the mattress. Between pains, she noticed it. She enjoyed it. She felt free.

By now, the afternoon sun came slanted into the side window. She was turned on her right side, facing it. She was working. She was onstage. Martin came back in. His face seemed familiar. They had not been married long enough. Or something-enough. . . . "I know you," she said, straight into his eyes, "it's your baby." "No, it's all yours, baby; take it!" as if he were an M.C. or something, she thought. "All right. Okay. OKAY!" she screamed, in the middle of a cramp. "Either gimme yer hand or get the hell out," she heard herself say. He reached out, took her hand, she felt briefly of its smooth skin, he gave the hand of the woman a friendly little squeeze, dropped her hand, and turned to leave. "O Jesus, that's not what I *meant*," she howled; but he was already gone. He was thinking, she doesn't look like anyone I ever knew. . . .

She wasn't. She was at her mother's table in the afternoon sunlight. She was onstage, wearing her deep alexandrites. She was terribly alone. Someone came and gave her a needle. Stared down at her across a chasm. She wanted her mother . . . she called for her mother. I am turning hard too fast, she thought, something is wrong, something is all wrong. . . . Something was wrong; the kind of pain was wrong. Without having experienced the process, she knew: her animal body knew. It had started too soon, maybe the baby wasn't ready really, maybe she couldn't do this, she was terrified, alone, alone, she called for Dr. Bob, she called for

Bob, Bob, Bob, and then for Martin her husband, she was screaming. No one came. Neither of them came. And then a strange intern strode in, and a nurse, but they were both soothing, "Now you just take it easy, everything's all right, everything's going to be all right, try not to shout, you know there are other patients to consider. . . ." She wanted to kill them. What the hell did they know. Superficial, evil bastards. What the hell did she care about the other patients. This was her own scene, she was onstage, she was furious, she was scared to death, alone. . . .

   Dr. Bob came. He lifted her great bulk and placed her in a squatting position on the bed. The pain changed. She screamed. He inserted his fingers into her vagina. "Gently, now . . ." A tiny pain, of a different nature from the other, and a welter of fluid coursed down her legs. Soaked the bed. There was no Alix in the room. No Alexandra. Alice leaned into the work and screamed. Martin's face appeared. "Get him out of here," she told Dr. Bob. "Okay. Sure." And Bob lowered her to her side again. He took her hand. The needle was beginning to take effect now. His face faded in and out. "What'd you do before you reached in? Was that the bag of waters?" "Yes. And I turned the baby's head. It was this way . . ."—he placed an index finger across the oval he made of his other hand—"and I turned it this way," so that the head was in line with her oval opening. "Okay," he said, "it's time to rest. Let me take over. You rest." He gave her another shot.

   As she lay dazed she watched him. Hand on her belly, on the baby. Hand gently inside her again. Less pain this time, but Jesus Christ, it was still a lot. How the hell did the animals go through this? Remembering the sound of a horse giving birth, the groans, the snorted breathing, the high whinnying of pain. Sound of the pigs. I'd rather be a chicken, she thought; that's funny, must remember to suggest that one to Martin. . . . "I want Martin." "All right." And when he came, and took her hand, she forgot whatever it was made her call for him. He looked so worried. So did Dr. Bob.

143

She suddenly felt like the Woman who invented this whole process. She must reassure this man, who just stood there looking more rumpled than she'd ever seen him: "It's okay, Marty, it's gonna be okay, it's just tough to do, ya see?" He stared at her. She had never called him that.

But then she was worried. It sneaked in behind the medication. That edge of fear like an inkblot, and the edge was razor-sharp now, cutting through the dreamy medication. "Sleep, baby," Martin was saying. She held his hand limply. And dreamed the dream: It was stillborn. The baby was a boy, too tiny, she was too tiny to bear it properly, it was born dead . . . she wept. In the dream

It was stillborn. Too tiny. Its tiny head not completed. She wept.

It was a girl: in the image of her mother. The face of Alice's mother Margaret. Shit.

It was a boy who looked like Martin. He took it away from her and smirked, laughed.

It was a beast of many parts, only some of them human.

It was triplets. Boys. What can I call them? Edward Harold Martin. My God. I will not do this.

It was born old, a sexless old man with no genitals. My God. Who did this thing to it?

It looked like her first analyst and like her own father and like Dr. Bob, but they would not let her hold it; it was made of glass, it would break, they said. She said she would be very careful, VERY . . . We can't trust you, they said.

It was twins. She stared at them and went quite mad. To know them for what they really were. Screamed.

It was a girl. A Scorpio girl who stared at her as if she hated her All colors spun in.   .

It was born hungry and she was not allowed to feed it and was forced to watch it starve.

shifting and shifting she watched the choices. None of them told her it was going well. At the end, she saw a dream in which she died giving birth. That dream was a dream of many colors, where the colors spun in, like the dream that she had

had a Scorpio daughter who stared at her. She moved effort-
lessly from the purple inkblot stains to the thick bitter purple
of her own color. And moved, surrounded by color and tears,
until she could no longer move. She tried to cry out, "Martin!"
but the best she could manage was "Marty," and it made no
sound.

1969

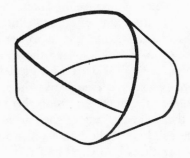

EVENTS OF A MARCH NIGHT

It was the end of winter, a bright and clear night in March. The wind was steady and even, moving the trees that stood above the roof of the old house. Branches would swing softly against the roof or the shutters, with a crisp brushing noise that fitted into the wind's susurrus. Everyone in the house was long asleep. It had been a busy and usual day: a day of tending to the animals, of seeing to the feeding of humans and animals alike, of talking over how the winter had gone, and how it was almost over, and what the spring would be like. In the barn near the house, the cows were freshening. Near them, the horses slept evenly. The house, dark and thick with age, sat near the top of a small hill, the only one marking miles of otherwise almost level land. And it was the only house, as well; the people in it had owned the land around them for many years and would continue to for many more years. They had no feeling about this, but lived with the land simply, with a kind of dignity which accepted the seasons and their courses. Across the acreage ran an old brook, shallow enough to use for watering the animals, and near enough to the house to provide it with good water, all the year round. Into its gently curved banks the same grove of trees which sheltered the house sent roots, here hidden and here revealed by the slight swelling of the current during the early spring. The children of the household would play among the roots, making them into caves and castles. There were often more than half a dozen children in the household, if you counted those who belonged to the servants as well as the owners.

On this particular night, the moon gave a yellow look to the night; it made its own patterns out of the trees, shaping the roots differently, providing a connection between those branches which did not touch the wide walls of the house or its stone fences. In one of these wide shadows, a man moved firmly. He was not afraid of the light, for he wore a pale jacket and his fair head was uncovered to the air. His breath was gone, he had run the last distances to the house, he had come a long way without a horse. A horse would have made his presence more obvious than it was. He did not want to announce himself; neither was he concerned, at this house, with whether he would be seen. He knew well the patterns of the household: everyone from the village knew, and knew as well all of the tender gossip about the family therein. There would be no one about at the hour of four in the morning. The old farmer and his wife would be abed; the dogs, having waited well past midnight for any noise of prowlers, would have sunk into the first false, deep sleep of their night.

The fair young man had keen senses: his hearing was acute, his eyesight keen and unerring. In the hunts of that locale, it was customary to drive up the game from three sides, giving the animals a chance to run off at the fourth. Those animals who, by some fate, came within range of the young man's weapon were not able to continue their quiet lives. But he was known never to kill for sport: he was a thoughtful man, and did not abuse his gifts of strength or skills. For him, having lived off the land had provided many deep lessons. And yet he was a man of some temper, he would not be put off. A man of great strength and with less than a perfect hold over it all.

He was moving steadily toward the old house. His goal was the dim oblong which indicated the window where the young couple, son-in-law and daughter of the household, usually slept. He knew that the son-in-law was absent, had gone on his seasonal trip to the city to make purchase of implements and supplies. And he had made certain that the man had indeed gone: he had a certain business with the young wife. That couple were oddly set into the ménage of the old house: both of them were quite deaf, and both of them were occupied with other fabrics of life than that afforded by the farming routine. One might assume that their world would be shaped differently, because they moved in a world whose moments did not depend on the ticking of clocks or the sudden footfall.

The fair man had once wanted the young woman, and had been discouraged from his suit: the old farmer had not thought it just to give his girl to a man in perfect physical condition; it might make a slavey of her in some way; at any rate, there would be an imbalance, and he wanted to wait a bit, to see what else might come of her life. And sure enough, within the year, another man appeared, a clock-maker, and as deaf as she, and therefore attuned to the same inner sounds which involved the girl. Yes, they had gotten along well: it was difficult for the rest of the household not to watch them, in their courtship, done as it was with hands and eyes and the most delicate of gestures. They meshed in their way of living, in a gesture which had little of will in it. He would come to the old house almost every evening, and would sit at dinner with all the family, and she would sit beside him, so that they could be heard, in a sudden lull, making their small guttural sounds, so much less than their gestures to each other. But no one made much of them. It was a world which involved the flesh of animals, there had been many different births in the time of the farm, and such animals had been included with the others, if they were reasonably able. It was a form of natural justice, and it made sense to them: why not keep the calf with the misshapen hoof, if it could still get around to its food? or the colt born without a mane? Its own kind accepted it; it had a tail, and could defend itself from sharp flies. And so the calf became a fine producer of calves, all of them with even hooves, and the colt grew, was the beloved pet of one of the sons, and eventually sired along with the others.

Well, as long as the two seemed suited, they were wedded. And all went simply and peacefully; the farm was known for this, the even pace in which the years and the next years came and went. Even this difference did not make a difference, when it came down to it. But the other man, the fair man of the village, was thwarted: he did so much want to possess the girl. He remembered her skin, and her dark eyes, so much like those of a doe he had not taken one spring. While he himself was like a roan horse: big and sturdy, with cheeks almost rusty in their color, and gestures of a big man. She had not made many gestures toward him, in that time before the other man had appeared. Her father had always stepped between them. But he wanted her: he only waited until he knew the time was on his side. He was, after all, a prudent man, and a man whose temper was almost always bounded carefully. It was not a question of patience. He himself was an official of the town, the sort of man who felt the power which was given to him, felt the way people were attracted to him because of his physical strength and his beauty; he sensed this power given to him and he had some ways of misusing it. His nature was not clear, even to himself. He could not have said when he had first begun to think about this night or the events he planned for it. His days had rather more paper in them than he wished, and fewer faces or bodies. His prudence of temperament prevented him from the kinds of sudden moves for which townsfolk the world over are known. But he was as much animal as any human: he lived in his belly, he felt from his groin, his thoughts were not always clear but had the sort of undefined edge to them sometimes that indicated they were based on the senses.

So he wanted the girl, almost suddenly; with the first changing of this season it occurred to him and the thoughts began to form. For her part, the young woman lived another way entirely. She had known of his interest and had not known what to make of it; it was a good thing for her when the other man had appeared; these days, she felt it was a good and reasonable life they had together. They had been married some months and she had never known another man. Her husband was her husband: she could not make comparisons. It was as if they had lived in another age, had been betrothed as children and moved naturally to all of this. When she looked at him, she saw her husband. What she knew about him was what she knew about the other men in the household, from watching and from sensing, and from the animals. She was a young woman of perhaps twenty years, with a look of a bird (whose way of hearing is also invisible), and the fine healthy body of a doe. She could not associate her husband and his ways with the ways of the other, fairer man; one was her husband; the other was a man of the village.

As the moon moved, the man moved with it, using the shadows as a bridge. Elms led him directly under the window he sought. The thick wall of the house shone chalky white in patches near him; a white patch set onto his jacket; the moon was at his back. He stopped a moment, utterly still in the almost-still night. He felt a stranger here, at this time, as though he moved in a dream, although his flesh firmed at the thought of why he was here. The window was a dark, silent oblong. On the old wall, chinks between the rocks of its texture afforded holds for his fingers and the ends of his boots. The bottom edge of the window was raised, as was the top. It was easy to raise them. He was quiet; the girl might not hear him, of course, but there were the dogs, and the many others asleep in the big house. Now he was inside the room. It was unfamiliar to him: he moved the curtain aside so that a bit of the moonlight would give him a view. Big old poster-bed, and a chifferobe as a dark mass against another wall, not a large room. And she was there, yes, her hair down, another dark mass as part of the rhythm of the room. He could smell her personal smell, that aroma he knew to fill any room where she was: female, but utterly herself. He was almost blind with wish. He moved noiselessly to the bed.

As he stood over her, staring, trying to see her clearly, she awoke: expecting her husband's face, and in that first shock or amazement at seeing the fair man, she made no sound. But when he put hands on her, her first small noise came. It was not enough of a noise to matter much, he thought, what with the roomful of clocks and their odd constant ticking. It covered her noise. He reached for her and uncovered her and took her. She was no longer surprised: somehow, immediately, from his expression and his first gesture of uncovering her, she knew what he was about. And so she was passive to him: it was in her nature, she was part animal, and knew what he was doing. In some way, in that quick way we think in times of stress of action or sudden activity, she was alert instantly, and then she was amused. That he should want her! Enough to come here this way! Really interesting! So she was, at the beginning, passive. And then it changed. After he uncovered her and saw that she was not going to struggle or defy him, he took the chance of uncovering his own body. He noticed that she watched him. She was quiet, focussed completely on his movements, following his hands as he dropped off his jacket and boots, as he shed his shirt and his hard coveralls. He noticed that she was smiling. Watching him in her birdlike way: the eyes were points of light in the bed. The way it was going surprised him. He had expected to have to fight for her, fight with her to get to her. But this! she was quiet, but that smile, and the eyes, and the smile again. It was disturbing. But not enough to change him or to put him off.

He saw now that she was not going to cry out or fight him. He moved to her, put his hands on her thick flannel gown, brought it up over her head. Christ! but yes, she had a beautiful body, he could see her, and the smell of her made him fill and grow. But she was watching him now. Not his face, but his belly, and the fine stand that grew below it, formed for her and from the months of waiting for this time. He was in shadow, turned slightly sideways toward her, over her, bent slightly toward or almost over her. She could see him, his body, with an edge of soft light along it, from the window where he had pushed aside the curtain. His smell reached her, it was different from her husband's smell, he seemed to be speaking, his lips moved as he looked at her body. But she was watching him. From his narrow loins, from the dark shadow between them, extended what she thought of as his pizzle, and she saw him as a stallion, no, he was certainly not like her husband, in God's name what sort of man was this, or was he half-animal, as he seemed now, as she had read about in books? But then there was no more thinking: he put himself next to her, and stroked her, and was sure that she wanted her body to move toward his, and there were no words: he kissed her, and kissed her, the hollow of the neck, and the wide breast, and the soft belly—and her hands moved across his back. He went to move into her. Until that second she had forgotten what she had seen: his enormity, his weight expressed in the manhood: but now she was forced open, forced to recognize him, his cheek grazed her lips and as he entered her she did cry out, she had to, and he had to cover her mouth with his own. No, she could not do this, it was impossible for a man to seem to have the organ of a horse, and if he did, then how could she open for him? O she would break in two! she screamed beneath his lips. No matter if she had wanted him or had been ready for him, this stranger. No way to take him in. But he was going in, steadily, firmly, not roughly, but firmly and surely. He had had a lot of women before her. He knew that they were each surprised with him, and he knew that many of them could not take him into them. But enough of them could and had. It was not really a concern of his.

But the young woman was stunned. She knew so little of men, and there was no room now for thought of what she did know of men or of animals: he moved into her, and filled her, and immediately she realized that in spite of the peculiar agony, she felt wonderfully wild, a way that she had never yet known. Part of it was this stranger who had entered her room and now was entering her body in this dramatic and firm way, no permissions asked of anyone. It might have been wrong of her father to keep her from this man and with-hold her from this possibility!—this fled through her mind as she laughed aloud with his motion in her. He was a firm and tolerant lover, aware that this girl had only known her husband before him, and how much could that skinny fellow have been to her! He knew he was attractive and he took her laughter as admiration for him. A fine horse of a man he was, natural and thick of the loins, and bigger than most or than one might even imagine, seeing him stride across a field or ride to the hounds. A horse riding a horse! she laughed again, giddy, and her laughter was natural and rich, not itself a sound made by a deaf girl: just simply a rich laugh. O her father might've given her a chance with him, just once! and then see which she'd have chosen. Both were thinking this thought.

When he thought she would leap away from him, with his motion, his mass within her, she moved further to him, encompassed him. All around them, the clocks continued, and in tiny spaces of his awareness he knew them. She went dark in her head, eyes shut, no memories, no thought.

And they moved together toward the great hill, moved up the side of it, and came to the top of it together. She had not known of this. The light there. After the darkness. Such light.

And he moved carefully to rest near her, only for a moment, long enough to read on her face what he needed to see. No, this was not an ordinary woman, he had been right to seek her and make this happen, a full and rich woman, this one! He touched her face and dressed and left by the window, as he had entered: quietly and firmly. The moon had changed its place, so the wall was darkened, his leaving was shadowed. She had laughed! that funny deaf girl, that beautiful woman, that doe; shocked or not, she had laughed and taken him in! O no, this was not at all what he'd expected: a fight, at the very least, a running, a chase: but not this perfumed thickness of her flesh as she took all of him to herself! No, it was not ordinary. It was as if she had outsmarted him, or maybe he'd outsmarted himself?—by letting himself plan it without accounting for her reactions. What a fine filly! except she was more a doe, wasn't that it, with her tight body and dark eyes and that funny gentle way. He moved out into the dark night, now unlit yet not somber. He felt fresh and whole, as if he had been caught suddenly in a rainfall and had soaked to the skin and had dried in the sun. His feet met the road-bed sharply, as if they were hooves, and he made the miles back to the village without losing his pace or his breath. At the town, he was not tired. He stood awhile near the fountain at the center; light was beginning to dawn. The village slept.

In the house where she lay, she was the only one awake. His leaving left her full and full awake. Her mind was at once chaotic and intensely calm. As she stood, the fluid he had left her coursed down her thigh, making her laugh again, a soft laugh of delight. She thought of her husband, of his ways, his gentleness, his face, his body. Not again could she be with him, after having given herself thus to the fair man.

This was an unshaped thought, a feeling. She could not at that time have declared if she preferred one man to the other. Why had he come to her? She moved toward the window, unthinkingly, in the midst of her own senses, her flesh still rich and fluid with the fair man's body. He was gone; he would be back to the town by now. And her husband would be back on the morrow. What if she'd known the fair man before this, before she'd married! Her hands touched her body: her breasts, where he'd put his mouth, and her dark fur where he'd entered her. She felt the calm of the house around her. Dawn was beginning over the trees, beyond the stream. Perhaps he would come for her, and perhaps she would go with him. But for now, she would sleep.

1966

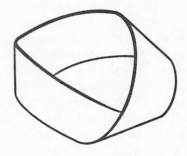

THE KITCHEN

It is morning, she comes into the kitchen. Spring, the windows are open a bit, soot has collected on the windowsill. She begins by getting a sponge and cleaning off the windowsill. She wrings the soiled sponge under running water and lays it on the counter, next to the bottle-brush, the rubber stopper, the rubber dish-scraper, the plastic food-scrubber. She sees that the children have already been into the kitchen, there are two bowls on the table, the bowls have remnants of cereal in them, there are milk-spots on the table. With the clean sponge she sweeps off the milk-spots, with the other hand she lifts one bowl, stacks it into the other, carries bowls and sponge to the sink. Starts the hot water, fills the bowls, washes out the sponge, wrings it, looks around the room. Turns on the flame on the stove beneath the coffee-pot. It is glass and shows a half pot-full of coffee left from last night. Sets out a cup on a saucer, picks it from a stack which is her favorite set, the ones next to it were a gift and are not in favor, they are rarely used. Goes to the refrigerator, gets out a container of light cream and the orange enamel tin containing the sugar, gets a teaspoon. Sits on one of the stools beneath the kitchen table. The table is at the center of the large kitchen. The table, fashioned by her husband, is made from a large piece of parquet flooring. He has cut it to the size he wants and lacquered it, the base of the table is an old pedestal they found together in a junkshop.

The coffee makes a small sound, she lifts it off, turns off the flame, carries the pot to the table, pours herself a cup. Everything is smooth at this minute. Let's see. The beds are made, what have I got to do today, Elsie is due in, the beds, o yes, I did them already, the damn kids are up already, aren't they, what next, it's Wednesday isn't it, he's still asleep, better get him up, lights another cigaret, looks at it briefly, moves toward the washing of the dishes, the dishwashing machine which contains the dishes from last night's late snack, stacks the two cereal bowls in it, spoons go into the silverware section, measures the detergent, pours it into its niche, starts the machine. A child has come into the room, makes a high whining noise like that of an insect, she brushes it away, sips at her coffee.

He comes into the kitchen, he is dressed for work, want toast? she asks, pouring him a cup of coffee, yes, moves across the room, opens the bread drawer in the cupboard, it sticks, the back runner and left side runner are broken or missing, the drawer won't close again properly, she turns and looks at him, surly, he hasn't fixed it yet, has known about it for months, every time this happens, ever since they moved in, with all the damn woodworking he does he could at least fix something she had to use so often. Damn him, least he could do. She clears away the coffee-cups, rinses them, sets them

aside, ready for the beginning of the dishwasher's next load.
Sponge across table again. Tidy now. The day begins.

Evening, the same night. She clears the dinner
dishes, she has eaten dinner with her two children and the
child of a neighbor. Her daughter has spattered soup on the
floor, the neighbor's child has scattered crumbs and crusts, her
son has left morsels of meat. She does not like to cook for children, she is a good cook and likes to cook, likes to prepare
ornate and interesting foods, but she is not a fine cook, because she lacks the real verve. She has too many cook-books.
Her favorite food is turkey soup, made from leftover turkey
scraps. The skeleton. She does not like fish of any kind, she
was raised a Catholic, she loves shrimp and clams, which she
calls 'seafood,' and tuna is not fish. When she buys butter, she
repacks it from its original paper into little white china tubs.
Her kitchen has old cabinets with new handles. New counter
which her husband made and a new table which her husband
made. She does not like her children, is afraid of certain
things about them, something about control, she does not give
hem much definition. They whine for gifts. I will let them
eat whatever they want if I am ready to feed them. But if I do
not want to feed them just then, they do not get to eat. This
kitchen is officially closed to them after their dinner. If I am
asleep in the mornings, let them wait or fend for themselves.
I won't spend all damn day in this kitchen. The three-year-old
girl has four linus-blankets. The five-year-old boy still takes
a bottle. He has a minor speech defect.

The kitchen floor has been enamelled over its lino-
leum. Then waxed. Epoxy paint in a dark brown, and then
wax. A hard glossy surface, washable, can take almost any
hard usage. The floor surface runs six inches up the walls,
covering the baseboard. She clears the dinner plates, rinses
some of them, stacks them in the dishwasher, puts the detergent in, turns on the machine. Sweeps the kitchen floor,
clearing off the remnants left by the children and by her own

cooking. Lifts the kitchen stools and places them upside down on the table in the center of the room. Her husband has come in, watches her from the doorway, sure you're not forgetting anything, what do you mean by that, she doesn't look up at him, continues to sweep, finishes, reaches for the mop, wets it, wrings it, damp-mops the floor. As every night. There is nothing on the floor now except the table. She has lifted the plastic wastebasket and washed it out, turned it upside down on the counter next to the sink, has placed the bagful of garbage in the incinerator outside, near the rear door, the delivery and service door to their $550-a-month apartment on upper West End Avenue in Manhattan. The door at the end of the corridor outside the kitchen. The kitchen is only one of a few doors off that corridor.

Another of the rooms is her husband's workroom. Where he built the counter and stools in the kitchen. The tabletop for her kitchen. Her husband is putting in a wine-rack in the pantry-corridor outside the kitchen. Near it will be a section of shelves for her many cook-books and her trays and her pitchers and spice-jars and grain-jars and pasta-jars. There will be display space here, as in the kitchen, for her considerable collection of basketware. She does not use most of them, nor many of the utensils and jars displayed around the kitchen on pegboards or hooks or shelves. Her husband built a rack on which she hangs her cooking-pots. He built it from a butcher's rack. Her pots hang from the huge hooks which used to hold carcasses. One of the pots is aluminum, with a Teflon lining; it is the property of her husband, who was born under the sign of Cancer, and it is not to be used or handled by anyone else at any time. The rest of the pots and pans hung on the butcher's rack are copper-bottomed or solid copper. They are usually polished and shining.

There are twenty-two cabinets and drawers of various sizes in and near the kitchen. They are filled with cooking implements and devices related to cooking. She has collected them in the ten years they have been married. Some of these things come into use only when they have company for dinner. The last dinner party was for six guests and cost a little over $80. She cooks for company herself: help is so dear. A simple dinner, just meatballs in wine over noodles, and she cooked everything, and served everything herself, but it did run up, what with liquor and a decent dessert and all. Even keeping it simple. It just runs up.

It is mid-morning now, she is sitting at the kitchen table, ordering her groceries. The household helper, Elsie, is listening, is watching, it is she who will do the shopping, at the corner supermarket. The young wife does not like to shop for herself. So the maid will go. She instructs to buy the store's own brand of cleansing powder, 'Marveline,' it is cheaper. And its own brand of butter. But that Elsie is to buy no other marmalade save Orange-Sliver which is imported and is the best. Not any other kind. She pays Elsie $1.75 an hour, Elsie is an affable woman who has been cleaning this woman's kitchen for the past several years, as well as her own kitchen in Harlem. She will also take care of these children today, while the younger woman goes out, goes downtown with her friend for luncheon. Or perhaps shopping for antique bargains.

The rooms near the kitchen are filled with different kinds of disorder and semi-order. In order, radially, they are filled with: sawdust, around a piece of woodwork the husband is building; children's toys; unsorted boxes full of household goods still packed from the move to this house; the husband's tools and implements; cartons of books across the length of the long corridor-shaped room at the entrance to their apartment. When they moved to this place, six months ago, each of the rooms had contained the signs and remnants of having been inhabited by different kinds of animals. The shit and smell of animals of different kinds. The kitchen had recently contained five rabbits, which had been permitted to run freely as they pleased: the kitchen floor and the floors inside the cabinets had been encrusted with rabbit-shit. The three bathrooms had been living-places for several snakes. Their leavings had become stuck to the tubs and seats, as a plague for the new couple who were trying to set the place to rights for themselves. But it had been such a bargain, they could not resist it. At that rent. In this city. What was a little animal-residue, after all, they would put it to rights in short order, some elbow-grease, Clorox, Spic 'n' Span, Lysol. Brushes, brooms, mops, sponges, newspapers, a big package of steel wool, they would get at everything but the smell. Pervasive.

The huge livingroom appeared to have held the former tenants' chickens. Their shit was, of course, whitish, in contrast to the dark pellets of the rabbits and the dried-slime tracks of the snakes. And all of these were unlike the irregular, high mounds of dog-dung heaped in random fashion throughout the many rooms of the apartment. It had taken the couple a long time to clear the place of the various residue. She was an avid worker, she would put on a surgical mask sprinkled with her own cologne and plow right into the job. He seemed much less sensitive to the smells and a bit less willing to do the actual cleaning, but he would carry out the cardboard cartons full of soiled papers. Afterward, once in a while one of them would suddenly visualize a particular area as it had been when they had taken the place. The young woman would get a vision of the rabbit-shit as she mopped the kitchen floor. The tile floor of the bathroom would be marred by a mirage of dark, encrusted slimy tracks. As if they could never really get all of it out of there. Try though they might.

Her husband had given up smoking and was at the same time trying to lose weight. He had had a scare that winter, a cancer scare. He would therefore drop his excess forty pounds, and would stop smoking. He had been smoking perhaps three packs of cigarets a day, with an occasional cigar on special occasions. Not an easy combination, to give up overeating and oversmoking. But he had his areas of determination. He insisted. He would come into the kitchen and drink many cups of coffee with Sucaryl, he would chew gum by the half-pack-full, he would come into the kitchen and take bits of lettuce, other raw vegetables. He would nibble at the semi-rich concoctions his wife lovingly prepared to substitute for the rich pâtés she had been used to making for him. He remained fat for a long while and his teeth were already stained by nicotine. He had an angry disposition and so did his wife. She was never really hungry and he was always hungry. He was Cancer and she was Virgo. There was never enough food in the world for him, never enough, on the table, in the fridge, in his bank, on his plate, to feed that hunger, and there was never enough order in their lives for her to feel comfortable. He was conscientious in his carpentry at home and on his job, and off-hand for all of his appointments, and he would gorge on non-fattening foods at his own table. The table that he had built. If he had done what he considered a good job that day, a well-made plan or a good deal, he would give himself a great reward: he would eat a rich, huge, non-diet meal, in a restaurant or in his kitchen at home, or in the great hall of a diningroom where they entertained visitors, at the trestle-table they had bought at auction.

The wife doesn't understand money but she does like it for what it gets for her. She loves clothing. Fine, expensive clothing in the height of fashion. None of it original in concept but put together so that it might appear original or clever. In quiet good taste. Conservative. A good black dress and a good costume-pin, simple, elegant; white denim jeans and a striped shirt. No fads except the proven ones. Nothing ethnic. Very American. This carries through into the decor of their apartment. Neither of them relates to their ethnic heritages. Their home is laden with walls and rooms full of antiques: plaques, emblems, prints on vellum, charts, maps, typographers' symbols and initials, shields, tapestries, an Indian goad of pure brass, all purchased, none Russian or Irish or English. A synthetic ethnos. The huge fireplace in the front hall does not work. Much oak and walnut, some teak and a bit of ivory, as inlay.

On her shopping list this morning is an order for two long loaves of white bread. She calls it 'plastic bread' because she knows it has little nutriment. It is the typical commercial white bread. She will not buy the available whole-grain loaves because they are too delicious, and she and her family would just sit around eating it, loaves of it, heaped with butter, and gaining weight, too much temptation. So she buys plastic bread. That way they will not be tempted, will stop at one or two slices. Her children are thin. They wear fine clothing and their ribs show. Their cheeks are sallow, they are city children, they go to the park nearby with Elsie or with their father or mother. In the kitchen the daughter whines: bring me my bottle mommy, bring it to me upstairs, and the mother does. Whatever the whine asks for, if it is the girl-child. If it is the boy, it may take a while longer or may not happen at all. She forgets. She is displeased with him and worries about him, he is not her idea of an aggressive boy-child. Not like his father or her brothers. The boy, five, is also taking a bottle with juice or milk in it. And he howls quietly for it. She does not know how to wean him or feed him. For the first three years of his life he lived on hot-dogs and milk. Once in a while pizza. Now he will get himself a plate of cold cereal, in this kitchen. And will prepare one for his sister. The girl loves sweets, in a short while she will have to have all of her teeth repaired in a hospital under general anaesthesia. Ice cream and candy. The boy will eat of the food at the table when it is made available to him. She has taken him to three psychiatrists, she knows he is disturbed with his life. The three turned her down before a personal interview because they considered the case too ordinary and not worth the time. She did not describe it to them correctly and there was no sense of urgency in her description on the phone. The boy is tiny for his age, bright in a deeply concealed way. His father loves him wordlessly. A Pisces child. A dreamer, a painter. The mother does not understand him and he knows this well. At night he asks for favors from his father. But she responds, bringing him a cup of nightmares.

The father, guilty and innocent, moves about the house near the kitchen, carpentering, smoothing, polishing, moving about with his rabbit-beaver stained teeth in the big apartment or in the big advertising agency. His place, his shell, his pride. While the mother moves about the big apartment, cleaning, cleaning, cleaning, endlessly washing, sponging, rubbing, mopping, mopping, soaping, polishing, sorting, opening, closing, wrapping, dishing, portioning, fastening, freezing, bottling, pouring, shifting, unwrapping, rewrapping, corking, slicing, grating, blending, mixing, ladling, dicing, slicing, grating, testing, moving, moving, moving. . . . Talking on the phone to her friends, reading recipes, talking to her house-helper, to her children, to her husband.

At the end of the day, the wife and the husband are still awake. They sit at the kitchen table with cups of coffee. Have been married for ten years. Have slept in the same bed for ten years. Have had sex together for ten years, had marital relations, have made love, have had intercourse, have never fucked, have been in rooms near their kitchen table but never on it, never on the kitchen floor in a flurry of excitement, always on their bed, never at the edge of their bed, never with some clothing on, never in the middle of the day, always in either of two usual positions, never the variations, never feeling each other till they came, never taking it in the ass, never with the loving mouths, always hidden from their own sight and from the sight of the lover. Not to be discussed. I do not want to know. It is not nice. We do not. Now they sit in their kitchen at the end of the day, it is quiet, the kitchen fan hums softly at the window drawing the air out, she has swept the floor, wet-mopped it, started the dishwasher, it hums at her right, a harder sound than the fan. He has eaten dinner out with his art director, they have accomplished a gratifying amount of work on a certain account, so he has eaten dinner at Pen and Pencil, he reports to her what they ate, but not before she tries to guess, knowing his favorite luxury meal: two very dry martinis, pâté de maison, filet mignon, baked potato, poire hélène, no, he says, went to the P&P, kept it simple, bourbon and branch, tried their chicken, wasn't any damn good, too dry, O too bad, she says. What'd *you* do today, he asks. Not much, she says, it was kind of . . . What do you mean, kind of, he says. O not much, she says, just my way of putting it, that feeling, you know, one of those kind of nothing days, Elsie came in, took the kids out, I had lunch with Sherry, you know, nothing much. Sometimes I just feel like, you know, just taking off and disappearing, she tells her husband, without looking at him. O you don't have to take off to do that, baby, he says, smiling. O boy you're in a lousy mood, she says, I didn't say that to aggravate *you*, you know . . . I just mean. I was just. Feeling like. I don't know what. Getting the hell. Out or something. Something. Sure, he says. Sure you do, baby. It's a tough life for you isn't it. All depends on who's living it, she says. Maybe it's a lot tougher than it looks to you from there. Maybe even tougher than Sherry's, and from what she told me today, she's having it pretty rough lately. Yeah, I'll bet, he says, there's a broad who really has it rough all right. Her old man makes even more dough than I do. Must be hitting fifty grand easy. What the fuck she have to complain about this time?

They're splitting, she says. I mean really. No *kidding*, her husband says. I mean, Sherry's sure she's getting out, finally. She told him so. Finally, he says. Yeah, she says. They both drink coffee a minute. Thinking. The kitchen quiet and humming around them. The noises of West End Avenue traffic soft around them, back of them. The floor gleaming. Bullshit, he says to her softly. That's all you two do when you get your heads together. Your little two-hour lunches. Well, *you* took two hours today, I bet, she says. Yeah, but that was work, he sighs, damn you. And that phone thing you do with her, he goes on. What the hell, always the same things, same bullshit, over and over. That broad is a real castrator. Took his balls off years ago. And now *she's* gonna leave *him?* That's a joke. Taking them with her like the silverware, I bet. O for God's sake that's not the way it is at all, that's not fair, the wife says, softly. In a pleading tone. She says Tom had no balls to begin with and that's why she's leaving him. If she had had a real man to be with from the beginning she thinks it would all have been different. Someone to lean on or something. Yeah, he says. Like hell. Tom's a good guy, I know him, I ought to, I *work* with him. Well, but you don't have to *live* with him, she says. O God, he says.

      The phone rings. It is on the wall outside the kitchen. The wife jumps for it. Sherry, she says, to the phone and to her husband. How're you? Jesus, at this hour? the husband says, how the hell do you think she is? direct into the wife's face. Same old bullshit, bet it goes on for half an hour this time, big lunch today notwithstanding. O Sherry, says the wife, if you had any concept of reality. If you told the man on paper he could have the apartment, you'll just have to get out. That's all there is to it, it really is as simple as that. Yeah, the husband says, loudly, aside, keep just one commitment, you made it yourself, you dumb castrating broad, I bet you can't. His wife puts her hand over the mouth-piece of the phone, O for Christ's sake, honey, she'll hear you. Yeah, he says, I wish to God she would, people like her make me gag. Why doesn't she wise up, or at least shut up and keep her goddam foolish ignorant head to herself. Spread the wealth, is her theory, okay, let her keep it off this house. Shut uppp, the wife groans.

      For her last birthday, her husband bought her a tin-and-copper mold for making pâté de foie. Other birthdays he has brought her other culinary accessories, from Le Bazar Français, or Mark Cross wallets or purses or gloves. Or he would bring her an addition to their collection of antique monograms. One of the first things they unpacked was their collection of antique W's, which were hung even before they had finished washing down the floors. They often spend a Saturday afternoon shopping for antiques of this sort for their home. They leave their children with one or another set of grandparents, both of whom live across town from them. They enjoy the shops and auctions of University Place and on Second Avenue near St. Marks Place and on Third Avenue near 90th Street. The wife enjoys decorating the apartments of her friends. She has begun to accept small honoraria for her help in doing this service. She does not understand money but she does like what it can do for her. She has said more than once that she believes in what she can buy. She says that her husband wins all of their arguments, because he is always right. She considers herself much less intelligent than her husband. But she is sure she is a good cook and a good decorator. She is sure she has good taste. She was raised lace-curtain Irish and she has fought for her good things and her good taste. It is very American. She likes the fine things which can be bought for money. Not the handmade things except if bought by her.

She knows she is not a good mother and she becomes nervous about it, every so often, but she always forgives herself. She is not really interested in being a good mother, the idea of nursing her children was revolting to her, she lost weight carrying the first child and he weighed just four pounds at birth. But she did have her figure back right away. Fitted into her usual stylish clothing right away. Her husband never goes down on her. She would not wish him to. After the cancer scare this winter they are both worried that he may have become sterile. She does not like the children she has, she is confused by them. Given the choice, she favors the daughter, but she does not like taking care of their needs. It is with great relief that she turns them over to her helper two days a week, or to their grandmothers on the weekend. But now that there is the possibility that her husband might have become sterile as a result of the cobalt treatments or from the presence of the malignancy itself, she has it in mind to become pregnant again. It would provide an emotional buffer for her, set between herself and the two children she already has. She considers adopting but will try to have one of their own first. Before giving up and going for adoption. From her kitchen, she has discussed all the aspects of this with her friend Sherry. She tells Sherry, I haven't been using my diaphragm. Neither she nor Sherry considers that the husband might be aware that her diaphragm is not inserted in her body. He is not aware that she is not using it. He has never placed his hand inside her body. And Sherry says to her, But you have such terrible pregnancies, how on earth could you think of going through another one. God I don't know but I feel like it would be good for him, if we had another kid now. Prove something. To him. As a man. You know.

       I know, says Sherry. About balls, she says. Effectiveness of same. I can't wait to get away from Tom. God but he's dull. I can't touch him any more. Not that he's reached out lately of course. I mean I can't even bring myself to wash his underwear. I mean I can't even put it into the machine. It's like it belonged to some stranger. A weird feeling, let me tell you. After thirteen years or whatever it's been. How could I live with him for all those goddam years. How'm I going to live without him now. It's such a goddam *habit.* Thorn in my side but I need that thorn, if you take it away now I might bleed to death. Know what I mean? Makes me alive, he's kept me alive, gives me something to bitch about really, now what'll I do, he made most of the decisions and I couldn't, only don't ever tell him I said that. Now what am I supposed to do, says that friend of his is going to take over our, I mean his, the, apartment, at the end of the month. I can't just get out. I need time to find another place. I mean, I'm *used* to the place. What I mean is, I'm used to the whole setup, by now. Even Tom. I'm so used to him. In a funny way. But it doesn't feel right. Like with the underwear. I can't . . .

Now that's what I keep telling you, Sherry, you're so impractical, if you would only face the fact that you signed it over to the friend on the basis of you and Tom splitting, and you really *are* going to split this time, then you have to just go ahead and get out. Find yourself another place, fast, where's your sense of reality? O Jesus, the husband says, from the stool within the kitchen, reality, what the hell. Shut up, his wife says again. What? says Sherry. Nothing, I was just talking to him, he's here, at the kitchen table. O, says Sherry, what does he think about all this. I don't know yet, she answers, we haven't discussed it much. Liar, says the husband. Listen, the wife says to the phone, why don't you look for a flat down in the Village. You've always wanted to live down there. No, not now, Sherry says, too tricky, I'm scared to death of it really in some ways, you know that, when it really comes down to it. Besides, I've thought about it, I'd have to send Eileen to school up here, it gets too complicated. You know I wouldn't put her into a public school down there. And those schools like Elizabeth Irwin, I don't think she'd fit. We're too conservative for that. You wouldn't do that either. Don't want her growing up looking like them. Or thinking there's only one political candidate.

They both laugh. Both the women laugh. From their kitchens, over the phones in their West End Avenue kitchens, their copper pots gleaming, their good dental work shining, copper roasting-pans, chafing-dishes, butter-spreaders, vegetable-knives, corers, peelers, juicers, graters, fryers, mashers, tubes, tines, handles, shining and glowing and flashing around them. Around their bell-bottom beige jeans and striped blue-and-white polo shirts and machine-made sandals. Around the scrubbed, shining faces of the two women in their thirties, in their kitchens. The womb-shaped bottle of vinegar on the shiny counter. The husbands standing or sitting somewhere in the background, just out of sight, just within earshot. The husbands in their casual after-work clothes, sitting near the kitchens, near their workrooms, near their trestle

tables, the trestle tables that resemble the think-tank idea-
tables in their Madison Avenue offices. The husbands, looking relaxed.

One day, the wife had forgotten a cigaret on the
edge of the counter, that counter which her husband had
spent three days finishing off, with sandpaper and with varnish and more varnish and a third coat of clear varnish. A
perfect job. The kind that made him feel entitled to some
ice-milk immediately afterward. Just had to be wiped off with
a damp sponge, he told her. By the time she grabbed at the
cigaret, there was a dark-brown stain, a semi-oval, terribly
dark against the even glow of the rest of the light-tan wood of
the counter. A scar. She felt a wave of panic. She needed to
ignore it, put it out of mind, but it was within her peripheral
vision. But that night he had noticed it, as soon as he came
into the kitchen, and he had almost hit her, she had thought
that he was going to hit her, for the first time. Who did this,
he said, up close to her face, did you do this, you dumb bitch,
what the hell do you think I put all that time and work in for
on this thing, for your goddam kitchen, that's what, not to
have you fuck it all up with your goddam carelessness, Jesus
you don't even have the goddam character to give up the
fucking cigarets, do you, do you, you dumb careless bitch, and
he stood that way over her, his finger pointing into her face,
less than an inch away from her skin, she just staring at him,
then backing away, this infuriating him, he starts after her,
she moves back again and away from his rage. Away from
him. Do you give more of a damn for a lousy counter than for
me, she says. O don't be a goddam idiot, he says, I made the
goddam fucking thing for you to begin with didn't I? O no
you didn't, you did it because you like to do that kind of
work, makes you feel good, nobody asked you for the counter,
I asked you I don't know how many times to fix the damn
bread-drawer and you don't do it, you just do jobs you like
to do and nobody in the world could get you to do anything
they wanted you to do if you didn't feel like doing it, maybe

you just made it so you could show it off when people come over, don't think I don't see you flapping about it, I never liked light wood all that much and you know it, you know I love dark wood. O really, he says, listen to her. That's rich. Is that why you burnt the frigging thing, baby? I didn't do it on purpose, can't you see that, she says, close to him, feeling a sudden lightness, waiting for his anger to break and fall. But baiting him with the edge of her own anger, her resentment of his anger, her fury with him and his anger. At his reminding her of who and what she is, and has been, and will be. The precarious roots. They both fell back then, back to not looking into each other's eyes often, and were in a mute trance before each other for the next few days.

The next day, when she was cleaning up the kitchen in the morning, after she had cleared away the children's dishes, wiped off the table, swept, damp-mopped the floor because they had spilled cereal and milk on it, she turned automatically toward the counter. The burn . . . She went into the husband's workroom. It was odd to her, right next to her kitchen but it was his province, she rarely went in there, the smell of the place was both foreign and familiar to her, it was his smell and the smell of his things, he would bring things out of that room to use for work on her kitchen or the new winerack and bins he was building, or he would bring things to this room from the rest of their house for repair. Most of his tools were here. On his shelves were jars he had gathered from her kitchen: she had saved them for him at his request: they had once been filled with strained or chopped baby-foods. Now they were filled or half-filled with screws, nails, brads, staples, washers, nuts, paper-clips, rivets, all the small metal used for connecting things to other things. Each size of each metal object had been sorted, was placed together with other objects of its kind and size and use. So that when he wanted to work on something, the right metal for the job was at hand.

On some shelves she saw cans of paint, varnish,

shellac, vinyl shellac, removers, solvents, thinners, and additives for the paint, shellac and vinyl shellac. It was difficult at first to decide which might be the right ingredients to use in repairing the burn. She ought to sand it first. There were square, round, large and small pieces of sandpaper, some of them had numbers, some seemed suited for the sanding-wheel attachment of his drill, some were light-tan-colored and might blend into the color of the counter, others were reddish and very fine-textured. She took up a piece of tan-colored fairly fine-textured sandpaper, marked 'fine' on the smooth side, went in to the counter, and began to rub gently at the burned area. In less than a minute she had erased the burn-mark completely. Apparently it had not even penetrated the vinyl shellac layers he had applied. It had not even gotten down into the wood. She had reached the bare wood already and the burn-oval had disappeared. Goddam him to hell and back for that goddam vicious mouth of his. She left the kitchen with the gummy piece of sandpaper. Went to select a varnish to cover the bare spot. It had to be that clear vinyl stuff he had used. Hoping the damn kids didn't come in and nag at her while she was touching it up. Elsie due in. It wasn't going to be so hard to do. What was all the damn fuss about anyhow. The room was in disorder but the shelves were arranged in sensible order, she found the vinyl shellac and a paintbrush which might do the job. And retouched the now-gone burnt spot. It all took less than six minutes.

He would be surprised that she had done that. Had taken it upon herself. Would he be glad? Would he be pleased. Probably not. His province. There would be something he would find imperfect about the job she had done. As compared with how he had done it originally. Or how he would have made the repair. Although it looked quite flawless to her. The shellac was viscous. Anything viscous was so tricky. Like sauces. The way some of them had to turn transparent. How the nature of some things was that they had to turn transparent in order to be good or correct or right or work out or taste good or be. Her husband was the kind of man who had quit going to his analyst after the third session, he told her later that he had been told things that would be too difficult to face or to follow through on. Kind of thoughts that made him uncomfortable. He didn't want to know about. He had no difficulty following through on his job, and he earned his $45,000 a year. He liked and understood money and what it could do for him, he liked good clothes and good whisky and good steaks and a big apartment. He could not own a car, he would borrow his father's car on the occasions when he might need the use of one. Although he could afford to rent one. He was deeply attached to his possessions and his wife was one of his possessions, so that he took pride in her soft, long strawberry-blonde curly hair and her quiet taste in clothing and their well-formed children. He is under the sign of Cancer, his wife is Virgo, she is attentive to the details of maintaining his possessions. There is a tacit agreement between them. He would glean and she would order. They have never discussed this.

The kitchen is rarely disorderly. One evening, there are friends over to visit, and in the midst of the evening, the wife decides to follow her usual routine of cleaning up the untidiness that has accrued around the room. She gathers used objects and napkins and dishes. She finishes. No one has observed her, she is only away from her guests a short time. A little while later, the husband goes into the kitchen for more ice and a few more limes and cocktail napkins. He catches a faint whiff of rabbit-shit. He opens one of the cupboards, in the group near the kitchen door. There is a small heap of rabbit-pellets there. He is incredulous and disturbed, interrupts his wife, calls her into the kitchen, what the hell's this, how could we have missed this? But honey, it's fresh, she points out, without considering the implications. What the hell, he says again, looking at it. Listen, you go back to Felice and the rest, I'll clean it up. And she does.

Later, they sit in the kitchen. Just as a point of

interest, he says, what's new with your dear Sherry today, I haven't heard her name cast about lately. Can the sarcasm, the wife replies mildly. Into his eyes. She usually knuckles under to him when he comes on aggressively. She laughs at his complicated verbal jokes and his brutish sallies. She has long, curly, very-dark-brown-almost-black hair of which they are both proud. Their children were born dark-haired and are now strawberry blondes. He does not wear a pocket-watch, nor, for that matter, any time-piece. One of his friends is going to Iceland and offered to pick up a watch for him, but his parents are going directly to Switzerland soon, and he has implicit trust in them, so he has asked that they pick up a Rolex Oyster for him, duty free etc., knowing that they will probably give it to him as a gift. What do you know about love, his wife says. Every pot has its cover, he says, quoting his mother. O goddam it that sounds like your mother, she says. In your kitchen you think I would have the nerve to mention my mother? he says, beginning to reach out for her, against her. Up your sainted mother's ass, says the wife. O you make me gag, he says, still reaching. It's bad enough you're not too bright, but when you try to be funny. I'm going out, he says. Have yourself an evening, she says, snarling. He doesn't go out. He takes his begun hardon into his workroom and slams the door. She sits on one of the stools in the kitchen, there is silence for a moment. The daughter comes in. She is still in diapers and she will be four years old soon. As she comes toward the mother, the smell of a bowel movement surrounds her. Well, what have we here, says the mother, in an absent fashion. She has a luncheon date with Sherry tomorrow and they plan to go on over to an auction afterward.

You know what Sherry told me? she asks her husband. No, what, he says, his mouth dry and puckered. She says the analyst made Tom walk out on her, that whatchamacallit technique. You know. What bullshit, says her husband. You don't understand, says the wife. They're both seeing the

same man now, remember, see? I know, says the husband, I
know. Well, she says, don't you see? Sherry started to walk
out on him two months ago and the son of a bitch shrink
tells her to stick with it, and then he sees Tom and tells him,
what's the matter, hasn't he got any balls, staying with
Sherry like that, starts putting Sherry down and getting Tom
to kick her out. Meantime she's just sitting still because the
shrink tells her to. Crazy, says the husband. Goddam fucking
bunch of shit, Sherry can't leave him I bet, he been holding
her into shape for years, even I know that. Some smart
shrink as I see it, baby. O no you don't, says the wife, he's
just another goddam shrink who doesn't like women, is all.
Why should he, her husband says, he had a mother and they
all do the same thing to a man, he has a wife too I'll bet. O
get off of it, she says, that isn't cute. Why does everything have
to be a war with you. No it isn't, he says. Well, she's much
stronger than Tom, really, you know that, she's a nutsy broad
for all that helpless act she pulls around you, and she can
always call you up and get all hysterical and unload her load
or get her load out at the shrink, and believe me Tom isn't
like that, he sucks it all in and develops an ulcer. I know.
Yeah, well, says the wife, you think you've got it all figured
out, but I still think there's something damn immoral in an
analyst doing something like that. Manipulating. O I think
it was great, says her husband. Great.

      The wife turns away from him toward the sink.
The dishes are stacked there after the dinner meal. She has
scraped the food from them into the plastic bag which lines
the white plastic wastebasket. Now she rinses most of them
and places them in their proper niches in the dishwashing
machine. Neither she nor her husband has ever broken a
bone or had a serious disease. Until the cancer last winter.
And excepting her difficult pregnancies. They have no friends
or acquaintances who are maimed, crippled, poor, widowed or
seriously ill. They make no further inquiry into their bodies
than seems necessary at the moment. They never discuss sex.

The Kitchen

They vote Republican and discuss their vote with the friends who will also vote Republican. Their children, ungifted, go to a fine private school nearby. They have many difficulties there. Elsie has returned from the corner market, she was unable to find Orange-Sliver marmalade but has fulfilled the rest of the shopping-list. We are conservatives, the wife says to Sherry's sister-in-law at a party one night. But we don't have closed minds. By this time the shit of animals has begun to appear regularly throughout the house. One need only open a cabinet or a sudden door to find the heaps of dung or pellets or trails. But the wife cleans it up, it has become an automatic gesture. Almost as though she assumes that this is what she will find when she comes into a room. Fresh deposits. So often that she glances at it slyly, a little half-smile, ah there you are again are you, and cleans up with the same broad tender ritual gestures that she uses in cleaning up the rest of the normal soil of her household.

1967–1969

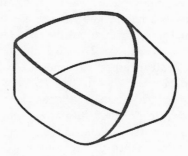

BLUE JUMP,
or,
The Inabilities

"And is it not strange . . . that one
says of a thing that it is full, when
it is not full at all, but not of a
thing that it is empty . . . when
one fills, one seldom fills quite full,
for that would not be convenient,
whereas when one empties one
empties completely . . ."
—S. BECKETT:
Watt

I.

Knew what she was about from the look of the car parked
outside the house. So he walked in without noise, just beauti-

fully cool (so stoned out and on music) and feeling very onto everything. Yeah, it was a bit, coming straight on through the door, but he did know the house, and he knew vibes. All the ritual going for him; all the cues. On.

He was late 30's and thought he was beginning to get it all together. Like music, or his work, or like that last trip, maybe. Now it was all running together; not all the time, not a filmstrip yet, but right now it felt good. And all of that feel walked into any room when he did. So everyone in a room (any room. this one.) dug that about him. He wasn't on any penance trip today, so his own vibes were silky. The god-ness in him. He thought part of it was having been near enough to the Western medicine racket to have shucked it—realizing you can't separate corpos from ethos from ethnos—a realization under mescaline which made several of his own varicolored segments slip silent and fast into place, soft thud and click, not a clank of metal because it was all about flesh and it worked itself softly like flesh. . . .

He'd reached "his" age, that age at which a man begins to be the realization of his self, toward which he'd been moving (not always knowing how, much less why). The age for approach to clarity, though yes, clarity is one of the enemies, and he had that number down by now—but felt himself having been beamed toward this age, this year, this point. All his experienced life. There were two sides to him and he still tasted the fear, it had a rich substance in his flesh, but he knew in his own skin that he had just begun "his" age, the fulfillment time; after next year would begin a softening, a falling away, a loosening out, a moving away from the hard edge of confrontation which was available to him now. His shoulders carried him, they felt their width. A frame.

He was vain; never considered his health or his mortality; once he speculated on Gene's sudden death, of MS, quick and young, but that wasn't really his bag, that kind of thinking, so he sped away from it. If he didn't like an idea, he'd get the hell away from it. And this showed in his walk. Firm toward, firm away from, and both times fast. He used this peculiar walk of his as armor; and he walked into this particular room the way he walked into the woods with his dog. The dog was with him now. A god-image of a dog, beautiful wavy-haired retriever, with eyes cut out of autumn nights and plenty of soul wisdom. He and the dog ate the same things. Ate out of the same plate, when they were out of the City. When Hackett went the macro route, the dog swung with it, those two months, and seemed even trimmer and more energetic than before, though Hackett got tense and skinny. They both agreed to go back to meat.

The woman was moving softly in the moody room he walked in on. She did not notice him, very caught up in what she was doing, busy with her tie-dyed mind. Her hands full of yarn and something woody. A very Cancer/Pisces-looking chick. Color all around her, all over the house, nothing like what it had looked like when he had lived there . . . she was all about color, wasn't she. And cloth and textures and wood. The great kitchen-pitcher stuffed with whisks and wooden utensils, Mexican and Japanese, looking like a weird bouquet—when she changed pads, and she did, often, looking for the righteous nest, everything fitted into the firm small painted cartons she used for stacked wall-cubicles. She had her number down by now. Everything travelled, everything beautiful went with her.

Like the kids did. Both of them blond, and Scorpio, like maybe twenty other kids they knew, friends' kids. If February had been that kind of good month for fucking, what with the winter depression, outdoors messy, spend all that time indoors, looking for reassurance, deep worry about fuel bills, bodies thrust toward each other, that month also called "suicide month" amid and after the long arduous four-month winter hassle, with two months to go of it all. . . . Thus all the Scorp kids, from one to ten years old—each family had at least one, like the *I Ching*. But the kids weren't planned. When would people plan their kids, for compatibility with their own signs. But is any of it an accident, he thought.

Watched her from the doorway, until she noticed him. He felt that there was no man in the house. The turn of her torso toward him, in response to his vibes, his smell. Yeah—she was good; good-looking, too, to him. So he pulled back into his hide and was wary. He was paying alimony to one ex-old-lady, moved alone now, all antennae, wary as hell. They were both trying people on like garments in a good shop, at Goodwill or a rummage: there was that leather jacket last month, this turtleneck shirt on Monday; too heavy, too light, too new, too old, the wrong size or fit; that pair of cords, bells, and you can imagine the vests, beads. Her eyes blurred; his had glazed over.

He'd pulled back by now mostly, or so he thought. She was still involved with the possibilities. Alexia was about thirty and not a line. None of it showed yet. She turned to face him from across her room. She'd known quickly he was there; there wasn't a sound of that place she didn't know, or on the land near it, but he walked like a friend and felt familiar. "Hey," she said (sound for a new man coming in), "how goes it?"

"You dig this house," he said, looking at it and at her in it. "I used to live here—you know, last year and part of the one before. It's a great house, right? I was just passing by . . ." He stood thus, feet apart.

"Coffee?" she wanted to know, and more. And the pot was on the table near the lit franklin-stove. To partake of: all of it very open, he could not mistake the warmth. Cancer must be her sign. The soft fire against the early Fall chill. Children making noise outside. His dog had run down to them, where they were messing in a stream at the bottom of the rise. The house, set up top, caught the dark sun of five o'clock.

He rolled a joint, lit up, walked slowly around the room, easing out. "She gives . . . too much?" he was think-

ing, and, "Good, what she's done with the house." Her weav-
ings and books, the music scattered over the little funky
piano.

"Why'd you leave here?" she asked, touching his
hand as she took the joint for a toke. Aware of him. The
maleness of his skin's scent beneath the pot's sweetness.

"Well, for one thing, it wasn't insulated then . . .
I had to hang a rug over that doorway . . . I huddled in this
room and the kitchen for a whole winter. Jesus. It was down
to 20 below that winter."

"But it was *good?* Because it's a good house. Good
vibes."

"I couldn't manage it after a while. There was a
settlement I had to meet—the old lady hung an alimony rap
on me that about broke my balls, really messed up my life,
which was I guess what she had in mind. . . . I had to spend
most of my time in the City hustling. . . ."

"Yeah," she said, feeling his pain. Imagine having
tasted living here and then having to give it up because of
someone else, someone with a real selfish push. "You couldn't
get out of it, I mean you tried everything?" And regretted
saying this. Of course he would have tried, and failed. Or he
wouldn't be saying all of this.

"Well, I tried to get out from under, but she had
this tough lawyer, and you know how the law leans toward
the ladies." His bitterness evident. She thought he didn't
know she would notice and feel she had to make up for this.
"It was either quit the whole work scene in the City, and try
to make it work out here and connect in the City (I do commercial art, you know, layout and illustrations), or maybe give
up the whole gig, run, split for Mexico, you know—I finally
figured I didn't have the guts to just split, or even to just try
to make it from here. And she knows me. She knew I couldn't.
I couldn't really cut out on the kids. I wanted to be able to
see them. And if I didn't pay, I couldn't. She had it set up.
What a drag."

"What's she taking you for? Is it child support plus?"

"Hundred fifty a week."

"God, that's a lot," she said, thinking of what she herself lived on with her two kids. "I bet she's living high on that. I'm lucky if I net ninety, most weeks," she told him. "I do macramé, by the piece, for a guy here in town, and other leather-work; meantime, my tapestries are in a gallery in the City, and if I'm lucky I sell maybe one every five months or so; but then somebody orders one special, you know, their colors, my design or something—"

"Doesn't the kids' father give you some?"

"When he can. He's a grad student and he hasn't got much. Sometimes a ten or a twenty. I hate to ask him." She heard herself saying it and felt the smugness; she would sound so righteous next to his old lady. Okay, but it *was* true.

He told her he was Taurus, moon in Capricorn. It figured. She knew it was all about earth. So it was double earth. Cancer rising. Good. Must've hurt him to give up this house, then. All ways. Out the window back of his head the sky was thick with clay-colored clouds; as he saw it, back of her head, the sun's last light was a bright, clear light blue, with no grey in it.

She laughed at herself. "I'd probably ask him if I thought I'd get it," she told him.

"I guess it's got to do with guilt," he said. "Depends on who quit who. I still feel that I could never have . . ."

"Yeah. But," she said, wanting it otherwise, interrupting him, giving him room, "I hate guilt; if there's anything worse than guilt, it's guilt payments. . . . They never stop. I don't think we originated them."

"I know. It's not a new feeling. My parents were aces at making us feel guilty. But I think I'm getting through it. Anyhow, 'some progress is being made,' just to give you the current report." They both laughed, but it hung over them in the sweet room. But they were feeling too stoned to stay with the down feelings. She had flopped on the couch; he was moving around the room, around her, keeping time to the music.

"I'd sure as shit rather have all this again," he told her, looking and moving. He means me too, she was thinking. Good. Great.

"You hungry? I've got a big stew going." She smiled lazily at him.

"Sounds great. Sure you've got enough?" and that naggling sound of *She's giving too much, she gives too much,* at the back of his head. He should have at least brought wine. But.

"Listen, there's plenty. I usually cook enough for two days or so; and besides, somebody's always dropping by." She went into the kitchen and he followed her. As she worked, setting things up, he gave her a hand; he knew where everything was, not just knowing the house, where the drawers were, but sensing where and how she made things work. Got spoons, forks, bowls together, while she threw together a salad.

She was amused, turned, smiled up at him: "Beautiful!" the way they were working together. It occurred to her at that moment to wonder how they would get along in bed. If it was anything like this, they had it made. But he was thinking that his ex was really clutzy in a kitchen. He hadn't been separated long enough from her to have lost the scabs on the wounds. He had always hated her inefficiency.

"Another five minutes for the stew," Alexia said. He went into the other room and she followed him. Walked over to the stereo and began it. The Stones. She moved simply to the shape of the music. Felt herself melting into the shape of his impression on her room, her space here.

"How many kids?" she asked, with a certain evil corner of her head. (She'd had two kids and stopped, and she was knowingly so damned vain about this; *she* would never use having kids as a weapon! and it was an easy guess he had more; his old lady was a bad type—) "Four," he said, wishing she hadn't brought it up. He might as well have said "Seven." It was that bad. She winced.

"Four," he said again, looking hard at her. Goddam her. Goddam both of them.

"Don't go on that trip," she told him, feeling that Gudrun side of herself emerging and then being pushed back. Jesus, I will not do it, I will not make him go that trip, she said to herself, harsh with herself, he's paid his dues, and probably more than that; why not let it be, it's *his* dues, fuck vanity. . . . I don't need another medal for good guessing. . . .

"Oh, Jesus," he said, "Okay." Touching her shoulder lightly and swinging with the feeling she had picked up on. Yes, he had slipped backward just then, slid backward on his own wheel (not realizing she had programmed the change). The kids had been born too fast, too often, while he was not paying attention really, his old lady was into some game then for sure, and they hadn't talked about having a kid before each conception. "Clever bitch," he said, now, to this woman, meaning both her and his ex-old-lady.

"Well, so she had to do that number . . . lost her game anyhow," Alexia said. Meaning to be soothing or something. But she still felt smug and she could tell he was ruffled. She leaned over to him. The easy noise of the stream, the dog, the kids a susurrus back of them. He leaned to her mouth with his.

"Consider," she said, beginning to come out of it.

"Oh, Jesus, I consider too much, you better believe it," he moaned, and it was true. They were on the daybed near the stereo, it was full dusk now, his hand firm on her firm left breast, warm feelings through the shirt. Both very high, and the stew done on the stove, the smell of it rich and sustaining.

After they all ate, everyone cleared up and he told her he had to split back to the City. "Call me, if you come in this week," he told her, writing his number on the kitchen pad. "Or if I can get away, I'll come by here." And left.

II.

As he shot south on the Thruway, thought about the friends he knew who were lushes, the bottle-babies, dying slowly of their own design, were they Zen-masters or something, trying to select the moment of death? What an idea—he knew he was still stoned. The things people choose to do themselves in while still staying alive, the pain gimmicks, he thought. Or is it just the disease of the perpetually alone, the constantly lonely . . .

His dog curled on the seat next to him, on an old blanket which covered a rip where the stuffing had sprouted. The golden dog's fur still damp in the chill night air. Ah, shit, let the evil bitch Joan keep the kids, the small dog and the big pad—he had got Morris, and the studio, and his freedom, he would keep that part of the world set up and he would survive. Even though she didn't want him to. She had told him she would as soon he died. But he knew she loved the fighting, she leaned into it with a rich old zest born of watching her own mother and father at it.

Still he dreamt of when it had been good with them, the first couple of years. The small jokes. When they'd gotten the dog, this one: what else to call a retriever but "Morris," short for Philip Morris, she always had called the dog Philip, but Hackett had always called him "Morris," as befit two men who were friends: a male game, covering tenderness with the gruffness.

Unreal City ahead finally, and down to the garage on Ludlow Street, where the rates were cheapest, and then the long, good walk north with the companion dog, to the block where his studio was. He walked a slightly different route every time, to see, to vary, to inhale the City. He was born on a farm upstate. He would never be used to the City.

And up on the boxy elevator to the wild skylit studio with its terrace leaning out toward space (the place where Morris could go to shit if he needed out too early or too late to be walked). The place cut sharp against lit buildings of the East Side in the Twenties. It suited. He was a romantic.

Hackett looked over the work on the easel and at the drafting-table. Still miles to go on this series. If the lines in the illustration went out, so, to represent the deaths in the story—he'd make it. And the Big Bread would clear this time. This time. Ah but Jesus, he was sore with trying to tough it through on this gig. He wanted out from under. Loved the work, but the striving was a mess. He turned on his lamps and went into it hard. Down the hall, his two assistants finished up on what he laid out. The days went into night. He kept the feel of that hot soupy stew, the crisp air of the woods and stream, and her soft flesh, the new chick; kept coming back to her and the idea of being with her, those few days. Imagine, she was in that house, the house that had been his shell, his place after he and Joan had split—the house where he had begun to heal. Funny. Good. How much that house had been to him. The kids came up to him sometimes and the long walks they had taken. And all the long hours alone. Safe haven and a sweeter reality.

III.

Four days had passed, and his phone rang. "I'm here," her voice said, sounding surer of herself than she felt. Her ride into the City had dropped her at 8th St., and she'd headed for the phone at once. Not even a coffee to cool out on. Because he had still been in her house, even after he left. His aura remaining.

"Good," he said. "Come on up. I'd like you to see the place."

It was late afternoon again. What seemed to be "their" time, the way this was "his" year. He was proud of his pad and of his work. It had something in common with hers. Working with color and texture. He introduced her to the assistants, who seemed not at all surprised. "Let's eat," he said to her. "How about Max's?"

They went to Max's. He'd known Mickey for years, at a reasonable remove (nothing more could be permitted: two Taureans, wise to each other). Mickey always wanted to know how Hackett was doing. He liked successful arty museum painters better than he liked Hackett, but Hackett spent some bread and some time at Max's, and Mickey thought he was a good guy. Mickey was far from being an artist but he had good snob mod taste in art, and kept work from his habitués around the place. Got something off being around the painters, the ones who were making it. Well, each of them liked to make money, in his own way.

Hackett was hungry, as usual, and as usual she was not: too excited with his presence, with being in the City again, and she wanted to make love with him, didn't like to make love after eating, eating took the edge off the radical hungers of the body. They both had a weird thing going about eating. Hackett ate only twice a day, out of some notion that this would control his weight, but what he did was to put away an enormous high-calorie breakfast at about 9 a.m., and a very substantial dinner at night; and the feeling he'd get of starving at about 1 o'clock every day gave him the illusion that he was burning up the food he'd eaten and was losing weight. Alexia, on the other hand, ate minute quantities of food all day long, often on into the night, as she'd done when she was pregnant. Felt comfortable digesting that way, and it gave her the illusion that she never ate very much, made her feel dainty in her own eyes. And it never messed up her feelings if she wanted to make it with someone. They both were being somewhat phony with themselves. But it was not an evil game. She ate a shrimp cocktail and crackers and a margarita, and he ate broiled shrimp, a baked potato, a huge salad, and two Tanqueray-and-tonics. Both feeling good about themselves.

He was careful to leave two of the shrimp and the shell of the baked potato and some salad—for a doggie-bag. People he knew, people he had done covers for, or illustrations for, passed the table and stopped. Fee Dorman stopped, and Donald Feltz, and he was caught in a Leo paw-hug from Fee and a too-long but tender Sag rap with Donald. He was glad that she could see his friends. A good dinner—quick bliss —she was or seemed to be comfortable and quiet, seemed to be listening to where he was at. He never thought about what would be next. Over coffee he showed her the problem with this new set of illustrations he was working on.

They left the place naturally and began the walk north to his place. She moved easily, following his lead, though he said nothing. When they got there, he watched her as she learned his areas. "A loner's pad," she said, not looking at him. Noting the cigaret butts in the ashtrays, the other old blanket on the floor at the foot of the bed, for Morris to sleep on. Morris, who was waiting nicely for the food he knew was there. The lighting was cool and unpretentious, functional, nothing was comfortable or uncomfortable. Lots of dust and roaches in the kitchen. Dust and pubic hairs on the bathroom floor and in the tub. "Someone comes to clean when I remember to call," he said, seeing it suddenly as it must look to her. Considering her clean, pretty house. And she was thinking, what did my house look like when he lived in it, did it look like this? And he thought, I hope she doesn't start emptying ashtrays.

"Coffee?" he offered. "If you're hungry any time, anything you see is yours." Opened the fridge for her to see. It was clean. It wasn't half as bad as it could have been. For a bachelor's fridge. His assistants kept a few things stocked: a quart of orange juice, half a loaf of whole wheat bread wrapped in plastic, a can of dog-food half empty and very old, can of olive oil, small jar of mayonnaise, a wrinkled lemon, a bottle of gin almost full, jar of Orange-Sliver marmalade, some country apples Hackett had brought back the time he had met her. The last of the half-bushel.

She made some fresh coffee while he walked Morris. She sensed he wanted her to wait, he needed the time to adjust to her presence. No milk in the fridge, so he said he would pick up a quart at the corner. He enjoyed the ritual of walking his dog. Two blocks away, he met the guy who owned the other Golden Retriever of that neighborhood and they stopped to talk. The dogs were from the same kennel. They had nothing else in common, the two men, but the dogs were a lot. They always stopped to compare notes. A good feeling. His neighborhood.

She poured herself a cup and made a setup for his return. He came in. Took his cup. She took a joint out of her purse. "I have some," he said, thinking about her always giving. "No, I know you do, but this is supposed to be dynamite. Gift from a very good friend. Someone who cares." "Okay, let's do it."

She lit it and he took it. They sat crosslegged on his double bed quietly and did the joint. He talked first, asking her what it was like in the country now. She sat curling her hair around her finger, thinking. Not quite responding. She was moving into a sensual mood. He said a few more things to her, watching her eyes, guessing at her legs under the woollen pants she was always wearing.

He got up and offered her a cotton bathrobe of his. Morris came in and curled up at the bottom of the bed on his blanket. This seemed enormously funny to both of them. Maybe to all three of them. He was watching them. Hackett got another bathrobe and put it on, his back to her, his buttocks firm toward her.

Turned and looked at her sitting there primly in

his bathrobe. Nobody had ever worn that robe till now but him. "I bet we could really get it on," he might have said, or/and listened to her saying it to him. Smiles and smiles.

She moved against his chest at an angle, softly and smoothly, and he accepted her fully. Took her mouth. His hand on her belly, soft skin, first through the robe, then under. Very high by now and getting to a good place. "Sweet body," she said, full of affection, smoothing his crisp-haired thigh and belly and then his prick. They moved into half-dark unaware hemispheres and were almost naked under the cotton blanket. He started to go in and lost his hard. She said nothing; held gently, then touched him, so, and it was good again and he went in strong and firm.

"Okay. Here," he did, and she went with it tightly. But they were in the City, with all its heavy and uptight, and they spun out. He came before she did, making a glorious series of noises next to her ear and into the nape of her neck, his wide waves also sound waves. "Okay," he said again to her, turned her and caused her to come around his body and hand, and then they slept. As he began to sleep, they both felt the muscles and nerves in his arms and legs twitch in that relax-out of the tension man of the City.

At 9 a.m. they were still stoned and happy as they put on their clothes. She was making an early bus back. They went to the corner for three plates of scrambled eggs and bacon. (One for Morris; "thanks, he's *had* dinner, you can take him to a movie," she thought, and told that familiar one to Hackett and he loved it.) The café owner knew Morris was a familiar and would never consider excluding him, health rules to the contrary and be damned. All heart.

She left for the bus. As she disappeared all of it crowded down on him again. He thought about her body and his, her soul and his, and he was worried. Worrying had become his usual province this year. Then he remembered her saying to him, "Why don't you love yourself?" at some time when they were together last night.

192

Signs of danger of impending disaster of panic. Suspend the moment of disbelief and its corollaries. This moment is now and forget the rest. Fuck the past. Forget the future. And all the honorary messages. No guessing allowed, no second-guessing allowed, but still everything is allowed. Allow yourself. Love yourself. *Anyone who says 'I don't know' when talking about himself is a liar.* The Biggest Con. And pan over to TIME's film about army wives of POWs, that one who said straight out she'd gotten horny as hell, hated war in general of course but specifically anything that kept her old man away from her for so long, but 'hadn't done anything she wouldn't be able to tell him about,' yeah, she had nothing bad to say about a society made her sit with legs crossed 2 years out of her pretty young life while her man went out to possibly get killt—Hackett choked on it. Caught in questions. The fake and the false of it. Where he was at. This man, extant in 'his' year. She had said, that wife, 'I'm tired of not really living,' read it to say 'fucking' which is what she meant, and he could say the same thing. He hadn't made it enough for years. In years. Goddam it to hell. Too much work to do and all the feelings.

He went back to his studio.

IV.

The highway spat out a tongue of dark toward the country town. On his way back there. A week later. They would play out another scene there but let it be on his terms this time. He felt she had had too much to do with the way it had gone down last time. He was bugged.

However, she felt it had all gone his way last time they were together, and was glad he was on his way up. "I may be up Saturday," he'd said, so she was looking for him to show up any time from Friday night on. Knowing a bit by now about his habits, his concepts of time.

Friday night came and went. On Saturday, she went into town to shop, wondering if he would be there when she got back to the house. Sure enough, he was sitting on the hillside halfway between the house and the stream.

He was not thinking about her. He was into his own head. For him, the place at that moment had its own old kind of peace, as if he still lived there alone. She was gone, the kids with her. The 'she' being just any she, right now. All the she-s.

But then there she was—this woman, this Alexia. And something animal in him came through the terror: he reached for her. But she did not move into his arms. Instead, reached and touched his cheek, and then a funny gesture: tapped his chest twice. What did that mean. She looked as if she knew. At that moment something went wrong between them. In the midst of the chill he said, "I stayed at Frank's last night." Knowing it would bother her. Glad that it would bother her, reach her. The way she did not reach for him. He had his anger.

Frank was on the other side of the town. An old friend, from the time Hackett had lived here. It had been easy to go to Frank's, cool out, hang loose, before going over to see Alexia. Somehow that was what he needed to do. He felt uptight about seeing her. It was good; okay, it was very good, with her. Maybe that was the trouble. But he didn't think about it. He just followed his feelings. Which told him to go to Frank's instead.

She turned from him, cold as stone and amazed at the weight of her feelings. He had been in this town, he had been at Frank's, and not even called? The stone turned in her gut. Not a jealousy, that was not it, she thought—a confusion, something felt wrong. But am I jealous, of what, of whom, of his having gone to Frank's? That's silly, that's not it. Why didn't he come here?

But she didn't ask. And he didn't say. She smelled his fear. His skin radiated it. He was filled with his fear, it had no other name, and they played animals, standing there in the hot sun, the cool air, each not speaking about what was happening.

"What the fuck," he said, one hand clenched. "I'm going to take a walk." He started away.

She turned silently and went into the house, carrying the groceries. He walked to the bottom of the ridge and stopped, his back to the house. He felt her eyes. She was frozen, too: at the door, yes, watching him, immobilized, trying to feel what to do, whether to act. Jesus, she was thinking, I hardly know this guy, what kind of dude *is* he, what am I feeling now about him. . . . It was too much. She didn't want to be filled with his fear, his feelings, her own responses. She said aloud, to the air in front of her, "I shouldn't give a fat rat's ass where he was last night, or where he goes now either for that matter. . . ."

Hackett watched Morris poking about in the brambly thicket, and he was looking into lined blankness himself. I don't want to see, he thought. I don't want to feel like this, I don't want to feel involved with her, I don't want goddam it to get fucking well involved with any broad now, to hell with all of them, who needs, who wants any of it!

:And between them, like the spinning of a tumbleweed on the moundy earth, all of the good feelings that had happened between them in the past couple of weeks. . . . She called down to him: "Want some company on that walk?" and he turned, relieved, the burden of the decision off him, turned to her quickly: "Sure, that would be great. Terrific." As she moved down the hill toward him he turned away again for a minute, looking at the familiar landscape, this place he knew and loved. And as she walked down, she touched and moved that tumbleweed with each step and moved it toward him.

On the walk, some of the time it was as it should be and as it had been for them. He would touch her, and then draw back. Some of the time he would seem to be pacing.

She was muted, trying to follow his lead. But he did not have a lead to offer. He was made of metal.

At one point, he challenged her understanding of astrology: "You know, I like most of the things you know, what you talk about, but when you start with that stuff, I just pull my horns in."

She had to laugh. "An apt phrase, my dear. . . . Well," she stalled, sorting it out, trying to appeal to his sense of the logical, "it's a reasonable system. Those trees, for instance. You can tell a birch from a beech, right? And an elm from a maple. First of all, by the leaves. And then all the other ways. That's what astrology's all about. Many kinds of people, with discernible differences, with individual classifiable traits." He did not like it. "It's still bullshit to me. A bunch of mystical mumbo-jumbo."

He felt her withdraw. And even he had to consider his choice of images.

V.

So now they knew each other's pads, and bodies, and some thoughts. And feelings. And the space between them had become familiar. They could have stopped seeing each other. But it would continue.

His children were not real to her; he would not let her meet them; he would not often talk about them. And he felt she gave too much, he felt encumbered by the occasional presence of her children.

The bodies could go well together. And they had this strange involvement with the house they each had lived in, that each had chosen from the many others. Not a coincidence.

He did not call her. A week went by. He was conscious of the time. She did not pick up the phone to him. Each of them thought of writing a note, and didn't. When she did call, finally, she was told by his assistant that Hackett was off to Canada on business for a week or so, was due back in a few days. He had left no message for her; had simply taken off. She had not expected this.

While she waited she went back into baking things and having people in for soup and bread and a smoke. Making the warmth into a form that would cover the waiting and the fear. There was something about him that demanded her allegiance.

The day after he was due back, she called, toward evening. "Hey," she said, softly, "it's me," playing that game. Being wary; frightened of his response either way. "Oh, yeah, babe!" he said, voice all bright. Not playing it straight. "Been expecting your call. You did tell Andy you'd call back, right? How you been? Everything okay?" She moved a step backward. He was moving fast. A funny feel.

"Yep. All's well. Temp hit zero last night. But probably that's nothing compared to Canada."

"Right. It was below zero up there. But it was a good trip."

"I'm glad . . ." She was caught. Didn't know what to say next. But then he, on an upbeat, jumped in with: "Boy, am I glad to get back. Hey, are you in the City now?"

And she could say, "No, but I have to come in tomorrow." Thinking fast, remembering she knew someone driving in tomorrow at about noon. She had had no plans to come in, no need to till now.

"Great, call me when you're finished with whatever you're doing. If it's before seven, we could have dinner. Okay?"

"Great. At the bar."

And so another dinner at Max's; her nibbling and his gorging. But afterward she was looking out for herself; she was tight; fond as he seemed to be, she knew what she knew about him. When they left Max's, he began to slouch into his easy, familiar walk uptown. But she asked him to walk her to the bus.

"I have to split for upstate. I've got a ride back."
Let him guess with whom. And so, of course, he reached for
her; it worked; the Tantalus game. He wasn't at all ruffled.
"I wish you could come stay with me tonight," he said, meaning it.

"That's the breaks," she said, delighted. It was good
for him, to have to reach. She took such joy in being tough.
If only to get there before he did. She felt good, leaving him
that way. She lost nothing by it, even gained, a certain stance.
Wow, he was thinking, what a weird change . . . But he did
feel lighter. She was doing a number; what the hell; he felt
good.

The next time she came into the City, she met him
for drinks at Max's at about five o' clock. He told her, at once,
gently holding her away from him, after her quick hello kiss,
"I have to talk to you. I think we ought to change the setup
we have going."

"Now what the hell . . ." she said, and their faces
were both masks.

"I think we should cut out the sex; just be—you
know—friends." (Revenge, she thought, because I wouldn't
make it with him last week, because I left. But of course he
wouldn't see it. He isn't into analysing things the way a
woman is.) And (She's too pushy, he thought, thinks she can
run the show, well, that's one way to be sure she isn't under
my skin.) "Well," she said, "Isn't that a gas," and then, giving
it the light touch, "Can we have a drink anyhow?"

He giggled. It had gone too easily. He was relaxed.
He felt in control. Had a drink, then two, while she was still
drinking her first. Then they both had another one. Fee came
by and bought them one of his specials, a "Dorfish," which
was a lot stronger than it tasted. Tony came past and stopped
to rap, and so did Ish. And Donald. And it was just past time
for the last bus back. She was cool, but didn't show it. He was
rattled. So, in a spaced-out, fairly drunken repetition of the
other times, they left Max's. He asked her to call friends who

lived nearby. She refused; it was too late. He acknowledged this. Neither of them could hold liquor gracefully.

Walking: she said very little. He began everything. Started every topic. He was very out-loose, she was very pissed off. He was keeping it his game all the way.

Then they were up in his pad. She went into the bedroom and stretched out, fully dressed, across the bed. Carefully on "her" side of it.

He stopped, as she had planned him to do. "You gonna sleep with all your threads on?" "Why not," she said, in what she hoped was a soft, sleepy, I-don't-care voice.

"Don't be silly," he said. "You don't have to be uncomfortable. Here's the robe." "Oh, hey, listen, man," she said, noting that it was *the* robe, not *your* or *my*. "Very cool. Very thoughtful." She was smirking into the semi-dark, the room that was again dusty and hairy.

He was feeling sorry for her. A nice chick really, and just now she looked sort of lost. After all, they had gotten sort of close. The first time she had come to this place, he had told her about himself. His past. He felt drunk and he didn't like it. He didn't feel in control. There was no control.

That he was all about walking, taking long walks, city or country, also meant he was all about walking away from. He knew that, without wanting to give it a name. "Now" became a safe "then" as soon as a step away from it was taken. Sometimes it seemed to him that each of his years since adolescence was like a blister that grew on his heel and broke. As when learning to hike: too fast, too much. And somehow the wrong shoes. The mistakes. He was still hating himself for them. Excoriation. They were therefore still happening to him.

And she, free, surly, competitive, enjoyed making comparisons, just to see if he would begin to realize what he was putting down on his own scene. Felt bigger by standing on other people's faults. . . . She was lying down now, and was standing taller than he. Knew he was in trouble. "These is troubled times we live in," she said softly, snickering and thinking herself Gudrun again.

For all the good that'll do, she thought, hot for him, lying cool across his bed in his, "her" bathrobe, on "her" side of his bed, waiting to see what his next move might be. She felt very drunk and very alone. The Women are not Lib, she thought. And I could be more honest with him. Well, he's probably going to reach; he's really programmed for it. . . .

He did, because they were both programmed for it, each by the other. Up on the high of not having been honest, not having declared the next move aloud. The subtle way he caused his thigh to touch her thigh and then averted but too slowly. Then the way she saw to it her scent reached him, and the wave of her arm as she "relaxed into a yawn" while he "got comfortable" while knowing she would be conscious of his torso at her ribs. Yeah—both hungry and both playing nature against the games. Something lush in making believe it wasn't going to happen when sure as hell it would, it was. There went the edges of the robes apart, a little offhand gesture, a hand that wasn't actually reaching but did brush sex flesh near it, and the bodies slid together, the mouths, good as they should be without the defenses, the thinkings, the angularities: all of it swung out right. They made it, the man and the woman, good, tough, sweet, with a reverence, without ideas, without hangs, and they made it together, and slept.

By morning's light he was cool again, today was not last night, the controls were on, "no comment" in effect; she was cool again, satisfied that he had broken his word to himself, been betrayed in his false rules. She left at once, not expecting anything further from him. And not getting anything. A void. No goodies.

VI.

All of his up was turning into a down. He thought he'd feel better by cutting back to the original setup—forgetting it wasn't cooled out originally, it had been warm and physical almost at once—he saw himself as doing better alone, in a kind of purity; he thought of it as Clarity again and got caught in a little shudder. . . . Well, to get where he had to go, he had to go it alone, at least for now, he wanted to; he felt threatened by the ease with which he melted into that house, that woman's scene. Took away from his alone godliness. If he couldn't do the thing right by being alone on some mountaintop, he could at least be gutsy enough not to give in to needing a woman again (only get burnt again), and so it went, around and around in his head.

In the middle of his big fat city, he would yearn for the openness—not just of that airy town, but of the easy way of the house she was in. Damn her, he thought, if only she could pull back, give less. Be less able. She never seemed like she needed him.—But when she did pull back, he felt it, and wound up feeling fear of getting burnt again, and hated himself. For following that part of his nature.

Music playing, "He ain't heaaaavy, he's mah bruuuther . . ." all along his roads, every time he rode the highway going anywhere, same song. The question being, was he his own brother, was he being good to himself. What was it she had said a while back, about his not loving himself enough? There was a numbness and a witlessness, a rhapsodic core of deathliness circled within him, a slow move contra life that had at its core no motion.

He had come so many miles since he had studied anything that interested or involved his intellect. Made him feel voracious. And even when he was in school it had had nothing to do with his own idea of himself. Always with someone else's ideas of who he could be, what he could do with his life. Only in this last couple of years had he begun to discover his own power as a man, his own power over his own life: the choices . . .

Now, he thought he wanted to help himself, and to help her, to reach out and give them both a bigger chunk of the world. Now, when it could all open out!—and it was all turning into control, that shaper of motions which is made of fear. . . .

Well, he thought now, making a safe jump, a jump more toward the dark blue sky and its nonboundaries than toward the real earth or real flesh on it, maybe he would just go all out for more help for himself. Just take, as long as she was so damn good at giving all the time. Someone had once told him to listen carefully to the first strong statement the other person made at the beginning of a sexual relationship —about how the thing was to go, or about what was wanted or needed—and then, *to read it backward.* ("I want to take care of you," would, for example, really read: "I want you to take care of me.")

So that now Hackett was playing around with this. Maybe, then, when he said over and over to her, "You give too much," he had really been saying, "You're goddam well not giving me enough—at least not of what I really need or want." And what, then, had she been really saying to him? He tried to think. What had she repeated, or said strongly, those first couple of times? Jesus, he couldn't remember one thing. Not one strong or memorable thing. To pin her down with.

That image. And he grew large at his groin, thinking about fucking with her. He had begun, before her, to get so far from his own body. It had all moved up into his head, away from his own animalness. Especially when he'd gotten into drinking, a while back. The tight way he was treating Morris was the way he treated himself. Certain loving indulgences, but withal an artificial life, stilted and limited and full of the pain of the cities. Sharp edges. There was more of the irritation lately, and it was not working through . . . just the gestures . . . maybe he did not want her to help him.

He was waking up alone wearing his own hair shirt; desperate with the named and nameless wantings. When he had been a medical illustrator, he had wanted to be a doctor. And now that he was a fiction illustrator, he wanted to be a writer or a painter. He wanted out. He was afraid of being free; he was afraid of being ripped off, of being fucked-over, of being had; day by day, while he worked hard and thought too much . . . tight into uptight . . .

She was due to meet him tonight, here at the studio. He would not face thinking about it any more. At four o'clock he got a call from someone who'd just hit town and had to see him about one of his jobs, an important one. "Okay, I'll be over right away." He would meet the man instead. When she called him, he would have his assistant tell her he was not able to meet her.

"Let me talk to him anyway, if he's still there," she said, and the assistant, not knowing better, put the call through. When he told her, she said, "Oh. Well. You going to be with him long?"

"Well, dinner and some," he said. "I *am* sorry, but this just came up."

"Listen, I have a few things I can do till later. How about ten o'clock, at Max's?"

He didn't fight her. "Okay. Ten." He was not willing, but he couldn't figure out any way to say no. He had to face her. See how he felt. It was confused, as is. And after a good dinner with Sam Brody, maybe he'd feel differently.

VII.

She had no image of his soul now. Had spent the last three days considering: he had been warm toward her, he was possible, he had some tenderness going. She would try for it. The big gamble. Her up mood leaned toward seeing him. She felt high, very out-loose, enjoying riffing out on the bus coming into the city. The phone call was just three minutes after she'd gotten off the bus—as usual. After she hung up, she mumbled softly, "Not to be believed," and sat down with some coffee to plan what she would do with her time until

10 p.m. (some five hours or more from then). She wanted to swing with him, let it all go with its own motion, be easy. . . .

She visited someone, then fell by St. Adrian's, then took a cab to Max's. He was not at the bar. She ordered a Bloody Mary for the first nourishment of the day, and savoured it, enjoying the novelty of being alone at that bar. Nodded to the few she knew through him. It was good being in the center of a cluster of people she didn't know and didn't want to know, with the security of knowing Hackett would arrive in a minute or so. He would be here soon; he was never late. Casual, but never late. Lately she felt how Hackett was hurting, the conflict he was in. But here—with the lights, the music, the little high she always got from this scene, look of the men's eyes on her, rattle of the city talk, being away from the kids, the realities of her life—ah, to hell with his or anyone else's pain, she was away from her own pain and worries for now.

When she ordered the second Mary he was almost twenty minutes late. What could she do. Just groove in behind the music some more, talk to the guy standing next to her, and get further into the neat high feelings where she didn't care if he showed or not. But there was the clock and the door.

A long time later, he walked in, cool, almost an hour late. Walked in looking very beautiful and into himself, but without his aura. Averted his eyes until he was right next to her. He seemed thickly set into his body, the shoulders narrowed to fit through the crowd. She stared at him, very direct. He hated it. It felt like full circle. But he couldn't get the hell away or out, and didn't really want to, at least not just yet. "Hackett," she said, not feeling brave or like challenging him. "Hi," he said. And that was all. Ordered a drink for himself. Her glass was full. Paid for her three and for his. The room was very crowded. That saved him.

"Listen, Hackett," she began, not knowing what she would say next.

"Tough day," he said, effectively shutting her off. He was thinking about the conversation he'd just had with Sam, and about how he'd have to spend tomorrow afternoon taking his kids to the zoo for the ninth time or something like that, so their mother could get her hair set and all that shit. He was not looking at the woman next to him.

She began to curl around her own insides, tasting fear. "What are your plans?" he asked her, without affection. "I thought I'd take the early bus back tomorrow," she said, smiling up at him, taking the big risk. She would pretend she felt close to him. She did not understand what was happening. The atmosphere between them was violated.

"Oh. Well, listen. I brought with me this stuff I was discussing with the guy I had dinner with, you know, the one from Chicago I told you about, and I have to do a rough for him of the new layout by ten tomorrow. I'll probably work on it all night, what the hell . . ."

"Well, listen," she said, trusting her own femaleness, "don't worry, I'll just hang in, I don't take up so much room." Thinking of the way it had gone a week ago, when he'd said he didn't want her, and he had turned to her and she to him, and it had been good . . .

"Yeah, well, okay. But I have to get this work out." He was annoyed. He had no name for it.

"You said it, and I heard it. Yes *sir*."

Jesus, would he ever begin to relax? In the whole world, there had never been such uptight vibes. He wasn't about to lean with her. At the end of his second drink, he said, "Let's go." Not much else to say between them, there or on that famous long walk up to his place. She was remembering some beautiful book she had read, long ago, about this place, "A Walker in the City" it might have been, written by some sensitive oriental about how New York looked, and illustrated with these great soft inky drawings in that Eastern way of seeing this purely Western city; she was trying to capture some of the romance of seeing the City that way, but the stiffness of Hackett's stride next to her, his silence, the caution of his joints, how he was on liquor, who he was on tension—he was an eraser of her mood; she thought of Robbe-Grillet and gave a laugh as they crossed the street, so that he just stared down at her, or was it out at her, and she just ignored him. But there was still some possibility.

The minute after they got to his studio he opened the fat black zippered folio and lit the lamps around his work area. She shrugged, picked up a book, sat down in a chair, started to read, and started to fall asleep.

"I'm going to be a long while," he said, "why don't you just get some sleep, babe." ("Not unkindly," she thought, wryly, half-asleep.)

She walked into the bedroom. It was empty. She was very drunk and hating it. Sat on the edge of the bed. Ah, where were the mates of yesterday . . . the blessed warm feet of whoever . . . she was remembering, finally, her ex, Ron, and the five years they had, good things often, the kids, there was a lot to be said for what they had, but then he was weak, in spite of being such a beautiful cat, weak in the stance of his pelvis; she had thought even then that he was definitely AC/DC, not to joke about, something Ron couldn't begin to face even now, and the sadness of having to be 'closet' anything, instead of straight-out whatever . . .

She undressed, slowly, alone, standing with cold feet on the blanket on the floor at the foot of the bed (Morris was inside, of course, with Hackett), and slid into the bed, alone, and for the first time noticed that there was only one blanket on the bed and that this room was chilly; not chilly, it was goddam ice cold—she kept her shirt on. None of this his-bathrobe jazz this time.

She heard the rustle of his papers. She stretched out long and lean on her belly, face away from the room where he was working, on the weird off chance that if you don't look, the wish will happen . . . She was dizzy with the drinks and immediately felt nauseous, but fell asleep in spite

of it. Didn't know she had fallen asleep until she woke. Cold.
Cold. Into a terrible cold, dark room. He must have turned
the light out. Alone in the cold dark bed. Slight noise of his
motions in the other room; feeling of the ghost of dreams
hanging like a pall, her own aura gone flat and cold; where
was she, a country called *Alone*, separate from her husband,
her parents, her children, her lover; and then, mercifully, she
fell asleep again.

And into a wild cold dream. Hackett was an eraser.
A soft one, like Oldenburg's. He was one big soft eraser, moving along inside a picture that showed their lovemaking, and
erasing it. Then he was himself, pale and removed and tall,
and the eraser was his prick, coming crisply from out of his
fly, looking very reasonable and alive, but made of something
like dry ice, and his come clouded the room with a vapor that
she knew would be as dangerous to the touch as dry ice.

And then her ex-old-man was there, too warm, too
sweet, too much, but gone, long gone; the kind of warm cloying that she had had to run from in order to feel the realities.
But the trouble was that neither Ron nor Hackett saw her,
and she had no means to make them see her, she was in the
same room with them but they did not talk to her, notice her;
and she was more alone in that kind of coldness, that tough
mist, that isolation of their terrible warmth (the one asexual,
the other hypocritically sexual) than she had ever been in her
awake life; O dear God what was this . . .

She bolted awake again, into the dark of a strange
room which was freezing cold, not her own pad's familiar
smell but an alien place, woke into crying without realizing
it, without being able to stop it, without knowing why, into
deep racked sobs—her flesh almost naked to the cold air, no
warmth around her body or beneath it where she had lain, no
warmth in the room, no light.

She walked blinded down the long corridor toward
where she knew Hackett's workroom was, feeling her way, sobbing, into the silence; the rooms were farther apart in the

darkness, the corridor was many aching miles long—Jesus, how she needed the comfort of another human's real flesh— came then to where he had opened the daybed in his studio, and was asleep on it, under one blanket, his portfolio next to the couch, papers issuing from it, his face peaceful and off to itself. Stood staring down at him, in the dull light of the fire-exit bulb at the end of that room. Morris was there, curled on bare floor at Hackett's feet.

She was still sobbing, not understanding, still in the midst of the nightmare of the Big Freeze, of which he was so much a part. She did not think of touching him or of reaching out.

He woke, or started: "Jesus, kid, what the fuck *is* it?"—coming out of his own world of nightmares of too warm and too cold. His own horror shows.

"Oh, Hackett, the dream . . . so *cold,* so terribly alone—I felt—I feel—so terribly alone—I don't know—so—"

"Well, don't we *all,*" he said, with a knifelike sar- castic slowness. So muddy, into the room; trying to be so bright and curt. The room filled with his anger. She stared.

"Hackett. Listen. A little *humanity,* for God's sake. A little warmth. I mean, Jesus, Hackett, we're both warm *bodies,* for God's sake, aren't we? Or what are you really made of?"

"I, for one, dearie, am made of extreme fatigue and the absolute knowledge"—he glanced over at the clock on his worktable—"that in just two hours, I shall have to face a fuller-than-usual work day, and I have been up most of this goddam *night* already." "I *know,* but—"

"NO buts," he said, quite loudly to her, "get some sleep, bitch," he said, baleful, all the irritation of the world in his voice. He hated her clutching at him. Felt as if she were taking his blood.

And still she had to reach out, as if toward the sun, wanting what he could not give her; as if toward another human with whom she had been close; as if any of this could

save either of their souls, as if tenderness could solve it all . . .
She went back into the bedroom and started to bring in the
one blanket from that bed, thinking that she might at least
simply lie on that desolate daybed with or even near Hackett,
who was a human man though not a source of heat or light.

"*Don't* touch that blanket," he hollered sharply out
to her. And then she was forced to notice it was an electric
blanket, connected by its umbilicus to the wall of the room
and thence to the City itself. A place where she was, after all,
a stranger and a visitor. She dropped the blanket.

Lost. She went back to the other room. No light,
no heat, Hackett already asleep again, the City asleep, nowhere to go, nothing to do, she got onto the bed, lay near but
not touching the man, there was no warmth coming from him,
she was only an inch from his feet but knew them as objects
rather than flesh; all of his male aura was cooled out and
shut off and he was as if plastic, finally.

He was as if unable to be affected by his surroundings now; this, then, would be the texture of "his" age, "his"
year, his ideal way of being, the core for which he had lived
till now, the year which would decide the shape and direction
of the rest of his life. This minute, then. In his dream, at this
moment, he had great pride, and some wisdom; he was showing his children how to fish, they were standing on an island
situated in a river where they had often fished together, an
island they had named after him, it was always "Hackett's
Island," though the children thought of it as "Hacketts' Island,"
as if it were also named for them, their last name; and the
children fished up the live laughing body of their mother, and
showed it to him, and then they were all laughing together in
the sunlight, at the river, the logically impotent ex-wife and
the freed ex-husband and their mutual blue-eyed permanently-
waved children, all at the banks of an island named with their
own name. Of course, in the dream the occurrence was not a
dream but was the reality, so in the dream Hackett saw nothing unusual in using pot joints for bait, or for the kids' fishing

out another woman from the water, and still another, and the other women had no faces, but did laugh as well. All the companionable laughter, and nobody even looked waterlogged. The children of the other women had no faces. But they could giggle. At that point it had turned into a nightmare. Sun under a cloud. Hackett woke, turned to find Alexia next to him, threw some of the blanket over her. They slept.

In the morning, Alexia woke before Hackett and dressed silently. He woke and went about his usual routine, which always calmed him. He asked her if she wanted some cereal, though he knew by now that she only took coffee until later in the day. She refused politely, as if to a stranger. They took a silent walk to the crosstown bus, Morris with them, they not with each other, and she boarded the bus alone, he having handed her the change. She would move toward Port Authority and would return home. He watched her leave and forgot her face. She watched him as he stood there with his dog, and forgot his face. Except in later dreams.

1971

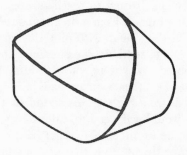

THE CHALLENGE

PO | Splitting Apart
. . . The inferior, dark forces overcome what is superior and strong, not by direct means, but by undermining it gradually and imperceptibly, so that it finally collapses. . . .

I.

He was drawn to her always, heavily and deeply, but he was a furious man, and so often the rage won out: the rage at her, at himself, at how his world was moving. For her part, she was attracted to him, even after all their time together. And repelled by him: she was afraid of him and of his holds on her—more than he knew. When he entered their house, where she lay asleep, she woke, judging the sound of his step, but did not show him she had wakened, did not go to him. Although often she wanted to reach through to him . . . Waking, she realized it was from a dream about him: she had been screaming at the woman with him, that strange girl with the familiar face, long red hair, she screamed and beat at the girl, flailing, sobbing, 'Why were you with him,' hideously angry, miserable that the other woman had lain with him . . . usually, no words from her man, he would stand off to one side, and then she would wake crying, full of fury; then, if he were near her bed, he would scoff, 'Forget it, this is the reality, isn't it, I'm here with *you*,' but that did not bring her out of it, she was not bought off, the bitterness felt natural to her . . .

He would not follow any of the available ways through to her. He moved about, most of the time lately, in his animal fury, not in the pleasure of being a man on earth, but the burden, his step too heavy and sullen, his smell too thick for her. In the woods, he could walk without sound; in their house, his step was insistent and brutal. And, of course, to her, as identifiable as his face: all of his nature and moods evident in that walk. She lay there, sometimes, some mornings, this night, listening to him as he moved through his familiar rituals: the coffee, the bathroom, the match lit, the door to his workroom as it was set well apart from her, the move toward sitting on the edge of that bed in there, so far from their bed-couch . . . the door, placing a muteness between them, and then, sometimes, the sound of his typewriter . . .

She was a richly fleshed, dark, large woman, while he was finely wrought, tall, light-boned, light-skinned, light-haired. Even so, these days he trod more heavily than she. There was no flesh around his Achilles'-tendon like a heavy fabric. When he was resentful of her, or of his world, he would stop bathing. His body-smells would accrue until they became a vicious cape that he swung violently around him. His usual body-smell was pleasing to her (they were both loving toward the body's natural liquids). But she could not abide his dreadful unshod feet when he had not bathed for a week. And his clothing bore the unpleasantness further. So then she would refuse to launder his clothing. So he would take to wearing his trousers without underpants. Then she would stop cooking for him. And then a pause, for half a day or half an hour. Each would sulk without snarling. Then the snarl would come, then the howling, they would hurtle at each other, in some roomful of misery, unable to get it said, repeating phrases, trying to cut out the rage with the broken glass each held; and then it would stop, finally, both exhausted, nothing resolved, and go over into a deep, unbreachable silence.

     He would get his own food, these days. Ate intentionally of the unnourishing, the oversweet, because he knew this would irritate her further. She kept good food there, knowing that he spent so much energy; he looked as if he were working hard, not the true energy of the labourer, but the bright spurts of useless frantic motion, looking busy, seeming involved, so as to expend his anger. It was what he needed to do. So she tried to stock up on high-protein foods, because he was always tired. ("How are you?" "Tired." "Yes, I know, but besides that?" was how it went.) And when he was into one stage of their quarrel, he would help himself to jam sandwiches, would buy and bring in candy-bars, ignoring the eggs, cheese, meats she brought in.

     At these times he would leave the sweets bottles out and open, with flies and ants collecting at their rims; the candy-wrappers, the empty beer-cans, bread-crusts would mix in a detritus of resentment around the kitchen. And the livingroom, where they slept when they were loving. Packages of supplies he had unwrapped and never put away. Burnt matches dropped where they were struck. And his used clothing everywhere, dark with a week's soil . . . carrying the despair further, making it visible. His caring about his leavings would add to his weight; he wanted to be as light as possible now. He had, of course, been fat, as a child; chubby, as a young man. Yet he did delight in her Rubens-like richness of flesh, and told her so, when he could. She was all ivory, soft, though she went angular and rigid when they fought. She was a cellist, he, a writer. Seeing her with her cello, he had wanted her, years ago; she was of a piece with its fine curves, its richness and tone. They had been together from the day they had met, some several aeons long gone; he was determined and possessive. But by now only two valences were left to them.

It was more than sex held them together. They were bound by their arts, and their arguments, and by their hunger for each other. They wanted to own each other, and at times they seemed to. It was unthinkable to either that they ever part—but for different reasons. He had to own her; he did not, had never had this feeling for another woman (perhaps this was part of the reason for the children). And she—wanted to possess his soul; a sort of domination, her insistence that she knew the best way to live the life. She would go blind with love and lust at the sight of him, and they had been together for a long while . . . it was always new. Perhaps the fighting served the purpose of renewing them. Sometimes they would swing wildly, bloodily, into lovemaking, mixing the two valences. He was adamant in his feeling for his own life, and it had nothing to do with what any woman thought.

They were both conservative, really, but each responded to the same stimulus in different ways. Her fabrics and manners were silky, and he could be so graceful socially. She hated blue, and he favored blue. And each responded to different words of the common language. He could not stand the word "suppose," which seemed to upset his precarious balance of emotion. Things had to be definite. He sought precision. She could not stand the word "never," since her temperament had to believe that everything is possible. Their fantasies were different each from each. He told her, "I would rather lose any sense but that of sight," and wept as he thought of the possibility. (If *he* did the supposing, it was all right.) She valued all the senses equally, but, in her tension, could not imagine living without being able to make music. She would have thought he'd have chosen "being able to write," but she did not understand that he kept that away from his most vulnerable concepts. He was Scorpio, of earth; she was Taurus, also of earth, but her way was slow, deliberate, richly thick, while his was quick, angular, uncontemplated, with a fine striking-power for mobility. But the motions of each were within a narrow band: conservative. Within which she was content; against which he strove. She would not go to Morocco or Tangier; he dreamed of these places. She would prefer the elegant, civilised cities of Europe. He came from a solid Republican family which had come generations ago from Wales and France and England; he took pride in the lineage-chart his mother had had drawn up. It traced his blood back to Welsh statesmen and English minor royalty. His mother collected Early American chairs. She, his wife, was the child of first-generation Armenian immigrants.

As a second son, he resembled his father, and he feared he would be less of a man, less of a writer, than his father. The father had been a successful, well-known novelist. Harry had had the grace to change his name, slightly, in trying to make his own reputation. This man, this son of that father, was a hunchback; he would have been over six feet tall were it not for this malformation; as it was, he stood only a bit less. He moved without consciousness of his defect. Without self-consciousness. His woman (whom we have met before) had bucked teeth, teeth that were also very large in proportion to her other features. Really a flaw in her otherwise luxuriously regular face. I describe these "flaws" of appearance to you at this point only that you may notice how impertinent, how irrelevant such usually over-magnified details can be. For the story, it is also important to tell you that the woman, of Armenian lineage, had long, thick, dark body-hair, abundant, and a line of fine, dark hair across her upper lip . . . and that the man had never been circumcised. Her abundant body-hair acted as cilia of pleasure between them, for both of them, in their lovemaking; and since he was uncircumcised, she feared his moody weeks of non-bathing, afraid of his taking her unthinkingly and infecting her body, as had happened once. He seemed not to care . . .

Watching him, her good feelings for him would start in her womb and all of her furred areas. She would watch him as he slept or as he sat across a room talking to someone else. The power of her feeling for him would surge through her body, part of it tenderness, part lust; she could not have described it except in terms of music . . . it was akin to a Chopin nocturne, deep and rich, or a certain section often unnoticed in the Trout Quintet, or *that* passage of the violin in the Wieniawski concerto. . . . They were so different, he and she. He moved solitary and crisp; she was gregarious, and devoted to sensing him. They did not resemble other couples near them, but resembled all of the other couples as well . . . everyone near them was involved in unexplainable, unreasonable arguments, in subverted violence toward each other . . . many couples were parting . . . a frazzled rope . . . or more like a cello-string going: a crackle, but with a sharp, animal-like whine, as a cry of pain . . . so many of their friends. Over in a second, but resonating, the vibration carrying, widening, touching the nearby lives with fear and sadness . . .

When it was good between them, when they were together and loving, his writing would go well. All of it would move. He could enter it—as he entered her—with a gusto and a quickness. And his entering her and fulfilling her would give her impetus: would cause a quickening of her motions, her will, she could move out afterward into her music, joyously. But then they would wrench apart or slip apart. She might reach out lovingly to him and he (caught in what corner of his mind) would not respond, or would pull back, ab-

stracted and wooden beneath her hand, and she would pull
away as if burnt by his coldness. And they would enter the
cold/hot desert. Still wet with their fluids of loving, they
would say the words that would dry them, and would become
distorted; they would become deprived of each other's joyful
lubrications. The life-givers. They would part while their
liquids were still wet on the bodies. Half an hour later, she
would notice one of his curled blond hairs on her skin, and
she would wonder how they had moved apart so fast, from
that into this.

He was angry right out of his dreams: he would
wake, realizing he had had one of his few dreams (she dreamed
often, every detail real; he said he envied her the experience
and the recall) and a-sweat with the dream-ordeal: his mother
had sent him out into the snow again, to school, after he had
protested he was sick, after the thermometer proved him right.
He felt the high fever again in the dream. She had not
wanted him at home underfoot. The parents had been stoics,
puritans, the father too busy always to leave his typewriter to
be with his boys . . . all those terrible, lonely structures he
had had to learn, to tolerate, until now he was wary of all
structures; they seemed strictures to him; he would push and
lunge at the simplest conventions as if they were bars he had
to bend in order to prove himself his own man. He was always sorting out. The sorting was a solitary process for him.
It forbade acknowledging the people around him; he shut out
his family. He needed always to be testing, whether they
would all be there at the end of whichever period of solitude,
whether she would still love him, whether he could achieve
his goal of the moment, his project of the moment.

This process interested her. She did not need to
test it in that way, did not need much solitude. She was utterly sure of herself, of whatever she was involved with at the
moment. Each involvement was total. She never fell asleep
angry, but always woke angry, and sorted things out for the
first half-hour; Harry took much longer, and needed to be

alone then. These days she was involved in hatha yoga. She could find one answer after another for the reasons, for The Cure, for the way through it all, one rationale after another, one god after another, each satisfying until it disappointed, and another available just after that. He had no patience with her utter confidence in this or that method or doctor or philosophy. Especially after watching the denouement of each in turn. She ran no testing; there was total belief in each device, in its time. But then there was her need to proselytize, to try to involve him in her current concept of how their lives could be better.

One of her constants was her deep need for him, for his involvement with her, for his approval, and he knew this and used this to bind them. And she needed the children. She would meet with friends once a week to play chamber music. She gave and took lessons. Took care of the house. She would play at home, softly, firmly, at odd hours, between the chores, in no particular pattern . . . she kept herself lovely, and cooked, and built on her slow defiance of him. He was, after all, not much interested in her kind of music. While, for her, it was breath.

As they move now wordless and sullen through their mutual rooms. Immured. Near the two children, both of whom have normal backs and straight even teeth. Can one visualize the areas behind the shut doors. The rhythms of their lovemaking. Though the life of them is silent at this moment, their live cells are wreaking the natural methods of carnal magic. On one particular angry night a month ago, she told him to get the hell out, and he went. But he returned, and she wanted him to return. This was their political affiliation. At some point, when he was fifty-five and she was close to fifty, they would kill each other, leaving a small amount of sincere affection and a large amount of life insurance to the children. Who had not known either of them well. Or they would outlive the children, who would have been killed in other wars. Or the children will have, despite genetics, married their logical mates, quietly but not well, and would need any money left to them. The late money.

II.

"I'm so *cold*," she said into the phone. "You sure are," he said. "But, Harry, you have no idea what it's *like* here, when you left there was still some heat left in the house, even though the furnace was off, and I built a fire, but it doesn't begin to . . ." "Suffer," he said, "or, better yet, hang tight and get it off bitching about it, or, better still, don't call me here. I've got enough on my mind, damn it. Did you have to call me here?" He was at his agent's office, in the City. "Oh, Harry, you are really being such a drag, you just don't give a damn that the kids and I are freezing here, Jesus, you have no idea what it is to have to put up with . . .' "Yeah," he snarled, "put up but never put out. Do you." "Very *funny*, Harry. And with Blartzin sitting there taking it all in. *Very* cute," she snarled, loving him. "You think he doesn't know what the score is? You crazy bitch. I know what, use some of that exquisite fat of yours to keep yourself warm till I just finish up business and toddle on home . . . you know, if you were rendered down, Chubby, like slab pork, there'd be enough to light all the lamps of goddam China. So how come you're complaining?" "I never met anyone like you," she said, lamely. She was well-paid. "And you're not about to," he said. "Lucky me," she said, smiling into the phone. "Imagine two like you . . ."

She hung up on him. Her mouth full of hard, dry bread-crusts. Ah, their cozy house, their house in the country . . . early today, he had left for the City to confer with his agent about the new novel. He was worried about the meeting, so he began to needle her. He said he was fed up with what he called her "Armenianness; all that ethnic shit," he spoofed her about all the *-ian* endings and all the lamb cookery and left quickly, leaving her aching. He knew the furnace was broken; he left anyway. He was involved with the game of goading her. Sunday, tomorrow, nobody could come to fix it, and she was waiting for him to come home, for him to fix it.

She ran from his sarcasm. The children were out of the house; she was blessedly alone. She picked up the cello and played a bit, but it could not hold her. In the middle of a passage, she ran out, left a note in case the children should return, took her car, and rode, alone, slowly and then fast, along the roads back of their house, watching the leaves, feeling the air, the season turning. Autumn. Turning, turning . . . thinking about his metabolism and hers. How different they were; he was so much himself, sharp and guarded, the attack, the defense . . . she touched her underarm hair lovingly with her left hand; the other hand managed the steering. When would he learn to drive with ease. Live with ease. That terrible tension he had to maintain. She shifted her throbbing Taurean weight on the seat. Her body, her thighs, her cunt were warm and pulsating (for him? for herself? she never could be sure). God help me if it rains tonight, she thought. The kids will have to be indoors and they might pick our own house. It's so cold, so damned cold. She spun along the road, loving herself, her way of being. She was gifted; she loved her own teeth . . .

The road was full of her music. What if each color had a note. Fine music, unbounded and unshaped. Such good, such fine music. She was tired of listening to his criticism of her music. Or his endless chatter when he told her about what he was working on now. Which was only noisy in comparison to his huge silences. But when would he be back. She did miss him.—For his part, in that other part of his world, he was still talking to his agent. Plans. "I am *not* interested in following your line with it, I am *not* concerned with your idea of perfect structuring," he was saying, "even though you think . . ." So the agent became annoyed. "I'm *simply* telling you that it won't *sell* this way, your way," he said, slowly, using sarcasm the way his client did, so as to be sure to reach him. He knew his clients well, or didn't take them on. They would earn for him. He would pick the ones who were conservative enough, outré enough, flexible enough, sensible enough . . . sensible enough . . . but then there were the types like Harry, who was good and who knew it, knew it too much, fought him hard; it was like landing a marlin . . .

"You can go to hell," Harry was saying, "I won't change it." "Wellll, we *could* try it your way, but I bet you my fee it doesn't sell." "How about that. You're on. How long you going to give it? But you'd better try with it, and I better *know* you're trying for it, you son of a bitch, at least as much as if I'd done it your way . . ." "Trusting soul, aren't you. How about two months. That fair enough?" "Yeah. Damn right. I bet it runs away within the first two weeks. This way. The way I wrote it." "Okay. Maybe you'll learn a lesson this time, Harry, not to be so sure of yourself, you know, you don't know everything, and this is my business . . ." "It's *my* business, goddam your ass, Blatzev, and don't you forget it, old buddy. I *know* what I did here. I know how this book's supposed to work, and it *does* work and it *will* work. Why are you sweating it? Why are you raising such a goddam stink? Swing *with* me, damn you, I *need* you behind me with this one! All you guys get your nuts off playing God with what other people know how to make, when what we really need is somebody who understands and knows enough to stand off and let the thing swing out of its own motion . . ." "All *right*, Harry, I said I'd give it two months, now let's have a drink . . ."

The trip home took less time than usual. On the trip he considered possible alternatives for handling the middle section. Maybe the damned fool was right. Could he be right. If he . . . If. He went through the war scene at the

beginning of the fifth chapter instead. If he turned that into
. . . If. If his wife would lay him, for God's sake. If after that
she would keep the kids out of the way when he tried to re-
work that chapter . . . after she laid him, if she laid him
. . . If. And then he ran out of gas. Near the clockmaker's
house (you know the one, Arthur Knapp's place, the yellow
house). Tarpaulin blowing bleakly over the woodpile, no
lights, nobody at home; here he was, on a road he knew well,
on the way to his own house, not five miles away, and out of
goddamn gas; and no lights, nobody home in the only house
in sight. What do my instincts say to do, he thought. Past that
curve is the pay-phone over at Peever's store. He called his
house.

      His wife answered. "I'm out of gas," he told her,
"What a rotten day it's been, shit, unbelievable." "Where are
you?" she asked. He could taste the flesh at the nape of her
neck. "Not far. Hey, babe, I don't remember the last time I
saw your belly," he told her, suffused with love, and then she
said, "Suffer," her hand clenched around the phone, "I don't
suppose it would *occur* to you to carry a full can of gas, the
way I do?" She was angry and smug. She felt valuable. "Are
you still cold, babe? Is the house cold?" he asked, wanting her,
wanting to be inside her. The wind was cold through the
broken glass of the phone booth. "Oh, you goddam bastard,
now what the hell do you think it is? You left it this w . . ."
"If you'd consider coming to . . ." "You're kidding, Harry.
That's *your* problem," she said, as precisely as his answers to
her earlier in the day. Her voice cold. "Oh, Jesus, you goddam
fucking *cello*," he said sadly to her. "Better than being some
kind of goddam artificial metallic fucking *machine*," she
shrieked, "at least you have the sense left to notice that I'm
made of something *natural,* not like *you,* you son of a bitch
cold robot," she finished, smirking. "And, in case you haven't
noticed, it's beginning to rain. *And* the kids just came in."
"They did. It is. Yes," he said, shaking his head, sad again,

turning his neck to notice the drops spattering the dusty road near him. Ah, that cartoon, he thought in the silence between them, where the woman is the house, is shaped like the house, reaching for the man to come home . . . but in the cartoon the woman is threatening, the house-wife-figure is menacing. To him, right now, she was all the warmth in the world. In that house. Poor lady he left in a cold house. He was repentant and horny. But then she spoke again and spoiled it all, with her "Suppose you" that sprang out at him again. "Ah, damn you, Sybil, goddam you," and she insisted on finishing it: "Suppose, just *suppose,* for once you had the goddam sense to fill up that gas can when you . . ." "Fuck you, goddamed bitch, stupid goddam irritating son of a bitch bitch." "But listen. Harry," she cried, delighted with herself, delighted with his response, she had really gotten to him.

"No." he said, and hung up on her. His mouth full of dry dust and vitriol. It was almost five miles to their house. Where my love lies awaiting, he snarled. And that snotty goddam Baltzin, with his ideas of how a novel should be rewritten. What a fucking drag. And even if he did get to the house now, the kids would be there with the noise going. Drag. But always the slim chance he could get to the typewriter, always the slim chance he could get inside his nice fat wife's sweet cunt, then be alone, try to work the problem through. . . . God, what a good feeling! To feel like fucking and to fuck, to feel like working and to work. The two joys. The double joys, the twin joys. Then the work would roll out of his hands, slipping from brain and groin to fingertips to paper—those times he felt like that elegant machine he'd seen at the Doubleday plant, curling an endless roll of handsomely printed paper. One paper, wide, smooth, endless, good, indivisible, with the liberty and freedom I need, he thought. Except for the fact that my goddam agent has taken it upon himself to rewrite the entire middle goddam section of my novel, he has. Has he. Would he. Keep his word. Try it my way. Or should I try it his, since he's already bent for me. And he walked out of the booth and into the rain. Back toward the car. He wanted his wife. His groin throbbed with the lust. He felt a quick hardness against his thigh. The damn bitch, didn't she know by now how to talk to him? Oh God, what a waste. . . . He sat back, he moved back of his own eyes. He walked slowly and straight, loving himself as no one else could. He was so gifted. . . .

The road spun out loosely in front of him. He was suddenly faced with being unable to drive. Forced to walk. Into the unwilling revelations. Those things he usually missed because he had to hurtle through fast. Leaves, the road was covered with them, slippery as ice when wet in this season, he had to watch out for them. They were wetted into a uniform buff color, like skin, all their individual brilliances melted together. The peeled skin of a season past, he thought. What if he told that to Sybil. She would probably find some fault or other. —For her part, she had removed herself from the children's orbit, she had her back to their room, her strange anger was moving her outward strongly into the music, she was working on a Mozart trio and the bowing was giving her trouble but it was all right. She was content that he would not be back so soon, the problem before her was interesting, not something she couldn't work through; it would have to take him at least three-quarters of an hour to get home, in this rain. She was immersed in the music. His arrival would only pull her out of herself and into his demands, would make her lose the purity of her effort. She had been more amused than he knew, that business about running out of gas. But it *was* funny, she thought, and giggled her revenge, and had to stop playing. How foolish he was, imagining her having to take his nastiness that morning without responding in kind. Imagining himself sensible enough to tell her how to solve problems when he was so utterly impractical. How absurd he was. How vicious, she thought, remembering this morning. And picked up the cello again; began to play.

III.

Walking, thinking. The middle section. I don't believe in the kind of form he was talking about. He's living in the 1800's in his head. Okay, I used to do what he's asking now, but I'm past that. If the work is itself, it has its own life. I never know how it's going to go when I begin it. I just know who the people are and then they take it over; who they are is how it goes. When they live, it lives. I believe in them. I believe in that. I believe in her too. Goddam goddess bitch, her belly and her cunt, rich as honey. They talk a damn sight better to me than her mouth does. I believe in them. But when she takes me in her mouth I believe in her mouth too. What sounds would that litany be, she would make it into music, I would respond. Why aren't any of the world's big fat religions based on penis-worship any more. Just the holy lingam and yoni. All these statues around, and all just people, why not cut out the middleman and go straight to the Man or our own bodies. My lady down the road knows of this. Her blessed cunt from which all blessings flow. Down her leg, down my leg now. Where she is is where I go to. But she says, she saith, No, my fat surly conceited bitch goddess. Goddam foreign interesting bitch. Gives yes but only so much and then no. And I want it all. All these years and I still haven't got enough of her, haven't got all of her, feel like I never will get to where she lives. . . . To be able to do whatever I goddam please in the life and make my own terms with the world and always to find her there in the house. Want. Her. Into this goddam anxiety about the work and here I am walking down a road with another or is it the same hardon. So many years, so many fucks with the same woman and it still happens this way. God, how I could give this gift to the world today. I could fuck the world and still have some left for the sun and moon today. I will smash across her beautiful belly and butt and take that hulk of her the mounds of her the curves of her beautiful rich round rare lovely damn

flesh and throw myself into her as if it were the first time a
man came into a woman. . . . Not about to happen, Harry
old boy. She'll stop it. She wants this, she wants that. Can't
she just leave me the hell alone. What's happening, Harry,
where were you, Harry, how are you feeling Harry, how did
it go today, Harry, talk to me Harry, Jesus, does that broad
bug me . . . hey, fuck off, broad, shut up and let me take
care of business, can't you, just lie down and give a little and
I'll do the rest.

     I *know* what I want to do. I want to make him
sell the book just the way I made the book. I want the book
to be allowed to be itself, like Clarence Schmidt's hillside,
big, wide, laplapping over at the edges, no boundaries, the
only structure its own nature, extending into time/space,
itself wherever it ranges, its own character, raw and fine and
pansy and tough and phony and terribly harsh all at once,
this place it's all the mess of civilisation and a foot away it's
all the sarcasm of nature. This isn't any of the books I wrote
before, goddam it, doesn't he know that? I want something
saintly and radical with this one. Jesus I was so fucking
scared when I first went there. Woods full of dismembered
dolls with heads growing from their feet, headless shards of
mirrors where I was reflected in the chaos of where I really
live, my own head torn off, my feet impaled, a thick nail or a
thousand nails through my belly fastening me to the top of
a fake tree that was once real like some gilt blossom, I was
all the artificial and real things that crazy willful old man
made, fake painted silver real wood, still am real branch with
fake flower coming out the end, is my come turning in me
toward out, spurty like yellow flower in the sun, next time I
come it'll leap out like a tulip or an iris and it'll lie there on
the sheet on the ground between our legs as if it were the
spirit of the next child. . . . Ah god, he lives in a goddam
old *car*, well then so do I and I'm still young, or I feel as old
and heavy as Clarence. Ah I don't like this walking, I could

live in my car too, starting today, get the hell out; no. Couldn't.

But *he* could and does. Has neither kith nor kin. She: looms, blooming, or that looming blooming house. I'll give her to Clarence and let her become one of the fat-sauce dolls he collects to win the world guess games, to show what a mess or dream we're all in. Would she keep house for him in that car. What would she become as he has in senile foment. Where would I. What will I. Where what when with the trees turning dark though silvered. Here the damn wind coursing over the rain silver road. Damn wind. The challenge. She is changing me. But I am more myself than I used to be. I remember the child that I was. My father's shadow then and now over me. Am still somewhere he. More my own feet on this road. She's not who she was either, was good but now's fine . . . hell with it. She should be wife and woman and to hell-o with cello, funny about form isn't it Harry old man, scoff and fall backward into traditional every time, if not in this then in that, want to break form, do you, but want your wife home and waiting unbusy with legs open every time for you, want agent to shut up and let be do you. . . . I remember pearls that were my boyish eyes, walking in woods like these, and miles to go, and I chose *this* road, and remember not guessing how it would go but knowing anyhow and having it go the right way by itself, but with me with it all the time all the way. If it don't fit, forget it. If it fit use it. If it fit good and it hold still, fuck it. Good. Ah, fuck it all! or what's this heaven about, Harry old bird, master cliché coiner of this world, snap to, hayfoot, miles to go before I fuck her, before I creep deep to where she lives and I come alive, alive-o, where I live that other life inside her warm dark places I know so well. . . .

My lady of the warm dark places, and isn't it cold as a witch's tit with this damn rain slipping down my neck like the kiss of vampires and the wind slick sideways, but

Jesus it's a real wind isn't it, it's real and it's good. How could I live inside my car when I live inside my lady, fat warm pretty lady who talks too much, pushy Sybil my Armenian, wants everything *her* way. And I am a goddam fucking impatient man, too impatient, hey, hayfoot, what wouldn't I give for a cup of goddam hot coffee right now, if I lived in my goddam fucking car I would at least have a hot-plate in it, but the old bugger Schmidt cheats, doesn't he, ego bigger'n that whole hillside, unnatural to live like that, somebody's putting him up in a motel I hear, can't say the old boy's genuinely humble can you. But he works every day. More'n I can say by a damn sight. But none of us is Georges Simenon. See, men, ong. Semen. Ong. My friend's kid who says nothing but "ong" and Sam says it's the kid's happy-sound, ong ong ong says the kid is feeling happy, and he who cherishes him says so, that's who, and so who am I to question. Happy is easier for that kid to come by, shit for sure harder for the rest of us, wish for coffee, image of coffee steam cup, smell of, I see it, cigaret instead, car passing me, don't want a ride, get there under my own steam or won't at all damn it, and it'll be all my own trip, my own. . . .

IV.

Playing. Thinking. The bowing on that last bar. Bad; in fact no good at all. Over and over. Too bad this is all that's available in technique, I'm so tired of following this form, these forms, it's like John Cage says, you separate out music from all the sounds of the world and it becomes like an imprisoned animal, and here I am, trying to duplicate other people's idea of the cry of imprisoned animals, all these notes between bars and here I sit, perpetuating the cages with this bow this soft wood instrument this stance . . . those leaves today were all the notes I need, no bars, wild, free, I heard what they had in their natures, damn lovely, but now the kids' voices loud inside, hers always that same C variant and his a full tone lower. But that turn of it means I'd better get something onto the stove for them, ten minutes before they turn into howling wolves. Wind howling around outside, too cold in here, more wood on fire. There. Better. How could that goddam stubborn fucking man do a thing like that, is it so goddam hard to remember to put a can of gas in the back of the car, too logical for him is it, I think he consciously tries not to think of what might be practical, what a drag. What if I did that, didn't keep any emergency staples around the house in case, boy would he get mad if there were nothing in the house for him to eat, but when he gets mad it sometimes turns me on, image of his face his belly his downy belly his prick, sweet edge of lust feeling coming between thighs, oh but I hate the bastard when he stands screaming at me over me, acts tough and wearing out all the good feelings, Jesus, he thinks all he has to do is. Thinks that's all there is to. It. To begin with. Quick hand on my breast and jumps me, doesn't make it go. But so long since we've been. I bear the grudge every time he rams on in, with all that goddam power and no smooth, tough not necessary. Remembering John, silky limbs and all gentle, bony sweet man so far from here in time/space, summer sun instead of this cold, room shady in daylight, magic of his 'let's go slow, sweet baby, and love it more, why go fast?' to teach me forever for learning how the slow goes, slippery and lovely, body into the soft easy magic and places full of aromatic and joy feel.

But if I give some of that now I get back the Harry sass snot ram push lust and cold. If he angry when he mad. He will does try to make it sad bad and make me sad. Ah but he could be that sweet man but he's afraid of too much. . . . Should I use the kohlrabi for supper for them or that frozen stew his mother gave us last week. Yes. That would be easier and no cooking tonight, give me another quarter hour playing time, that is if the kids. If I dare ask him again when he gets here how it went with Blarmis in town. He'd

probably shriek at me mind your own business bitch. But
want to know how it went for him. Okay so we're out of
money again in three days exactly I figure. Wonder if he had
the balls to ask for the advance, hope so, ah yes, but hope
looks like an inverted light bulb. Teardrop, all lit up. The
Maybe Syndrome I will call it. Maybe . . . you'll think of
me . . . when you are feeling . . . blue, Christ but that's
lousy music set in with this kind of music, or is all music
just music and the same, glad I had a father played the violin,
the Armenian Jack Benny wasn't he though by God. Better
get the stew into oven into pan warm water yes. Okay.

      Was that his car; no. By god if I'm not getting into
a shitty paranoid mood. Why. Not-so-free-floating anger. Left-
over anger. Parataxic anger. Goddam fucking lack-of-fucking
anger. Oh and I will make a casserole of all my left-over
anger and throw it bloody well in his face, like the time he
dumped that turkey casserole across the floor in his rage, in
my face, in front of the kids, fine dish I had made with love
for him and them, we had to eat goddam cornflakes later,
damn him o goddam that son of a bitch to hell for that,
other day when he got to me and got me crying finally said
what's the matter I said free-floating pain but he couldn't
understand wouldn't. Would he believe how my music buys
off the pain, only certain notes representing all that pain and
others for the anger, or is it sounds and not notes at all.
Considering Charlotte Moorman whence also is the body a
cello, to play and to play, if she could if she would live like
this like me and also play but what would she play and how.
Or is my composition my body or my children. Are all these
musics my children. More perfect than I could compose. Perfect notes like leaves. Windsound, rainsound or fury melody.
Furry melody. I want him now. Here. Now. Bastard that
runs out of gas wants sympathy and here am I out of heat.
But in heat now, for him. Big talker big runner, runs too fast
when all of us in car, yeah, everyone has to speed on through,
big tailgate expert, runs roads like he runs my body, how

much can he risk without getting killed, push up sharp hard against the edge of life testing how hard before death and keeping life sharp thus. Tough game, not many women into it, makes me frantic for peace and a soft way through or down any road . . . on this road, in this place are we odd or just like the others. If we made another baby with the next come it would set me to running set him hard against the edge again or more so, better watch out for it . . . I'd like to try but not with that for a father, they turn out lovely but he is too cold to them, Jesus but this house is cold, and colder still without him . . . Miss him. Miss my other cities, miss the children I lost and never had, he wouldn't go when I went away last time and I wouldn't when he, when will I see Paris again, maybe never if it is up to him, could get there without him again, under my own steam, set up to go with Alice and Steve and we could get some concerts set up, but if I went it would be not asking him for a goddam thing, and it would be all my own trip, all my own . . .

V.

He was too thin now. It had been too easy, back then, for him to begin the writing and make it work. Not so much struggle then, when one's father passes along the talent *and* the connections. But he knew that his novels, till now, till this one, lacked blood; they were his father's idea of how the novel ought to be, and carefully avoided incorporating Harry's soul. They were thin-blooded and successful: formula stuff, easy to make, for him; easy to sell; easy to read. And during those years, Harry was well-fleshed. Now, it had changed, was changing; the fleshy fat had dropped off him and was going into the work and the life, finally. He was beginning finally to feel like his own man. And his fat, rich-fleshed Armenian wife, his pushy wife, was part of it. The confrontation . . . he had always wanted this, but had never known how to get through to it. He had seen the lives of those around him, and his own life, as if through frosted glass. But she would not let him escape. She, with her odd wisdom, had become one of his prime edges. His honing edge.

She would say to him, how far have you gotten from what your own soul is? and: What are you so proud about? That book you just finished has nothing to do with you. You're still writing your father's idea of a book. and: You sure you want to write novels like that? You really want the world to take a look at you through your books and see a carbon copy of your father? I mean, don't you want to do something just for yourself, or maybe even for us, something different, all your own?—and he would contort in misery, he would become infuriated, hearing her, knowing; at the beginning, in the first year, he would hear her as if at a great distance, and the only way through for him was to slap out, which he did, often, howling at her with his pain, his shapeless, nameless anguish. In the years between, the distance between them lessened, as the distance between him and his own soul was lessening. So that in this last year, while he was thinking about and then working on the new novel, she could reach him more quickly; but she had given up on trying it as much, because of his anger. The frosting on the glass between him and his world wore away in patches; seven months ago, a tough clarity hit him, and he began and then finished the novel.

It gave him trouble, all the way; it was the most difficult act he had ever attempted; he had never thought of not doing it. She thought that his marriage was the real challenge; the marriage was the big challenge to both of them. To be married. To such a man as he, being with any woman would be a great demand, the moreso with her, a woman not from his own background or class, a woman with her own ideas, with her own acts of integrity and of creativity and of independence . . . but after all, wasn't that why he had chosen her . . . At the beginning, in the early years, he

would reply to her challenges mildly, smoothly, at first:
Listen, baby, I really *like* the way I do things, it *suits* me, I've
earned my own way, *I* write the books, in spite of Dad, in
spite of his ideas, in spite of his money. And she would reply,
Yes, Harry, in spite of, in spite of, in spi— Until he reached to
slap at her in his fury.

But she liked their parents' money, and so did he.
They both liked the security it gave them, to take their artis-
tic risks, in the early years. She had never thought that part
through clearly; she knew that he had never had to do without, truly, and that he would still lean on the possibility of
asking the parents for money if they were really strapped.
She wanted him to be sufficient to himself; she wanted him to
be malcontent, not realizing that his poverty of soul was sufficient as a goad for him. She thought that poverty would do
for him what it had done for her; she had worked at menial
jobs from her teens onward, and she coveted for him the
nervous hunger of trying to make it on one's income and
not ever being sure there would be enough money for food.
The money provided invisible softening for the edges of their
lives, these days. Lately, they did not ask for it. There were
checks at birthdays and on holidays, and the parents had
joined to help them with the down payment on the house
they were living in. To help them get out of the City. Once
in a while, they had helped meet the mortgage payment. The
children got small checks, "to teach them how to save, and the
value of money." Sibyl liked and resented all this. Harry
simply enjoyed it. He felt no guilt and no involvement. He
felt he did not "care who was his Guggenheim Foundation,"
that his talent justified his means, that he was working
through well and hard; he was satisfied that he was a pure
artist and a good one, even during the years when he was
turning out novels to his father's taste, after his father's
image. He would not want to hear Sibyl's exceptions: he was
sure that holding down a regular job would prevent him from
being creative in his art.

But he wanted the parents' help; he thought he deserved it!—and Sybil really liked having the money, because, after all, wasn't it she who had the bulk of the 'real' work to do, taking care of the house for all of them, the table, the children, the laundry, shopping, in addition to keeping up her music, and teaching when she needed to . . . To her eyes, it would be more their house if Harry had built it with his own hands. But he would choose an old house, which was also to her taste, and, with help, had done some of the remodelling; he would not take the time from his writing to build a new house, he said. They fought. He designed and re-built a fireplace in the house, and it did not turn out as they had discussed, foreseen, planned, and she accused him of ruining the look of her favorite room. She had a vision of exactly how she wanted things to look. To be. Or to come out, after planning. As did he; but in this, he was more able to compromise, more flexible than she. What did it matter if the fireplace was half-a-foot narrower than she had visualized? It still worked, didn't it?—but she had had her concept; she had *counted* on it, she wailed; that was a four-hour fight. . . .

Some of their products were not planned together, of course: the work, each unto each exclusive (he never commented on her work, much as she felt bound to comment on his, whenever she felt the urge), and, more or less, the children. But Harry, at the beginning, would try for dominance, even in this. When they did not conceive the first year, he wanted to apply to adopt a child. Running through the incredible excruciatingly stupid small bureaucracy of a small agency. (Each had thought the other incapable of producing the child; this was the first of the many seemingly unsolvable endless fights, the hours of subtle or brutal accusation, tears, the howling, the cleverness: he would mock her when she would bring in great bunches of tomato plants for their garden, heaps of house plants for their kitchen, and she would leap back at him, "If you don't give me a baby, I have to have something to love, something to raise," and he would rage at her, she helpless in her hunger, he helpless in her accusation. At the adoption agency, Harry, still then possessed by his lost innocence, and deluding himself that he had a lust for Truth, told the insipid and curious worker about Sybil's eccentric rages, implying that they were of an almost psychotic texture (for surely he was not at all to blame in all of this; and neither of them had been tested for fertility; though they told the worker they had!). Then Sibyl was interviewed, and when the worker asked some of the questions that Harry had obligingly provided as trigger material, Sybil predictably blew up. So their application was turned down. Ostensibly because of her unfitness to be a mother. He did not tell her about this at the time. She had never mentioned his rages; she was too willing to accept the slur, the blame, the fault. To her, his rages were not pertinent.

Much later, when they did conceive, she realized that Harry had made that bad gesture in order to avoid encroachment, the immediacy of the pressures of a child in their lives just then. The following year, they had conceived their daughter. She was not the child either of them would have designed or chosen; Harry would have little to do with her; it rested with Sybil to try to smooth a way between the three of them for survival. Then she was to introduce the idea of the boy, their son, to Harry, two years later. Harry was never close to it all; he was never involved, past the original lovemaking. He kept a distance. Some pride; no reality. He was glad they were *his* children, though. He would not like to have had to adopt. His pride went against it.

VI.

Now they were set into the midst of a weird, tough, painful siege: many of their friends, here and in the City, couples they had known for years, couples they had met just last month, were breaking up. Splitting like geodes under a chisel. Snapping like dry branches of the season. As the stories appeared, on the phone, at their door, in letters, day by day, sometimes late at night, Harry and Sibyl were living in awe and in horror. They had become afraid, during this last month, clutching at each other, taking in the news, gasping, they could count nine, and then fourteen, and then, for God's sake, twenty-two couples they knew or had met, here or in the next town or in Toronto or in the City, people they knew well enough to have had over to dinner, people whose ideas they knew, people each had gone to school with—split apart. And in each case there remained, after the separation of the couple, two solitary, terribly separate Giacometti figures, strained, hewn of natural material but put through the chastening heat of parting, so that the metal had an unnatural iridescence . . . each standing alone. Alone.

Having forgotten how it was, being alone: born alone, walking and sleeping and thinking alone as they had done as children, separate each and each in the skull. The parents of their daughter's closest friend: just this week; a phone call. The couple from whom Harry and Sibyl had bought this house, earlier in the week. The owner of the restaurant they often ate at, last week. Sound of fraying and of snapping. Sound of splintering. Echo of 'alone': sound of brain shocked in skull like concussion. Three other couples they knew, some time last week. Four more, the end of last month. The couple in the second house down the road from them (surely *they* would have lasted!—everything in common, and told it so, fondness for each other, six children to indicate loving, they seemed to have taken nothing for granted, they—). And the woman who played first violin in Sibyl's Sunday group and the man who interviewed Harry when he reviewed his last novel and who appeared one night at their doorstep, half-crazed into booze and pot and the franticness of a man gone suddenly unexpectedly single . . . they took him in for three days. It did no good. Some good. Hard to tell, they said after he left, if he would come through it or would bend under the weight and snap.

The man and the woman were caught in the panic of their friends and acquaintances. Theories abounded. One friend was sure it was cosmic: this business of tampering with the Moon, for one thing; and the shifting from Piscean to Aquarian eras . . . well, why not, Sybil said, they thought, talking it over; and still it was not an answer. It was a medieval plague with no known cure, with hideously recognizable deathly results, the cries of the afflicted were loud on the cold air, no list of symptoms by which one could form preventive techniques. . . .

One night, they sat together over coffee, feeling fond of each other, feeling bound, feeling threatened, this was last Monday, the children were safely asleep, the fireplace crackling near them, their quarrel over its precise size long forgotten. Sat, at right angles to each other, edge of her hand touching his . . . she was reciting the names of the couples, in a solemn recitatif of mourning . . . its rhythm a chant . . . as if to ward off the demons . . . the list was stunning: Rochelle and George, Diane and Tony, Peggy and Richie, Gary and Lynn, Eva and David, Ed and Lynn, Peggy and her David, Joby and Bob, Tom and Marge, Toren and Tom, Jackie and Michael, Danny and blonde Lucille, Rachel and Isaac, Dave and Anne, Bob and Peg, Pia and Frank, Estelle and Sy, Susan and Jerry, Jim and dark Lucille, no more hyphens between their names now, blood between the names now, each name representing a bleeding wound, some of them joining with others in frantic beds, lonely beds, double beds with half empty, Christ, some gone solitary into a supposedly purifying aloneness, some terrified as bare bones in their beds, some noisy, some silent, into drink, into drugs, into other friends' houses, some travelling, most with children left gaping and confused, two rooms out of four in so many houses turned dark and empty and unable to be faced, to be entered . . .

A scourge, they agreed, reciting the names, not of the dead but of the alive who were bleeding, whose lives would continue, who might form new liaisons, find other ways, other guises for survival, "all together now, shift and change your partners," or solitary . . . aaaahh, they sat, feeling each other's soul; contemplating each couple as their names were said, considering the possible reasons, or the obvious reasons, none of which might be true or all of which . . . a pause; Harry looked at Sybil intently, silently, deeply, wondering, loving her more than he could ever define or announce; she meantime listening to the soft sounds of the house surrounding them, feeling the breath of the children in their beds, feeling the small current passing where her hand rested next to Harry's; feeling his fear, feeling her own, without being able to define it, loving him clearly and well, in this time of menace that was upon them . . . how long will this last, will we survive, what have we got, what about this house, these children, how would he/she do on an alone path, nothing is permanent, one cannot count on anything, anyone, what is there to be sure of, not one goddam thing on this earth, and I am part of earth, what right have I to look for security in this other human animal: the world is turning too fast, some of us are spinning apart, nothing is sure. I'm a piece of God but I'm not God and there probably is no scheme to it or if there is, I can't see it, when does the list end, Bobbie and Tom, Carolee and Jim, Irma and Jack, Maxine and Jerry, Janet and George, John and Elinor, oh Christ, it used to be one out of five, this feels like the ratio is reversed, Alice and Lou, Sam and Elly, Arlie and Linda, Alan and Carol, Arlene and Peter, June and Carl, Phyllis and David, Ruth and Bill . . . what can we do, all that blood, can we mark the doorposts with blood, whose blood out of all of these, is ours required, what is the magic, how shall we take this, my God.

When had it started. Less than a year ago. And most of them since Spring. News reached them from all over

the world. It did average out to two a week or more. And
meantime they could only name two couples who had met and
joined during that period. Those months. "The times, they
are a changin'," Harry intoned, slowly, sadly, blowing smoke
at the lightbulb above them. This night, sitting quietly,
drinking coffee, sitting together as man and wife, passing the
sweet smoke between them, there was no room for argument
between them. They would use the other couples' names to
weave a protective circle around them, around their marriage.
Let it not happen to us as it has happened to our friends, we
do not know the name of what we have and we slap out
against it and against each other, seeming to revile what we
have, but heaven help us as nothing has helped our friends,
let there be a way to survive this . . .

But part of Harry's mind was wondering, even as
they were listing the names of the friends, about each of the
women who was now free and alone: what kind of lay would
she be?—and Sibyl, in turn, sought the natural form of each
of the ex-husbands: what sort of man was he really? in the
world, to his woman, in his work, in the bed? And when the
friends had come by, some after calling or writing the news,
some just turning up, they would reach out to Sibyl and to
Harry: a few drinks, a few meals, a meal, a drink, a joint, an
hour: needing to avoid the empty two rooms in their own
houses, needing to talk, to listen, to feel loved, to eat, to turn
on, to sleep without waking into the cold, alone nightmare of
"it's all over . . ." There was talk then of the weird medieval
plague that was upon this modern world now. Theories. And
through it Sibyl would wonder, while she was grateful for
Harry, even looking at Harry across the room or table or bed,
if one of the newly unattached men would have more of a
sense of adventure in the life, would be affectionate with her
and the kids, would be able to remember to fix things that
needed fixing, would be more casual than was Harry. Or
what would it feel like to be with another man in bed after
all the years with Harry, all the familiar landscape, pattern.

She realized sharply that it might feel very good to be alone for a while, just with the kids—and skittered away from the thought as soon as she recognized it, and before she could give it a name. With no children, it looked easier . . . but it wouldn't be painless, even then. *With* children, it was a horror. Always.

Elinor had told them about her twelve-year-old's reaction and response: "Oh, he's furious with me. He wonders what kind of person I am; this was my second marriage (he's from my first, you know; Evvie is from this one, with Don). He says this makes him feel like I'm a born loser, or really have some screws loose, and I'm not sure myself any more. But I tell you this, I'm feeling awfully good these days, I mean once the initial shock was over, maybe it's a phony reaction, but for the first time in *years* I feel like I belong to *myself* and not to somebody else, not to whichever man I happen to be married to. I mean, I don't even think about the word 'love' any more, it's a question of alternatives . . . I've got no guilt that I should be doing something else right now other than exactly whatever I happen to be doing at the moment—time is such a *luxury*—I'm sleeping better now than I ever did with Don—I mean, his snoring and all. I mean, I was into the 'boys' thing so young, and then I married Alex before I knew what the hell it was all about, and then I went from that marriage right into the ever-lovin', waiting arms of Don (remember how he was just sitting around like some kind of weird bird, waiting for all the shouting to die down?) and you know something? I always thought I couldn't stand living alone, couldn't possibly stand life without being made love to, without circling around a man—big motivation thing for me—and you know—I can! and I think I like it! It finally feels like my own life I'm living. Nobody's setting up the structures but me. Oh, it might change—once I get horny enough. But right now I don't even want to make love. I just want to be alone. —But when Teddy said that, I mean about my being a fuckup, it really worried me: is that how he really sees me? Well, I thought about it, but not for long. I told him, 'Okay, babe, so that's how it looks to you. You've got a smart head for twelve, but you're still twelve, and you don't see my side of it, and even if you live to a hundred you won't, because I'm a woman and you're a man-child. Anyhow, you're going to have a long life ahead of you, and you can make all your own experiments and all your own mistakes, and I can bet there'll be plenty of them. But in the meantime, what I think I'll do to prove your point is, I'll just run out and marry the first six men I meet, all at once.' So he said, 'If you do it one at a time, I could give you away!' which gave him back to me, I mean, it's his sense of humor that was missing, and once we got to that again it was all right again. And it was okay. And it's been okay ever since, with us. At home. It's harder to work alone—but I've never felt this *free*—"

But in two months Elinor was back, came to them, burst in at midnight, stoned and sad and ready to brim over, flung her auburn head across their table and sobbed, sobbed, "I just—can't—stand it—alone any more—I just want to get laid—Letter from Don—he's fifteen hundred miles away and I—wish he—were here now—I just—can't stand it—anymore. . . ." and Harry, uncompromising, male, sensible, said, "Where's all the thrill about being so free, having all this energy to go do your own thing, lady? Gone with the wind?" And Elinor looked at him with hatred; Sybil remained silent, knowing both sides of it well. Her life and Harry's were so disparate now. Stretched thin. Under the fear which kept them clinging. Adding tension to their arguments. Harry was into smoking a lot of pot lately. The new book was giving him trouble. Barlintz the agent was giving him trouble. He was in trouble. He didn't relate to the kids at all. He jumped on Sybil for anything, real or imagined.

And Sybil was dreaming the terrible dream again. The one with the fair girl who had been in bed with Harry. Waking furious and frantic. Reacting toward Harry as if the dream had been truth. Edgy and jumpy. She couldn't discuss the dream with him; she was afraid; he might take it as tacit suggestion. Maybe he already had, somehow. Maybe he considered it 'droit du seigneur.' He was so arrogant, always on the edge of violence lately. Maybe the fear was pushing at him too; she didn't know. Why the sulks, though? The rage was something she had grown used to. Not these long silences. But at other times he was clearly with her, making the effort to love. But that was rare. And that was it: for him, it was an effort, now, to be, toward her, the way she thought ought to be natural: loving. She had no difficulty being affectionate with him; the fear made her even moreso. And this often pushed him away. He felt drained by her: her affection, based on nervousness as it often was these days, clung to him, made him feel sticky, made him want to pull back. Free himself. Making her reach all the more. . . .

She puttered about the kitchen, checking the stew in the oven, setting out sticks of carrots and celery and wedges of tomato and glasses of milk. The children were mercifully calm, in and out of the kitchen with only small, kitten-like noises. They were content in the livingroom, playing with toys near the fireplace. Reassured always by her presence in the kitchen. They were still too young to touch any of the larger questions. They would watch their father's rages with feelings that were never verbalized. He inflicted a kind of impotence upon them. He had very little affection to give them, very little attention. He, who knew so much about woods and fish and animals, had never taken his boy fishing, or tracking, or camping—she resented this bitterly, for the boy's sake. But when she mentioned this to Harry, he turned on her. 'That would be out of character,' he told her. 'Besides, I don't have the time. Not this week. You know that.' His answers to the boy were perfunctory; less than that to the girl. She seemed to add to his discomfort with her presence. Sibyl remembered his face, at the hospital, when they'd told him it was a girl. He had not changed since then. Even though the daughter resembled him. He was disinterested. He avoided her.

Sybil felt rotten when she thought of the relationship between her husband and her children; she hated him
for his coldness. Lately she would place herself between them
and him, as if to prevent their being hurt by his rejection. His
defenses against their joyfulness, their natural affection, their
noise and overtures of playfulness. She was miserable; furious.
The anger was growing, around the fear of losing the whole
marriage. She did not want the boy growing up thinking
this was how a man behaved. Elinor's Don, for example, had
always taken out his temper on objects rather than on the
people around him; when Elinor and Don had finally had
their most furious fight, he had broken up most of the furniture which she had brought to the marriage, and had thrown
the broken wood and cloth out onto the grass before their
house; but he had always been affectionate to the children,
even then, his own child and the child she had brought to the
marriage . . . The man didn't take out his misery or his
anger on the kids.

So that's it, thought Sibyl, I must want finally to
leave him. I must want that, more than I am afraid of it. I
don't see what else I can do. Or, she thought in her tidy way,
more accurately, I don't want to leave here, or even leave him;
I want to leave the way he is, and I want to stay here. But it's
not that I want him to leave. Or is it. Oh, yes, that *is* it, I do
want him to, that's why I keep thinking how peaceful it is
when he's not here, how peaceful it would be without him,
even now I have the jitters thinking he's coming back soon.
Braced for whatever horrors he'll bring. His goddam City day
with his goddam la-de-da agent. Good Christ, how I don't
want another scene with him. I've turned into some sort of
warped diplomat and I don't like myself for that. I've almost
forgotten who I am. And he does things that are driving me
mad. Why should I have to stay here—in the middle of this—
doing this—taking this. I love the man. Or do I. I need him.
Yeah, like a bed of nails. Yes, but I *want* him—I'm so trained
to his ways of making love that I probably couldn't make it

with anyone else by now . . . ah, but Jesus, when he pulls
that I-won't-bathe bit and walks around reeking and stinking;
boy, could I live nicely without that. The time Don said to
me and Elinor, Harry looks like the kind of man has well-
groomed hair and dirty underwear. How'd *he* know. Or is a
type that obvious to everybody but me? Maybe I got stuck.
Maybe I'm stuck with Harry. Maybe people are wondering
why I don't leave him. I can't change anything about him;
moving that man is like trying to move a goddam mountain.
Forget it. If anything changes, it'll have to be me. He doesn't
listen ever to me. He won't hear me. I can begin and try and
he turns away because he doesn't want to hear me . . . he
only hears himself. Maybe. Sometimes. Oh Jesus, why . . .
While she fed the children, she drank coffee and smoked cigarets and listened for his car. For his step. Wanting and not
wanting. He would be due any minute now. Quite soon now.
Afraid. Wanting.

VII.

He was not far from his house now. There was the Andersons'
place. Someone was driving slowly along the opposite side of
the road. Looked like Arthur Knapp's girl, Margery, from
here . . . it was. She seemed not to see him, but drove very
slowly past him, in the rain. Without thinking, he waved and
hallooed. After that, it was all too easy. She stopped quickly.
"My car's out of gas, back down by the Corners" (he would
not say "back by your house") "and I'm soaked to the bone!"
"Oh, I see, sure," she said, with a sideways glance and then a
direct look into his face. "How are you, Mr. Fowler? Where
you been keeping yourself? I been just down to the Andersons' place, why don't you hop in?" Why don't I just, Harry
thought, smirking. It was all so easy. He was so furious with
Sibyl. This girl, much younger than Sybil, much younger than
he, had the same sort of thick body as his wife, heavy-breasted,

wide-hipped, the car was filled with her musk and he was
again feeling the tough hot hardness against his leg. He
would try. He slid his arm along the top of the front seat, in
a gesture he remembered from his high-school days. This girl
wouldn't be too far out of high-school; the gesture might feel
familiar to her, rather than audacious. And she couldn't mis-
understand him. Not that she was about to, he thought. She
was talking. On and on. ". . . and then they was saying
they'd have to put a new roof onto it, if it was to last the
winter, that is if we had another winter like 1968, which'd be
the end of us . . ." Harry flinched. What the hell. If she
couldn't talk and couldn't think, she could probably at least
fuck; she was built for it, like any good farm animal . . .
that didn't require much thinking. He didn't need any more
goddamn intellectual types right now. All they gave a man
was questions and arguments and standards of behavior that
were too far from reality to be considered. He was angry.
And very pleased with himself.

They had turned the car around and were driving
toward her house, toward his car. When his car was in sight,
"I'm freezing," he said, feeling like an obvious fool, "I walked
all that distance in the rain. How about stopping at your
place for some coffee?" There were still no lights at her house.
"Oh, that's a good idea," she succumbed, lightly. Ah, Harry,
he thought, you buffoon, you crafty, subtle oaf, you brilliantly
subtle cratfsman, and all of it wasted on this clod, if only
someone like Sybil could see it, hear it . . . but what good
was all this? Would subtlety reach Margery Knapp? Would a
quick fuck save the soul of Harry Fowler? Yeah, tune in in an
hour and find out, he thought, absolutely charming himself.
Okay. He smiled at her (engagingly, he thought), hoping she
felt the warmth of his hand on her shoulder through her coat.
He despised her. He was doing his xenophobic bit. He was in.
Nobody home, and she was answering, "Why, you poor man,
you must be wet to the bone, walking all that way in the
rain!"—knowing, as she did, of course, that his own house was

just a few thousand feet farther on along the road where he'd been walking. Where she'd been riding. Where she had stopped for him. Made him notice her in her car. She knew what she was doing, she did. She was not exactly being had. He felt no guilt. They walked silently up the path to the dark house. While she was putting water into the coffee-pot, he lifted the thatch of dark-red hair across her back and put his mouth to the nape of her neck. If it had been Sibyl, you could have said that he had kissed a woman's neck. Now, he simply wanted to confirm and take in more of the musky smell of her in a hurry, and to arouse the strange woman further. To make himself clear; that was it. To her. And to himself. This would make him clear. Would clear things up. Would clarify his position in re . . . Oh well, much confusion for such a simple act; he hoped the preambles wouldn't have to last much longer; he couldn't stand much more. He didn't want to do anything phony: no promises, not much conversation.

She let him take off her shirt, and reached for him in a most appreciative way. She seemed to be all lust, and all the way through; the surface was the same as the underneath. No virgin, this chick; great. He missed the feel and smell of a new unfamiliar female. It had been quite a while since he had taken anyone but his wife. He had been inclined sometimes but had not needed to. Well, he needed now, and here it was. "It," for God's sake; an edge of disgust as he noticed his own phrase; she was, then, nothing but an object for him . . . well, okay, what else could she be? Stupid broad. Easy and stupid and very very con-able and here she was. So easy and so great. Responsive, too, wouldn't you know! She was all over him. He was forgetting his mind. They were in her room, upstairs; the doors were open throughout the house behind them; no one was due; they had all the time they wanted. . . . He stepped brusquely onto her all round parts and into all her oval parts, all of her hot and damp and thick with her scent; she had a really delicious body, this fat redhead broad, this hick broad, didn't she, and he stopped thinking and he came, and wrestled around with her, nibbled her breasts and came again, and they rested, without talking, and began again, more slowly but even less tenderly, and this time both of them came, loudly, firmly, together. And fell asleep together.

VIII.

Full night out the window. Migod, where was he? Leapt up and into his clothing. "Oh, but, Mr. Fowler," she was saying, the poor fool, the blithering idiot. For God's sake. Isn't that too much. "Let's go," he cut in. "Let's go get the gas. I have . . . some work to do." She did not answer, but put on her clothing quickly, and started quickly down toward the car, walking in front of him all the way. Her hips swinging. She felt good. She knew what her power was. He would be back, some time, she thought. They went together to the station, bought a can of gas, brought it to his car, filled it. He sat, watching her leave. For a while, he just sat, in his own car, in the car which was not big enough to hold the kids and Sybil and the driver, would just hold himself and one other person, and with bucket seats so that there was a distance between himself and that other person when he drove. . . . They would have to use Sibyl's old Tempest wagon when the family went anywhere together. "Together"—when was that—what was that. Where was he. He was in his own groin. He was filled with joy. His body was sweet to himself, he felt the dried juices along his thigh. How great, not to feel horny, to feel fulfilled. He felt as if he'd been horny for the past year running. And running was what it felt like. Goddam her, it did drive him. Damned if he'd save it for that goddamn bitch of his, with all her no and no and no. With all her nagging. Too long since he came three times in a night with her. Her with her goddam supposing.

But still he had to go back there. Where she was.

He had a frantic feeling, wanted to see her, anyhow, whatever. —For her part, Sybil, too, was frantic; leaving her senses. Here it was, full night, past nine o'clock, many hours after he'd called from down the road. She was afraid of him, yes, but she was also afraid for him. She had called two of the neighbors farther down the road where he'd said the car was, and, when they told her they hadn't seen him, she'd called the local police, much against her will or taste—knowing that he would resent her having done so, if he was indeed in any conscious state when he turned up or was found. . . . There would be another scene in any case. How he hated the police, she was thinking, one of the worst things about him, part of his whole goddam paranoia . . . okay, some of that was justifiable, but he had this way of being sure the worst would happen, thereby often causing exactly that to happen by virtue of his mental accident-prone syndrome, as Sybil called it. He always would blow up at the telephone operator who'd interrupt to ask for another nickel, or at the machine which didn't give him his brand of cigarets promptly enough, or the matches with them; or at the waiter who was dilatory (a loud scene, always), or at the insurance investigator . . . just doing his job, she would protest to Harry, but he thought the man was asking more than he needed to, he was into a terrible invasion-of-privacy thing these days, said, Well, there had to be a point at which those people had to leave a man to his own business, for God's sake, and he wanted to be the one to draw his own lines . . . But Sybil countered, as always ready with her logical argument, There had to be *some* kind of structure, didn't there? and there had to be people to do those jobs or the way all of us lived would fall apart, wouldn't it, and couldn't he be practical enough, just for once, to understand that there were a lot of details these people *had* to know, and that there wasn't all that much *private* about their lives, they weren't that different, after all, from everybody else around them . . . She was remembering now, over coffee, how he had behaved when they had gone into the bank to work out the mortgage payments. How he had blown up at the bank officer and the real estate man who were working with him. God, what a scene.

　　　　　She was so disgusted with him then and so furious afterward. But she had said nothing about it all at the time, in the bank. Well, if you were so goddamned disgusted, why didn't you say so then? Why save it the hell up and let it out later like this? he howled at her. If your tongue works so goddamn well now, how come you kept your stupid trap shut then? when they had come back to the house, when dinner was on the stove, when she started quietly to try to talk about the whole thing, hoping to find an alternative. Ah, shit, all you're concerned about is what kind of a name we'll get in this goddam small town and not about whether I was right or not. Well, baby, I was *right,* he hollered, leaning over into her face, "and that motherfucker institutional-grey computerized creep was *wrong,* the fucking automaton, the goddam cretin, and here *you* are, without beginning to see what I was trying to accomplish for *us,* because you see I'm *on* to how the bastards operate, and I *know* we could have gotten a lower interest rate, and they thought, the both of them, that they'd gotten themselves another goddam sucker fresh out of the city who doesn't know anything about land or property up here—and here *you* sit, dumb bitch, putting me over the coals in your own inimitable slow tender little way, yeah, pick, pick, *pick,* for Christ's sake get off my back, bitch! Harry. Listen. Harry. Very quietly. Almost calmly. Harry. Get off. Stop leaning into me. I can certainly hear you perfectly well and I do understand how you feel . . . You goddam fucking patronizing bitch. I was just trying to find out . . . Find out. Find. *Out.* You and your findings out. What the fucking hell you know about real estate? You know how you sound now? Like a fucking mosquito, is how. If you know so goddam much, why the hell didn't you speak up and try to 'find out' more, as you so delightfully put it, while the goddam event itself was taking place? Because it wasn't the time or the place to . . .

He was enraged. Is *this*? After the fact, after the whole thing is done? You want my balls? You want to go into the bank by yourself and do the thing instead? No. You want to sit here now, later, *now*, saving it all up till now, and you think this is the time to come at me with all this niggling shit? and he reached out and slapped her full across the right cheek. She averted the blow and stared at him, and turned, and stopped the questions. She was pale with fury and frustration.

But they had then somehow eaten dinner quietly, together, with the children, each thinking, each silent; and they made love later, and when they were lying wetly together afterward he said, into her face again but sweetly this time, 'I'm sorry for that.' 'I know.' She had hoped for much more from him. She had hoped for him to have had some insight into what had happened at the bank. But if he did reach that insight, he would never tell her about it. She loved him, if that was the name for all of this. She worried about him. Would he mellow, ever. She put down the coffee-cup and called the local police again. Yes, they had spotted the car; it was empty, though; they would take a look around, don't you be worried, it's probably all right, he might've stopped in with one of the neighbors for coffee—the usual reassuring speech to wives.

As the time passed, she avoided looking at the clock. Her tension passed itself on to the children, who became irritable and tired and whiny. She put them to bed. It was well past their bedtime anyway; she'd let them stay up, kept them up, to keep her company in her wait. When she was alone finally, the tension and the questions and the anxiety turned into sexual feelings: she became aroused, she was wet again with wanting him; she could feel her furred lips moving sensually together when she walked across the kitchen or sat down in her chair. She had all she could do to keep hands off herself. She would wait for him and they could be together. Hadn't he said he wanted her, on the phone before. Much better that way. It was good to remember he wanted

her and could say so. He did. She had not missed the direct-
ness of his phone-call, but she could not remember her own
harsh response, her own sarcasm. Did not want to.

She drank three cups of coffee, trying to keep
awake, and smoked six cigarettes. Walked into the livingroom, picked up the cello, put it down. Took a magazine over
to the kitchen table. Left it open; saw the dinner dishes,
washed them (they usually sat until morning). Then she sat
down at the kitchen table, fell across the open magazine with
her head on her arms. And there was the evil dream again.
Harry was standing with a strange woman across the room
from Sibyl. They were standing in intimacy: the woman's
hand was proprietary on Harry's arm. Sybil felt it beginning,
and was running across, screaming, crying, "Who the hell are
you, that's my man, get away from him," clawing, slapping
at the woman while she just stood smiling, and then beating
at Harry's chest while he just smiled, looking satisfied . . .
She woke to the quiet empty kitchen and the feeling of rage
and impotence which had no boundary. Its fierceness was unlike anything in her world. As if she could kill. Them both.
As if nothing she did would make any difference.

IX.

A while later, she heard the motor of his car. No one else
shifted that way; no other motor sounded like his. And then
his step. Moved her hand nervously through her hair and
tried to dismiss what she knew was her anxious expression.
Which usually aggravated Harry. (If she looked calm, unconcerned, as if nothing were out of the ordinary, it might go all
right. If she looked anxious or unusually concerned, he would
feel imposed-upon, threatened, and would act accordingly.)
She remembered what she had been like before she met
Harry. Concerned about her looks, about her loveliness, as
now, but never about her expressions and the response of

others. With him, she had become too aware, too self-conscious. He imagined too much, he exaggerated, he became irritated. And then he would howl at her or needle her. —For his part, he was always sure she was on the verge of mocking him, or of doubting his ability; she was always over-solicitous. He felt bound, unfree, imposed-upon when she worried about him. But in reality he was usually flattered. He was confused about this: he liked that she worried, and he was annoyed because he thought the concern would extend over into his province of personal freedom. Because it seemed to remove something of him. To demand something he was unwilling or unable to give.

She opened the front door; his hand was on the knob. She must not ask, "Where have you been, what the hell happened to you?" but instead must look calm and as if his lateness were not unusual; otherwise a scene. Besides, she wanted him, she wanted to make love as soon as possible. But this moment was like driving on slick ice. Had to be handled with knowledge and with caution. Damn him, for putting her through this, just to be with him!—and the panic, the horror of the dream pushing her from the recent past, so that she was almost out of control. Ah, why can't I just say and be the way that I am, why can't you understand, why can't you love me as I am, why is this the price of peace . . .

His blue eyes met her hazel eyes. Waiting for her inevitable questions. In anticipation, his face took on tension and his eyes changed focus. He looked around at his home with an objective stare. At his wife. But the furniture was too familiar to him. So he slid the familiarity aside, as if to turn a lens intentionally, so that he could see the room through his writer-eyes . . . no use; this woman, this room . . . he had betrayed her, he thought, all the joy gone out of his groin, the guilt swimming in coldly to his guts. And, with the guilt, alongside it, in came the old anger, red-hot, and uncontrollable. "Well, so, I'm late, what the hell," he said into her impassive face, "I had to do *something* after that session with Bartzlin. I just decided . . ." But his expression was odd. I didn't have to say that, he thought. I don't have to explain anything. Why do I constantly feel I have to explain things I do to her? ('Con brio,' she was thinking. Double play on 'con brio.') She put her hand on his forearm. (He's fore-armed, she was thinking.) "You didn't get too wet. I'm glad." "Now what the hell's that supposed to mean? Of course I'm wet. It's raining, isn't it?" The menace in his voice. "Shit," he said, pushing her hand away. It was all a knife that could cut her; a knife that sometimes was loving, that could cut away rotten stuff, could have healed more than it severed . . . "Listen. Harry. I only meant . . ." her voice trembling and controlled. She was being a metronome.

He moved across toward the kitchen, to the stove. Coffee would be good now. Jesus, how he wanted some coffee. He felt cold inside, he felt isolate. Not just late. Iso-late, he thought. She was following him (she thought of it as being pulled along by him. He felt it as being followed). As he reached down to turn on the flame beneath the coffee-pot, she put her hand on the nape of his neck. In their familiar way. But as he had done, he thought, hours ago, so many hours ago, to Margery. 'Don't do that,' he snarled, pulling back as if the gesture had surprised him. 'Hey, Harry, what is it?' trying to sound casual. Feeling the knife of the rejection, the hurt. It had been such a totally tender gesture. She kept the dream at her periphery: a part of her wanted to rip at him and scream. 'Leave me alone,' he said, in a tight voice. 'I just want to think and be alone.'

'Leave you alone?' she said, tasting it. She felt melted, she felt like runny ivory and honey, she wanted him: he did not want her. What was it, it eluded her, it was there, something, it had happened before this way, where, real and imagined, that cold-fear feeling—he had not been alone. That was it. Instinct and reduced-cue and then it was all there, and the ice-cold fear/fury slid through her body. Not wanting to believe, but knowing.

Harry turned, looking down at her. Into her face. Marjorie comes all liquid, he was thinking. Sibyl comes all warm and firm and pulsing and not so liquid, just enough, like a tender hand around my prick, along body skin, all of her. Jesus, he thought, Sybil can see it, it must be all over me like ink, the other woman's scent, the other woman's come, it's like invisible ink, lemon-juice kind we used to use when we were kids, the kind that appears at will with heat . . . Ah, goddam them both, with their hungry cunts and their demands of a man. What a mess. I thought it would all clarify. But there she stands, my wife, with that wounded-animal look of hers. Damn it if she doesn't know . . . if she gave it to me when I wanted it, I wouldn't have to . . . 'Harry,' she said, wanting not to plead, hearing it in the bass register of her voice, despising it, it was the old game again, he wanted her when she didn't seem too eager, he liked to chase after her sometimes, she didn't always know which way, which angle he was coming in from. She wanted to be contradicted. Nothing in the world would comfort her now as would his body; it would be the contradiction she needed. If he would now reach for her, all light and dark between them, her need and his need the way it had been so often, the endurance of their bodies' way together.

But: 'Shut up, Sibyl,' he said. Turning away from her. From her eyes. Her body. 'I want to make love,' she said, thinking Please let's make love, please take me now, don't tell me anything, I don't care if it's so or not, tell me with your body that it's okay, just give me you back, the reassurance, I was so worried, I am so worried, the dream, that dream . . . you're here now and it's probably true but I can't even tell you, I can't say any of this to you . . . And then he said, at right angles to her again, 'Yeah. *Now* you want to. Not when *I* want to. Never when I want to. Well, sweetie, right now I don't want to. Here,' he said, grabbing her by the arm and turning and forcing her face into his armpit, 'haven't you been counting the days since I had a shower, Love? It's easily a week since I took a shower. By that shall ye know, damn bitch, and I'm not here on earth to please your highness' ideas of the fastidious. Remember,' he said, with that smile, 'our boy Auden's little speech, '. . . *nor, above all, make love to those who wash too much . . .*' I wouldn't inflict myself on you, dear girl. I wouldn't, in fact, touch you. Don't worry. Just let me the hell alone.'

She moved away from him. The coldness, the confusion eddying from him froze her thighs, dried her wetness. She was driven toward him, driven away from him . . . it was impossible. Had become, finally, impossible. She was frantic and impotent. All of this had become too familiar to her, like the furniture of their lives, like the furniture in their kitchen, their livingroom. All of it represented him. This moment and too many others like it. She was innately comfortable with the furniture of her life but not with his, with him. All of it was stained with him. By him. If this continued, in this way, she thought, by the time they were in their late fifties they would undoubtedly kill each other (though she was certain he could kill her, she would never have the courage to do him in, even if the inclination grew proportionately through the years . . .) and whatever was left would go to the children. By the time the children were grown, or even teen-aged, chances were good, she thought, that the institution of marriage would be on its way out, if not out, for the middle and upper classes at any rate . . . Okay, well and good, but what does that leave me with now. It's still in fashion even though it feels like some kind of Russian roulette to me. The dissonance is more imperative than the accord. Trouble is, he thinks he's right and I think I am; it's so different from the way the work goes mutually making music. In music we can work together for something. I can let the others be right. But when he's always right, I'm always wrong, and I can't stand that. I don't have a philosophy to cover this minute though . . . I don't know what comes next. I know what comes next. The next step is, I have to leave him. I mean I'm going to quit this. I'm going to have to leave him. It's all wrong. I've got to. No alternative left. That's it.

'I'm leaving this,' she said, aloud, to the roomful of livingroom furniture. To nobody in particular. To everyone; everything. She would seek the warmth in some other way. Become a statistic. One of the names on the list she and Harry had recited. All the people in that gifted circle of 'I can't anymore.' Number 38 on the list of couples who split up. Part of a liturgy. What were the possibilities for her. Limited. Unlimited. Not clear. Nothing was clear. Just 'out' and soon. Maybe that way, alone, things would clarify, it would clarify her. Right this moment all of her being centered at the pinpoint of light that was her self: that place where one is alone always. Made now of fear and of calm, but of light.

She was not so heavy-bodied when she had something definite to do. She could make decisions. She was capable to decide for her own life. Harry would show the world only his profile. She felt she saw him full-face and head-on, and it was not pretty; he was not a handsome man. In the town where he was born, many men were called Laverne, with never a nickname; some were called 'Wayne,' others, named 'Arlington,' were called Arlie—and he was the Harrington in town, named for his grandfather (after whom the Syracuse family farm was named as well)—his father had been Henry, of course, and so he became Harry. The son of Sybil and Harry was called Henry H. Fowler. Young Harry did not masturbate until he was past sixteen; he would be put to bed earlier than the other boys on the block, for reasons he has not yet ascertained, and would 'kick himself to sleep,' as he puts it, by kicking rhythmically at the covers and sheets in a sad gesture of rage and of impotent misery. Cars became his escape. Until three years ago he was faithful to Sibyl, but after the first move away from her he found other women occasionally; he has many fantasies about infidelity; he has never done anything radically his own except this most recent novel, and his marriage and these children . . . He does not love the children, but he does love his work, his wife, his car. And that he does not believe his wife, when she comes quietly into the kitchen where he is drinking coffee, and tells him that she is leaving him.

X.

Did he develop an ulcer. Did he become even more of a loner. Did he buy an Austin-Healey. Did she wear the same clothes for a week and stop washing her body, to see if he had somehow had the secret of expressing misery. Did he move into a solitary cabin at the other end of their own property in order to save rent money. In order to deceive himself about motives. Did she stay put in the same house they had shared, now that she was without him; did she begin to sleep around, neglect her cello, drop some of her friends, have two abortions within nine months. Was he lonely. Where the pipes froze in winter. Forgot to go to see his own children. Did each become an image of a child. Did he fulfill an old dream and learn to play the violin. Was each his own child for the first time: with the knowledge of an adult. To honor the self, to love to understand to indulge to treasure. How. What to do with so much to live. Feel.

Feeling of desperation. Unable to fall asleep alone, without the lover's darling rump and feet to console. Feeling of flushed come alone or with a strange lover (that newness) or did he lose his hard with the first and second but not the third woman he took to bed. And did she find herself unable to come with anyone save her own man. Unable to trust a new strange man with her deepest feelings of openness. Of vulnerability. In both of them the white fear, blossoming in the gut like a mushroom, dreams bursting open into nights of awake aloneness . . . into shut-off, the darkness.

Or leaning hungrily into life after trying for too many years to change to someone else's idea of who one is or could be. Or meeting the great new person down the road, around the corner, in the bar, in the next city, who turns bitter or dull within ten minutes, an hour, a week . . . The exciting new lover whose walk is too light, whose scent is too easy, whose laugh rings spurious suddenly, whose ideas of heaven are one's private ideas of hell. Ah all of them. The men after prestige, the women after money, the rebounds, the pill-freaks, the innately furious, the acid-heads, the infantile, the self-deceitful, the desperately willing: did this man and this woman separate and meet them all. And refer back in the mind and the groin to the partner long lived with and just lost. And be as unable to take in a new woman's children from an earlier man, as one had been unable with one's own. And be as unable to make the gestures of loving with the new woman. Or did she cut off her long hair and begin to use depilatory wax on her upper lip and have herself fitted for a diaphragm. Did he go on a diet of spaghetti and ketchup and lose seven teeth. Did he age physically ten years in five months. Did she age emotionally a hundred years in one night.

He heard her saying she was leaving him. He could not turn to face her. His face had no expression. She left the room. He turned toward the porch off the kitchen. The porch doors had twelve panes of glass. She was not there. She was leaving. Him. He made a fist and put his fist through one, two, three, four panes of glass in the door nearest him. She did not come running at the sound of breaking glass. He walked out of the house, his fist streaming blood and still clenched. Down the hill-path at the back of the house and around to where the cars were parked. His car next to hers (theirs). He was so precious to himself. He considered himself made of ambergris. The elegant end-product of a beginning which might be diseased . . . where would he go. Another birthday and what else. To have to rip apart his study that had taken him these years to set up just the way he needed it to work. Even now, the being away from her, the beginning of feeling free, was making him feel high. Maybe there was something wonderful happening. The hand began to hurt. He decided to drop by at the doctor's office. She had a hell of a nerve leaving him. One of the most talented men she could ever hope to meet. A good man if not a great one. She didn't know how much she was losing. The bitch, the ingrate. Who would be laying her. He knew every hair on her cunt, goddam her. Inside his belly bloomed the two heavy grotesque cancers, Fear and Anxiety, white, mushroom-shaped, hideous, dull. . . . Who would be laying her . . . Was this what she had dreamed, when she had woken clutching at him and weeping and howling 'No, no, stop it' . . . Christ. No way to cope with this feeling, the white mushrooms burnt cold in his gut like dry ice . . . He walked toward the doctor's office in a blindness. He would try to escape. He would ignore. He would step gingerly and refuse. Part of him knew that this feeling had little to do with reality. But if I screwed the Knapp broad who am I to say she shouldn't make it with anyone, the guy at the gas station if she chooses, anyone . . . He twitched, his cut hand curled into a fist again, he looked into the white-hot center of the double blossom that lay in his belly and he recoiled . . . Ah, they would engulf him. Their thickness was drawing him in.

Three years ago, the last time she had tried to leave him, Harry was balling his best friend's wife. And it was good—it was what he needed. He had believed then that Sybil was leaving him. But then: once, in that house, as he was entering the other woman, he wondered: where was Sybil now, and my God, where was Jerry, whose wife he was now taking . . . Could it be that Jerry was with Sibyl . . . was Sibyl with Jerry? Was Jerry . . . And the inside of Harry's head exploded; he jumped away from the woman before he came; threw his clothing on and ran out half-buttoned . . . Ran to a bar and drank and ran and drank again. Toward the end of the day, as he was walking toward the bus stop, he saw the bus coming, he saw Jerry standing there, waiting for the bus—Harry leaned toward the man and started to push Jerry into the path of the bus. But at the last second realized that that man was not Jerry at all. A stranger. And he leapt back, aghast at what had almost happened, at what had not happened, what could have been. He had almost murdered. His best friend; or a total stranger . . . another man. With the force of those feelings. About Sibyl, possibly. About the possibility of Sybil. And he had gone back to their apartment, with the taste of- personal violence thick on his tongue; had gone to where Sibyl was (in her momentary innocence) and had beaten her, smashed her nose till it bled, bloodied his hands with his wife's blood even though it was evident she had not been with Jerry. Or, for that matter, with anyone. That day. It did not matter. In his head, she had been; could have been. The thought was his, the deed was his, the anguish was his, the guilt, the fear—the goddam fucking double-standard, he thought, crazily, looking at his wife as she sobbed, bloody, across a room from him. His misery was spent; he would justify it to himself, to get away from how he felt: if it hadn't been Jerry, it would be someone else.

And now. He was sure she meant she was leaving him. This time. As the doctor repaired the hand, he felt no pain. The fear was an anesthetic. He had counted on her. Why didn't she understand. The damned bitch, with her automaton answers for any and all problems. Knew everything. If so, why keep asking those damn questions. Which he hated. He was glad she was leaving him. Now he could work without interruption. Now he could screw whenever he wanted to, without guilt. No more mosquito-whine sound of someone wanting him to be somebody he wasn't, didn't want to be, never would be . . . but my God, she was *leaving* him. Blast her damn hide for beating him to it: he should have left her long ago. What the hell, oh Jesus God, what would he do now. He would walk the streets with his head down thus; he would leave the doctor's office and . . . and what. Seek the

warmth. He could not go back to his own house. There was
no way through to her, nothing available. He was drawn now
to her, wanting to seek solace from her who had inflicted the
terrible wound. The fury; the impotence . . . a heavy burden; the world was turning unfamiliar. He was very frightened. He was elated; he was free.

XI.

She moved about the house, seeking some solace. He was gone.
There was a trail of blood-spots and shards of glass. How like
him, she thought. To act it rather than saying it. Ah well, it
was done. This would be the last scene, hopefully. And she,
at least, had said it out. He would always avert his face, giving
only the profile . . . The curtain in the window directly above
the hot-air vent blew gracefully toward her. To be able to
have to herself her own soul, not to have to watch what she
said, not to have to distort anything, not to worry about irritating the man. The children had wakened and were near her.
She sent them back to bed, not wanting them to have to share
the blood, the glass. Wanting as well to sort out the feelings,
alone. It had not been like this three years ago, when she had
said she would leave him. That had been bluff, she knew; this
was firm. There was no available way through to him. She
was burdened and laden with his ways. Her instincts were
sure now; he had been with someone else; it did not matter to
him that she wanted him and said so; he was satisfied and he
was guilt-ridden, and she had no better answer for dealing
with any of this than to leave him.

And did she begin to see other men, all of whom,
each of whom, followed in the pattern of Harry: laconic men,
self-absorbed men, men who slapped out at her, who were
hostile to the children, who had little medium ground available, the screamers, the howlers. And did healing occur thus.

Or did he absolve her, did he also confirm his love for her or hatred for himself by choosing women after her who were each and each directly opposite to Sibyl. Thin, carefully wrought ladies who did not ask questions, who shaved their armpits, who came from Wasp small towns. The Empty Ladies, he would call them, the Carbon Copy Ladies of Offices . . . All the fullness would have been with Sibyl: his own Lady. For her part, all the fullness could have been with Harry: his angularities were so needed, next to her roundnesses. The men she had met before Harry. The ones she wanted had often not wanted her. David on the violin, fuller-fleshed than Harry but with that same odd, quiet, cold glaze beneath the warmth (was it a kind of fear) had interested her. She had wanted to stay near him. They had been too young, in one way or another. With Harry (for Harry?) she had come alive, she had been challenged, it was a delight to be able to work next to him, she had been pleased with their differences. She had been lonely.

And for Harry: how many women were there in the world, from whom to choose. He thought that sentence, over and over, putting the emphasis on 'many' and on 'were' and then on 'world,' considering the possibilities. Such a narrow stratum, this, where they lived—that brightness back of them which bred the jutting-out into life, the good edges, the lack of caution that led into the finer adventure . . . both of them questioners, both challengers, both took nothing for granted, and all of this they shared: it was what had namelessly drawn them together at first and had kept them together for these years. Both so American: their faces, his books, her music . . . God, how they had been so drawn to each other! and not for magical reasons. But, for most of their time, when the flesh was not communicating, the deeper urges pulling them through their skins, they could communicate only in sharpness. Even their silences were designed to cut at each other.

XII.

It was always easier to talk to others. Harry would go to his agent. He trusted the other man. As the doctor finished bandaging, Harry asked if he could make the drive to the City. I think so, the doctor said, take this pill for the pain, you've got mostly superficial lacerations, no veins or arteries involved, but be sure to get back for a change of dressings tomorrow, I want to have another look at it. All right, Harry agreed, unwilling to think about coming back into town in tomorrow's light. I'll do that. And he called Blamertz from the doctor's office, collect. Woke him. "What? Harry? That you? What's the matter?" They had become friends. "I have to see you. I'll be in town in two hours. Everything's wrong. Yeah. I'll tell you then. Can you put me up at your place tonight? Okay. Good." And left at once. Stopped on the highway for coffee and a tunafish sandwich. It tasted like dust. He felt as if he were driving on ice. But he made it, to the City, across town, and up the elevator to his agent's apartment on West 55th Street. The older man's face blanched at the bandaged hand: the blood had soaked through.

"Only when I laugh," Harry said. "Pour me a drink. Roll me a joint. As you can see, I can't do anything worth a damn with this hand." He flopped into a chair. "I don't know what the hell to do. That fucking broad is leaving me. Leaving *me*. *Leaving*. Now what the hell do you say to that." "I say, join the crowd. I say, let's drink to it." The men had been working together for several years. They were, after a fashion, friends. "Jesus, Harry, what else do you want me to say? Either she will, or she won't. Whichever way it goes, you're not about to lose hold like you think you're going to. The main thing to do is to get hold of yourself . . ." "With one hand?" Harry couldn't resist it, even now. They both snorted. "You should have seen me driving in. Good thing I've got automatic shift switches." "So, she leaves you; what the fuck. The world's full

of fantastic broads." "Oh, Jesus, I've been married to the broad
for over six *years,* I thought we had something going . . ."
"Don't tell me you really believe you can count on anybody
else for anything sure, old man. There isn't any goddam
person in the world you can count on, outside of your own
skull . . ." "Yeah, smartass, that's why you live alone; big phi-
losopher, you're so hip, how come you're not getting laid?"
"Because I don't *want* to, that's why." "That does not compute,
as my son would say. You don't want to be alone any more
than I do. I mean, I'm all for being certain kinds of alone,
I'm even grateful in a way, for all of this, but I like being
alone when I know someone's there, for when I'm finished
needing to be alone . . . you know?" "I know. You've con-
veniently forgotten, secluded in the middle of your very own
pain as you are, that until early this year I was a very, *very*
married man . . . But if I lived through it, so can you."

By now, both men had killed two drinks and
shared a joint. The diction was fuzzy. "I'm having the time of
my life now. A different restaurant every night, if you dig
me." "So how come when I call at eleven at night you're alone?"
"Man's gotta rest sometimes, you know. I keep a couple of
nights to myself for catching up. Besides, it took me a few
months to get back in stride. Now, I'm getting fussy. I don't
just go out for pussy. I don't see a broad more than once unless she's really terrific. And I mean in and out of the sack,
both." "What do you mean, special?" "Well, the number one
thing is, she's gotta be a different type from Susan. That's the
first thing, and once you got past that, if she happens to be
smart and pretty, that's a lot. But the first thing is, not being
anything like Susan. Not in any way. Not talking or walking
or screwing. So simple. Just no memories of dear old Susan.
One chick, I remember, she never knew what she'd done, but
out she went on her ass. Turns out she had one of those funny
little laughs, you know, the thing Sue used to do when there
were a lot of people around and she wanted to be cute and
look like she was having a great time. That phony giggle."

Harry had been smiling and then stopped. Sat silent and thinking: what the hell, should I go through life looking for women who won't ever remind me of Sybil? Shit if I will. "Shit if I'll go through life like that," he said to Blavertz. And then there was that long silence.

"So," said the agent, slowly, in a kidding but kind way, "how did it happen?" "You mean the hand? Yeah. Well. The hand. I screwed this local piece. Before that, after I was here seeing you, I called Sibyl and she was pissed off as hell at me (I ran out of gas again) and along came this really built piece, lives down the road from us—what was I going to do?" They smiled. "Then I went home. Later. And when I walked in, Sybil knew. I mean, she smelled it on me. You know . . . and she went into the other room. Then she came in and she said she was leaving. Jesus Christ, it was like this glass wall was going up, so I tried to put my hand through it." "Yeah. I know. They *do* know. Listen, I knew too, like when Susan put the horns on me, I knew every time. . . ." "But—oh, shit, I don't even know why I did it; I was just so goddam fed up with her goody-two-shoes routines, and along comes this stupid broad, big chick like Sybil, but a redhead, one of those really dumb local types, couldn't even spell her own name until she was fourteen, but Jesus Christ, what a lay . . . what a great lay . . ."

The two men sat in silence. Reverence for The Great Lay. What could one say. The Great Lay, who doesn't happen to be one's wife this time . . . It amused Blavits to hear Harry talking about a country woman that way; the agent knew Harry's background; what a reversion, he was thinking, that was probably the same kind of local girl Harry first got laid with; in fact, I bet he kept some of that memory and put it on Sybil, with her big, luscious build . . . if he splits with Sibyl, wonder how long it would have to be before I just happened to come a-callin' on her, jest bein' neighborly, thought I'd drap by an' see how yer feelin' Miz Fowler . . . Shit, I'd better not. All's fair, but he'd kill me. Even later.

Look at that hand. This time he took it out on himself. This time. He'll never get over Sybil. He thinks *I* can advise him? I haven't gotten over Suse yet. And me with two marriages behind me, before Suse. He's a goddam amateur. He'd never make it living here in the City. He'd crack for sure. "Hey listen, Harry. Why don't you call her up?" *"Call* her? You mean call Sybil? Now? You're off your nut." "No. I mean it. I'm saner than you are and I say, pick up the phone and *call* her." "Ah, fuck you. She wouldn't talk to me. She's burning up. You don't know her. No. It's too late anyhow." "It's only 3:30 in the morning, sap." "That's not what I meant. Oh. I see. Well. No. She's always asleep by now; she's asleep and feeling very pleased with herself and what she'd probably do is fill me up with all this righteous shit . . . Oh, sure; that's just what I need right now . . . forget it." "Okay, it was just an idea. You could think about it . . ." "Yeah. I'll take the couch. See you."

He did not call. The next day, he stayed holed up in Blatzen's apartment, smoking a bit and watching television and eating a bit and trying not to think or feel. While he thought and felt. —For her part, Sibyl had done what Harry had guessed: gone to bed at eleven o'clock, after he had left for the doctor's; she knew she had to be up with the kids early the next morning. She had gone to bed feeling good, feeling lighter than air; then the dreams hit; she woke with the taste of fear in her mouth, cold as ice, no anger, just the fear. At 8:00 A.M. she called Elinor: "Listen, can I give the kids breakfast with your kids and let them all leave from your place? I have to talk to you." Her tone reached Elinor. "Okay. Will they eat French toast? That's what I'm doing now." "Yes." "See you in fifteen minutes."

XIII.

After the kids were off to school, the two women went to the laundromat. A comforting place. Familiar ritual. All the machines whirring. Elinor thought that being thére might be good for Sybil. But Sibyl saw the machines as machines today. "There they sit," she said, "chewing on our clothes, listen, listen to them, Harry's filthy goddamned socks, damn their filthy selves, but they're all I've got left of him," then she began to sob, Elinor didn't know what to do, awkward, there were a couple of women there who knew both of them . . . "That —goddam man—and his—machines," she said, her breathing shallow and menacing. "If it wasn't the typewriter, it was the car; he'd as soon have either one than the kids or me . . ." "Oh, Sybil, cut the crap. Is that what this was all about? You told me yourself you've got a good bed scene with him. A man who's got it going good in bed hasn't got it going into the machine thing, you know they're usually mutually exclusive." "Ah, but you haven't been to bed with dear Harry. Put it this way. He didn't used to have it going in bed so good. Only crude. That whole upstate thing. When he used to put it all into machines. Model radio in the garage. Hot rod to escape and lose oneself in one's asshole. Snowmobile too. Ice races. Drag races. Father was crazier about his new electric power lawn mower than about the wife, and you could see it. And understand why too. Oh, I don't give a fat rat's ass, the thing is, when I met him, he *wanted* to be with me, he *wanted* to be good in bed with me, so it was changing, and it just shaped up this past year to where we were really enjoying each other . . . He's no dentist, you know, or those types, not really; besides, those types aren't born, they're made . . ." "Hold on there, lady, are you attacking or defending?" "I'm *hurting*, is what I'm doing. Out loud. And maybe explaining too." Both staring not at each other but at the mindless round motion of the sudsy machines; nodding to the women they knew who came and went around them, speaking of more casual matters.

      "I think I'm losing my mind," Sybil said. "You should be so lucky. When Don and I split up . . ." "*Don't* lump us with you!" "Don't *snap* at me! All I meant was, when any couple splits . . ." "Who says we've split?" "Shut up, can you, baby," gently, "I know you're scared. Look. Either you've split with Harry, or you haven't. If you haven't, maybe you've got more of a problem than if you have, if you see what I mean. After all the kissy-face making up and re-discovery trip, when each of you thinks you've got the only priceless pearl in the world and how could you have done such awful things and said such terrible things and it'll never never happen again, you're back into the same old shit again, maybe after the first week of a second-honeymoon-type thing where every-thing's all rosy . . . and neither of you has really forgiven what started the last fight, and one or the other of you is hold-ing a grudge secretly, maybe even as a secret from oneself. I mean, whatever made you split is still *there,* and nothing I know short of an encounter group (which Harry isn't about to go to, if I know your Harry) would get it out in the open, and anyhow you're both stubborn . . ."

"It's impossible to live with that man. I mean, just look how he is toward the kids. It tears me up. They've never had a father, just a piece of furniture around that sometimes pushed them out of the way and once in a while spoke to them . . ." "And which is better," asked Elinor, "to have a really great, affectionate, interested father like Don, who had enough love to give for kids who weren't even his own kids, and have to stand around watching him break up all the fur-niture in the house one day and then split? Disappear utterly. I knew why, but he didn't bother to tell the kids, of course. Teddy's been absolutely shot down since Don split. He mopes and sulks and won't talk to me about it all, except for that brief thing right after it all happened. I'm really afraid for him, he's sucking it all in." "Listen, what you're telling me is, one way or another our kids are bound to be fucked up by what's going on with us . . ." "All you can say is, it's a different *kind* of being fucked up than we are. We lived through the lots-of-money-and-no-love thing, and the don't-I-give-you-everything thing, and the parochial-school-thing, and the my-son-the-doctor thing, and the I-want-you-to-be-

better-than-I-was-thing, and the kitchen-table-abortion thing, or the there-isn't-enough-money-don't-you-know-this-is-The-Depression thing . . ." "And our children have the should-I-try-acid thing and the should-I-fuck-when-I'm-fourteen thing . . ." "Yes. Et cetera. It's all made of the same fabric, really. Who was it said, 'Growing up in these times is difficult; but then, it's always been.' "

The machines whirled with the almost-alive clothes, the human skins, cleansing them, readying them for the next bout, the next days or nights on earth. The people of the town moved around the bench where the two women sat. "Where could Harry be?" Elinor asked. "I don't know. I'm really not sure. Maybe he went into the City. Maybe he's still around here somewhere. He might have gone to Barvetz' house." "Listen, why don't you call him there. To see if he's there. To see if he's okay. I mean, with that torn-up hand . . ." Sybil saw it and felt like retching. In compassion; in confusion; in horror. His flesh torn. But he did it. To himself. The Big Gesture. That sort of thing disgusted her and made her angry. But his beloved flesh, torn and bleeding. It hurt her. She did want to know how he was. She loved him, maybe. She loved herself more. She hated his self-put-down gestures and his rage. Had he smashed his hand because he loved her and she was leaving. Not likely. Had he done it because he hated himself, something about himself. More likely. Or because he couldn't talk to her. That was probably it. But he had most certainly been with another woman. As in the dream . . .

Elinor, trying to find out how much feeling there was left to build on, to build with: "Listen, you know you want to know how he is, there's no harm in making a phone call . . ." "Oh, what a joke. Yes, there would be. If he *is* there, he'd think I was following him, or being nosy, or, at the very least, being oversolicitous. You don't know him. Besides, if he is there, he's not awake yet, and waking Harry up is a hideous process. Not for me. Not now. If he is there, he's probably just gotten to sleep, matter of fact. Probably spent the night getting laid again, or getting drunk with Blametz, or getting high, and either he's sleeping it all off or still awake. Besides, if I woke him, there would be all that goddam guilt and anger of his. Forget it," she said. "Okay," said Elinor. "Just an idea."

During that long day, neither Harry nor Sibyl moved to the phone.

1969